THE
HUSH

By Skye Melki-Wegner

THE
HUSH

SKYE MELKI-WEGNER

Sky Pony Press
New York

First published in Australia by Penguin Random House Australia Pty Ltd, 2015.

This hardcover edition published by Sky Pony Press, 2017.

This is a work of fiction. Names, characters, places, and incidents are from the author's imagination, and used fictitiously.

Sky Pony Press books may be purchased in bulk at special discounts for sales promotion, corporate gifts, fund-raising, or educational purposes. Special editions can also be created to specifications. For details, contact the Special Sales Department, Sky Pony Press, 307 West 36th Street, 11th Floor, New York, NY 10018 or info@skyhorsepublishing.com.

Sky Pony® is a registered trademark of Skyhorse Publishing, Inc.®, a Delaware corporation.

Visit our website at www.skyponypress.com.
Books, authors, and more at www.skyponypressblog.com.

www.skyemelki-wegner.com

10 9 8 7 6 5 4 3 2 1

Library of Congress Cataloging-in-Publication Data available on file.

Cover design by Anthony Morais
Cover photo credit © iStock

Print ISBN: 978-1-5107-1248-5
Ebook ISBN: 978-1-5107-1249-2

Printed in the United States of America

For Brooke: sister, friend, and co-conspirator
in all my earliest adventures

PROLOGUE

FROM THIS ANGLE, THE WORLD LOOKED LIKE A TREBLE CLEF. A HILL curved high on the horizon. A swirl of ink. A symbol on a song sheet.

"Head down, boy," said the sheriff. "Head on the block, and we'll keep it quick."

Chester twisted his neck, eyes fixed on the hill. If he focused, he could almost ignore the shake of his limbs. The churn of his stomach. The choke of his throat.

The glint of the ax.

The prisoner before him had wet his pants, and the stage stank of urine and blood. Even now, red liquid pooled around Chester's knees. Would this be the last thing he felt, the last thing he smelled?

His fingers trembled. He swallowed hard and fought to keep them still. *No.* He would not let them see his fear. He would grit his teeth, and clench his fists, and never let them see it. If only his damned fingers would stop shaking . . .

"Any last words?"

The voice was oddly distorted. Almost from a distance. As though Chester heard the words through liquid, or from the bottom of a well. His breath fluttered. He tried to move his tongue, to form words, to say something, anything. But the words stuck like toffee in his throat, and all he heard was the roar of the townspeople, like the distant jeer of a thunderstorm.

"Chester Hays," said the voice. "You are found guilty of illegal Music. You are found guilty of connecting to the Song without a license. Your sentence is death."

The crowd roared even louder.

Chester knew that sound. He knew it in the depth of his lungs, in the tightness of his bones. He had heard those cheers a hundred times before, in saloons, in markets, in fairgrounds. As soon as he picked up his bow, and his fingers pressed the fiddle strings . . .

Just another performance, he told himself. *Just another crowd.*

The people cheered. His fingers shook.

The ax crashed down.

PART ONE
THE SONG

CHAPTER ONE

IT WAS A GOOD-SIZED TOWN. THE ROAD ROLLED IN LIKE A BRACE between fields of corn. With every step, dust puffed around Chester's boots. He was small and lean, his black hair a rumpled mess, his features tan. He ran a hand through sweaty hair then used it to shade his eyes.

A lone sign greeted him, rusting tin on a wooden post.

WELCOME TO HAMELIN.

High above the town, a pair of figures rode pegasi. The horses' wings arched long: crescent moons in the sky. Right now, Chester would trade his tongue for a horse. Even a common galloper, without the wings of the pegasus breed. Hell, he'd settle for a donkey. Anything to keep his feet off the ground and his weight off the blisters.

He plodded on.

Chester's shirt clung to his chest, his armpits. It had been a long day's trek from the railway track. He'd ridden overnight in a cargo train after sneaking aboard in another little no-hope town. Taminor, had it been called? Something like that. Hard to remember, nowadays. Another night, another town, another saloon. Hopefully the locals here would like his music and throw enough coins to let him fill his belly.

And hopefully they would know something about the vanishings. About the people who had started disappearing, just over a year ago. People who vanished from their beds during the night, leaving their families behind.

People like his father.

Chester's knees ached and his palms burned. He'd jumped when the train had slowed at a bridge, tumbling in a rush by the side of the track. Now he nursed his hands as he walked, dribbling drops from his waterskin onto the grazes. His throat ached, but his hands came first. If his hands were injured, he couldn't play fiddle, and if he couldn't play fiddle, he couldn't eat.

Besides, there would be a saloon in town. Chester could refill his waterskin, and maybe wrangle something stronger—though he couldn't prove he was of age yet. Had he turned seventeen by now, or was he still sixteen? Chester's father had never been sure of his son's birthday ("Sometime around harvest," he'd always said, with a careless wave of the hand). It was harvest time and Chester had been alone on the road for months. Perhaps he'd turned seventeen and didn't even know it.

It didn't matter, really. If he played a decent fiddle tonight, the barman would give him a drink. They always did, when the music was flowing. It might have been a while since a fiddler passed through this town. Chester could even be the first in months. Hamelin was a good-sized town, yes, but it wasn't well connected to the railway. It was a farming town, surrounded by cornfields, and mostly self-sufficient.

A fiddler would be a welcome distraction. A cheery little tune, a few well-chosen ditties, and he'd have them dancing past midnight. And tomorrow, when they'd decided Chester was a friend of Hamelin—not a thief, or a member of the notorious Nightfall Gang—he could fish for information. The same routine he'd performed in countless other towns.

Has anyone around here . . . gone missing?

6

Maybe this time he would find out something useful. Something concrete. Someone might have seen one of the victims vanish, or heard a ruckus in the night. An intruder in the shadows, or a scream beneath the moon. Something. Anything. Even if it was just a rumor, Chester would take it. Anything to find his father.

Chester passed the outmost buildings: wooden shacks and shops, with dusty curtains blowing in the wind.

He paused to fish his fiddle case from his travel sack. Then he walked on, carrying it separately in his grazed left hand. If anyone saw him approaching, they would know he wasn't here to shoot or rob them. He was here to play for them.

"Boy!"

Chester spun, startled by the voice. It was mid-afternoon, and harvest season—surely most locals would be out in the fields? But he squinted, adjusting his eyes for the sunlight and dust.

A man sat on a nearby porch, rocking quietly in a wooden chair. He wore heavy trousers and a dull white shirt, stained with dust and sweat. A pistol rested on his knees, and a bronze badge gleamed on his chest. *Sheriff.*

Chester forced a smile and waved. He exaggerated the motion, holding his fiddle case aloft. "Good afternoon, sir. How's the day treating you?"

The sheriff's gaze flicked from the fiddle case to Chester. "You looking to play for folks tonight?"

"That's the plan, sir."

A gust of wind blustered down the street, stirring the dust into eddies. Chester tried to maintain his smile. There was nothing illegal about regular folk music. He was just a boy—the sheriff could see that—and clearly he couldn't play real Music. Not the kind of Music that came with a capital "M." Not Music that teased sorcery from the hidden melody of earth and air.

7

Finally, the sheriff nodded. "Been a while since we had a fiddler in these parts. Couple of the boys like to strum a bit, but they couldn't hold a tune to save their lives. You any good, boy?"

"Hope so, sir," Chester said, "or I won't be eating tonight."

The sheriff laughed. "Truth enough in that." He pointed down the street. "You'll be wanting the Barrel o' Gold, then. Keep heading straight, and you'll see her on your left."

"Thank you, sir."

Chester gave a little nod of respect then hoisted his fiddle case back up under his arm. It pressed against the sweat of his shirt. He took a deep breath, unclenched his fingers, and trudged on down the street.

He felt the sheriff's gaze on the back of his neck, following him.

✳

The Barrel o' Gold was a two-story saloon, painted in whitewash and grime. When Chester swung its batwing doors, a bell jangled overhead. He inhaled a whiff of bourbon and old curtains. Tables dotted the room inside, streaked by shadow and backed by a long wooden bar.

"Comin', comin'!" called a voice.

Behind the bar, a redwood cabinet held shelves of alcohol. Whiskey, brandy, cactus wine. The bottles gleamed dark against the wood, tinted by a crimson sorcery lamp that hung from the rafters. An old woman bustled through a doorway behind the bar, a glass in one hand, a polishing cloth in the other. She wore a sweep of heavy skirts, and gray hair fell in ringlets across her shoulders.

"You'll be wantin' a room?"

Chester held up his fiddle case. "I've got no money, ma'am. But I've got music for your customers."

8

The old woman placed the glass and cloth on the bar, studying him. Then she nodded. "Play from the dinner bell till midnight, and I'll give you a room."

"And a meal?"

"Well, that goes without sayin'. Can't have you fiddlin' all night on an empty belly." She gave him a long look. "Picked a good night for it, boy. Got a big crowd into town, you see—Execution Day tomorrow."

Chester frowned. Could it already be the last day of the month? Surely he'd just witnessed an Execution Day a few days ago, back in Jubaldon. Or had it been in Euterpe? He couldn't remember. All these towns, the days on trains and the nights in saloons . . . they blurred together. An endless railroad journey, thrummed to life by the music of his fiddle.

If it was truly Execution Day tomorrow, it had been a whole month since he'd been in Jubaldon. A month since he'd stood in another town's square, and watched its prisoners die. The idea made Chester's stomach clench. But on the other hand, Hamelin would brim with people tomorrow. Farmers would trek in from their fields, and workers would flock from smaller towns in the region. There would be hundreds of people to speak to, to question. Hundreds of people who might know a secret or a rumor about the vanishings.

"How many prisoners lined up?" he asked, trying to sound casual.

The old woman shrugged. "Only one, far as I know. Fool got caught thievin' horses from the mayor's own stable. Still, always draws a crowd, don't it? Plenty of folks to play for tonight." She eyed him, frowning. "What percent you offerin' if I let you play in here?"

"Twenty percent of my takings," said Chester. "That's my usual deal."

She shook her head. "Fifty."

"Thirty."

"Forty."

"Thirty-five?"

The old woman scowled. "All right, all right. Thirty-five'll do it." She tossed him a key from her pocket then gestured up the wooden staircase. "Room Three, end of the corridor. I'll expect you down here at seven, after sundown."

"Thank you, ma'am. I'm Chester, by the way. Chester Hays."

"Call me Annabel," she said. "And make sure that fiddle's in tune. Last bloke we had playing in here sounded like a bunch of howling cats."

✳

Room Three was small and crooked, and there was a faint stench of vomit, as though a former guest had expelled a night's drinks onto the floorboards.

Chester opened the shutters. Daylight rolled inside, unfurling like a melody in a major key. He closed his eyes for a moment, letting the afternoon breeze wash over his skin.

When he opened his eyes, Hamelin stretched out below him. A dusty road lined with wooden buildings, and two riders soaring on pegasi overhead. One horse was white: a living cloud against the blue. The other was chestnut, with wings and limbs as tan as the cornfields below. They looked so quiet. So peaceful. Just hooves, wings, and sky.

Chester had always longed to ride one. To gallop faster and faster, churning dirt and dust until those wings lifted them up and the world fell away. But pegasi were for rich people: mayors, lawyers, Songshapers. When Chester wanted to travel, he only had one choice: to sneak aboard a cargo train and pray he didn't get caught.

With a sigh, Chester shuffled back to the bed. He opened his fiddle case and stared at the gleaming wooden instrument, polished and obsessively cared for. It was sheer luck that Chester knew how to play. Most poor children never learned music. Few could afford the training. Children of rich families were sent to expensive music lessons. They piped away on flutes, and banged their piano keys. They strummed violins and hooted clarinets in the desperate hope of being admitted to the Conservatorium. Poor kids worked in the fields or baked bread or ran errands in the streets.

As a boy, Chester had dreamed of studying at the Conservatorium. But it was only a daydream, as realistic as sprouting wings and flying to the moon. He was a laborer's son, without a penny to his name. He could never pay the audition fee, let alone the years of tuition, board, and food. He didn't have a noble heritage to call upon, or a vault full of gold.

But he had been lucky. He had worked at an instrument shop, and the owner had taught him to play. Chester could pluck out a tune on many instruments, but the fiddle was his favorite. It was the only instrument he owned, bought after months of scrimping and saving. Its music made his fingers sing.

He picked up the bow and tightened its hair, until the gap between hair and wood was the width of a pencil. Then he lifted the fiddle, pressed the chinrest onto his shoulder, and ran his bow along the strings.

He played a C major scale first, then a G major. Slowly, he melted from scales into melody.

The music calmed him. It was slow and steady, like drops of falling rain. Chester closed his eyes and fell into the sound, the run of notes, the thrum of double stops. Sometimes, when he played, Chester felt as though the music was his breath. He breathed in the song, and the song breathed back.

Chester's veins tingled. His fingers sped up and felt hot, fast, like the sparks of a sorcery lamp. They were more than flesh and knuckles. The world was spinning around his ribs, down his throat, into his stomach, until . . .

It wasn't his music. It wasn't the music of his fiddle, or the patter of his breath. It was something deeper. Something primal. Something . . .

Chester froze. The music snapped.

It was happening again. By the Song, it was happening again.

He shouldn't be able to sense the Song. He wasn't a trained Songshaper; he hadn't studied at the Conservatorium. Chester was untrained and unlicensed. He shouldn't be able to sense the Song, and he sure as hell shouldn't be able to play into it.

If Chester played into the Song itself, he'd be guilty of blasphemy. A capital crime. They would drag him to the square tomorrow. They would place his head on the block. They would raise the execution ax, and . . .

Chester swallowed. There was just the silence of the bedroom, and a breeze over the windowsill. He could still taste vomit in the air. He dropped his fiddle onto the bed and crossed back to the window.

He took a shaky breath then leaned on the windowsill, rested his chin on his hand, and tried to distract himself by surveying the street outside.

Most of Hamelin was made of wood. It was a town of shacks and cabins amid a dusty sea of ramshackle cottages. A town of grimy farmers and washerwomen, cobblers and grease-stained blacksmiths. A town where children shucked corn in the fields, and laborers tried their hand at anything from slaughtering hogs to mending fences. A town where life was hard but the people were harder.

Only one structure was built from stone. A grand manor adorned the hill that loomed over Hamelin. Dark bars crossed the windows: probably a recent addition, based on rumors of the Nightfall Gang. In the last year or so, as the gang of thieves had gained notoriety, aristocrats all across the country of Meloral had ramped up their security.

Even from here, Chester could see why the building might be a target for thieves. Compared to most of Hamelin, the manor seemed an extravagant palace. As he stared at it, a small curl of envy filled his belly. If he'd been born to a life of riches, Chester would have had a chance to study at the Conservatorium. Seven years of training. Seven years of schooling, of playing tunes, of memorizing scales and chords.

For centuries, the Song had played. It held the world together. It sang the trees from their seeds, and the clouds into the sky. It was a quiet rhythm, a pulse in the earth, the seas, the wind. Scholars called it the heartbeat of the world.

Students of the Conservatorium were trained to hear the Song in everything, in the touch of a petal, in the fall of a raindrop. They didn't dare to disrupt its beat, but by studying the Song, they learned to play sorcerous melodies of their own, to enhance the beat of the bars around them.

To play *magic*.

Chester tramped back toward the bed. He sat down heavily and picked up his fiddle. He took a long, deep breath. Then he nestled the chinrest onto his shoulder and pressed his bow against the strings.

CHAPTER TWO

FORTY MILES AWAY, IN THE TOWN OF BREMEN, SUSANNAH KEMP HUNG from a windowsill. Her fingers burned.

This wasn't how the job was supposed to go. It was meant to be a quick supply run: sneak in, grab the loot, sneak out again. The plan certainly hadn't involved a furious pair of guards, let alone hurling herself out the window.

She could hear the guards inside, rummaging through cupboards, searching under beds. Good grief, did they think she was stupid? Susannah hadn't considered "under the bed" to be a decent hiding place since she was five years old. The only real escape route was the window, yet these buffoons hadn't even *thought* to check outside.

Unfortunately, there was a good reason for that. Susannah shifted her weight again, straining to ignore the burn in her fingertips. Three heavy sacks of silver dangled from her belt. Her gang had chosen to strike the mayor's house, which had the distinct benefit of sitting on the outskirts of Bremen . . . and the distinct drawback of being four stories high. If she fell, she would splat like a peach on the cobblestones.

But then again, no one could climb like Susannah. She'd taken the burglar role in this job for a reason.

She swore under her breath, shifting the weight between her fingers. The sun wasn't helping. It was a hot day and the heat slapped her from two directions: reflective stone and glaring sky. Her pants felt glued to her skin as she scrabbled for a foothold.

She was too exposed here: a human figure on gray stone, with a mane of flaming red curls. If anyone took a stroll outside and glanced up at the outer wall . . .

There *were* cracks in the stone. If she ditched her boots, perhaps her toes might fit into the lines.

Susannah gritted her teeth and began to kick at her left boot. It took three or four tries before it fell to the cobbles with a deflated thump. She winced at the sound, but the guards inside the room were making too much racket of their own to hear it.

She set to work on the other boot. It fell with another flump onto the cobblestones below. Susannah held her breath.

Silence.

She prodded around with her toes, searching for a foothold. Her fingertips burned and her muscles strained. But she sucked down a sharp breath, counted a silent rhythm, and tuned out the pain.

Down, down, down. Susannah moved like a crab across a rock: slow and scuttling, her limbs splayed to reach the best possible holds. Hopefully the others had escaped safely. Travis was a brilliant actor—he could bluff his way free from a bank vault. He was playing the role of an aristocratic visitor from Weser City: an honored guest, who'd distract Bremen's mayor while Susannah snuck into his silverware collection.

But that part of the plan would now be finished. By now, Travis should be at their rendezvous point by the back of the courtyard. Susannah craned her neck to peer across the yard. No sign of Travis. Her skin prickled.

And what about Dot? The tiny blonde girl was the team's sole Songshaper, and her role in this job should also be complete by now. Dot had kept watch while Susannah snuck inside; if any guards proved too nosy, she was supposed to signal to Susannah, who had one of Dot's sorcery lamps. When activated, the lamp would play the guards into a doze. Why hadn't Dot spotted the guards and warned her?

Susannah let off a string of whispered curses. Where *were* they? Even if she made it to the ground, she couldn't sneak back into the Hush with half her gang unaccounted for. This plan had been too reckless. She'd become overconfident. Too cocky, too arrogant. She'd heard the embellished tales of the Nightfall Gang and she'd let her pride swell too much. When you led a gang of thieves, pride was a route to the chopping block.

"Hey! Hey, down there!"

Susannah whipped her head up, just in time to see the guard. He thrust his upper body out the window and pointed down at her, calling for his comrade. A moment later, his pistol fired and a bullet shrieked down the side of the building.

Susannah flung herself to the side. Her fingers slipped and one foot jerked loose, but she rammed it into a nearby crack, ignoring the agony as her toes struck stone. Why had she tried to burgle this place in the middle of the day? She should have hit later, when the locals would be distracted by the Sundown Recital . . .

The pistol fired again, and Susannah jerked aside with a huff of wild breath. Her body smashed against the wall, but she swiped to grip a handhold. There were more shouts from inside the building now: guards calling for reinforcements. Susannah knew she had only moments to flee. With her mass of red hair against the dull stones, she might as well paint an enormous bull's-eye on her scalp.

There was only one option left.

Into the Hush.

Above her, the guard disappeared from the window. Just for a moment, he turned inside. Just for a moment, she was unwatched.

But that was all she needed.

Susannah clung to the stone bricks. She wanted a solid anchor to hold when the world melted around her. She closed her eyes and began to hum. It was the four notes of the Sundown Recital, hummed in reverse order. The tune sounded strange this way—unnatural even—and if anyone heard, there would be cries of blasphemy. It was bad enough to eschew the recital each night, but to twist it backward for another magical purpose . . .

Well, that was a capital offense if there ever was one.

As the notes rolled off Susannah's tongue, the air around her stirred. There was a strange wrench inside her belly, in the deepest flesh around her spine, and the world spun like melting caramel. A whip, a blustering, a churn of wind and cold and darkness . . .

And she was in the Hush.

Susannah opened her eyes. She still clung to the wall. The same courtyard lay below her, she knew, and the streets and houses and fields of Bremen. But she couldn't see them. She hung in a bubble of faint light; all that ebbed at its edges was blackness. All was shadow, rippling with strange rain. The liquid was silent. Unnatural. It curled and twisted, snaking black tendrils toward her, but it didn't leave her wet. Just cold and in the dark. Alone.

The guards were gone, left behind in the real world. Susannah knew they couldn't follow her. Only the highest ranked Songshapers knew about the Hush. Susannah herself certainly shouldn't know of its existence, let alone how to access it. It was her secret weapon, and the only thing that had kept her gang alive. Of course, entering the Hush brought dangers of its own . . .

In the darkness, something screeched.

Susannah froze, clinging to the stone wall. She held her breath. There were creatures in the Hush. Creatures of twisted magic, formed from the remnants of real-world sorcery. The Hush was a dumping ground for the leftovers, the residue, dregs of Music and broken tunes . . . they leaked into the Hush, and the Hush came alive with their poison. The air here tasted cold and bitter, with a faintly unnatural tang, as though Susannah had licked a rusty sheet of metal.

She waited five long seconds. Silence. Finally, she began to descend. One hand, then the next. Her crab walk was more gradual now. In the Hush, she couldn't risk drawing attention to herself.

Susannah's feet hit the cobblestones. Her bubble of light had shifted with her, so that now she could see the stones and air around her body. She retrieved her boots and yanked them on. When she stepped away, the wall faded into swirling black behind her. Soon there was nothing but rain and chill, and the touch of cobbles beneath her boots. Susannah liked the cobbles. They were a reminder for her to keep her feet, and to keep her wits.

The rain fell on, tumbling and dancing, but the cobblestones did not grow slick. They remained dry beneath her, as parched as dust. This was the Hush. Its rain was not water, but shadow: a rain of leftover sorcery.

Susannah took a deep breath. She should find a hiding place and slip back into the real world. The sooner the better: it was safer to deal with guards than the perils of the Hush. She crept across the courtyard, heading for the rendezvous point . . .

Then she heard the scream.

Susannah jerked. That wasn't the scream of an Echo, one of the howling creatures that prowled the Hush. That was the scream of a human.

Dot.

Susannah's muscles flared with adrenaline as she charged toward the noise. *No, no, no* . . . What was Dot doing in the Hush? This wasn't part of the plan; her gang was supposed to hide at the meeting point, back in the safety of the real world . . .

She burst from cobblestones onto the grass of the little garden

18

at the edge of the courtyard. It looked eerie in the Hush. The trees were dark shadows and twisting limbs; the flowers curled black and faded, half-drowned in the crawl of the rain. The world streamed past like a trail of faded photographs.

Dot stood in the center of the garden. Travis stood beside her, eyes wide and alarm written upon his dark face. His spectacles were askew, half-falling from his nose, and his usually impeccable clothing was torn and rumpled.

And before them stood a Songshaper. She was a woman in her thirties, thick with muscle, with brown hair in an intricately braided knot atop her scalp. She wore a silver pendant in the shape of a nautilus shell: the symbol of the Songshapers. She aimed her pistol at Dot's head, and her lips curled upward into a very human smirk.

Susannah froze.

How had this happened? How had this woman chased them into the Hush? Dot and Travis must have fled into the Hush to escape a pursuer, but this Songshaper had known how to follow them . . .

Susannah's stomach churned. The woman hadn't seen her yet, but she was too panicked to come up with a plan. All she could think was *my fault, my fault, my fault.*

She'd been so stupid, so arrogant. Thinking she could waltz in here and rob the mayor in the middle of the day. Thinking she could deal with any low-grade, small-town Songshapers that might live nearby . . .

Susannah charged.

She burst through the darkness and hit the woman's side with an *Oomph!*, tackling her into the grass. Shadows tilted and roared around them in a rush of rain and fog and flailing limbs. A bullet screamed past just inches from her face. Susannah punched the Songshaper hard; the woman's nose snapped, and she let out a cry of pain. Susannah kicked her hand and the pistol skittered free; Dot darted forward to retrieve it, then aimed it at the Songshaper.

No one moved.

The Songshaper breathed in short, sharp gasps of pain. Susannah almost felt a burst of pity for her—until she realized what this woman was. This woman wasn't just a local Songshaper. She knew too much—about the Hush, for a start. No, this woman was a high-ranking Songshaper from Weser City. When Susannah realized this, it took all her self-control not to punch her again.

"Are you both all right?" she said, her eyes still on their captive.

"Yes, Captain," Dot said.

"Travis?"

"Oh yes," he said. "I'm just peachy. In fact, when I woke up this morning, getting chased through the Hush by a homicidal Songshaper was number one on my list of goals for today."

Susannah let herself relax slightly. "All right," she said. "Dot, keep that pistol steady. We'll just have to . . ."

Then she heard it: a faint whistling from the Songshaper's pocket. Susannah bent down, not taking her eyes from the woman's face, and retrieved the object: a glass globe, sized to rest in the palm of the hand. Its whistle grew shriller as she held it, and the glass felt hot against her skin.

"Show me," Susannah whispered.

The glass rippled with color—red, then blue, then gold. Inside the globe, an image began to form. A bird's-eye view of a town, streets awash in afternoon sunlight. For a moment, Susannah thought it was Bremen, but the streets were smaller, and the buildings were made of wood. No, this was a different town.

A word entered her mind. It seeped through the glass globe into her body; a whisper of knowledge, an answer to a question.

Hamelin.

20

Susannah frowned. Hamelin was a farming town, about forty miles away. And this was a radar globe. It would be tuned into a particular magical frequency, built to detect connections to the Song itself. This woman must be here on a mission, scouring the towns for a certain individual, a fugitive . . .

Someone had been detected illegally connecting to the Song. That had to be it. This woman was on the hunt for an unlicensed Songshaper.

Susannah's lips curled into a smile as her fingers curled around the globe. She would tie up this woman, and take her radar globe. She would return to the echoship with her gang, and then send someone out on a little trip to Hamelin. Someone to test this fugitive, and bring him back into her clutches.

An unlicensed Songshaper?

This was exactly what she needed.

CHAPTER THREE

At sundown, Chester peered out the window. The pegasi had vanished from the sky. Crimson light bathed the streets of Hamelin, painting the dirt a murky red.

Time to perform the recital.

Chester knelt in the center of the room. The floorboards were hard beneath his shins, but it didn't matter. This would only take a moment—just a single bar of music to reconnect his soul to the Song. All through the town, he knew, people would be doing the same. All over the region. All over Meloral. The recital brought the nation together. Wherever the sun was setting, people would be dropping to their knees, the notes of the Sundown Recital like honey on their lips. It was the nightly moment when every soul—no matter how rich or poor, how strong or weak or exhausted—shared a moment of music. A moment when all able-voiced folks sang that same run of notes, or sang it into the ears of those too sick or young to perform it themselves.

Chester hummed a low note. His lips tingled. As always, the tune stirred a quiet little twist in his gut. The run of notes spiraled upward, higher and higher. Downstairs, he heard other voices humming. It had to be Annabel, and perhaps her bar staff for the evening shift. Their voices rose together: that same run of notes. As they hummed, the air came alive with the vibration of their music. *One, two, three, four.* The beats of the bar thrummed like a pulse beneath the tune.

Chester breathed out. The run ended.

The recital was complete.

*

At seven, Chester headed down to the bar.

He wore a clean shirt and trousers, and a freshly scrubbed face. His dark hair was clogged with dust, and he suspected that he stank of the railway car, but his audience would be farmers coming in from a hard day's labor. Hopefully their stink would drown out his own.

"There you are." Annabel had finished polishing glasses, and a hopeful scent of stew wafted out from the kitchen. She slid a plate across the bar toward him. "Eat up, boy. Folks'll be here soon, and you'll have a whopper of a crowd to play for."

Chester threw himself onto the nearest bar stool. The stew was hot and spicy, with a pleasant kick of pepper. He slurped it down fast, and then—when Annabel had vanished into the back room—dared to lick the bowl clean with his tongue.

She returned to find him mid-lick, and let out a chortle. "By the Song, boy. Don't they teach manners in the other towns no more?"

Chester wiped his mouth on his sleeve and offered his most charming smile. "Oh, certainly, ma'am. I just couldn't resist the wonders of your stew. You could charge five bucks a plate for that."

Annabel raised a gray eyebrow. "So you'll be givin' me a bigger cut of your profits tonight?"

"Hey, hey—I said you *could* charge more for the stew. In the future. Can't change a contract that's already been shaken on."

The old woman snorted and took his bowl. "Tune up your fiddle then, boy. Folks'll be here in a jiffy."

Chester dragged a stool into the corner of the room. He opened his fiddle case at his feet: a velvet-lined mouth, hungry for coins. He had barely placed his fiddle beneath his chin and picked up his bow before the batwing doors swung open.

A horde flooded into the room. Bodies collided as people elbowed each other, the crowd brimming with backslaps and curses. There were farmers the size of tree trunks, dripping with sweat and stinking of cattle dung. Boys with cuts and grazes across their knuckles. Women massaging aching arms.

Some would be locals, but others likely hailed from smaller towns nearby and were here for Execution Day. They slopped like water through the bar, peeling off in different directions toward stools, tables, the bathroom out back. Men knocked each other aside, jostling for prime positions at the bar.

"Get us some supper, Bel!" one bellowed.

"All right, all right—keep your hair on," said Annabel. "You ain't about to starve if your stew's a minute late. Besides, I got a treat for you folks tonight." She stood on tiptoes behind the bar, and gestured at Chester to begin. "Go on, boy."

Chester pressed his bow to the strings. Few people had noticed him yet, hidden away in the corner, but now the farmers swiveled to face him. A few elbowed each other and pointed.

"Fiddler! Look at that, Jim."

"By the Song, how long's it been? Months and months, I reckon, since—"

"Well, good for Bel, I say—"

Chester tuned out the voices. He tuned out the stink of the room, and the heat of the air. He gave the bow an experimental slide across the E string and let the note reverberate. The closest tables were silent now in a skeptical sort of hush, as they waited to judge how well he could play.

And Chester let the music take him.

He began with a folk ditty, common enough in this region. He'd learned it a few weeks back, in a saloon called the Gabbling Goose, and clearly the locals in Hamelin knew it. Soon they were clapping, cheering along, and a couple of women linked arms in a dance. They threw back glasses of cactus wine, as the smell and sizzle of frying sausages wafted from the kitchen.

When Chester pushed the song up a notch into an even faster tune, foot stamping reverberated through the floor and sent Annabel's liquor bottles into a quiver. People scrabbled at cards, shoving piles of coins back and forth across the tables. Barmaids bustled around, sliding trays of drinks across the bar, and men called, "Another whiskey, darlin'!" or "How's about some fried potatoes?"

Chester couldn't help noticing, however, that the good cheer was not universal. One boy—perhaps two or three years older than himself—sat alone at a table to his left. He was a large boy, thick with muscles, and as tall as any of the full-grown men in the room. He picked at his plate of stew, and didn't order any drinks. A cowboy hat perched atop his head, angled slightly downward. He peered out beneath the rim, his eyes fixed on Chester.

Of course, that was fair enough. Chester was a performer; the whole *point* was for people to watch him. But for some reason, this felt different. Worrying. The boy didn't smile, or tap his toes, or nod along to the music. His eyes were an eerie pale blue, focused like bullets. He just stared. Silent. No blinking. No movement.

That was the difference between this boy and the others. Everyone else was watching Chester's performance, his music. But this boy was watching *Chester*.

Still, at least the rest of the bar seemed in high spirits. Annabel brought out plates of stew, and barmaids passed around mugs of warm beer. People chewed cornbread, slurped their drinks and sloshed their supper onto the tables. Chester sped up into another verse, faster and faster, and copper coins skittered into the fiddle case by his feet.

He slowed on the final verse, letting one note linger well past its right. People around him held their breath, hands poised in mid-air ready to clap. Chester grinned, dragging his bow to extend the note, teasing them. He stretched it and stretched it, letting the moment drip.

A man tossed a coin into the fiddle case.

"Ha!" Chester shouted, and he launched into the final chorus with a frenzy. People laughed and clapped him out to the end of the song. When he finished, the room broke into applause and Chester took to his feet, bowing.

"Thank you, thank you," he said. "Ladies and gentlemen, any requests?"

A woman nearby shouted "'The Captain's Cat!'" to general cheers of agreement. Then a man requested a bawdy song about a cowgirl and her whip, and his wife responded with a tirade of irritable whispers. A few people laughed, shouting support for his request.

Chester waved his bow, encouraging more suggestions. Song titles flew around the room, and he nodded and laughed at the ruder choices. But he found his gaze drawn inexorably back to his left, to the hulking boy with the cowboy hat. The boy had finished his stew, but he was still watching him. In the dark of the corner, his pale blue eyes looked like the globes of sorcery lamps.

" 'The Nightfall Duet.' "

The boy's voice was deep. Quiet. But somehow, even over the rustle and cheers of the crowd, Chester heard it. His throat tightened. His eyes met the boy's, and there was a long moment of silence between them.

"The Nightfall Duet."

The song had once been called "The Thieves' Duet," but it had been renamed in honor of the notorious Nightfall Gang. Over the past year or so, the gang had become legendary for their daring robberies, fleecing the wealthy and giving to the poor. And as their reputation had grown, the tales had grown ever more elaborate.

Some stories told of the Nightfall Gang stealing forty pegasi from a rancher's stable, or robbing the grandest bank in Weser City. Some people said they were ghosts in the night, waging a war on behalf of the poor. Others claimed they were evil sorcerers, who twisted the Song to gain their unnatural powers of thievery.

And for a gang who pulled off the most difficult of burglaries . . . well, only the most difficult song could be named in their honor. "The Nightfall Duet" was a punishing piece of music, designed to be played by two instruments. It was filled with tricky little runs of notes and even—unusually for a fiddle—a sequence of three- and four-note chords. When Chester's old boss had taught it to him, the man had barely been able to play it himself, and he'd had decades of practice in his instrument shop. It was a song to test a musician's mettle.

It was no accident that the boy had picked this song. This was a challenge. If Chester was good enough, this song could bring the audience to tears. But if he wasn't up to scratch . . .

Well, knowing the horrific squawks that a fiddle could produce, there'd be tears of a different type entirely.

Chester stared at the boy a moment longer. He forgot the cheering men, the laughing women. He forgot the sloshing beer and the pockets full of coins. There was just this moment. This stranger. This challenge.

He closed his eyes. He pressed his bow to the strings.

And he played.

The music flowed soft, then louder. Chester kept his eyes closed and his mind focused. He was vaguely aware that the room was quieting down, settling into confusion at his choice of tune. This was not a bawdy folk song. It was raw and rich and melting, like butter on the strings, and it dripped down Chester's fingers into the fiddle. He felt his skin tingle oddly, as it sometimes did when he played music. A tightness grew in his stomach now, a sting pricked in the back of his eyes. The rhythm called to him. He could feel it in the room around him. He could sense it in the fiddle strings, taste it in the air, feel it prickle and blister, heating his skin.

No, not just the rhythm.

The Song.

Chester played his music and, for a moment, the Song played back to him. It played quiet and refined through the floorboards: a gentle waltz. It played wild and raucous through the farmers' bodies: a folk song made of foam and waves. It played through Chester's own body: a stuttering tune in his fingers, a beat of drums in his pulse. He was barely aware of what was happening. All he knew was that he felt *alive*. His fingers were flying. Music poured from his fiddle to mesh with the Song, to bend into its ebb and flow and run like syrup . . .

"Get him!"

The shout blasted through Chester's mind. His eyes snapped open. The Music faded. It was like waking from a dream. He realized that the bar was silent. Everyone was still. The air puckered, shifting, as though an invisible hand had flicked a ripple through reality. The air rolled with smoke, which smelled faintly of warm honey—and through the smoke, they all stared. Pale faces. Slack jaws. Horror dawning in their eyes. Gradually, the air stilled.

Then he heard the shout again. "Get him! Someone get the sheriff!"

It was Annabel.

A rush, a shove, a flurry of cries. And before Chester knew what was happening, arms grabbed and pulled and shoved him down, crashing him into the floor.

CHAPTER FOUR

THE ECHOSHIP WAS QUIET.

Susannah sat in the cabin, one hand on the steering wheel. Huge glass windows rose around her, swirling with unnatural rain, mist, and shadow. The Hush.

This was how the Nightfall Gang traveled, invisible to the real world, roaming like ghosts across the country. It had taken weeks of planning to acquire this ship—they'd nicked it from the Songshapers' fleet in Weser City—but now that they had it, travel was infinitely easier. Echoships existed only in the Hush and were powered by the residue of magic that leaked through from the real world. The *Cavatina* hovered just above the earth, the size and shape of a sailing ship. Huge masts rose above its deck. Its sails were massive: high and flapping, a trap for the sorcerous air of the Hush.

Susannah had grown up in Delos, in the middle of Meloral's wide southern coast. As a child, she'd dreamed of being the captain of a ship, just like those she watched sail into port. She'd dreamed of the wind in her hair, the salt on her tongue, the sun on her skin. But now she captained an echoship, and the Hush rolled around her like a sea of darkness. It swirled across the windows, black and cold.

Susannah stayed alert for any sounds of creatures in the distance.

"Hello, Captain."

Susannah turned to see Dot enter the cabin. The girl was sixteen, only a year younger than Susannah herself. But Dot still carried a child's look in her eyes sometimes. A distant stare, a wisp of a daydream. Susannah envied her that. The Songshapers had taken her own dreams away a long time ago.

"Hi, Dot. Everything all right?"

"Yes, Captain," Dot said. "There was a minor fluctuation in the engine, and I had a theory that the melody was running a semitone off, but I readjusted the Musical calibration coil and—"

"Whoa, whoa," Susannah said. "In normal words?"

"The engine was a little off-key," Dot said. "I fixed it. For now, at least."

Susannah raised an eyebrow. "For now?"

"Well, ideally you'd have a couple of trained Songshapers to replay the Music into the engine from scratch, but . . ."

Susannah sighed. "But you're the only Songshaper in the gang. I know." She offered the most reassuring look she could muster. "You're doing well on your own, Dot. I know the ship's maintenance is designed for two people."

"Maybe this Songshaper from Hamelin can help," Dot said. "If Sam manages to nab him, I mean."

They stared out the windows into the dark. Susannah kept her hands on the wheel, steering slightly to the right. Normally, two emergency echoboats would be strapped on top of the vessel. However, since Sam had taken one of those boats to Hamelin, the *Cavatina* was a little off balance. Susannah was careful to over-steer, compensating for the loss of weight on one side of the ship.

"No sign of Echoes?" Dot said.

Susannah shook her head. "It's quiet."

"Too quiet, if you ask me. Normally we would've had a couple of close scrapes by now, so close to a town like Bremen . . ."

30

Susannah nodded. The Hush was at its most dangerous near towns and cities, where plenty of Musical residue leaked through from the real world. At its worst, this Music could turn the ground to molten silver, or blow eddies of deadly gas into its victims' lungs. Other times, it mutated into deadly creatures, driven by the strength of broken melodies.

Once, Susannah had slipped into a nest of scuttling spiders, whose legs were built of glass and shadow. In Weser City, a sprawling vine with metallic thorns had tried to smother her in the dark. Another time, she had fled in agony from an unnatural bird, which had screeched an explosion of Musical pain into her lungs. It had melted into darkness as it flew, its feathers dripping oil and starlight.

And the Echoes—the most terrifying creatures that stalked the Hush—were the most likely of all to congregate near townships. They were more likely to find prey there: humans, mostly, slipping into the Hush. The fact that the Nightfall Gang had escaped Bremen without a single murmur from the darkness was unusual. And in the Hush, "unusual" was enough to set Susannah's teeth on edge.

She gripped the wheel tighter. Perhaps she was being paranoid. After all, she still felt twitchy from the afternoon's mishap. It had been too close. Bremen was supposed to be a routine burglary. Just a local mayor's house: nothing special, no hard security. They should never have been in any danger. Yet Susannah had put all their lives in jeopardy . . .

But they'd escaped, hadn't they? They had knocked the Songshaper unconscious, tied her up, and left her in the courtyard. Sam, their getaway driver, had been waiting nearby with the *Cavatina*, ready to sail through the Hush. It had all gone too easily, considering.

Like clockwork.

Like a trap.

A prickle ran up Susannah's spine. They shouldn't have been able to overcome a high-level Songshaper, not without more of a fight. A real struggle. And now, the Hush was suspiciously clear of Echoes. Too easy. It was all too easy.

"Dot," she said. "You don't think . . ."

Above her head, a bell tinged.

Susannah froze. She raised her eyes with a sense of dread, not sure she wanted to know which bell had rung. A row of tiny bells hung along the ceiling, connected via pipes to the various sensors in the *Cavatina*'s hull. Only one thing could set a proximity bell ringing.

Another echoship.

The bell rang again. This time, Susannah's gaze locked onto it. Her breath suddenly felt as cold as ice. There was a moment of silence.

The bell chimed again.

"The third bell," Dot whispered. "Isn't that . . . ?"

Susannah nodded. The third bell denoted a Songshaper's licensed echoship. Just a small one, by the softness of the tone. Probably a single-person boat, designed to dart like an arrow through the Hush . . .

"The Songshaper from Bremen," she said, her throat tight. "She *wanted* us to get away so we would lead her back to our ship. She's following us."

Dot paled. "I'll tell Travis. He's in the—"

"Go, go!"

Susannah wrenched the wheel, adjusting their course through the rain. The *Cavatina* was powerful, with an engine dome large enough to fit a person inside. Because of the echoship's sheer power, they should be able to outrun the Songshaper's echoboat. But the smaller craft would be nimble and quicker to turn.

Susannah glanced up at the illuminated map on the ceiling. They were still within the sorcery range of Hamelin. She yanked a communication globe from her pocket with her left hand, guiding the wheel with her right. She raised a leg to kick one of the levers down, and the ship clanked into a higher gear. The globe tingled against her skin.

"Sam!"

No response. Had Sam taken his own communication globe into Hamelin? Or had he left it on his echoboat when he ventured out of the Hush? If it was in his pocket, it should be tingling against his skin right now: hot and buzzing, an indication that its paired globe was trying to make contact.

"Come on, come on," Susannah muttered. "Pick up, damn you."

And finally, he did. The glass began to shine pale blue. A face appeared faintly in the depths of the globe then slowly solidified into Sam's familiar features. Pale blue eyes. Cowboy hat. A surly expression, and a hard-clenched jaw.

"Captain?" Sam said.

Susannah hesitated. She could never predict what kind of mood Sam would be in. His personality fluctuated with more buoyancy than an echoship. It wasn't his fault, of course. It was the fault of the Songshapers—the ones who'd twisted Music through his brain. But still, it made him difficult to deal with. Which Sam was she speaking to at the moment? Angry Sam, friendly Sam, judgmental Sam?

"We're on the move," Susannah said. "We've got trouble. Change the rendezvous point to Linus, all right?"

Sam's eyes widened. "Hang on, I'm coming to help you—"

"No!" Susannah said. "Stick to the plan. We need that Songshaper in our gang, Sam, if we're going to pull off the Weser City job."

"He's gone and got himself arrested," Sam said. "He's as good as dead, Captain, and I ain't risking my life for no filthy Songshaper. I'm coming to—"

"I want him," Susannah said sharply. "That's an order, Sam. I don't care how you do it; you save him, and you bring him to me. Linus. Understood?"

"Captain, I—"

The globe fizzled, and the signal cut out. Sam's face vanished and the blue shine faded. Susannah cursed and dropped the globe back into her pocket. She had sailed too far from Hamelin, beyond the range of Sam's communication globe. There would be no more talking to Sam now—not until they met in Linus.

Assuming, of course, they survived that long.

Susannah leaned forward to crank another pair of levers. The ship gave a groan, vibrating as a hundred cogs and pulleys jingled within its hull. She peered through the dark windows. There was no way to navigate the Hush using her eyes. Not when all was darkness, and she couldn't see an obstacle until she was a yard from plowing into it. The windows were used to spot immediate attacks, not to navigate the swirling black ahead.

No, she had to use a map. That was the only way.

Even so, Susannah hated steering by maps. She liked to see where she was going, to plan every step with her own eyes. Teeth gritted, she watched the glowing lights of the sorcery map overhead. A tiny shining dot marked the *Cavatina*, illuminated like a speck of flame. She knew the map was playing Music—a rolling waltz, to conjure up the sorcery of motion and momentum—but Susannah would never be able to hear it. Not even if she devoted a lifetime to studying Music.

Not after what the Songshapers had done to her.

The door flew open and Travis sauntered into the cabin. Susannah glanced back at him then returned her gaze to the map. She couldn't afford more distractions. "What?"

Travis didn't answer for a moment. He glimpsed his reflection in the echoship's front window and paused to adjust a crooked button on his waistcoat.

Susannah sighed. Travis had only joined the gang a few months ago and he was still finding his place. They needed a doctor and a good con man, and having spent his last few years at the prestigious medical school in Weser City, Travis Dalton fulfilled both those requirements. He was smart. He was young. He was an excellent actor. After growing up in luxury, he was quite content to strut about in ruffled sleeves and silken waistcoats—and he was handsome, too, with his shining spectacles and flawless brown skin. All in all, he was a perfect addition to the Nightfall Gang.

And, unfortunately, he knew it.

"Well," Travis said, "I'm loath to interrupt at such a crucial juncture, but I'm afraid Dorothy asked me to deliver some rather bad news."

Dorothy, Susannah noted. Only Travis ever used Dot's full name.

At first, Travis had seriously rubbed Susannah the wrong way. She'd doubted he would risk even his waistcoat to protect the others, let alone his life. It wasn't just his posh Weser City accent; after all, Dot spoke with a city accent, too. It was the vanity in his voice—he spoke as though he thought he was better than they were. More refined, more fashionable, more distinguished. As if he was constantly bored by Susannah's plans and as though it took all his patience to play along with her silly little jobs.

But in recent weeks, she had begun to catch glimpses behind the mask. A twinkle in his eye or a crooked smile on his lips. She had begun to realize, finally, that Travis wasn't entirely serious in his preening. It was more of a game than anything. And when she considered the truth about his history and his real motivation for joining the gang . . .

Well, it had cast a whole new light on his attitude.

"What news?" she said.

Travis flicked a speck of lint from his sleeve. "Well, Dorothy took another peek at the engine. It's still suffering a few fluctuations in its Music. It should hold out for the next few days, but she asked me to request that you avoid any sudden jolts or turns that might throw the Music further out of tune."

Great. How was she supposed to outrun their pursuer if she had to keep the *Cavatina* steady? It might take days to shake the Songshaper off their trail. If Susannah couldn't lose her before the engine gave out . . .

"I'll do my best."

"Make sure you do," Travis said. "I doubt Dorothy alone has enough Songshaping ability to reignite a broken tune and I rather doubt we'll get far if the engine's Music snaps and it starts playing 'The Captain's Cat' or some such—"

"Why don't you go and help Dot with the engine?"

Travis adopted a look of pure horror. "Me? Go into the engine room? Why, I just cleaned the stains from today's job off my spare trousers; I couldn't possibly get grime all over these ones, too. What on earth would I wear tomorrow?"

Susannah snorted. "Oh, I don't know. Maybe some humility?" She wrenched another lever, ramping the echoship up another gear. "Either go and help Dot in the engine room, or go and get some sleep. I need to concentrate."

Travis gave a dramatic sigh. "Alas, I appear to have been rejected. Oh cruel world, why must you taunt me so?"

"Because you're a massive pain in the rear?"

"Ah." Travis took a moment to consider this. "That would do it, I suppose."

He flashed her a grin, smoothed back his hair, and sauntered back out into the corridor.

Susannah sighed. Despite everything—his vanity, his mockery, his unbearably posh accent—she couldn't help but like Travis Dalton. He was a constant reminder not to take life *too* seriously.

Susannah checked the proximity bells. The third bell had stopped ringing. Good. Their burst of speed had increased the distance between the *Cavatina* and their pursuer. She would stick to open fields, where she could risk higher speeds, and keep her nerves in check. They would have to take shifts at the wheel, and hope like hell that they didn't run into any Echoes.

With a bit of luck, by the time they reached Linus, Sam would have a Songshaper ready to fix their engine's tune.

CHAPTER FIVE

THE PRISON WAS DARK, BURIED DEEP BENEATH THE SHERIFF'S OFFICE. It was quiet. Just the scent of mildew, and the crawling damp of earth around him. Chester sat at the back of his cell, knees pulled up to his chest.

The crowd had taken everything. His fiddle, his earrings, even his boots. All he had left was his shirt and pants. He heard sniffling from the opposite cell, where a grizzled old man sat moaning in the light of a sorcery lamp. This must be the man who'd stolen horses from the mayor. The man who was to be executed tomorrow.

And now he wouldn't die alone.

Chester's stomach rolled, and he pulled his legs in tighter. How had this happened? He hadn't meant to connect to the Song. He hadn't meant to perform sorcery or Music or whatever the sheriff had arrested him for. All he'd done was play his fiddle, and something had happened that he couldn't quite explain . . .

"I didn't mean it, sir!" he'd said, when the sheriff dragged him down into the dark. "I swear, I've never trained in Songshaping, I didn't mean to—"

"Oh?" The sheriff slammed Chester against the bars and loomed up close in his face. His breath smelled like hot beer and sour meat. Any hint of friendliness had gone, shattered by the gravity of Chester's crime. "How'd you connect with the Song then, boy? Can't do that with no trainin', even I know that. We ain't all fools 'round here."

"I was never trained!" Chester said. "I was only ever taught how to play music, not how to . . ." He stopped, panicking. "I mean, do I look like I could afford training? I'm not rich enough for—"

"Oh, I'm sure you weren't trained official," said the sheriff. "Couldn't afford the Conservatorium, not a little brat like you. But you been trained by *someone*." The lamplight flickered, drawing eerie shadows around his lips. He leaned in closer. "You been trained illegally, boy. Black-market tutorin'. Blasphemy."

"I didn't—"

The sheriff struck him. The blow sent Chester backward, and his head crashed against the bars. He let out a cry—he was dizzy with pain—as the sheriff flung open the cell.

"You got a license?"

"No, I—"

"Seven years of trainin', it takes. Seven years before society trusts you to conjure Music—let alone mess with the Song itself. And a little brat like you figures you can do it? You figure you can risk all our lives, just 'cause you've had some black-market trainin' on the sly?"

He shoved Chester into the cell and slammed the door behind him. "You got good timin', boy, I'll give you that. Eve of Execution Day and all. Saves us the cost of keepin' you."

And then he was gone.

Chester's head throbbed and his belly churned. He wanted to call the sheriff back, to explain what had happened. But how could he? He couldn't even understand it himself, let alone explain it to another.

Stupid. He had been so stupid. For years, when Chester had worked at the instrument shop, his boss had claimed he was

39

impulsive. *As brash as an out-of-tune banjo,* the old man had said, with an irritable snort. And he was right. Chester shouldn't have played "The Nightfall Duet." He shouldn't have risen to the bait. He had let his ego—and the challenge of a stranger—coax him into public blasphemy.

It was bad enough to conjure sorcery without a license. For reasons of public safety, it was illegal to play Music without years of study at the Conservatorium. But to connect that Music to the Song, to brush his melody against the very heartbeat of the world . . .

Well, that was a whole new level of illegality.

Only the very highest-level Songshapers were allowed to interfere with the Song—those with decades of training and certification. Most of them only ever listened to it. They studied it, yes, but they didn't twist it or mangle its beat. They contented themselves by creating their own Music, and leaving the Song uncorrupted.

His throat tight, Chester remembered the unnatural ripple of air in the saloon. *He* had done that. His tune had touched the rhythm of the world itself . . .

And his connections to the Song were growing more frequent. It had first occurred a year ago: a horrifying rush of power in the instrument shop. For a long time, Chester had half-hoped he'd imagined it. But two months ago, it had occurred again. And this time the connection was even stronger.

One year ago, two months ago . . . And now, twice in a single day.

Chester let the darkness wash over him. His breathing sounded harsh down here, in this cell below the earth. Discordant. He focused on the music he'd been playing in the bar, "The Nightfall Duet." He strained to remember the exact point when the music had changed, when it had melted from an ordinary melody into Music, then into the Song itself . . .

A sorcery lamp dripped bluish light through his cell. Looking for comfort, Chester reached up to touch the glass. It was warm, but not hot enough to burn his fingertips. As he brushed it, a familiar melody crawled from the lamp into his skin. It was a common nursery rhyme, used by Songshapers to enchant simple objects: lamps, kettles, carriage wheels. The effect of the magic depended on how the Music was played, and the color of the light came from the creator's own power.

Chester pressed his fingers to the glass. He could feel the Music. It ran like water across his skin and sank into his flesh. Down into his bones. It ran from his fingers to his wrist, from his forearm to his elbow, up through his shoulder and into the rest of his body.

He had always been able to feel Music like this. *A gift*, his father had said. But it was also a secret. Only Songshapers were supposed to be able to sense the tune of things in a physical way. To let the rhythm flow like honey through their bodies. The fact that Chester could do it without formal training was another form of blasphemy. It wasn't as serious as what he'd done in the saloon—meshing his own fiddle's music with the Song—but it was still illegal.

Not that it mattered. He would die tomorrow anyway.

Chester stamped his foot against the floor, frustrated. His head still ached from its crash against the bars. But he couldn't give up. He had survived on his own for months, from train to train, town to town. Sometimes he'd been lost in the wilderness, wandering far from towns or rail tracks. On the hottest days, he had lain in the shade of scraggly vegetation, sucking his lips and letting sweat paint trails across his skin. He had clutched his stomach, sworn under his breath, and struggled on through dust and desert.

And he hadn't given up.

Chester had lived hard, lived alone, and survived. He had set out to find his father, Wyatt Hays. After Chester's mother had died in childbirth, his father had sacrificed everything to raise Chester on his own. And no matter what it took, Chester was going to find him. He'd seen more of the world than these Hamelin folks, who'd likely been born on the same farms as they would die. Chester wouldn't let them take that world from him. Not without a fight.

He pulled his foot away from the floor. Peels of dirt were stuck there, and he brushed them away as he turned. He pressed his hand against the earth. Cool. Damp. Malleable.

Chester began to dig.

He pulled and scrabbled, driving fingers deep into the dirt. It wasn't as soft as he'd hoped, but he grunted and dug his fingers deeper. Dirt crammed under his fingernails, driving painful wedges between nail and flesh. A chunk collapsed under his fingers, spraying clods across the floor, and he smelled newly disturbed mildew. Chester allowed himself a moment of hope. Hamelin was just a small town—perhaps their jail cells were really this rudimentary. He could dig and dig, all the way up to the night sky and freedom . . .

Chester's fingers struck something hard. Shock shot up his fingertips and he gasped in pain. He scratched away the surrounding dirt and squinted in the light of the jail's sorcery lamps.

It was brick.

Chester's stomach dropped. He pressed his fingers against the brick, and another little shock ran through his skin. Not just brick, but brick imbued with Music. Chester bent down and pressed his ear close to the stone. If he closed his eyes and strained his ears, he could hear it—just faintly. The distant echo of a Songshaper's melody, played into the brick itself.

Chester flung himself at the metal bars of his cell. He grabbed the bars and pulled, strained, groaned. He kicked at the padlock and yanked again and again on the bars until his arms felt like fire.

Nothing. The bars refused to budge. He was distantly aware of the other prisoner laughing, bitter and broken in the opposite cell.

"No point, boy," he said. "Think I ain't tried that?"

Chester clenched his fists. He couldn't die here. If he died, who would continue his search? His father had already suffered so much. He had survived a war, lost his wife, and raised his son alone in poverty. He had worked until his knuckles bled, just to keep a roof over their heads. And finally, he had vanished.

Chester had spent months trying to block out those final days but now, in his despair, he couldn't suppress it any longer. The memories rushed back to him, cold and unwelcome. His father had writhed in a fever, racked by nightmares, sweat and shadow. He had tossed and turned. He had lain with fluttering eyelids, a jumble of whispers on his unconscious lips. *Hush*, he had whispered. *Hush, hush, hush* . . .

Then he had vanished from his bed.

Now, Chester sat alone in the darkness. Something had given his father those nightmares. Something had taken his father away. He sat, chest tight, and fought against the silence. He would not give up. He would not let them win.

He reached for the bars and pulled, again and again, again and again, until his arms throbbed and his fingers burned . . . but still he kept pulling, gasping, fighting uselessly into the night.

✱

They came at dawn.

It was the sheriff who fetched him, with a stranger in tow. The stranger wore a twisting little goatee and a coat of olive green. For a long moment they stared at him, faces half-concealed by shadow.

Chester knew how he must look. His arms ached and his fingers throbbed. He had broken half his fingernails and strained every muscle in his body against the bars.

But he knew all about the value of performance. He knew about false confidence. Chester had grown up in Thrace, a rough-and-tumble city where men brawled on the streets and violent muggers lurked in alleyways. When he was seven years old, running errands for coins, Chester had collided with an enormous man in a rifleman coat. The man had leaned down slowly, his expression tight. "You scared, boy?"

Chester had managed a nod.

"Well, that's a secret you can't trust to nobody." The man's voice had been coarse, as cold as the bricks of the alleyway. "Here's a tip for you, boy. You want to survive in this town, you don't let no one see you're afeared of 'em. You show folks you're weak, and they'll use it to break you. Convince the world you're strong and you're halfway to being there."

And so, just as Chester had learned to play fiddle, he had learned to play the game of bravado.

Now, exhausted and ragged, he forced himself to his feet. He would not give in. He would not lie in the dirt of the prison and let them judge him.

The sheriff placed his hands on the bars. "I've been talkin' to Bel. She says your name's Chester Hays. That correct?"

Chester met his gaze. "If I tell you, will you reconsider chopping my head off?"

The sheriff snorted. "You've got gumption, boy, I'll give you that." He turned to his green-coated companion and bowed his head. "All yours, sir."

The stranger pulled a gleaming badge from his pocket. He thrust it into the light of the sorcery lamp, so that Chester could see the words inscribed on the metal.

44

Nathaniel Glaucon. Accredited Songshaper.

Chester's belly clenched. For the first time, he noticed the pendant around the man's throat. It was a silver nautilus shell that boasted his status as Songshaper.

"Took me seven years to earn this license," said Nathaniel Glaucon. "Seven years of slaving away at the Conservatorium. Classes, lectures, exams. And even after seven years, half my class-mates failed the final assessment." He leaned in closer. "It isn't easy to become a Songshaper, boy. You have to earn it. You have to bleed for it."

Chester privately thought this was a little melodramatic. The closest he'd come to bleeding when learning a musical instrument was a few blistered fingertips before he'd grown callouses to press on the strings.

Nathaniel Glaucon, however, seemed deadly serious. He held up his badge as though it was evidence of a divine miracle. "I fought for this, boy. I earned it. I am qualified to play Music, to summon magic from the air. I can even touch the Song itself, if I'm careful not to disturb its beat. But you?" His lips twisted into a scowl of disdain. "You commit blasphemy."

Chester stepped forward to grab the bars. "Hang on, wait! I'm not . . . I mean, I didn't mean to—"

Nathaniel raised a hand to cut him off. "I sensed your crime all the way from my home on the hilltop. A decent Songshaper can always sense nearby disruptions in the Song. Do you deny that it was you?"

"No, but I didn't mean—"

"Intention is irrelevant, boy," said Nathaniel. "You're guilty. It's for the sheriff to decide your sentence."

He dipped his head and hummed a few notes of the Sundown Recital, a quiet little prayer to the Song. The sheriff joined in, obediently bowing his head. The underground jail filled with music. When they finished they snapped their heads back up and stared at Chester.

Silence.

"For this most heinous of crimes," said the sheriff in a chillingly official tone of voice, "I sentence you to die this day, this last day of the month."

✱

They bound his wrists and dragged him up into the dawn. Chester blinked in the glare of the sunlight. He stumbled to his knees, but the sheriff hauled him up by the back of his shirt.

"On your feet, boy," he said. "Unless you want to die in shame." He fingered the pistol at his belt.

Chester eyed the pistol. For a terrible moment, he considered it. If he stopped here, the sheriff would shoot him. Perhaps that would be better. A fast, clean death. His head would remain on his shoulders.

But it would mean giving in. Chester still had minutes to live, precious minutes, and he wasn't about to give those up. If he truly was as brash as a banjo, then he'd damn well keep plucking those strings until the very end. *Convince the world you're strong and you're halfway to being there.*

He clambered to his feet.

In the square, a crowd had already gathered. They broke into cheers as the prisoners approached: Chester and the horse thief, bound and helpless in the growing light. The thief whimpered and cried, and Chester caught a whiff of urine as the man lost control of his bladder. The sheriff shoved the man in the small of his back. The man stumbled forward, then tripped into the puddle of mud that had formed in the dust around his feet.

"Get movin'," grunted the sheriff.

A minute later, they stood in the center of the square. The crowd roared. A pair of local farmers grappled with the horse thief, forcing him to kneel, his head upon the block.

"Thomas Malkin," said the sheriff. "You are found guilty of theft from a government official. You are found guilty of denying your crimes, and attempting to flee from justice. Your sentence is death."

The man called Malkin was sobbing like a child. When the ax came down there was a terrible crunch of flesh and bone. The crowd cheered. Chester clenched his eyes shut, breath like fire in his throat. He couldn't watch the head roll away, or the blood splash across the platform. He couldn't . . .

"Next!" called the sheriff.

And then he was up there. Chester didn't even remember those final steps across the square. All he knew was that his head was lying on the block, and the other man's blood was smearing his cheek, and liquid was pooling around his knees, his shins . . .

"Chester Hays. You are found guilty of illegal Music. You are found guilty of connecting to the Song without a license. Your sentence is death."

He could see the hill. With his head at this angle, it curved like a treble clef. Chester thought of his fiddle. He thought of the Song. *This is just another performance*, he told himself. The crowd was just an audience, enjoying his music, dancing to his fiddle as his fingers ranged across the neck. He was pressing his bow to the strings. He was coaxing a melody from its touch. His heart was fluttering because the music was so pure, so perfect.

Someone was shouting, a blur in the crowd, pushing toward him . . .

He would not let them see his fear. He would not—

The ax came down.

And just before it hit his neck, the world stopped.

47

CHAPTER SIX

CHESTER DIDN'T BREATHE.

For a moment he thought he was dead. The ax had come down, his neck had been severed, and this world of blurring light was just the final scream of a dying mind. But he could feel his hands. His legs. His chest.

The world was gray: the sky had tipped a bottle of ink across Hamelin, turning the town to shadow. Chester took a cautious breath. His lungs inflated. The air tasted bitter, with an odd tang of salt, and it moved like molasses in front of his eyes.

Slowly, Chester twisted his neck around. It was still attached to his shoulders, as far as he could tell. He rolled his head to the side and looked up. The executioner was gone. The ax was gone. He struggled to his feet. If he focused his eyes, he could make out the remains of the square. The cobbled streets. The execution platform. Faint silhouettes of buildings loomed behind the unnatural rain. But there were no people. No voices. No sound. Just empty sky, as dark and smoky as the world to his sides. Rain fell, tumbling and swirling, but it didn't leave him wet. It spilled around and around, like a fistful of colorless leaves.

Perhaps he *was* dead. Perhaps he—

"Chester Hays?"

He whirled. The speaker stood beside him, cloaked in a swirl of rain and shadow. Chester strained his eyes to make out the face.

It was an older boy, about nineteen: a bulk of height and muscles beneath his leather coat. He wore a cowboy hat, tilted slightly downward, and had pale blue eyes that glinted beneath the rim. With a rush, Chester remembered the blurred sight of a figure running, shouting, shoving through the crowd toward him . . .

It was the boy from the saloon. The one who'd suggested "The Nightfall Duet." Had he known what would happen when Chester played? Had he somehow guessed, in that whirlwind of music, that Chester would accidentally connect to the Song?

Chester took another weak breath. "Who are you?"

"Samson Walsingham's my name," said the boy, "but most folks call me Sam. And you'd better hurry. Ain't safe to be in the Hush without no training."

"The what?"

"The Hush." Sam gestured at the gray expanse of air. "This place."

Something stirred in Chester's memory. *The Hush.* He was sure he'd heard that term before . . . but his mind felt muddled and he couldn't think clearly. His brain was strained with fear and panic, adrenaline still pumping after the horrors of the execution, confusion at the swirl and whip of this unnatural gray world.

"Is this the afterlife?" he whispered. "Am I dead?"

Sam snorted. "No, you ain't dead."

"Well then, what is this place?"

Sam shook his head, impatient. "It's hard to explain, all right? But you ain't dead, and the Hush ain't no afterlife. It's just . . . somewhere else. Somewhere to escape to." He waved a hand. "Look, you gotta come quick—no time for spelling it out."

Chester backed away. "Why should I trust you?"

"Cause if I hadn't yanked you into the Hush," Sam said, "your head would be taking a vacation from your shoulders right about now."

"Good point."

They hurried across the square and down a street. As Chester moved, the patch of visibility around him shifted: the square vanished into rain behind him, as the road ahead formed nebulous shapes and shadows. It felt as though he was walking in a bubble of light, deep underwater, with a boundary that ebbed and shifted.

"What did you mean," Chester said, "about it not being safe here?"

Sam grabbed his sleeve. "Hurry up."

Chester stumbled, startled by the larger boy's speed. Sam's legs were powerfully long; for every stride he took, Chester was forced to take two. The older boy glanced around constantly, checking from side to side. His eyes were intense, pale, and glinting beneath the rim of his cowboy hat.

Occasionally, a strange noise echoed in the Hush: a huff from their left, or a shriek in the distance. Whenever this happened, Sam would yank Chester behind him. He would thrust out his hands protectively, as though to ward off an attack from the dark. There would be a long pause. A silence. Chester would hold his breath.

Then Sam would yank him forward with a new burst of speed.

As they hurried down Hamelin's main road, Chester glimpsed the looming bulk of the Barrel o' Gold through the gloom. But here in the Hush, the saloon was no longer whitewashed wood. It was gray and distorted, shrouded in rain and smudged by darkness. As soon as Chester passed, the building faded: just another vanishing ghost in the Hush.

Chester's throat stung and his breath felt sharp. They passed through the outskirts of the town, hurrying onto the road beyond its boundaries. Cornfields rose on either side of them: tall and faded, swirling with gray. Black paint seemed to splatter the sky.

Sam jerked him to a stop. "Touch the ground, and close your eyes."

"But—"

"Just do it!"

As Chester knelt, he kept his muscles tense. If the larger boy attacked him, he would be ready to run. But Sam did not attack; instead, he knelt and pressed his own right hand into the dirt. Then he grabbed Chester's shoulder with his left hand.

"What are you—?"

"Easier if we're touching," Sam said. "I had a hell of a time yanking you into the Hush before, when you were under that ax. Had to yell the blasted notes over the crowd and grab you at exactly the right moment—used up every damn speck of concentration I had."

There was a moment's silence.

Sam whistled.

It was a low, deep whistle. It echoed and rolled, like the howl of a wolf. It faded. Sam let out another whistle, then another. And suddenly, Chester recognized the tune, The Sundown Recital. But instead of humming the notes in order, Sam was whistling them backward.

Chester recoiled. *Blasphemy.* An abuse of the Song. He jerked away, but Sam tightened his grip.

A flash. A compression of the air. Chester felt as though his skin had been pressed in, pushed against his bones and flesh. His eyeballs ached and his nails crushed like knives into his fingertips. The air whirled and whipped, as though to pull him away, and he dug his hands desperately into the dirt of the road, as though the dust and soil was an anchor in a stormy sea. The air around him sucked backward, a whiplash, and then . . .

51

It was over.

Chester blinked. He was kneeling on a dusty road, with Sam beside him. Hot morning sunlight beat down on his frame. The darkness was gone; the fog had vanished. They were on the outskirts of Hamelin, by the edge of the cornfields. The grass crackled a little in the rising heat, and he heard the buzz of insects in the fields nearby.

Sam rose. "Come on."

Chester struggled to his feet, trying to keep his balance. He felt dizzy—almost drunk—as the last few minutes caught up with his brain. He had almost died. He had almost *died*. But Sam had saved him. Sam had pulled him out of the normal world, and they had escaped through the dark unreality he'd called the Hush . . .

Suddenly, Chester knew where he'd heard that phrase before. The memory returned like a slap. His father, tossing and turning in the night, his forehead streaked with sweat, his eyelids twitching, lips muttering. His father in the throes of a nightmare. *Hush, hush, hush* . . .

Chester felt a sudden coldness. "Sam, what's the Hush?"

"Told you, I ain't got time to explain. It's too—"

"I have to know!"

Sam grabbed him by the shoulders. "Listen to me, Chester Hays. If you want to know right now, you're gonna end up dead. I'll tell you, I swear, but not right now. We gotta get out of here first, get someplace safe. You hear me?"

"But—"

"There's a blasted Songshaper in that town," Sam said. "He'll know you headed for the edge of town—where else are you gonna run? If you want to live long enough for answers, we gotta go."

Chester's stomach twisted. Sam was right. Chester couldn't help his father if the townspeople killed him. He could hear them now, quite close: shouting, yelling, barking orders. Their cries rang out like gunshots in the quiet morning air.

"This way!"

"Get him! Someone's helping the little—"

"There's trails in the dust, look!"

The shouts grew closer by the second: a bustle of noise, yells, footsteps. All coming from the center of the town. All surging toward them.

"They're coming," Chester whispered.

Sam swore under his breath. "I didn't save your neck to have it blown off by a pistol."

But to Chester's surprise, Sam didn't charge down the road. Instead, he twisted aside and plowed down a tiny trail into the field of corn. Stalks swayed higher than his head, creating a labyrinth of green and gold.

Chester darted along the path, suddenly grateful for his size. He'd always wanted to be taller and stronger, but he was well-suited to this narrow path, clearly designed for a nimble farmer to navigate his crops. Chester could dart and weave, twisting and turning with the loops of the trail. Sam, on the other hand, was the size of an ox. He crashed along without the slightest hint of caution, smashing corn stalks as if they were toothpicks.

Chester hurried forward. "You're leaving a trail."

"Oh, really?" Sam said, gruff with sarcasm. "I hadn't noticed."

"I just thought, maybe you could run sideways . . ."

"And *I* just thought," Sam said, "maybe you could start showing some respect to the person who saved your Song-cursed neck."

There was a shout from behind them. It was closer this time. Too close.

Sam grabbed Chester's arm. "Come on!"

They plunged down a path to the side. Chester spluttered as leaves and stalks smacked him in the face. Then they were running, smashing through the field. Broken stems slipped under Chester's feet and every oversized leaf seemed determined to whip his eyes.

"Couldn't we . . . just . . . go back into the Hush?"

"No!" Sam was sweating now, but his breath held steady. "Too many dangers, and you ain't trained to deal with 'em."

They burst into a clearing: a long, wide row of corn that had already been harvested. Chester stumbled into open sunlight, doubled over to clutch his knees, and sucked down a lungful of air. Then he straightened up, taking a moment to get his bearings.

In the distant blue sky, a pegasus circled.

Chester swore. It was a chestnut horse with wings of golden brown. Its rider was just a silhouette from this distance, but it wasn't hard to guess why he'd taken to the sky.

"What?" Sam said.

Chester pointed. "They're hunting us from above."

Sam squinted up. "This way."

A dozen wider paths trailed off into the corn. They didn't take the widest path or even the one that led farthest away from town. Perhaps Sam thought that would be too obvious—although, privately, Chester would have settled for obvious so long as it took him away from Hamelin.

The hillside sloped lower, painted with fields. Every breath he took tasted of dust and half-dried cornhusks. They swerved left and right, navigating forks in the path, weaving ever downward.

As the morning wore on, the heat thickened. Air slapped hot on Chester's face, his neck, his forearms. Insects buzzed. Chester felt as though his shirt itself might dissolve into sweat. He wished for a river, a creek—anything to wash the dust and salt from his body. But there was nothing. Just the smother of the sun, and the crackle of dried husks underfoot.

He could still hear shouts, but they sounded more distant now. Perhaps the townspeople had chosen the wrong path in this endless maze. Chester shielded his eyes, took a shuddering breath, and almost allowed himself to hope.

Then he glanced up. "Sam, get down!"

They collapsed into a heap under arches of foliage just as a sweep of chestnut wings crossed the sky. Chester held his breath and fought to keep still. If he rustled the stems, a jolt would travel up the corn stalks and toss their highest leaves into a quiver.

But he risked raising his eyes, just a little. There was still an arch of darkness above, circling, as though the rider thought he might have spotted something, and was looping back around to double-check . . .

Chester felt Sam beside him, torso pressed against his shoulder. The older boy held his breath. He kept as still as a boulder, silent and steady in the leaves.

Finally, the shadow was gone.

Chester raised his head. The path through the corn was clear. He took a deep breath then slowly began to unfold his limbs. As he did so, he angled his neck for a better view of the sky.

"Gone?" Sam whispered.

"I think so."

Chester crawled forward onto the path, where he could move more freely. Then he looked up properly and shaded his eyes.

"He's leaving," he said quietly. "But I think we should wait a minute, to be sure."

Sam slumped back onto his elbows. Chester followed him back into the crook of the corn, where they'd already trampled the foliage. After a while, he lifted a hand to shield his face from the sun. He wished he had a hat like Sam's, with a rim to cast some shade. The skin on his knuckles and his arms stung raw with sunburn.

When he could no longer stand the silence, he asked Sam: "Why did you save me?"

There was a pause.

"Why's it matter? You're alive, ain't you? No cause for complaining, if you ask me."

"I don't see why you'd risk your neck for a stranger."

Sam hesitated. "I'm working on a job with some friends of mine. We've been . . . recruiting, I guess you'd call it."

"Recruiting?" Chester turned to stare at him. "And you want me?"

"Well, you passed the test."

"What test?"

"Last night," Sam said, "in the saloon. You hooked up to the Song, all on your own." He made a sound that was half-laugh, half-scoff. "Just what the captain's been looking for. When she sees what I dragged in for the job, I bet she'll offer me a pay raise."

"That's why you saved my life?" Chester said. "You want me for this . . . job?"

"Hell no," Sam said. "I don't want you for nothing. I don't trust Songshapers, and I sure as hell weren't hankering to save your neck."

"Then why—"

"Cause orders is orders, and I do as I'm told. Captain wants you, and Captain gets what she wants." Sam glanced up at the empty sky. "Come on. Better move before that blasted horse comes back."

"But the Hush—you were going to tell me—"

"Later."

Chester forced himself to swallow a retort. This wasn't the time to argue. They were still in danger, and Sam still held all the answers. This boy might even know the reason for his father's vanishing. But if Chester pushed too hard, or asked too many questions, the older boy might clam up completely.

All he could do was follow and trust that the answers would come.

CHAPTER SEVEN

THE FIELDS WERE EERILY SILENT. CHESTER TRUDGED WITH A STITCH in his side. There was no wind, no breeze, just heavy air, as hot as stew, and the sound of their own progress. Huffing. Stomping. Snapping twigs and heaving breaths.

And suddenly, a shout.

Chester stiffened. It wasn't a distant yell from some far-flung corner of the maze. It was barely a hundred yards behind them.

"I found 'em! Get the sheriff!"

"Hey, over here!"

Chester whipped his neck around. He couldn't see the speakers. But when he thought of all the stalks they'd broken, brushing the sides of the path, he felt sick.

"Come on," Sam whispered. "This way."

Chester fought to keep his footsteps light, but it was hopeless; every strand of dried grass or broken stalk crunched like a firecracker. And Sam, despite his speed and strength, wasn't built for sneaking. He blundered along with all the noise of a wild griffin, sparking cracks and huffs and snaps into the silence.

"The Hush!" Chester said. "We can go back into the Hush, can't we? Just long enough to get away from—"

Sam shook his head. "Can't do it out here, even if we wanted to. You need some Musical residue in the air, for breaking into the Hush."

57

"There's none here?"

"Nope. It's not like in the middle of town, near that Songshaper's house."

Chester felt a weight settle in his stomach. Without even realizing it, he had been relying on the hope of the Hush. The knowledge that if worst came to worst, they could slip back into unreality, safe from the sheriff and his bullets.

But they were trapped, with no way into the Hush and no way out of the cornfields. Their pursuers probably included the farmers who owned this field. They would know every twist and every turn. Chester, on the other hand, was lost. Ahead, nothing but endless green and tan. Above, just empty blue. There were no landmarks to judge by, no way to keep track of the town or the horizon. He couldn't see over the tops of the corn stalks, which loomed like soldiers over his head. He tried to steady his breathing, to hide the terror that wrenched at his belly. *You show folks you're weak, and they'll use it to break you . . .*

They swerved around a corner. Chester skidded on a few dried corn husks in a wild attempt to avoid crashing into Sam. The larger boy had jerked to a halt, slapping one hand up to keep his cowboy hat from flying off his head.

"What . . . ?"

And then he saw a man, ten yards ahead.

Nathaniel Glaucon.

Chester's throat closed. For a long moment, he didn't breathe. He stared down the path at the Songshaper, at the sweep of his olive-green coat framed by walls of corn stalks. At the chestnut pegasus by his side.

At the pistol in his hands.

Sam whipped his own gun from its holster so fast that Chester barely heard the click. There was a blast of gunfire and a bullet smashed into Nathaniel's chest.

58

Chester jumped, shocked by the roar of the gun. His ears rang, warping sound in and out like the chokes of a dying man. Nathaniel jerked back and Chester stared, waiting for the Songshaper to topple.

He didn't. Blood poured from his chest, spreading a stain across his olive coat. His breath was ragged, as though the bullet had pierced one of his lungs. But there was no cry of pain and no falling body. Instead, a flittering tune escaped his lips: a hum of notes, pouring Music into the air. A wisp of dark smoke curled up from his chest, as though his humming had scorched a melody into the wound itself . . .

Healing, Chester realized. Nathaniel was using a melody to heal himself. Chester knew that a trained Songshaper could be powerful, but he had always pictured wild, brutal blasts of power. He had never realized that such finesse was possible: the skill to stitch your own flesh together with a song . . .

Nathaniel fell silent. He stood there, a gun in one hand and reins in the other. His pendant—the silver nautilus shell—glinted at his throat.

The pegasus, which had let out a terrified whinny at the gunshot, was straining and rearing now, fighting to break away. Its wings flapped and its nostrils snorted, panicked by the roar of the bullet.

Nathaniel fixed his gaze on it. He hummed a slow, quiet tune under his breath. A tune of control, perhaps, to tranquilize the beast.

The creature's wings sucked downward and vanished into its spine with a slow, crumpled slurp. Its legs stopped straining; its nostrils ceased flaring. The magic fizzled into its veins, its hooves, its bones, its withers. And slowly, inch by inch, the beast calmed. It stood silent and still, just an ordinary chestnut stallion, its mind drugged into a doze.

Silence.

Nathaniel raised an eyebrow at Sam, and kept his own pistol trained toward them. "Now, now," he said. His voice was hoarse, but with every word it sounded stronger. "You can't have expected that to kill me, boy. I am protected by the glory of the Song."

Sam scoffed. "You ain't protected by nothing but your own damn spellwork, you filthy—"

Nathaniel Glaucon cut him off with a laugh. "Oh, very good." He took a step closer. "Very good, boy."

He dropped the reins. Behind him, the horse just stood there, silent and numb as stone. Nathaniel's gaze wandered to Chester now, and he adjusted the angle of his pistol. It pointed directly at Chester's face.

Chester froze. He stared down the barrel of the pistol, at the hole where the bullet would emerge. Beside him, he felt Sam's muscles tense. The silence stretched. No one moved.

"Now," Nathaniel said, "this is interesting." His eyes flicked back to Sam, but his pistol stayed trained on Chester. "For someone who knows so much, you took a great risk coming here. All to save this brat from his rightful execution. Why might that be, I wonder?"

Sam didn't respond.

"I know what you are, boy," said Nathaniel Glaucon to Chester. "But this is my town and we play by my rules. I won't let an unlicensed Songshaper run out of here alive."

He pulled the trigger.

The next few seconds were a blur. Sam crashed into Chester's side and he was falling, stumbling, smashing down into a wall of stalks and leaves. Chester's ears were ringing again, but this time pain accompanied the roar. His left arm burned hot, slick with blood.

Sam lay half on top of him, heavy and gasping. But a moment later he was up, firing wildly at the Songshaper. Five sharp cracks smashed down the path. Every bullet shrieked, and Chester felt as though his ears might blast right off his head.

Nathaniel staggered and dropped his weapon.

Sam fired again and again. But he wasn't firing at the Songshaper's chest. With a jolt, Chester realized that the older boy was firing at Nathaniel's *ankles*. The man toppled with a cry. His own pistol slipped from his fingers as he struggled to catch himself. He collapsed, flailing, into the tangle of his own coat.

"You might be hard to kill," Sam said, "but good luck standing with your ankles in shreds."

Nathaniel fished something from his pocket—another gun, Chester thought in a panic—but no, it was a miniature flute. The man pressed the instrument to his lips and began to conjure a huffing, panicked melody. As the notes poured out, smoke spiraled up from the end of his flute. The path began to tingle, alive with Music, and the dirt beneath Chester began to dissolve. With a gasp, he felt himself sinking, as though the dirt was sucking him down into his grave . . .

"Oh no you don't!"

Sam charged. He forced the Songshaper's head down onto the path, and eddies of dust rose to mingle with the smoke. The flute skittered away and Sam swiped it up, along with the man's lost pistol. Chester scrambled for a patch of solid earth just as the entire path snapped back into rigidity beneath him. On the ground fumbling in pain, he fought to rip his sunken knees and ankles free from the dirt.

Nathaniel snarled up at Sam. "That's mine!"

Sam clutched the flute tighter, holding it beyond Nathaniel's grasp. The Songshaper began to hum, pushing furious Music through his lips and teeth. Sam blasted a bullet into the man's throat, just above his silver pendant. Blood poured from Nathaniel's flesh as he choked and writhed in the dust. But his fingers pummelled the dirt beside him, with a certain regularity to their beat. He was tapping out a rhythm, Chester realized: a weak, halting beat to slow the bleeding in his wounds.

A curl of dark, unnatural smoke rose from Nathaniel's throat, and the skin began to slowly blister. But this time, the healing was sluggish. A rhythm, it seemed, was less effective than a melody. For a while, at least, Nathaniel would be in no fit state to attack them.

And behind him, the chestnut horse just stood there. It remained numb and silent, drugged by sorcery, its wits as lost as its vanished wings. The sight was unsettling: an unmoving statue in rising clouds of dust and smoke.

Chester struggled to his feet. He had to help. He had to do *something*, he couldn't just lie there. But as soon as he rose, his head swam with dizziness. Pain shot down his upper arm, where the bullet had struck. He clutched the wound, fingers tightening, and fought to stem the sticky flow of blood.

A moment later, Sam was by his side. "All right?"

"Yeah." Chester gritted his teeth, and tried to look braver than he felt. "I'm fine. Better keep moving."

Sam grabbed his arm and examined the wound. He swore under his breath then stumbled back across to where Nathaniel writhed on the ground. The Songshaper struggled to rise but his bullet-ridden ankles made it impossible.

Sam ripped off the man's coat and tore a strip of fabric from the vest he wore beneath. Then he was back with Chester, tying the fabric tightly around his injured arm. Chester cried out when Sam gave one final yank to tighten the bandage. It felt like a whole new bullet through his flesh: a sharp shock of pain, followed by the burn of heat and seepage of blood. Chester clenched his eyes and let a hiss escape his teeth.

"Will he be all right?" he whispered.

"Who?"

"The Songshaper."

Sam glanced back toward Nathaniel. "Yeah, he'll be fine. Might take a few hours of healing, but a man like that don't die easy." He looked at Chester. "You, on the other hand . . ."

Chester swayed a little, trying to fight back the dizziness.

Sam grabbed his face. "Look at me."

Chester blinked and tried to focus.

Sam stared into his pupils for a moment then nodded. "All right, we gotta move. You feel yourself getting too dizzy, you let me know. Don't wait until you're falling off the damn horse, all right?"

Chester gritted his teeth. "Yeah. All right."

They staggered across to the chestnut horse. Sam vaulted onto its back and gestured for Chester to get up, too. Chester winced at the stab in his arm, but stuck a foot in the stirrup and launched himself up in front of Sam. With a gasp of pain, he found his balance.

The horse remained utterly still. Apart from the inflation of its chest when it breathed, they might as well have been sitting on a statue. The Music used to numb the creature had certainly worked.

"Here." Sam reached forward to pass Chester the miniature flute. "Can't bring its wings back without the right training, but at least you can wake it up."

"You do it, I don't know how—"

"Gotta be you," Sam said. "I can't play Music. Just play something cheerful. Something alive. And do it fast."

There were other footsteps now. Other shouts and cries in the fields around them. Suddenly Chester remembered the farmers, the townspeople, the sheriff. They would have heard the gunshots. They would have heard the shouts, the cries, the shrieks of the panicking pegasus . . .

Any moment, they would be here.

Chester raised the flute to his lips. He took a deep breath, struggled to tune out the agony of his arm, and blew a few test notes to get a feel for the instrument.

Finally, he launched into the music.

For the first few bars, there was nothing but the rollick of melody. The shouts behind them grew louder and there was the sound of running footsteps. Figures burst out onto the path behind them, and Chester heard the angry clicks of cocking pistols while the horse remained still and silent.

Chester played harder. He built up the pace, the lilt, the thrum of the music. He scarcely dared to take a breath, except to suck back a note along the curve of his tongue. There was another tune now, echoing at the back of his head, that took the rhythm of his heartbeat. He stuttered, panicking slightly, as he recognized the Song.

No! He couldn't afford to connect to the Song. He had to focus on his own tune, his own Music. He clenched his eyes shut and blew the flute harder, focusing with every last ounce of concentration on the melody. The tune rose higher and higher, louder and louder. The horse jerked. It shook its head and a whinny escaped its lips. Its nostrils flared and it stumbled backward, tripping away from Nathaniel's bloody body on the ground.

"That's more like it!" Sam reached around Chester's sides to grab the reins, and gave the horse a kick. "Let's get of here."

The horse bolted.

There was a frenzy of bangs and shouts. Hamelin locals poured down the trail and started firing in their direction. Sam kicked again and Chester clutched at the horse's mane, his heart thumping and his arm throbbing. The world was a clatter of hooves and the shriek of bullets.

They rounded a bend in the path, building to a gallop, and the world flew by in a whirl of green stalks and blue sky. Dust roared up from the horse's hooves, and Chester coughed and spluttered as it puffed into his mouth. But he kept his eyes open and his body tensed. Another bend, and another. The horse charged and panted, an engine of sweat and muscle. The cornfields fell away. With a final crash, they plowed through a patch of young stalks.

And then they were out, charging downhill with reckless speed into open fields and sunlight.

CHAPTER EIGHT

IT WAS ALMOST NOON WHEN THEY HIT THE RAILWAY LINE, A GLEAMING trail of hot metal and wood. It ran into the distance, on and on, seeming to narrow as it trickled away. On the western horizon, it vanished into a shimmer of heat under midday sky.

Sam reached out to help Chester dismount. For a moment Chester was insulted, but the burn in his arm won out over pride. He allowed Sam to grab him around the waist and lift him down.

"All right?" Sam asked.

Chester nodded, although he still felt a little dizzy. Blood trickled out under the bandage Sam had made and he suspected the horse's jolting had dislodged it from the proper pressure point. But he took the reins in his good hand and gave the firmest nod he could muster. "Yeah. I'm fine."

Sam bent to examine the railway track. His boots scuffed the dirt as he knelt, placing a cautious hand on the hot metal. He frowned then shuffled sideways. Little puffs of dust scraped up from the drag of his coat in the dirt. He pressed his fingers to the metal again. He bowed his head, cowboy hat tilting toward the tracks.

"What are you doing?" Chester asked.

"Concentrating."

Chester wasn't sure whether that was an answer to his question or an order to shut up. He decided to go with the latter and took a few steps parallel to the track. He stared down the line. An endless line of wood and metal. Endless fields, endless sky.

The Meloral railway line had only sprung up over the last decade or so. It began in Weser City, on the southwestern coast, and stretched thousands of miles to the eastern port of Leucosia. In recent years, other tracks had begun to branch off from it, casting a spiderweb of lines across the country.

Unfortunately, this progress had come with a cost. Hundreds of workers had died to lay the tracks, collapsing under the scorching sun in the remotest areas of Meloral. Only the most desperate of men would take a job on the railway. In many towns, going off to "work on the tracks" was a euphemism for poverty or running from the past, and it meant dying young.

Sam dusted off his hands. "Right," he said. "Train's coming soon."

"How do you know?"

"Can feel it vibrating. The whole damn track starts to wake up when there's a train coming."

Chester peered up and down the track. They were in the middle of nowhere—no station, no bridge, no fork in the line. Nothing that might slow a train long enough to jump aboard. Just flat, empty track. If a train came through here, it would come at full speed.

"How are we supposed to jump on?" he said.

"Huh?"

"Onto the train, I mean. It'll be going too fast to—"

"We ain't here to catch a train."

"Then where are we going?"

"Back into the Hush," Sam said.

Chester's insides froze. "What?"

"You heard me," Sam said. "We're going back into the Hush. We'll need a hell of a Musical push to break back through. The trains're powered in part by Music—normally they give enough of a push."

"You said I wasn't trained to go there yet." Chester tried to hide the sudden twang of nerves in his voice. "You've changed your mind?"

"Nope," Sam said. "It's too dangerous for you to run around the Hush on foot. But lucky for you, I got transport waiting." He gave Chester a long look. "How'd you figure I got to Hamelin so quick yesterday?"

"I thought you just happened to be in town . . ."

"What, for a blasted harvest party?" Sam snorted. "Yesterday morning, I was in Bremen. There was a Songshaper there, tracking you with a radar globe. If you keep joining up to the Song," he added, in response to Chester's startled look, "sooner or later, you're gonna get yourself noticed. The radar picks up interference in the Song, see, and it sends an alert if your Musical signature ain't registered . . ."

Chester swallowed.

"Anyway," Sam said, "the radar said you was over in Hamelin, so the captain sent me to check if we'd found a real rogue Songshaper, or just a glitch in the radar."

Chester's mouth tasted dry. "Last night in the bar . . . you told me to play 'The Nightfall Duet' because it was a hard song. You were testing me. You *wanted* me to slip into the Song again, in front of all those people!"

Sam didn't deny it.

"You could have gotten me killed!"

"Would've happened eventually, anyway," Sam said with a shrug. "You was teetering on the brink of it as soon as you started playing. Lucky for you, it happened when I was there to save you."

"That doesn't mean—"

Sam cut him off. "Want to know about the Hush or not?"

68

Chester shut up. He realized with a surreal detachment that he was on the brink of losing it. After the horrors of his prison cell, the near execution, the dark of the Hush and the chase through the cornfields, he felt oddly fragile, like a shard of pottery on the brink of shattering. But then he thought of his father and pushed his own pain out of his mind. This oversized boy in front of him—with his cowboy hat and pale blue eyes—might hold the answers.

"All right," Chester said. "I'm sorry. Just . . . tell me what to do."

Sam took a moment to process his apology, then nodded. "Get behind the trees. Train'll be here in less than a minute, I'm guessing."

The trees—a tangle of trunks and lines of shadow—would hide them from the tracks. Chester led the horse gently by the reins to the shelter of a nearby clump of foliage, thankful that it didn't pull too hard when he had only one arm's strength to rely on. Unlike Nathaniel, Chester didn't need Music to calm the beast down—the exhaustion of the ride had done that for him.

A roar bellowed down the track.

Chester peered through a cluster of branches. A train thundered down the line toward them, black and crimson, blasting clouds of smoke into the sky. It chugged, it roared, it rattled. Its wheels played a clackety racket of drumbeats—and amid the smoke and chaos, it piped a whirl of music into the sky.

No, not just music, but *Music*.

It was a rolling tune, a rollicking rhythm. It was churning wheels and grunting brass, the charge of a horse, the screech of a griffin. It pumped through the engine of the train, up into smoke and sky and sunlight. But the Music would only be there for a moment—at the exact moment the train passed by. Would they be close enough to harness its power?

"Ditch the horse," Sam said.

"What?"

"Just do it."

Chester released the reins. The horse stumbled backward, a little skittish, away from the roar of the train.

"Right," Sam said. "Now, you gotta trust me. No matter what I do, no matter how crazy it seems. I ain't about to let you die, all right? Not after all the blasted trouble you've put me through."

Chester nodded.

"Swear it," Sam said. "No matter how crazy it seems, you do exactly what I do."

"I swear it," Chester said.

Sam stared at him, as though trying to decide whether he was trustworthy. Then he nodded. "All right. Let's go."

Sam dashed out from behind the trees. Chester followed, his heart shuddering like a loose fiddle string. They hurtled forward— and with a terrible lurch, he realized where Sam was heading.

The track.

The railway track, right in front of the train.

The train blazed toward them, gushing and roaring and pouring smoke into the air. Music pumped up through its smoke, and Chester fought down an insane urge to laugh. It sounded almost like a folk song, distorted with fire and power and engine grease.

This is crazy, Chester thought. *This is crazy!*

His entire body was trembling. He shouldn't be here. He should be fleeing toward another town, searching for clues about his father's disappearance. Perhaps he could slip away from Sam, escape the townsfolk on his own and make his way alone . . .

But he felt faint from the blood loss and he had given his word and he had no idea what else to do. He had no money and without his fiddle he couldn't earn a living. Nor could he charm people into spilling their secrets. Besides, at the moment, Sam was his only real lead to finding his father.

Chester took a deep breath. He tensed his muscles and hurled himself onto the track.

When he touched the metal, Chester let out a cry. Lit by the morning sun, it burned hot on his flesh. Sam grabbed his shoulder and began to whistle. Chester could barely hear over the roar of the train but he caught a few notes and realized it was a reversal of the Sundown Recital.

The train was almost upon them. Its brakes screeched: the driver must have spotted them on the tracks, but it was too late. The train's shadow fell across their bodies and Chester felt the world grow cooler, until all was smoke and screeching and metal and shadow and—

It was gone. A churn in the air and a yank behind his gut. The world turned dark, rain exploded in blackened twists around his face, and dark fog rippled out from their position on the track.

Silence.

Chester was shaking. He raised his head, almost unable to breathe.

Darkness stained the world around him. He still knelt on the railway line, but the metal beneath his knees and hands felt like ice. Rain swirled through the air, the sun replaced by dark gray sky. There was no train, just silent track. He was back in the Hush.

Sam yanked him to his feet. "Come on, hurry. Gotta get the echoboat started before that train's finished passing . . ."

"Echoboat?" Chester stumbled along after Sam. The rain parted as they crossed the track, throwing light onto a new patch of darkness.

And suddenly he saw it. It sat on the railway track: a strange beast of sails and lumber, crouching on its nest. It was the size of a large wagon, built of wood and metallic cogs. A yacht's mast rose from its top, sails fluttering in the dark. Its windows were made of glass, an expense almost unheard of, except in Weser City.

"What . . . ?"

"Echoboat." Sam clambered up a short rope ladder and onto the deck. He heaved open a trapdoor and began to descend into the boat. "Get moving, will you? Gotta use the train's residual energy to jump-start the engine, or we'll be stuck here until another damn train comes along."

Sam's voice faded as he vanished inside, swallowed by clanking machinery. Chester scrambled after him, clambering down into the innards of the boat. He dropped down into a sort of driver's cabin, a cubicle that brimmed with wheels and levers. The trapdoor slammed shut overhead, sealing them inside.

"How can I help?"

Sam yanked an enormous wooden lever. "Get out of my way!"

There was a grumble around them and the cabin began to shake. The train's Music played on, still leaking through from the real world. But it was fainter now; the whisper of a dying song. Sam swore then pulled another lever. He pressed a button and yanked a copper chain on the ceiling.

"Hold on," he said. "This ain't gonna be the smoothest ride."

The echoboat jolted and Chester slipped. He grabbed the wall with his good arm to steady himself. The vessel vibrated, shaking with magic and Music. The echoboat heaved itself up slowly, like an old man rising from his rocking chair. It groaned and grunted up into the air, until it hovered about a yard above the railway track.

"Yes," Sam hissed, cranking another lever. "That's my girl!"

The echoboat lingered for a moment, motionless, then shot forward with a *whoosh*. Sam grabbed the steering wheel and wrenched it sideways. The machinery groaned but the boat twisted around and jerked to the side. And suddenly they were flying, out into the dark expanse of rain-streaked fields.

"Just like I told you," Sam said.

"What?"

"Too dangerous to run around the Hush on foot. But when you got transport waiting . . ." Sam twisted the wheel again and the echoboat turned a sharper left. "Well, you'll see why this place is such a secret."

Sam waved a hand at the window, toward the swirling black ahead.

"Welcome," he said, "to the Hush."

CHAPTER NINE

Inside the echoboat, all was still.

The initial roar and rumble had died away, replaced by a serene kind of hum. Chester couldn't decide whether the sound was an engine or the barest hint of Music in the machinery. He squeezed his eyes shut but couldn't pick out a melody.

"Why don't you take a look in the back?" Sam suggested. "I gotta focus on steering."

Chester's mouth felt dry as cornmeal. He wanted to ask a thousand questions, but he saw the look in Sam's eyes now: the focus, the pressure. The older boy's gaze fixed squarely on an illuminated map as he wrapped his hands around the steering wheel. His knuckles were white.

Chester forced himself to be silent.

In the back room, a chain of sorcery lamps hung from the ceiling, casting a shimmer of pale orange light through the air. Wooden cupboards filled the corners, a hammock slouched from one side of the room to another, stacks of books posed like makeshift furniture behind the door and a dog-eared sofa hogged an entire wall. The air smelled faintly of honey and ashes.

Chester looked down at his hands. He was vaguely surprised to see that they were shaking, so jittery that they felt disconnected from the rest of him. *Shock*, he thought.

74

As he stumbled forward, a lamp glinted in the corner of his eye. Chester had a sudden flash of the ax crashing down. His entire body jerked, a marionette yanked sideways by the memory.

With a ragged breath, Chester reached up to touch the lamp, hoping that its tune might calm him. The glass was hot beneath his fingertips. Its Music rolled down his fingers like sweat: the tinkle of piano keys.

Oddly, the tune was unfamiliar. The Songshaper who had enchanted this lamp hadn't played the usual nursery rhymes that formed the magic of most ordinary lamps. They had created their own song, playing a little of their own Music into the glass. The tune was warm and sweet and unsettling all at once.

Chester sank onto the sofa, fighting to calm the choke of emotions in his chest.

All right, so what did he actually know?

There was another version of the world, called the Hush. It looked like the real world. It had the same buildings, the same fields, the same railway lines. But it was dark, filled with fog and rain. Unnatural rain. Rain that fell in swirls and sheafs, yet left those it touched as dry as bone . . .

And not *everything* that existed in the real world existed here. The train, for instance. It had existed in the real world, but not in the Hush. Here, its only remnant was its Music, the sorcery that powered it. Nothing else had leaked through.

He also knew that there were dangers in the Hush that he hadn't seen yet, dangers that frightened even gruff, burly Sam. And strange magic existed here, like the echoboat. An unnatural hybrid of sails and machinery, designed to sail through the Hush like it was a sea of shadows . . .

Chester closed his eyes. Of course, there was one more thing he knew about this place. *Hush, hush, hush* . . . His father's final words before—

The door banged open. Chester opened his eyes.

"On a straight course for now," Sam announced. "Nothing to crash into out here, just a bunch of fields, for miles and miles. Should be all right without a driver for a while."

"What . . . ?" Chester tried to speak, but his mouth felt too dry to let the words slip through. "What is this thing?"

"Echoboat," Sam said. "I already told you. Just a small one, though. It joins onto our gang's main echoship, the *Cavatina*. That's where I'm taking you, to meet the captain."

"Echoship?"

"Floating ships, I guess you'd call 'em," Sam said. "They only exist in the Hush—I ain't never seen one in the real world. But here, with all this residue of magic and sorcery sloshing about . . ." He shrugged. "Don't really matter how it works. It's Dot who knows all that stuff, not me."

"She's in your gang?"

Sam nodded, then crouched beside him. "Gotta look at your arm. Captain won't be happy if I bring back damaged goods."

"Might mess up your hopes of a pay raise?"

"Something like that."

Sam pulled Chester's arm into the light. Chester sucked his teeth, clenched his fists, and tried not to show how much it stung. *Just another performance*, he told himself. He had to prove his strength to these people, to earn his place in their gang—and ultimately, to earn the truth about his father.

Sam unwrapped the makeshift bandage and tossed it aside. A hiss of disapproval escaped his teeth. "I ain't been trained to deal with this, you know."

He sounded irritated, almost angry. Chester felt as though he was expected to apologize—as though it had been his fault that he had been shot, and left the older boy with damaged goods on his hands.

"If you hadn't told me to play 'The Nightfall Duet,'" Chester said, "I wouldn't have gotten shot in the first place."

"You're the one who chose to play it, not me," Sam said. "Back on the ranch, my pa used to say 'It takes a fool to squat with his spurs on.' You make a mistake, you can holler all you like, but don't go blaming the world for your own damn recklessness."

"But you—"

"Besides," Sam added, "if you had more control over your own powers, you could've played your merry way through 'The Nightfall Duet' without getting caught."

"But I don't have any powers! I'm just a fiddler, I swear."

"Then how did you connect to the Song?"

"That was an accident; it happens sometimes when I play something tricky . . . I don't know why it—"

"I'll tell you why," Sam said, pointing a finger. "Because you're one of them."

"One of what?"

"One of them blasted Songshapers," Sam said. "And don't try denying it," he added, when Chester opened his mouth to protest. "You did it again before, up in the cornfields. Played a tune on the flute and woke that horse up from a calming spell. That was Music with a capital 'M.'"

Chester stared at him, his mouth open. Sam rummaged through a nearby drawer and pulled out a small wooden box. He opened it to reveal a medical kit, with bandages, drugs, and syringes.

"I'm not a Songshaper," Chester said. "I've never gone to the Conservatorium. It takes years of training to—"

"To get your official license," Sam interrupted. "That don't mean that other folks never learn on the sly. Black-market tutoring, illegal instruction books . . ."

He filled a syringe with dark liquid. The needle glinted in the light of the sorcery lamps. "I'm not a fool, Hays. I know you learned off someone, but you don't gotta lie to me about it. In case you hadn't noticed, I ain't working on the side of the law."

"I didn't learn illegally from anyone! It just happens, all right? I can't control it. If I'd had actual lessons, do you think I would've connected to the Song right in the middle of a saloon? I'm not suicidal."

As the words tumbled out of him, Chester realized that what propelled his outburst wasn't fury. It was fear. Even though sticking with Sam was the best way to get information that might lead to his father, every instinct screamed at him to flee, to return to the real world—a world of fresh air, of sunlight, of dangers that he could understand. Not this unnatural world of dry rain and cold and darkness . . .

Sam grabbed his arm. "Hold still."

He jabbed the needle into Chester's arm, right below the bullet wound. Chester gasped at the pain. "What . . . ?"

"Stops infections," Sam said. "Travis always makes us take a jab when we get cut up."

"Travis? Is he another member of your gang?"

Sam scowled. "Captain hired him as our doctor, not that long back. Useless at fighting or thieving, but he knows his way around a medical kit." He yanked the needle out of Chester's arm. "Most of the time."

"It doesn't sound like you like him much."

"I don't like no one much," Sam said, "unless they're handing me a bottle of whiskey."

He pulled out a flask of clear liquid. When he uncorked it, Chester caught a strong whiff of liquor. Sam sloshed it over a cloth and began to clean the wound.

Chester closed his eyes. The alcohol burned and he desperately wanted to yank his arm away. It took every inch of self-control to keep it in place and to allow Sam to keep wiping it with the cloth.

After the initial sting, however, he was surprised to realize that Sam's touch was almost . . . gentle. The boy cleaned the wound with soft dabs, not the violent scraping Chester had expected.

"What's your job in this . . . gang?"

"I fight. I steal. I do the dirty work." Sam gave the wound a careful wipe. "I steer the ship. I pick up any scraps and junk we need for jobs."

"And me? Where do I fit in?"

"Like I told you," Sam said, "scraps and junk."

Chester jerked his arm back. "I meant, why am I being recruited? What does your gang want me for?"

Sam snorted. "Been on the lookout for an unlicensed Songshaper for a while. Captain wants you for a job in Weser."

Chester's gut clenched. "Weser City? But I . . . I've never been to the city before."

"First time for everything."

"And it's a criminal job?" Chester said.

"Well, it sure ain't picking daisies in the sunshine." Sam began to bandage the wound. "Don't you start acting all high and mighty, neither. We all gotta eat, and we only steal from rich folks. And in case you hadn't noticed, you're a criminal yourself now."

"I didn't say I wouldn't do it," Chester said. "But I'm not killing anyone, if that's what you want."

Sam gave him a condescending snort. "As if a weakling like you could kill anyone. It'd have to be a little old lady in her rocking chair—and even then, I figure she'd knock you out with her walking stick."

"I'm not weak! I've survived on my own for months, and—"

"Oh, I'm sorry," Sam said, tight with sarcasm. "Did I jump to a conclusion about you without knowing all the facts?" He gave a pointed look. "Since we're on that topic, I'll have you know we ain't a gang of thugs. We don't go around killing people."

There was a pause.

Sam pulled the bandage tight and began to tie it. "We rob 'em blind," he said, "but we leave 'em breathing."

After that there was silence. Chester felt a little dazed. It was as though someone had shoved a wad of bandages through his ears and muffled the thoughts that should have filled his brain. He slouched against the wall, watching blearily as Sam tidied the medical kit.

Chester's vision was oddly blurry. He blinked a few times and tried to sit up. He managed a brief struggle upright, but his body folded and he slumped back against the wall: his muscles didn't want to work.

A peculiar warmth was spreading through his body. It emanated from his arm, where Sam had jabbed the needle . . .

"You . . . you drugged me!" he choked.

"Oh, didn't I mention that?" Sam said. "What a shame."

Chester threw him the nastiest glare he could manage. Considering that his eyes were already slipping closed, it was probably more of an eyelid flutter. He gritted his teeth and managed, "You had no right . . ."

"You gotta rest," Sam said, "and I gotta concentrate."

Chester blinked again, struggling to focus on the older boy. Sam dumped the syringe and old bandage into a wooden bin then headed for the door to the driver's cabin. His silhouette was hazy and tilted to the side . . .

And with that, Chester slid out of consciousness.

CHAPTER TEN

AT SUNDOWN, THEIR PURSUER VANISHED.

At least, Susannah had assumed it was sundown. It was impossible to know for sure in the Hush, where darkness hung like a constant blanket. No night, no day. Just blackness. But when the clock in the driver's cabin had announced sundown, the Songshaper in her echoboat had fallen behind, fading to a faint blip on the map, a subtle tinkle of the proximity bells. A faint chime, almost a whisper. And finally, she was gone.

"Why's she stopped following us, Captain?" Dot peered at the bells. "She's letting us get away! Do you think her Music's broken, or—"

"Sundown," Susannah said. "She had to pull out of the Hush to perform the recital."

"Oh yeah." Like Susannah, Dot had momentarily forgotten the significance of sundown. She looked down at her fingers, twisted them together and said quietly, "Can't believe I forgot."

"It's easy to forget when you're in the Hush," Susannah said. "And you're weaned free of it now, remember? You don't have to stress about it anymore."

"I know," Dot said. "It's just . . . it still feels wrong, sometimes. Boycotting the Sundown Recital, I mean. It's like . . ." She

81

waved a hand. "Like a thousand tiny insects are flying into my brain and flittering their wings on my skull."

Susannah raised an eyebrow but didn't respond. Dot often made odd statements like that. The girl would speak of moon-beams that played poker with the stars, or invisible dancers on the *Cavatina*'s deck when the rain splattered loudly.

"I have a theory," Dot said, "that the symptoms we get when we withdraw from the recital aren't just a physical thing. It's guilt. It's forgoing everything we've ever been taught. That's why it hurts so much. That's why it makes us sick."

"Maybe," Susannah said.

She wrenched the wheel clockwise, steering the *Cavatina* down a nearby slope, then reached up to touch the map. At her touch, the image zoomed in quickly to focus on a close-up of their immediate surroundings.

"I thought we were heading to Linus," Dot said.

"We are." Susannah gave the wheel another turn. "But this could be our chance to lose the Shaper. If we can hide before she gets back into the Hush . . ."

Their echoship spun into a hash of curving lines on the map. Through the windows, the Hush looked the same as always: black air, swirling rain. But from the map, Susannah knew they were on the edge of a steep hillside. If they sailed down the hill and through the valley, perhaps they could escape unseen.

The Songshaper would have to perform her recital before she returned to her echoboat in the Hush. By then, the *Cavatina* would be beyond the range of her proximity sensors and she would have no idea that they had snuck off in a slightly different direction.

"Good idea," Dot said, catching on. "Should I tell Travis we're taking a detour?"

Susannah nodded. "Go on."

Dot flounced out of the cabin and the door swung shut behind her. Susannah let out a quiet breath, angling their ship down the slope. She had to be careful on slopes—if the ship scraped an unexpected boulder or a farmer's fence, she might find herself with a massive hole in the hull. Not to mention the noise of a collision, which could lure out certain denizens of the Hush.

What was the Songshaper doing now? Had she finished her recital and returned to the Hush? The proximity bells were silent, so the woman clearly hadn't cottoned on to their ruse yet. Perhaps she was panicking, fumbling around for signs of her quarry in the dark.

Or perhaps she was cold. Emotionless.

It was easier to think of Songshapers that way. Easier to explain what they had done to Sam. What they had done to *her*. If Susannah thought of them as heartless creatures, twisted by their Music, with all human instincts wiped away, it became easier to rationalize their actions. They were just machines. Sorcery shells. Rabid dogs that knew only how to inflict pain and misery.

But if she thought of them as human . . .

Well, it became more difficult. She remembered their faces as they loomed above her. Their cold eyes. Their needles and buckles, the Conservatorium ceiling, the *thrum, thrum, thrum* of their machines . . .

Susannah sucked down a sharp breath. She wasn't a victim anymore. And more importantly, she wasn't alone. Even now, she heard a gentle chatter of voices from the kitchen down the corridor.

Dot. Travis. Two of her gang.

The gang had started almost a year ago—just her and Sam, at first. They had begun by robbing the wealthy, stealing everything from jewels to echoships, from pegasi to communicators. They had stolen from those who supported the Conservatorium, those who gave it money and borrowed its prestige. Those folks who, like the mayor of Bremen, sent their children to study in its hallowed halls. Those who funded the Songshapers' cruelty.

And their robberies had fed the poor. The gang pawned most of the goods they stole, converting flashy trinkets into coins. With those coins, they had bought boots for the beggars in Bremen, and coats for the orphans in Delos. They had left baskets of bread on doorsteps for starving workers in Jubaldon. They darted in and out of the Hush, shadows in the night, and they turned the word "Nightfall" into a word of hope for the impoverished and fear for the aristocracy.

But it wasn't enough. It would never be enough.

Not until they hit the Conservatorium itself.

Not until they rectified what the Songshapers had done.

✳

When Chester woke, the echoboat was dark. Sam had extinguished the sorcery lamps, leaving only a single orange globe to dapple shadows on the ceiling. The effect was eerie: lines of dark and light, slicing and glinting on the glass of its neighbors.

The pain in his arm was dull now, more like an ache than a burn. Clearly, Sam hadn't been telling a complete lie—the injection must prevent infection as well as being a sedative.

Chester rose to his feet, a little unsteady. He touched the orange lamp and let its melody flow down into his fingers. The Music was warm and welcoming and it filled his veins like a shot of whiskey.

In the driver's cabin, Sam adjusted the wheel. "Awake, are you?"

"Either that, or I'm sleepwalking."

"Feeling any better?" Sam swiveled on his stool, looking him up and down with a critical expression. "Told you a bit of rest would do you good."

Chester's mouth was dry. "What time is it?"

Sam shrugged. "About seven at night, I'd guess. Hard to tell in the Hush, since it's always so—"

Chester jerked. He felt as though someone had shot another needle through his body, but instead of dispensing a sedative, it flooded his veins with a cold rush of horror. "Seven? But sundown . . ."

"What about it?"

"I haven't done the recital!"

"Good."

Chester gasped. "What?"

"You gotta wean yourself off it at some point," Sam said, "and I figure it's best to go cold turkey."

Chester stared. He couldn't believe what he was hearing. He had hummed the Sundown Recital every night of his life. When he had been too young or too sick, his father had hummed it for the both of them. That was how it worked. You couldn't stop performing the recital. It renewed your allegiance to the Song. It kept you alive and healthy. It protected you from evil magic. And if you failed to perform it . . .

"Calm down," Sam said. "Looks like you're having a heart attack."

Chester dropped to his knees. He covered his eyes and tried to focus. Was it still sundown? Was it too late? Either way, he had to try. He summoned up the tune in his mind and began to hum. The notes rolled upward, one after another, until—

Sam clapped a violent hand across his lips. "Shut up!"

Chester squirmed, trying to break free. The older boy's hand was rough and calloused, but Chester kept humming the melody, pushing its muffled notes through the folds of Sam's palms.

"Shut up!" Sam said. "Do you want 'em to find us?"

Out in the darkness, something shrieked.

Chester froze. He stared at Sam, as the older boy slowly withdrew his hand. Sam's eyes glimmered in their usual pale blue, but there was something else in them now. Was it fear? Sam reached up and wrenched a lever beside the steering wheel. Around them, the echoboat shuddered and jerked to a halt. It lay still and silent, a bulk of lifeless wood and sails. It was as though Sam wanted to hide their Musical signal from someone . . .

Or something.

Another shriek. Chester's lungs seemed to curl inward, shriveling up at the sound of the cry. It wasn't a human shriek. It wasn't a scream.

It was the cry of a beast on the hunt.

"What . . . ?"

Another cry, and another. They didn't come from the same direction: some howled from the left, while others shrieked from the right. And with a terrible chill, Chester realized the question he had been about to voice wasn't "What is it?" but rather "What are *they*?"

There was a patter out in the darkness, almost like a roll of drumbeats, and the faint whistle of a broken tune. The tune played in and out, like the wheezing breaths of an asthmatic. A snatch of music, a gasp, silence. Then another tune rolled in, and another, each from a different direction, as though a pack of living melodies was prowling through the dark.

Sam grabbed Chester's shoulders, pressed his mouth against his ear and began to whisper, very quiet and very fast. "They're called Echoes. They're blind, but their hearing's damn sharp. Can't touch me, but if they get their hands on you, you're dead. One little touch and you've got Musical venom melting the flesh off your bones. Got it?"

Out in the darkness, there was another chorus of shrieks.

Chester swallowed. "Can we fight them?"

Sam gave a tiny huff of breath, right against his ear. "I can't. They can't hurt me, but I also can't fight 'em. We sort of . . . cancel each other out."

Well, that made about as much sense as the second verse of "The Captain's Cat," but this wasn't the time to demand any details. The Echoes' tunes were growing louder.

"What about me?" Chester said. "Can I fight them?"

Sam shook his head. "You ain't been trained yet. Keep quiet. They might pass by . . ."

Hardly daring to breathe, Chester rose to his feet. Outside, he saw an endless realm of darkness: swirling rain, churning shadow. But the sounds of the Echoes were fading now, seeping like fog into the darkness. Their shrieks grew distant, one by one. A howl stuttered and faded like a fiddler playing a broken string.

Chester allowed himself a slow release of breath. They were safe. The creatures had given up, they had gone. And then . . .

There it was. One last Echo lingered in the black. It came right past the window, pale and translucent, floating from the dark into their bubble of Hush-light. It was humanoid, but eerily distorted: no face, no eyes, no distinctive features. Its entire body glowed white, like the shine of a colorless sorcery lamp. When it moved, it blurred like liquid. The Echo had its own tune, its own melody: a requiem that trickled down its limbs. The tune looped, again and again, wavering like a broken music box.

Chester's lungs burned. He didn't dare take a breath.

Beside him, Sam shifted a little sideways, moving his weight to his other foot. There was a creak in the wooden floor. It was the tiniest sound—more like the meow of a kitten than the creaking of floorboards.

But it was enough.

The Echo whipped its head around. It rushed to the window, pressing its limbs against the glass. Then it began to melt. Chester felt his breath catch, cold and horrified, as the creature started dripping through the window. It was like watching a candle melt, except the candle was a pale human body with clammy translucent hands that seeped like wax.

Sam swore. "It's coming."

"What?"

"It knows we're here—it ain't gonna give up!" He turned to Chester, panic in his eyes. "Listen, you gotta fight it; I can't touch the damn thing."

"How?"

"Where's your fiddle?"

Chester shook his head. "You know I don't have it! The sheriff took it, back in Hamelin . . ."

"Damn!" Sam said. "All right, maybe you can whistle or hum or—"

Chester hurried into the back room and produced the miniature silver flute they'd stolen from Nathaniel Glaucon. "I can play this."

Sam, who had followed him, nodded. "Good, good. Better than whistling. You gotta listen to the Echo's tune and cancel it out. Echoes run off their own Music, it's like oxygen to 'em—if you reverse their tune . . ."

There was a sharp sucking noise from the window. Chester glanced through to the driver's cabin and his stomach curled. The Echo was making progress, melting through the glass. It squeezed slowly, like apple pulp seeping through a burlap sack, but wisps were already beginning to ooze into the cabin.

"Listen to it, dammit," Sam said, as pale as Chester had ever seen him. "Listen to its tune."

Chester listened. He heard the creature's Music clearly now: a strong, steady melody. A four-bar requiem. It echoed through the cabin, playing off the ghostly limbs that had melted through the window. Those same four bars looped, again and again, like a child learning to play his first sheet of music, practicing the

88

first line until his fingers blistered. Chester couldn't identify any particular instrument playing the tune, it was simply *there*. All instruments and none.

Sam leaned closer. "Play it backwards. Cancel it out."

Chester raised the flute, fighting the tremble in his fingers. His wounded arm burned, but he couldn't play the instrument one-handed. He pursed his lips, as though to kiss the air above the metal mouthpiece. It took a steadiness to play the flute, to control his lips and the rhythm of his breathing. He closed his eyes and tried to force his lungs to behave. If the notes were squeaky, or staccato, or broken . . .

"All right," Sam whispered. "Go."

Chester played. He began at the end and flipped the tune on its head. From the final note of the fourth bar, he played backward to its start. Then he plunged into the third bar, and the music rolled like an uncomfortable itch from the metal of his flute. It sounded odd, played backward; the timing tasted wrong, and Chester winced at the mess of the melody.

In the driver's cabin, the Echo kept coming. It let out a scream—a warbling, shaking scream that was punctuated by silence as though it was suffering bursts of pain. But it sped up its melting and pushed more forcefully through the glass window. Soon its torso was through, and then its thighs. It sped up as it went, gaining momentum, as the bulk of its body surged into the driver's cabin and left only the tips of its toes outside.

But as it spilled into the echoboat and jerked forward, its movements were no longer fluid and smooth; it didn't float through the ship but *wrenched* itself forward. It flickered, jumping ahead in little sharp movements. One moment it was in the driver's cabin by the window; then, with a flash of unnatural shadow, it was in the doorway. Chester stumbled backward, still playing, and suddenly it was in the back room.

Chester tripped back and fell onto the sofa. The creature reached toward him, its translucent hand gleaming like the tentacles of a jellyfish in the dark. Sam swore and thrust himself in front of the creature, but it began to seep through his body as if he was just another pane of window glass.

"Keep playing!" Sam said. "You gotta keep up with it!"

The Echo's melody was faster now. Chester sped up his own reversal, desperate to match the pace of the creature. He played against it, loop for loop, ending the first bar whenever it ended the fourth. The melodies clashed.

The Echo was barely a foot away now. It seeped through Sam's body, its grasping hands as pale as starlight. Above, the sorcery lamp reflected eerily across its skin.

And suddenly, the music . . . clicked. His music became Music and locked against the Echo's tune. It was like trying to pick a padlock with a pin, or completing a jigsaw puzzle. It was the moment when that final effort slotted into place.

There was a rush. Cold air blasted out from the creature's body. Chester scrambled along the sofa; there was nowhere left for him to go, and his head crashed against the wall. But he kept his eyes open though they streamed with liquid from the sting and blast of the wind. The creature gave a terrible howl, like the cry of a tornado, and its Music shattered. A wild tumble of notes exploded outward, a storm of sound, a burst of white light. The Echo was melting, dissolving into the dark of the Hush. Chester scrunched his eyes shut, but he could still see the shine through his eyelids. He dropped the flute and raised his hands as a shield, breath catching, lungs seizing . . .

The room fell silent.

For several long seconds there was nothing, not even the sound of breathing. Then he heard Sam release a long, slow breath. Chester opened his eyes.

The Echo was gone.

The shock rang in his ears and his wounded arm throbbed like hell from holding up the flute. "I'm all right," he managed. "It didn't touch me."

"I know. If it'd touched you, you'd be a corpse by now." Sam said it so matter-of-factly that the words sent a prickle down the back of Chester's neck. "Deadlier than rattlesnakes, those things."

"Why couldn't it touch *you*?"

Sam didn't meet his eyes. "Long story."

Silence.

"I gotta get back to steering." Sam turned toward the driver's cabin. "I can stop the boat for ten minutes or so without too much damage, but if I don't start it up again soon it's gonna lose all its charge from the train."

Chester followed him. "Then what will happen?"

"Then we'll be stranded out here with an uncharged echoboat," Sam said. "Here's a free bit of advice, Hays: if you're anchoring an echoboat, do it on a railway line. Easiest way to recharge the engine with Music when you want to start it up again."

He wrenched a lever and the boat shuddered back to life around them. The cogs clanked, the metal thrummed, and they blasted like a cry into the dark.

CHAPTER ELEVEN

After dusk, the warning bell chimed.

The *Cavatina* was passing through a line of empty fields and Susannah had left the wheel unattended for a minute—just long enough to grab a plate of dinner. The echoship's kitchen was a comfortable room, lit by sorcery lamps and warmed by a crackling stove. Pale floral wallpaper decorated the walls and the scent of sweet syrup and hot corn griddlecakes wafted through the air.

Susannah skewered a fork into a griddlecake and drizzled a hefty serving of syrup across the top. They had stolen the corn from a wealthy farmer in Bremen. The flour had come from their food pantry, which was regularly replenished with the proceeds of minor thieving jobs.

"Mmm," Susannah said, as syrup burst across her tongue. "Nice job, Dot. You're officially the queen of griddlecakes."

"Oh, it wasn't all my doing, Captain," Dot said brightly. "I have a theory that cooking pixies sneak under my fingernails and direct the best ingredients into the mixture."

Susannah snorted. Personally, she tended to put Dot's behavior down to an overactive imagination and leave it at that. Travis, however, stared at the tiny blonde girl as though she was a bow tie that he couldn't quite figure out how to knot.

"I do hate to break it to you, Dorothy," he said, "but there's no such thing as cooking pixies."

"Oh, I know," Dot said. "They just appeared tonight, especially for me."

Travis just stared at her. As the newest member of the gang, he was still uncertain how to deal with Dot's peculiarities. Finally he shrugged and settled for slicing off a petite segment of griddlecake with his knife and fork.

That was when the bell chimed.

Songshaper.

Susannah almost choked. "Dammit!"

"What is it, Captain?"

"Proximity bell," Susannah said. "Someone's picked up our trail . . ."

Susannah and Dot hurried back into the driver's cabin, the griddlecakes forgotten. Susannah nervously ran her fingers along the levers, down a row of buttons, and glanced upward. The bell was stirring again. Now that the initial warning chime was over, its volume would fluctuate to indicate the distance of the danger. Right now, the bell was merely trembling—a faint little quiver of metal, barely enough to produce a chime. But something nudged at the edge of its range . . .

"What do we do?" Dot said, alarmed.

"We go faster!"

Susannah slid into the driver's seat. She cranked up a lever and the echoship lurched forward; Dot grabbed the wall as they shot onward with a new burst of speed. There was a distant crash and a shout of indignation from down the corridor. Clearly, Travis wasn't thrilled by the lack of warning.

The bell chimed again. Susannah swore under her breath. "How the hell did she catch up?"

Dot shook her head, eyes wild. "I don't know, Captain! Her boat must be a newer model; it's a lot faster than ours."

Susannah cranked up the speed, changed gears, and shoved a handful of levers forward.

"We'll have to hide from her sensors," Susannah said. "We've got a decent lead . . . if we can just find a place to anchor and let her pass by . . ."

Travis raised an eyebrow as he entered the cabin. "I'm not sure whether you've noticed, Captain," he said, "but this is quite a large ship. It's hardly a prime contender for the national hide-and-seek championship."

Susannah ignored him. Heart pounding, she checked the map. A cluster of trees and boulders lay ahead, marked clearly by illuminated symbols. Out of sheer luck, a shining line ran right through the middle. "There," she said. "A railway line, just up the slope."

"But Captain—"

"We can't outrun her." Susannah glared at Travis. "She's too fast. Too nimble. But her sensors will only pick up active sorcery, so our best hope is to hide and hope she passes by. Got it?"

Travis hesitated. "Very well, Captain."

Susannah eased the ship around in a gentle loop, avoiding the obstacles, and then carefully sailed uphill toward the railway line. The *Cavatina* hovered for a moment, like a roosting bird, before it slipped onto the tracks with a gentle bump.

Susannah powered down the engine. The less Music their ship produced, the less likely they were to turn up on the Songshaper's sensors. This option, however, carried risks of its own. They had an hour, perhaps, until the *Cavatina* would lose its Musical charge. If they lingered too long, they would have to wait until a train passed through in the real world and hijack its energy to restart the vessel.

Hopefully it wouldn't come to that.

Susannah flicked a trio of switches. Lights flickered off and machinery fell silent until all that remained was the sorcery lamps.

Although Susannah couldn't hear their Music, she had memorized the tune to extinguish them. She brushed them with her fingers and hummed the required notes, leaving them to slowly dim. Soon she stood in a darkened cabin, with cooling globes of glass above her head.

"If she finds us," Dot said, a little quieter than usual, "she won't bother with handcuffs, will she?"

Slowly, Susannah shook her head. They weren't in a town or a city. There were no judicial processes here—no sheriffs or judges to decide their fate. The only law was the barrel of a gun. If the Songshaper caught them, they would die.

In the dark cabin, all Susannah could see was the circle of light that surrounded her in the Hush: a bubble of faded gray, just enough to illuminate the others' faces. She could see they were tense and strained, their eyes wide and their expressions haggard. It had been a long day, and it was about to get longer. All they could do now was wait.

Somehow, Susannah had to distract them. She had to keep the danger off their minds, and keep the nerves out of their bellies . . .

"Dot," she said. "Can you fetch my blackboard?"

The blonde girl looked as pale as an Echo in the unnatural ebb of light. But she nodded and scampered back toward the kitchen, where Susannah kept a small blackboard and chalk at the end of the table. A moment later, she returned with the board under her arm.

"Okay." Susannah yanked the cover off the blackboard and balanced it on her knees, within her weak pool of Hush-light. "We need to talk about yesterday." Usually, she liked to do a review of every job, to assess what their strengths were and the areas where they could improve.

"Is this really the time, Captain?" Travis said.

Susannah glanced up at the proximity bells. They remained silent in the feeble light. The Songshaper hadn't found them yet and no matter what, she had to keep the others calm. Right now, their greatest threat was panic.

"No time like the present," she said, as lightly as she could manage.

"But shouldn't we wait until Sam's back, Captain?" Dot said.

"Sam's bringing an unlicensed Songshaper with him," Susannah said. "I don't want to let a stranger in on the details of our plans until we know he's trustworthy."

"Pardon my curiosity, Captain, but do we know anything about this Songshaper?" Travis said. "We're all rather young in this gang, you know. Personally, I've been finding the youthful angle rather refreshing; I hope we're not going to be joined by an old curmudgeon with a grudge against—"

"Whoever this person is, he's clumsy," Susannah said. "He let his unlicensed Song connection be picked up on a radar, and now Sam says he's been arrested."

"So?"

"So he's probably young," Susannah said. "I can't imagine anyone living long if they're making mistakes like that."

"Perhaps it will be a beautiful lady," Dot said, in a daydreamy voice. "With eyes like peacock feathers, and hair the color of sunlight, and colored skirts that swish when she walks . . ."

"I hope not," Susannah said. "We've got enough peacocks around here as it is."

Travis waved her remark away with a scowl. "I wouldn't say no to a beautiful lady in this gang, either. Tell you what, Dorothy— I'll fight you for her."

"Don't be silly," Dot said. "You could never take me in a fight."

"I'll have you know," Travis said, "that I was Senior Boys' Boxing Champion for three years running at my old—"

"I'm sure you were," Susannah interrupted. "But Dot would build some kind of super peacock-wrangling Musical gadget from spare parts in the engine room, and you'd be on your champion arse in ten seconds flat."

"Five seconds," Dot said. "I'd just play an explosive waltz into the nearest sorcery lamp and light it above his head."

The others stared at her.

"What?" Dot gave an innocent smile. "All my sorcery lamps are explosive. You never know when you might need a bomb on short notice."

Susannah felt her jaw hanging slightly open. What other little Musical tricks had Dot hidden in her sorcery devices around the echoship? After a moment's reflection, she decided she didn't want to know.

"Right," she said. "Well, I don't think—"

The third bell stirred.

Susannah froze. It was only a faint sound, the weakest tendril of a whisper, but a moment later it chimed again with a little more certainty. Dot and Travis stiffened beside her, their bodies tight and tense in the darkness. Then the bell sank back into silence and a trio of quiet breaths escaped their lips.

"We should run for it," Travis said. "Captain, we should—"

Susannah shook her head. "No," she said forcefully. "It's too late now. We just have to keep calm and wait it out. As long as we don't panic . . ."

There was a long pause.

"Um . . ." Susannah said eventually. "So we were talking about what went wrong yesterday, weren't we? In Bremen?"

The others looked at her, visibly torn between exasperation and gratitude. They knew full well what Susannah was up to; she wasn't exactly being subtle. But even so, they seemed willing to play along. After all, what was the alternative? It was better than waiting in silence for death.

97

"That's right, Captain," Dot said. "And I know exactly what went wrong. A high-grade Songshaper showed up when we weren't expecting her."

Susannah nodded and wrote *Weser City Songshaper* on the board. "She's obviously on the trail of a fugitive," she said. "Hunting down that unlicensed Songshaper. Why else would she be lurking around with radar equipment in Bremen?"

"It was supposed to be a simple job," Travis said, perking up a little. He leaned over to peer at the board through a haze of grayish Hush-light. "I played my part perfectly, by the way. The mayor was utterly convinced of my credentials as a traveling aristocrat. By the end of the meeting, he was ready to offer me a permanent position as his—"

"Yes, all right," Susannah said. "That's one good thing, I suppose. We can add your acting skills to our list of what went right."

She drew a line down the board, dividing it into *Successes* and *Failures*, and wrote *Travis's acting* in the first column.

"You missed a word," Travis said, squinting at the board. "I believe you mean *Travis's excellent acting.*"

Susannah snorted. "Don't push your luck."

"*Travis's spectacular acting?*" he suggested. "Or how about—"

"I guess you didn't have a chance to use my sorcery lamp, Captain," Dot cut in, looking a little anxious. "It works, though—I deliberately chose a quiet tune so the guards wouldn't hear you."

Susannah shook her head. "Yeah, the Songshaper had gotten to you by then." But she added *Dot's lamp* to the first column on the board.

In fact, the entire plan had worked fine: except for the unexpected Songshaper, it had all been so simple, so easy. They had planned a dozen scams like it before and they had always gone off without a hitch. So few people knew about the existence of the Hush, the gang could slip in and out of their victims' buildings like ghosts . . .

The bell tinkled.

Susannah took a tight breath and glanced up at the ceiling, half-afraid of what she might see. The bell was vibrating slightly, nudging back and forth in faint little quivers of alarm. Not close enough to produce a clear chime, but still too close for comfort, as though the Songshaper was prowling the dark, skirting at the edge of their proximity sensors . . .

"She's going to catch us," Dot said quietly. "Isn't she?"

"No." Susannah forced her gaze away from the bells, away from the vast black maw of the window. "As long as we don't try to run for it, we'll be fine. If we can just hold our nerve and keep the engine switched off until she passes . . ."

"She caught us in Bremen," Travis said. "And we weren't even using an echoship."

"She must have sensed us on her radar," Susannah said. "If it's sensitive enough to pick up tiny fluctuations in the Song, it probably picks up other random bits of nearby Music, too." She frowned at Dot. "But I didn't use your lamp . . ."

Dot shook her head. "Even if you had, those radar globes only hunt for fresh pieces of Music. They have to tune out existing sorcery objects or else there'd be a false alarm whenever anyone used a lantern."

"I hate to say it, Dorothy," Travis said, "but you're the only one capable of Songshaping in this gang. You must have done *something* to set off the radar." He waved a hand. "In a town like Bremen, I'd imagine that even a tiny speck of decent sorcery would seem suspicious."

Dot looked confused, as though struggling to remember what she'd done. Then she blanched. "Oh!" She clapped a hand across her lips. "Oh! I didn't think! Captain, I'm sorry, I didn't know anyone nearby had a radar!"

"It's all right, Dot," Susannah said, seizing this new opportunity for distraction. "Just tell us what you did."

Dot looked down at her fingers, twisting them together. "Well, I was keeping watch, like you said, but I'd seen whip marks on some of the servants. They looked so miserable, you see. They had bloodstains on their shirts! I thought the mayor should pay for being such a horrible person, so I . . ." Dot twisted her fingers tighter. ". . . I hummed an allergy spell into his flower garden."

"You what?"

Dot looked embarrassed. "Just a little personalized tune," she said. "It won't affect anyone else, I swear. Just to make him sneeze when he goes for a stroll outside."

Susannah stared at her. Despite everything, she found herself fighting back a laugh. Of all the things to have given them away . . .

"Oh, for heaven's sake, Dorothy," Travis said. "That's not how you seek revenge on a wealthy man. You should have made him allergic to his money, or cravats, or shoe polish, or—"

"Wouldn't do much good to make him allergic to his money," Susannah said, "seeing as how we stole it."

Dot brightened. "How much did we end up with, Captain?"

"Three sacks of silver, and a pouch of fancy jewelry," Susannah said. "We'll pawn the jewels in the next big town we hit. I was thinking Linus, actually, since we're meeting Sam there."

"A splendid idea," Travis said. "I like Linus. They have an excellent tailor there; I've never had finer trousers sewn than in Mr. Beaumont's establishment."

Susannah squinted at the blackboard, hunting for an excuse to extend the conversation. Right now, she knew, nothing was more dangerous than silence. Silence led to doubt, and doubt led to restlessness. If they could just hold their nerve a few minutes longer . . . "All right, gang," she said. "I think we learned something from yesterday." She looked at Dot. "Dot, if we're in a small town, don't risk any Songshaping in the real world unless it's crucial for the job. In a place like Bremen, it sticks out like a sore thumb."

Dot nodded. "Yes, Captain."

"Travis," Susannah said, "if a job goes wrong, don't run off in a panic and assume it's all over. If you'd kept the mayor distracted a little longer, we might have found it easier to get away."

Travis clapped a hand to his heart, as though he was deeply wounded by this remark. "Ah, the vicious pangs of criticism! My self-esteem shall wither and perish under the weight of such a blow."

Susannah raised an eyebrow. "Done?"

"Yes, I believe so," Travis said, more cheerfully. "What about you, Captain?"

"I should plan better for emergencies," Susannah said. "It was my fault we didn't have a backup plan. As captain, I take full responsibility for the danger you were placed in yesterday. And for that, I'm sorry."

"It wasn't your fault, Captain," Dot said. "It was—"

Above them, something moved.

Susannah looked upward. It was the third bell again, quivering with the promise of danger. This time, however, it failed to chime. It didn't even tinkle. It simply swayed a little to the side, like a half-drunken cowboy, before it collapsed back into stillness.

Susannah let out a slow breath. "Well, what do you think?"

"I think," Dot said, with a fresh note of hope in her voice, "that she might've just gone past us."

"And I think," Travis said, "that you might be right."

Susannah allowed herself a small smile. When it came down to it, they were a good team. And once Sam returned, their gang would be complete again—and with a new member, too. A new member for a new job, the job Susannah had been waiting for. They were so close now to the big one.

So close.

"All right," she said. "Five minutes, and we'll leave."

The others nodded. Susannah knew they were itching to leave right now. It was hard enough to stomp down on her own impulse to flee. They couldn't linger too long or the *Cavatina*'s charge would wind down and they'd be stuck waiting for a train to jump-start the Music of the engine. But the longer they waited, the farther the Songshaper would draw ahead, and the larger the distance between them, the better.

"So," she said, "the next job."

"The big one?" Dot said eagerly.

Susannah shook her head, a little regretful. "Not yet. Soon, I promise—but we're not quite ready."

"But Captain, there are only a few weeks to go," Dot said. "And we've found an unlicensed Songshaper now. That means we've got almost all the pieces we need to—"

"Yes," Susannah said, nodding, "but we'll still need to train him—"

"Or her," Dot said.

"—and we've still got to pick up more supplies. We don't know how skilled this Songshaper is, and we don't know . . ." Susannah trailed off. "We don't know how *willing* he'll be to join our plan."

"I wouldn't blame him for bowing out," Travis said. "No offense, Captain, but this job is suicidal. You'll be throwing this fellow to the sharks and crossing your fingers that he performs his role before they tear his head off."

Susannah wanted to argue, but he was right. This would be a dangerous job for all of them. But for the Songshaper in particular, it would be deadly. Would any sane person agree to play the part she was going to assign to him?

It had taken months to find an unlicensed Songshaper. Generally, folks who learned to play Music on the black market were savvy enough to keep it a secret. Now that she'd found one, Susannah wasn't about to let him go. Dot was right. The deadline for this job was only three weeks away. If they missed it, it would be an entire year before a chance arose again . . .

She would have to ease him into it carefully. Tell him just enough of his role in the plan to pique his interest. Let him feel comfortable in the Nightfall Gang. Let him see what riches were offered to the members of the gang, and what amazing new skills they could teach him to survive. She would give him a few weeks of comfort aboard the *Cavatina*, with its cozy cabins and hot meals. And then, when he was wrapped around her little finger . . .

Well, you couldn't catch a shark without bait.

PART TWO
THE GANG

CHAPTER TWELVE

THE NIGHT WAS LONG.

As the hours wore on, Susannah paced through the *Cavatina*, tired and nervous. She ventured up onto the deck, straining to make out the shape of their enemy in the distance, even though she knew there would be nothing but blackness and the cold fingers of the Hush on her skin.

Normally, every few nights, the gang would leave the *Cavatina* on a railway line and camp beneath the stars of Meloral. It was unhealthy to dwell too long in the Musically contaminated air of the Hush without a break, and there was always the risk of an Echo attack. Susannah had hoped to sleep in the real world tonight, but they had to keep moving. The Songshaper was still out there, hunting for them.

Back inside, the corridors seemed to swallow her: the throats of patterned wallpaper, the tongues of carpet, the teeth of glinting sorcery lamps. Oddly enough, it was Sam of all people who'd insisted that the ship look less like a machine and more like a home. She would never have guessed it. Sam, who stomped around in cowboy boots and scowls. Sam, who was more comfortable with a pistol than a paintbrush. Sam, whose emotions fluctuated with unnatural jerks and sways if he so much as wandered beneath a badly tuned sorcery lamp. Yet it was Sam who had persuaded them to convert the echoship into a comfortable living space, complete with cushions and picture frames.

"It's home, ain't it?" he'd said. And that was all the explanation Susannah had managed to wrangle out of him on the subject.

The ship felt empty without Sam here. Susannah had never been interested in him romantically—they were both too damaged for that, and reminded each other too sharply of past ordeals—but she still loved him. Like a brother, almost. A brother with all the layers of an onion, and just as much ability to bring people to tears. They had first met in a grimy bar in Weser City, both reeling from recent trauma. When they had joined forces to create the gang, Sam had insisted that Susannah be the captain.

"You're good at dealing with folks," he had told her with a wistful smile. "I'm only good at fighting 'em."

Right now, though, Susannah felt too exhausted to deal with anything more complex than a griddlecake.

"Any trouble?" she said, entering the driver's cabin.

Dot shook her head, focusing on the sorcery map. "Bells are quiet, Captain. Want to stop when we hit another railway line?"

"No, keep going," Susannah said. "There are a lot of fields around Linus, and Sam's only got a small boat. We might have to hunt him down."

Dot readjusted the wheel a little. "Good. I'm sick of sitting still."

Susannah smiled at her. She had that much right. Apart from Travis, none of the gang was particularly good at sitting still—or even staying more than one night in the same place.

"You all have such itchy feet," Travis had once complained, when they were preparing to move on from a comfortable city hotel after only one night. "Couldn't we stay long enough to . . . I don't know . . . savor the local flavor?"

"The local tailors, you mean," Dot said.

"We're thieves," Susannah said. "Going on the run is part of the job description. Besides, we've got to give these coins to the beggars in Jubaldon, remember?"

If she was honest with herself, though, it was more than that. As much as she valued the work they did as part of their "wealth redistribution program," as Dot called it, it was partially just an excuse to keep moving. While she waited for the final job, Susannah *had* to keep moving. She had to keep roaming. She couldn't stay in one place for too long; the same buildings, the same trees, the same locals . . . It drove her insane. Some small part of her felt the constant urge to flee, to run, to escape, as though somehow this might save her from the horrors of her own upcoming plan.

Another part of her constantly worried about what would happen if she was caught. She had good reason to feel that way. Susannah wasn't just a fugitive for leading the Nightfall Gang. Her outlaw status, like Sam's, went back a lot further. All the way back to the Conservatorium, and that terrible night when—

The third bell jingled.

Dot scrambled aside as Susannah cursed and seized the wheel. She squinted up at the sorcery map, where a thin line of light trickled across their path. "That's the Linus River up ahead! She must've known we'd never dare to cross it here, so—"

"—she doubled back to look for us," Dot said, nodding.

Susannah kept her gaze on the map. Beyond the river lay the glowing dot of Linus. They were so close. If they could just hold out long enough to reach a safe crossing point, maybe—

"Left!" Dot cried.

Susannah obeyed, not taking time to figure out what the problem was. Dot, who usually spoke in the soft tones of a daydreamer, wouldn't scream like that unless there was a genuine threat.

The *Cavatina* surged left just as Travis burst into the driver's cabin. At that moment, Susannah spotted the danger. A huge tree reared in the darkness, close enough to scrape the right-hand side of their ship. If Dot hadn't screamed at Susannah to turn, they'd have hit its trunk like a glass lantern hitting stone.

"It's not on the map!" Susannah gasped, staring through the window. A wall of bark flashed by, distorted by the dark and rain of the Hush. Then it was gone and the window refilled with blackness.

"Must've grown over the last few years," Dot said anxiously. "Those are fast-growing trees, those leafshiners. The map must be out of date . . ."

The proximity bell rang again.

"Songshaper?" Travis said.

"Yep," Dot said. "She's catching up, too. That last ring was louder than before. Captain, I don't think hiding's an option this time . . ."

"I know." Susannah cranked a lever up into a higher gear. "We'll have to outrun her."

"Oh, naturally," Travis said. "You know, when I was choosing how to flavor my oatmeal this morning, I wasn't aware that 'suicidal recklessness' was an option for the day. Where do you keep that one, Captain—behind the sugar jar or the box of dried cranberries?"

Susannah glared at him. "Got a better idea, pretty boy?"

Travis pursed his lips, but didn't respond.

Susannah flicked her gaze from side to side, checking the other windows. No sign of trees, but would she even know in time? She could barely see a yard through the dark of the Hush—would she see an obstacle coming and have time to avoid it, or simply smash right into it?

Another bell tinkled. This one sounded different: a higher, warmer pitch. Susannah wrenched up her gaze, startled, and saw the fifth bell in the collection was ringing. "We've got an echoboat in range!"

"You think it's Sam, Captain?"

"One way to find out!"

Susannah dug into her pocket with one hand, keeping the other on the wheel. She pulled out her communication globe and clutched it tightly, waiting for that familiar blue shine . . .

And there it was. The fog within the globe shifted, congealing into a familiar face. Cowboy hat, heavy jaw, pale blue eyes.

Sam.

✳

Chester ate breakfast in the dark.

"Is it morning yet?" he said, peering out the echoboat windows. It always looked the same in the Hush: a black morass of rain and fog.

"Close enough," Sam said.

An icebox squatted under the sofa, filled with bread and cheese. Chester ate his sandwich in huge chunks, ripping it with hungry teeth. The bread was a little stale, but the cheese was sharp and peppery on his tongue.

As he ate, he kept his eyes on Sam. Despite his best efforts, he still wasn't sure how to read the older boy. Chester didn't like it when he couldn't understand a person—it was like being faced with a song he couldn't play.

Usually, Chester prided himself on reading people. There were all sorts of folk in the towns of Meloral, and Chester had met hundreds during his travels. Nervous fidgeters, headstrong barmaids, gruff farmers, jovial washerwomen, gossiping errand boys, and draconian sheriffs who used their guns and badges to feel better about their . . . inadequacies.

Sam was different. Whenever Chester thought he was getting a read on him—*Tetchy? Ruthless? Distant?*—another bubble of information would rise to the surface. Sometimes Sam seemed ruthless, like when he'd blasted those holes through Nathaniel Glaucon. But other times he was gentle, like when he took the care to clean Chester's wound—then a moment later he'd be angry and snappish again. Sam could be fearless or paranoid. Vicious or panicky. The boy owned a dozen different temperaments, and he flittered from one to the next as though he was merely changing outfits. Perhaps that was why Sam's body was so huge—he needed room for his wardrobe of personalities.

And thanks to Sam, Chester had missed the Sundown Recital.

He still couldn't believe it. Never in his life had he missed the recital. Even now, he could feel his skin prickling and the rush of hot blood through his veins. He told himself it was just the shock of the Echo attack or a slight concussion from banging his head on the wall.

But he knew it wasn't really. It was withdrawal.

He'd once been told about a senile old woman who'd lived down the street. Chester had only been six or seven at the time, but the story had shaken him to the core. When the woman had run away from home for two nights she hadn't performed the Sundown Recital—and of course there had been no one to perform it for her. By the time the sheriff had found her, she was a huddling twitch of limbs, sobbing and screaming with fever in an alleyway.

"Withdrawal," the sheriff had called it. "I seen it before. First day, you just get a bit of pain. But the second day, you're screaming and hurling your meals back up. And if you ain't strong enough to cope with it, you go insane. Lose your allegiance to the Song forever, and start babbling nonsense . . . kindest thing you can do is a bullet to the skull."

Now, Chester fought to ignore the thrum of heat that tingled through his veins. He had been tempted to perform the recital at least a dozen times overnight, but he knew it wouldn't work. It was too late. The Sundown Recital only worked at sundown. There was no way to cheat the system. It would be like trying to cheat the moon, or the stars, or the Song itself. It was blasphemy.

Besides, he still remembered the horror in Sam's eyes.

Shut up! Do you want 'em to find us?

Those words rolled around Chester's skull like cold marbles. It was his fault the Echoes had found them. He had somehow called them, through the hum of the recital. But he couldn't go without the recital forever . . .

A bell rang.

Startled, Chester turned to Sam. "What's that?"

Sam dropped the remains of his sandwich and hurried into the driver's cabin. Chester followed, his skin still prickling faintly with the thrum of his missed recital. It wasn't pain—not yet, at least—but if he skipped another sundown . . .

Don't think about it, he told himself.

In the cabin, the bell chimed again. Chester hadn't noticed it the day before: a little metal bell, hanging from the ceiling above the wheel. It was made of copper, or maybe bronze, with a swirl of intricate carvings on its surface.

"What does it mean?"

"We're in range of an echoship," Sam said.

Sam produced a small glass sphere, the size of his palm. He held it up to the sorcery lamps and it glinted, cool and translucent. Yet as he held it, its color shifted. It melted from being clear to a vivid green: the color of the prairie after rain.

"That's Susannah's color," he said.

"Who?"

"The captain."

Chester stared at the globe. It looked a little like a sorcery lamp, but there was no hint of light from its surface. Just shifting

113

colors, like paint on a wall. Inside, a wisp of fog swirled in the same bright green as the glass. The fog solidified, twist by twist, into the shape of a human face.

Suddenly, Chester realized what was happening. "That's a communicator!"

"Yep," Sam said.

"But . . . how can you afford . . . ?"

Sam snorted. "We didn't *buy* it."

Chester stared at the globe. He'd heard of such things, of course, but never expected to see one with his own eyes. Communicators were worth a fortune; only the best of the Songshapers could enchant them, and only the highest ranks of nobility could afford them.

The fog settled into its final shape: it was a young woman. If Chester squinted, he could make out a few details: a long nose, a tangle of curling red hair. This had to be Susannah, the captain of Sam's gang.

"Sam?" She sounded urgent and snappish. "Sam, can you read me?"

"Here, Captain," Sam said.

"Did you get the Songshaper?"

"Yeah, I got him," Sam said. "Just a runt of a kid, though, and he ain't been trained too well."

"Dot can help with that," Susannah said. "Are either of you injured?"

"Boy got shot in the arm, Captain, but nothing Travis can't fix."

Susannah nodded. In the depths of the globe, her face was too small to read her expression. "I need you back here quickly, Sam. But be careful—we've had a hell of a night, that Songshaper from Bremen's on our trail. If she catches us, we'll have to—"

A snap of sound, and the globe went blank.

Sam swore under his breath. He clutched the globe more tightly and shook it. Nothing happened—it stayed just a clear glass ball in his hand.

"What happened?" Chester said.

"Lost the damn connection." Sam gave the globe one more shake, his lips tight, before he dropped it with a curse into his pocket.

"What's wrong?"

Sam yanked a lever, blasting them forward with a new-found burst of speed. The older boy looked suddenly pale. "Only two things can break a connection like that," he said. "Either falling out of range—which don't make sense since we're heading in the right direction—or . . ."

There was a pause.

"Or what?"

Sam let out a slow breath. "Or the person you're talking to is under attack."

CHAPTER THIRTEEN

THE *CAVATINA* CROUCHED IN A GULLY, BLACK RAIN SWIRLING LIKE A symphony around its hull. Its marker blinked on the map, guiding them forward.

Chester stared at it, stunned. The echoship was thirty times as large as Sam's boat, or maybe forty. It was the size of a mansion, not a wagon. A faint shine emanated from its outer skin: a hint of Music, trapped in wood and metal.

If Sam was pleased to see his home again, he didn't show it. His face was drained of color and his eyes were wide open.

"What's wrong?" Chester whispered.

Sam pointed.

A shadow lay beneath the left side of the echoship. Not a normal shadow, like the constant darkness that swirled around the Hush, but something deeper and blacker. Like an ink-stained jaw opening up to consume the base of the ship, licking its tongue around the wood, pressing its lips up toward the windows . . .

Sam swore. "How could they be so stupid?"

Chester glanced from the ship to Sam, then back again. "Um . . ."

"Why the hell'd they try to cross the river?"

Chester looked at the crawling darkness. It didn't look much like a river to him. Whatever it was, it certainly wasn't water. "That's a river?"

"In the real world, it's a river," Sam said. "First rule of the Hush: never ever fly your echoboat over water."

Sam wrenched a lever and turned the steering wheel, and they began to cautiously edge toward the *Cavatina*.

"Can't trust water in the Hush," Sam said. "Not when it's in a big mass, anyway. It's reflective, you see? Got Music all of its own . . ." He shook his head. "The ripples, the gurgles, the way it sloshes on the shore—all of that's making a tune. A melody. In the real world, it's just water, right? But in the Hush, if a chunk of water's big enough to catch your full reflection, then . . ."

Chester's throat was dry. "What?"

"It grabs you," Sam said. "Drags you down, tries to suck you into its own damn melody. Water's got too much natural Music. It ain't quite right in the Hush." He swore again. "And the captain just went flying over a river big enough to reflect the whole damn *Cavatina*."

"Maybe someone attacked her and she swerved the wrong way," Chester said. "Or maybe she was distracted, talking to you on the communicator, and—"

"If she was talking to me, she should've had one of the others steering." Sam's expression darkened. "I bet it was Travis. That weaselly little rat."

"I don't see any Songshapers," Chester said, trying to find something positive.

Sam shook his head. "The Shapers ain't fools. They would've seen the crash; they'll know this is their chance to take us down, once and for all. Bet they've hopped back into the real world to gather reinforcements. Give 'em twenty minutes and they'll be back here shooting every soul on the blasted ship."

Sam angled their boat toward the *Cavatina*. The ship took up almost the entire breadth of the river; barely a foot of water lay between the edge of the vessel and the shoreline. Not enough water, thankfully, to reflect their own tiny vessel.

"Hold on tight."

Chester steadied himself against the wall. Sam wrenched a crimson lever that Chester hadn't noticed before. With a mechanical groan, the echoboat shuddered—and then it began to rise.

"Can't do this too often," Sam said, in response to Chester's startled look. "Waste of engine power. But we got no choice if we want to dock the damn thing."

With a rattling clank, their echoboat ascended to the *Cavatina*'s upper deck. A large platform, circular and smooth, lay beside the ship's masts. The proximity bell jangled, louder than before, but Sam ignored it. His entire mind was focused on landing.

They touched down on the platform. A jolt—then a gentle little bump—before Sam jerked a lever and their echoboat fell still.

"Come on," Sam said. "We gotta hurry."

Chester followed him out into the swirling chill of the Hush. They stood atop the deck of the echoship, with their own small boat at rest beside them. The *Cavatina*'s masts rose high above, sails flapping in the dark.

As soon as they had clambered down from the platform, Sam wrenched a lever on a nearby railing. There was a clanking sound, followed by a hiss of steam, and a trio of metal claws shot up from the edges of the platform. They angled inward, slotting neatly into the grooves of the echoboat, and clicked down to secure it in place.

Sam and Chester hurried across the deck of the *Cavatina*. Sam unlocked a metal trapdoor, and gestured for Chester to follow him down the ladder below. "Home sweet home," Sam muttered as he slipped down.

And so Chester took a shaky breath, and followed him into the ship.

The *Cavatina* was not what Chester had expected. A dark green carpet snaked along the corridor, and the walls were patterned with floral wallpaper. Sorcery lamps dangled from the ceiling—mostly orange, punctuated by the occasional blue or red—and the air smelled of honey and cinnamon. If he concentrated, Chester could almost make out the Music of the lamps: a myriad of overlapping melodies, tingling in the depths of his ears.

Sam shoved open a door at the end of the corridor, revealing a spiral staircase. The staircase cavity was a little cold, but Chester admired the rich wood paneling of its walls as they descended.

They hurried along a hallway, passing a couple of doorways. Chester wanted to ask what lay behind them, but this wasn't the time. He could see now how the river had begun to take hold: the entire echoship was being consumed by shadow. Already the corridor was angled strangely, with a sharp tilt downward on the side where the ship was sinking fastest.

The driver's cabin was huge, at least six times the size of its equivalent on Sam's echoboat. Chester stepped inside, skin tingling. Three of the walls were composed entirely of windows, so that for one terrifying moment he felt as though he was falling forward into the dark swirls of the river. The ship was tilting more and more as black tendrils crawled up toward them. He heard clatters and crashes from other rooms as loose furniture slid across the floor and dishes tumbled from shelves.

Then he saw the blood.

One window of the *Cavatina* was splintered into shards. On the floor a young woman sprawled in a mess of curling red hair and blood. She wore a rumpled white blouse and a pair of men's trousers with a thick black belt. A wound pierced her torso, staining the blouse with a blaze of liquid crimson. She couldn't be older than seventeen.

"Captain!" Sam hurried toward her. "What happened?"

Susannah was breathing but her face was pale. "Song-shaper shot me through the window. She'll be back soon, with reinforcements." She grabbed Sam's sleeve. "Get us out of here, Sam."

"Why'd you steer into the damn river?"

"Wasn't deliberate," Susannah managed. "Lost control of the wheel, when . . . when she shot me."

"Where are the others?"

"Trying to fix the engine," Susannah said, in a rasping voice. "It got knocked out of tune when we crashed. Dot's doing what she can, but . . ." She trailed off, eyelids fluttering.

Sam swore, pressing a hand to staunch the flow of blood. "Dot ain't got enough power to reset that engine!"

"I know," Susannah said. "But we can't just sit here and sink . . ."

"Can I help?" Chester said.

They both stared at him. Susannah's eyes were unfocused, but he noticed for the first time that they were a pale, ghostly blue. Just like Sam's. Under the tendrils of red hair, her face looked almost ethereal. Chester knotted his hands behind his back and attempted to look more confident than he felt.

"What are you gonna do?" Sam said. "You ain't been trained."

"I know," Chester said. "But if Dot tells me what tune to play, maybe . . ."

"You ain't going into the engine room," Sam snapped. "Not when the Music ain't stable. I just risked my life to save your neck, Hays—I ain't gonna waste all that effort to let you kill yourself."

"I'm going to die either way, then, because this ship's sinking!" Chester said.

His fear was rising to the surface now, colored by frustration. He might not know about the Hush or echoships or Musical engines. But he had survived for months on the road and he had never given up. Not when his money had been stolen in Leucosia, or when he'd been forced to beg on the streets in Jubaldon. Not when a bitter old man in Taminor had told him he was on a fool's errand and that he should give up his father for dead. Not even in the prison cell, down in the dark under Hamelin. If Chester was going to die today, he would do it on his own terms.

"Where's the engine room?" he said.

Sam looked away.

Chester tightened his expression. Hopefully his scowl was one of righteous indignation, rather than an expression of the reality of rapidly congealing panic. *Convince the world you're strong and you're halfway to being there* . . .

"I've gone along with you for a day and a night without arguing or asking questions you didn't want to answer. But if I'm going to die here, I've got a right to fight for my life."

Susannah gave a hazy smile. "You did well with this one, Sam. We could do with a little fighter."

"I'm not little!" Chester said. For some reason, her patronizing tone stung more than Sam's outright refusal. "I'm not a child! Tell me where the engine room is, and I'll get your engine running again. I swear it!"

"Don't make oaths you can't keep," Susannah said, suddenly looking serious. She coughed, and a little spurt of blood trickled over her lips.

Chester felt his frustration fade, and guilt welled up in his stomach. What was he doing, snapping at this girl? She was dying. "Look," he said, "please, just tell me. It's got to be worth a try."

Susannah made a small sign to Sam and, finally, Sam pointed. "Down the hallway, to your left. Just keep heading downward."

✳

The doorway to the engine room was so low that even Chester had to duck his head. Opening the door, he was struck by a set of discordant tunes: a mixture of music, a jangle of wild noise—like a gunfight between melodies. Tunes ricocheted around the room, off the machinery, and back into one another, colliding with an explosion of sound.

Chester took a deep breath and scrambled inside. The air hissed with steam. He collided with various prongs of machinery, banging into clockwork contraptions and metal canisters, tripping through the dark and smoke as he navigated the increasingly tilted floor of the sinking ship. Black smoke blasted from pipes and metal spokes clanked like teeth across the ceiling. He barely ducked in time to avoid a mechanical arm that moved like a blade, slicing the air with a hiss of steam.

No wonder Sam considered this place dangerous. If you didn't know how the machinery worked . . .

A jet of steam blasted toward him. With a cry, Chester dove to the side. He smashed his injured arm against a metal tank—but he considered it a better option than having his face burned off.

Taking the opportunity to look around, he saw a pair of figures down in the darkest depths of the room. One, a young man, was tall and slender, with brown skin, and wore a pair of spectacles. He hunched over a segment of machinery, folding his spindly height beneath the low ceiling. He puffed awkwardly into a harmonica, looking about as comfortable as a librarian in a slaughterhouse.

The second figure was a girl with a crop of short blonde hair. She was banging away at the keys of a piano accordion, but the sound was lost in the din.

Between them sat a massive glass dome, buckled down with metal straps. Light fizzled through its innards like a thunderstorm with indigestion. Chester knew instantly that this was the source of the clashing music. He felt it in his fingers, in the static that tickled his neck, in the prickles of each tiny hair on his arms. Not just music, but *Music*. This was what gave the echoship its power. This was the engine.

And it was all going wrong.

"Hey!" Chester staggered forward. "Can I help?"

The strangers looked up at him, alarmed. The young man staggered backward, as though Chester might be an attacker, and the girl almost dropped her piano accordion.

"Sam brought me here!" Chester said quickly. "I'm a musician. I thought maybe I could help reset the Music . . ."

A look of horror crossed the boy's face, which Chester thought was a bit harsh. Then he realized that the expression wasn't directed at him. The boy raised a frantic hand to point behind him and, instinctively, Chester threw himself to the floor. With a fresh rip of pain, wet blood spilled out of the bullet hole in his arm. *Stupid, stupid.* He had reopened the wound, just when—

A metal beam clanked above him. It sliced the air with a violent hiss, missing his head by inches.

Maybe ducking hadn't been so stupid, after all.

"Over here!"

Chester crawled toward the glass dome, beyond the reach of swinging metal, and clambered shakily to his feet.

"It's safer here." The boy's accent was rich and a little pompous. "There isn't any moving machinery near the dome—it's rather fragile, you see."

It was a little less smoky over here, although the air still ran thick with steam. The discordant sound of the engine made Chester clap his hands over his ears—he had never heard Music so raw, so wild, so . . . *not like Music.* It didn't sound like a melody. It was noise. It was chaos.

"You're a Songshaper?" The girl's voice was high and light. In a quiet room, it might have sounded sweet, like a bird or a lullaby. In here, though, it was barely audible, and Chester strained to decipher her words.

"No . . . I mean, I've played Music by accident before, and I've got a flute . . ."

"We have to reset the right melody for the ship!"

"What is it?"

She handed him a rumpled folder. Chester thumbed through the first few pages, squinting in the darkness. It seemed to be a manual for operating the echoship. Then he hit a page titled "Engine Maintenance," with a run of staves, treble clefs, and notes. Sheet music.

Chester read slowly, letting the notes drip through his head as though he was playing them. Automatically, he imagined their sound on a fiddle—then readjusted his mind to hear them on a flute instead.

"Got it?" the boy said. His glasses had steamed up and he wiped them clean with fumbling fingers. "I'm afraid I can't play real Music so I'm just adding a few background notes to boost the tune. I went to medical school, not the Conservatorium; my father always said my talents lay closer to mindfulness than musicality, you see, and—"

"Got it," Chester said.

They all raised their instruments: flute, harmonica, piano accordion. Chester's arm burned and he felt the blood crawl across his skin, but it was more a dribble than a flow. The injection Sam had administered the day before must have had a substance to clot his blood, as well.

Ignoring the pain, Chester balanced the flute below his lips. He began to play with the others, pressing his fingers on the keys. He could barely hear himself over the din. He pursed his lips into a breath and focused on the music.

Dah, de dum dee dee daaah, de dum dee dee . . .

It was the tune of wheels clattering on a road. The tune of horses' hooves, or hailstones on a tin roof. The sound of movement, of power.

The sound of an engine.

Chester let the sound wash through him. It trickled from the flute into his fingers, into his wrists. It was the sort of tune that built on itself, that grew layer after layer. It was strong and stout and powerful.

The rest of the world seemed to fade away. The steam, the hissing, the clanking metal . . . it all faded, like smoke on a breeze. There was just the engine song. It flittered from his flute. It strained and plinked from the piano accordion, and it wheezed—just a little off-tempo—from the boy's harmonica.

And then the tune *caught*. For one glorious moment, they all played in unison, their shared note lingering in the air, and it snagged like a fishhook on the dome. Chester felt it happen; he felt the Music wrap around its players, and he stumbled, yanked by an invisible rope, toward the engine. His eyes flew open and he saw it, just for a moment: a wild stream of light around the dome.

A flash of brightness. A flash of sound. Suddenly the engine was playing their Music back to them. The cacophony of the broken tune vanished, and there was just the pure, powerful roll of the engine's rightful melody. It rolled around inside the glass, like flakes of glitter in a child's snow globe.

Around them, machinery shrieked. Lights flashed in speckles, and sorcery lamps flared around the room. A field of fireflies, waking into life and light. Chester could now see the others' faces clearly: nervous, sweaty, with foggy glasses and drooping hair.

The girl's eyes lit up. "We did it!"

The machinery bellowed and she gave a wild laugh. It wasn't a laugh of fear, exactly, but the cackle of some crazed pixie in a fairytale. It bubbled up from her lungs, light and frothy. "Gosh," she said. "It's so pretty, isn't it?"

Chester followed her gaze toward the dome. It was pretty, in a way, he supposed. In the same way that a griffin could be pretty from a distance—but up close, it would happily claw your brains out of your skull.

"Shouldn't we move?" the boy said. "I don't like the air in here."

"Nonsense," said the girl. "The air's toxicity won't reach a deadly level for at least . . ." She paused to consider. "Twenty more seconds."

There was a moment of silence.

The girl said, "Oh. I guess we'd better move then, right?"

And then they were running for the door: three stumbling figures in a haze of steam and machinery and curses in the dark.

CHAPTER FOURTEEN

CHESTER BURST BACK INTO THE DRIVER'S CABIN, PUFFING A LITTLE. The darkness of the river had risen. It crawled up over the window glass, like a stain of oil or seeping mud, as the *Cavatina* tilted down to meet it. A pair of lovers—ship and shadow—in the coil of breath before a kiss.

Susannah clutched a syringe, piercing her own flesh near the bullet wound. Its end led to a tube, which fed into a strange glass globe propped up in a medical kit open beside her. Whatever the globe was pumping into her, it was clearly working: Susannah breathed more steadily now, and her face looked more determined than pained.

"Engine's fixed," the blonde girl said.

"We know that," Sam said, yanking a lever sideways. "That's why I'm trying to fly this thing! Five minutes ago, it wouldn't even give a grunt of power."

"Don't let it touch you!" said the boy with the glasses.

"What?" Chester followed his gaze, confused, until he spotted the threat. The darkness had reached the broken window and was seeping through the cracks. It drizzled through chinks of shattered glass, which lay glinting on the floor.

"The water!" the boy said, pointing. "Don't let it touch your skin." He paused, looking Chester up and down. "Well, I suppose you could if you really *wanted* to, but it would be a shame to waste those charmingly rustic cufflinks."

Chester jumped back: now that the swirling water had come in, it was flowing even faster. "Can't we just reverse its tune or something? Like when I fought the Echo?"

"Oh, are you volunteering to throw yourself in?" said the blonde girl.

"What? No, I—"

"You'd have to touch the water first, to hear its melody," she said, apparently thinking aloud. "Then you could play it backwards on your flute. But of course, it would start dragging you down as soon as you touched it . . ." She brightened a little. "You know, I think it might work! It would be a horrible death, of course, but you *might* temporarily disrupt the river's Music while it consumed you."

At this, Chester decided not to offer any more suggestions.

Sam stomped back and forth between wheels and levers, swearing occasionally under his breath in his attempt to gain some lift. There was a ravenous growl from the bowels of the echoship, more ursine than mechanical, and the cabin began to shake.

"Sam, head west," Susannah ordered. "Last we saw of the Songshaper, she was on the eastern shore. Her echoboat's tiny— she'll sink if she tries to follow us across the river here, and it'll take her at least a day to reach the next decent bridge."

"You know," said the blonde girl, who was still considering the river, "another option might be throwing in a Musical creature, like an Echo. It wouldn't be a perfect tune reversal, but the combination of its dying life-force and its own inherent Music should theoretically—"

"Dot?" Susannah said, through clenched teeth.

"Yes, Captain?"

"Have you got a pet Echo to throw into the river?"

"No, Captain."

"Then shut up, would you? Sam needs to concentrate. And the rest of you, find something to hold onto."

Chester grabbed the wall, barely suppressing a shout of pain as his wounded arm jolted.

"Hold on tight!" Sam said. "This river ain't keen to let us go."

The *Cavatina* creaked and moaned as they ascended, fighting against the water that clutched at them: desperate fingers, refusing to release. Sam steered sideways, struggling away from the river's line of reflection . . .

And suddenly, the shadows retracted.

The whole world jerked; the *Cavatina* righted itself against the tilt and they slid backward in a clatter of limbs as the ship arced up onto the western shore. Chester glanced out the window just in time to see the river disappear behind them. Tendrils of black slowly drained from the cabin, seeping back down through the broken window.

"Gosh," said the blonde girl, looking excited. "That was quite an adventure, wasn't it? You know, I've always wondered what a reflection trap might feel like. I have a theory that—"

"Okay," Susannah interrupted. She pushed herself up onto her elbows, visibly fighting a surge of pain. "Time for chatting later, gang. Sam, I need you to get us the hell out of here."

"On it already, Captain."

"I want a decoy, too. Launch the Musical automation in one of the echoboats and send it north, with just enough sparkage to leave a trail." She shook her head. "I don't like to waste an echoboat, but it's better than being chased by a bunch of Shapers."

Sam wrenched down a fistful of levers then flicked a series of knobs and dials. A shudder ran down through the ship, as though something heavy had been dislodged from the upper deck.

"Good," said Susannah. "Dot, help me and the new boy into the medical room."

The blonde girl glanced across at Chester, startled, as if she had forgotten his existence. Then she spotted the roughly bandaged wound on his arm and saluted. "Yes, Captain!"

Susannah turned to the boy in glasses. "Travis, you've got a pair of invalids to deal with."

Travis looked down at his clothing. He wore a pair of sleek plum trousers, a white cotton shirt, and an expensive-looking waistcoat. A silk cravat adorned his neck, gleaming crimson under the sorcery lamps, and a gold watch dangled from his pocket.

Despite all this splendor, the outfit was a little scuffed and smoke-stained. Travis gave a melodramatic sigh, running his hands and eyes across the fabric's injuries.

"Travis!" Susannah said. "You have your orders. I need you to dress our wounds. I hired you on the basis of you being a doctor, didn't I?"

"Yes, but—"

"Are you afraid of getting blood on your clothes?"

Travis shook his head. "Oh no, certainly not. I just . . ." He waved a hand, clearly struggling for an excuse. He clicked his fingers. "Ah! It's unhygienic, you see."

"It's what?"

"Oh," Travis said, "it's a new concept in medical training. I really ought to change into a clean shirt first." He paused. "Sam, may I borrow one of your shirts? Mine are all so unsanitary—all those decorative elements are simply *havens* for disease . . ."

"Is this to protect your patients or your clothes?" Susannah said.

Travis gave her his brightest smile. "I'll meet you in the medical room, okay?"

He sauntered out of the cabin, boots clacking until they were silenced by the carpet of the corridor.

"Oh, don't worry about Travis," Dot said, turning to Chester. "He's just a vain little peacock. Spends half his time chasing pretty girls and the other half ironing his shirt sleeves." She paused. "You know, I've always had a few quibbles with the use of the peacock as a symbol for human vanity. If you ask me, a better analogy would be the—"

"Yes, yes," Susannah said. "Just get us to the medical room."

Dot saluted again. "Yes, Captain!"

She helped Susannah to her feet. Chester couldn't help but be a little impressed as he watched the captain stand. She held the syringe in place herself, even as color drained from her face. She swayed a little but Dot steadied her.

"That's it, Captain. Just down the corridor . . ."

"I know where the medical room is," Susannah snapped.

"Just trying to be reassuring, Captain."

✳

The medical room was small and cramped. Chester stepped aside to allow Susannah to take the bed, and stood back in the corridor to await his own treatment.

Travis appeared in an oversized flannel shirt, which swam across his skinny torso like a bedsheet. He tied the loose folds of fabric into a knot and rolled up the sleeves to his elbows.

"I see you've bravely sacrificed Sam's shirt to the cause instead of your own," Susannah said.

"What, this thing?" Travis looked down at the shirt distastefully. "Oh, it's checkered crimson already. The big lout will hardly notice a few little blood spatters."

Travis pushed Susannah back to make her lie down on the bed, whipped open a cupboard of medical supplies, and set to work. Chester watched through the doorway, a little queasy.

Queasy? That was odd. He'd never had a problem with the sight of blood, or even death. Once, he'd shared a cargo carriage with an old man who had died of fever in the middle of the night. When the train had stopped, Chester had carried the body down off the train and buried him in a stand of thistle trees near the railroad track. Sickness and death were just a fact of life.

But still, Chester felt sick. Clammy. And it grew worse by the minute. His breaths felt shallow and he clenched his fingers to steady himself.

"What's your name?"

He blinked, startled by the sudden voice. "Chester Hays."

The blonde girl nodded. "I'm Dorothy Pickett, but everyone calls me Dot. In there, that's the captain, Susannah Kemp, and Travis Dalton." She eyed him, clearly curious. "You all right? You look a little . . ."

"I'm fine." Chester took a deep breath, and then fought the urge to vomit it back up again. "It's just . . . I think I might be coming down with something."

"Ah." Dot's expression cleared. She tapped him on the chest with a smile. "It's withdrawal, isn't it? From the recital?"

Chester started. In the chaos of the morning so far, he had almost forgotten about skipping the recital last night. No wonder he felt sick.

"Not to worry," Dot said. "We all went through it. As long as you can get through tonight, you'll be all right." She laughed. "I bet Sam was cranky about it though, wasn't he? He gets like that sometimes, when . . ."

"When what?"

Dot hesitated. "Not my place to say."

There was an awkward silence. Then, from inside the room, Susannah—who must have been listening—said, "Let's just say

132

that Sam's emotions are . . . unpredictable. If you're going to join our gang, I suppose you've got a right to know what you're signing up for."

As she spoke, Travis poured a vial of greenish liquid onto her wound. It sizzled and Susannah flinched, hissing the last few words through clenched teeth.

"I know what I'm signing up for," Chester said. "You're a gang of thieves."

"No, we're not."

"Then what are you?"

"Well . . ." Dot waved a hand. "We're what you might call *specialists.* We've got a reputation, you see. In the industry."

"The thieving industry?"

"We prefer to see it as a wealth redistribution program."

Chester snorted. He'd heard that one a lot recently. Stealing from the rich, giving to the poor. Ever since the Nightfall Gang had become famous, it seemed that every thief in Meloral had used that line to justify their actions. Unlike the infamous Nightfall Gang, however, most criminals didn't genuinely give their earnings to the poor—unless by "the poor," they meant themselves.

"We give half our loot to those who need it," Dot said, "and we only steal from people who deserve it."

"Such as . . . ?"

"Aristocrats in Weser City. Songshapers in little towns who lord it over the common folk and take half their earnings to line their own pockets."

"Of course," Chester said sarcastically. "I'm sure you're a bunch of real heroes—just like the Nightfall Gang."

"Oh good," Dot said, "you've heard of us."

"What?"

"I said, 'you've heard of us,'" Dot said brightly. "The Nightfall Gang. I was the one who came up with the name—you know, since we boycott the Sundown Recital and all. It's got a nice flair, don't you think?"

Chester stared at them. Were they joking? The Nightfall Gang was the most notorious crew in Meloral. They had broken into Songshapers' mansions. They had scattered sacks of gold to the needy in Jubaldon and given new boots to the beggars in Linus. Some people were convinced that the Nightfall Gang used griffins to pull their getaway coaches; others that they were ghosts who only appeared by night to wage war on behalf of the downtrodden.

They were heroes. They were legends.

They weren't a bunch of bickering teenagers who crashed their echoships into rivers.

"No," Chester said, "you can't be the Nightfall Gang. I've heard stories about the gang; you're just a bunch of kids *pretending* to be—"

Susannah sighed. "The stories are exaggerated, Chester. That's what happens with stories—they get retold and they shift a little. Change their clothes, you might say. Haven't you ever heard a rumor spread through a town?"

"There is no way in hell," Chester said, "that you broke into a rancher's stable and released his fleet of forty pegasi. I don't believe it."

"Only four pegasi, actually," Susannah said, "and we only stole them on principle. The rancher was using them to spy on his workers. If he caught anyone resting, even for a moment, he'd whip them bloody."

"Poor things," Dot said.

"So you just broke in and released the horses?" Chester said skeptically. "How? I've seen the security that folks put on their pegasi stables . . ."

"We went in through the Hush," Susannah said, "and we rode out on the pegasi."

Chester stared at her.

The Hush.

And suddenly, he wasn't so sure she was lying.

The Hush explained everything. It made sense, didn't it? It explained how the Nightfall Gang could infiltrate the most tightly guarded buildings, how they could sneak into banks and mansions without anybody noticing, how they escaped with the loot, unseen and unheard, like ghosts in the night . . .

Chester stared at them. Could it really be true? For almost a year now, he had heard tales of the Nightfall Gang. They'd even had a song renamed in their honor—"The Nightfall Duet." All across the country, he'd seen the growing panic as aristocrats installed bars on their windows and increased the security of important buildings. If this really was the Nightfall Gang, he was in the presence of legends.

And they wanted him to join them.

"What . . . ?" Chester wet his lips. "What do you want me for?"

Susannah gave a slow smile. It wasn't a happy smile. It was a hungry smile. "Well," she said, "we're planning a rather special heist. And for this heist, we need an unlicensed Songshaper." She raised her head a little, and looked right into Chester's eyes. "One who's never been to the Conservatorium in Weser City."

"I'm not trained."

"Good," Susannah said. "That's the point. We have a very special target in mind and we need someone who won't be recognized there. Someone to go in undercover."

Chester stared at her, his stomach tightening. Surely, she couldn't mean . . .

"We're going to rob the Conservatorium," Susannah said. "We're going to fleece those scoundrels for all they're worth." She gave him a long, hard look. "But for our plan to work, we need a man on the inside."

"Me?" Chester said, mouth as dry as newspaper. "You want *me* to sneak into the Conservatorium?"

"Oh no," Susannah said. "We don't want you to sneak in."

There was a pause.

"We want you to audition."

CHAPTER FIFTEEN

CHESTER LAUGHED. HE COULDN'T HELP IT. THE SOUND BUBBLED UP inside him, panicky and shocked. Him? Audition for the Conservatorium?

The room was quiet. Chester stared among the gang members, waiting for someone to admit to the joke. Dot looked away and Travis made no attempt to meet his gaze.

"You're joking, right?" Chester said.

Silence.

Susannah gave him a serious look. "We need someone inside the Conservatorium, Chester. We only get one shot at this. They only hold auditions once a year and they're just under three weeks away. Do you think you're up to it?"

Chester stared back at her, stunned. He didn't know what to think. Hell, he didn't know what to feel. Six months ago his answer would have been *Yes, yes, yes!* He'd always dreamed of attending the Conservatorium. Of learning to craft true music and turning it into Music. Of playing sorcery into lamps, and songs into the night . . .

Of becoming a Songshaper.

But now? Now, he didn't have time for selfish whims. His father was still missing and Chester had to find him. Even if the auditions were only weeks away, the job itself might take longer. For all he knew, it might take months. And what if he was caught? It could even cost Chester his life. Then who would look for his father?

Chester took a deep breath. "I've got another job already."

"What?"

"My father's missing—his name's Wyatt Hays. He vanished from his bed and I can't . . . I mean . . ." He shook his head. "Look, I have to find him."

The others threw each other startled glances. Chester looked among them and a chill passed across his skin. They knew something. They knew something about the vanishings.

"You know what happened to my father?"

"A lot of things might've happened to your father," Susannah said carefully. "He might have abandoned you. He might've interrupted a burglary and been dragged off. Or maybe—"

"He used to be a soldier," Chester said. "A conscript, in the War of the Prairie. And when my mother died, he raised me on his own. He worked whatever jobs he could get, just to keep a roof over our heads. More than anything, he believed in family." Chester hesitated. "He would never just abandon me. And I . . . I can't abandon him."

"Maybe he—"

"He was having nightmares," Chester said. "Fevers and bad dreams, for days before it happened. And in his sleep, he kept talking about the Hush."

Susannah blinked, but didn't move. No one spoke.

"I didn't know what the word meant," Chester said. "Not until I met Sam and he dragged me into this place."

Silence.

Unexpectedly, it was Dot who finally spoke. Her voice still sounded light and lilting, but with a more cautious edge to it now. "What happens to the vanished ones is officially a mystery," she said. "Originally, I was working on a theory that it was an imbalance in the sorcery levels in the atmosphere, which inter-fered with the natural Musical tuning of human flesh, but—"

"You *were* working on a theory?" Chester said. "So you're not working on it anymore."

Dot opened her mouth, then closed it again. Finally, she shook her head. "No, not anymore."

"Because you found out what's really going on?"

"That's enough," Susannah said sharply. She pushed herself up onto her elbows and her shirt slipped back down to cover her wound. "You haven't earned our trust yet, Chester Hays."

"You know what happened to my father."

"Maybe." Susannah met his glare with a cool expression. "Maybe not. But I don't see why we should share our most valuable information with a boy who refuses to help with our plan."

"You can't trick me into helping you," Chester said. "For all I know, you could be lying. That's what you do, isn't it? You scam people—con them—and steal from them. You're nothing but a bunch of—"

"Thieves?"

"Exactly." Chester stepped into the room. "A few days ago, I turned up in Hamelin with a fiddle in my hands and a hope of finding my father. Now what've I got? No fiddle, a bullet-hole in my arm, and a bunch of near-death experiences—all because of your gang. And now you want me to risk my neck again, just so you can steal some jewels from the Conservatori—"

"The Conservatorium," Susannah said, "is responsible for what happened to your father."

Chester fell silent. He stared at her, mouth slightly open as it hung off the broken last word of his tirade.

"This job isn't just to steal jewels, Chester," Susannah said. "It's about justice. You're not the only person who's been hurt by these vanishings."

"You lost someone, too?"

"Something like that."

Chester felt a tense sort of tangle in his stomach. He took a deep breath. "If I prove myself, you'll tell me everything?"

"Of course."

"And you'll treat me like a full member of your gang? Not just some tag-along for everyone to kick?"

"Of course." Susannah hopped down from the bed. She was remarkably steady on her feet, despite the injury. "If you want to be part of our gang, though, I'd recommend that you start addressing your captain with a little more respect."

There was a long pause.

Chester lowered his gaze. "Yes, Captain."

The word felt odd on his tongue. "Captain" was a common title among only three groups in Melorian society: sailors, guards, and gangs of thieves. Chester had never belonged to any of these groups. The rigid hierarchy of the gang would take some getting used to.

"Well then," Susannah said, "Welcome to the Nightfall Gang."

They shook hands. Susannah's hand was warm and slender and Chester found himself gripping it a moment longer than necessary. He fumbled backward, silently cursing his own awkwardness.

This wasn't just an ordinary young woman. This was the captain of the Nightfall Gang. This echoship belonged to the most famous group of outlaws in the country.

And now, he was one of them.

∗

Susannah stepped into the driver's cabin, her mind churning. Once the swirls of black water had drained away, Sam had boarded up the broken window with a sheet of metal. The other windows glinted, slick with the song of a moonless night.

"So," she said eventually. "You all right?"

Sam nodded. "The doc fixed you up?"

"Yeah. I've had worse." Susannah pressed a finger to her torso. Her wound had already begun to scab over, stitched together by the Musical strength of Travis's injections. "Another set of jabs tonight and one in the morning and I'll be good as new by tomorrow evening."

The injectable healing tunes were shockingly expensive, but Susannah had insisted that the *Cavatina* be well stocked. In such a dangerous line of work, the medicine was worth its weight in gold.

Sam adjusted the wheel a little, turning the ship more sharply westward. On the sorcery map, the town of Linus blinked up ahead. "Lucky it was you, not me."

Susannah didn't respond. How could she? After what the Songshapers had done to Sam, he reacted badly to the mere presence of Music, let alone having a melody—even if it was a healing melody—pumped into his flesh . . .

She stared at the nearest window. Her reflection stared back at her, showing tangled red hair and a face pale with blood loss. The injections would heal her quickly, she knew—but her wound was only a bullet hole. There were other kinds of wounds . . . wounds that couldn't be healed so easily.

Her gaze slipped across to Sam. The older boy sat tense and quiet, his fingers tight on the steering wheel. Susannah would never admit it aloud—least of all to Sam himself—but he had been acting . . . strangely. More strangely than usual. He had been reckless lately: always the first to charge into danger, to throw his life on the line. And it wasn't just the recklessness of a boy protecting his friends. It was the recklessness of someone who didn't care anymore. Almost like he was past caring, past suffering. Almost like he just wanted it all to end.

"Are you all right, Sam?" she said quietly.

"I already said, I ain't hurt. New kid got shot, not me."

"I wasn't talking about that."

Sam looked at her. His eyes were blank: pale blue, almost eerie.

"Sometimes . . ." Susannah took a deep breath, then shook her head. "We're so close, Sam. So close to getting justice."

"I know that, Captain. Only thing that keeps me going, some days." Sam twiddled the wheel, spinning them deeper into the dark. "It's getting worse, though. Like a slow sickness. Every day it hurts a bit more."

Susannah glanced up at the sorcery lamps on the ceiling. "I've asked Dot to change all the lamps on the ship. Are you saying they're still not—"

"They're better," Sam cut her off. "But it still ain't like living before, Captain. I can still feel it in my head. All the time. Just the Music, running over and over and over . . ." He stared into the darkness. "I'm gonna be the one who takes 'em down, you know. Whatever it takes."

Susannah watched him for a long moment, disquieted. She didn't know what to say. Finally, she wet her lips. "What do you think of our new recruit?"

"He's a Songshaper, Captain. I don't trust scum like that."

"You know why we need him."

"Don't mean I gotta like it," Sam said. "My pa used to say that tossing your rope before you make a loop don't catch a calf."

"What the hell does that mean?"

"It means we'd be damn fools to get ahead of ourselves."

"Dammit, Sam, we don't have time for this! In a few weeks, it'll be too late to—"

"So what?" There was anger in Sam's voice now, and he stood up with a flare of ice in his eyes. "That don't make it right to risk everything we've worked for."

Susannah opened her mouth to argue, then closed it. There was something . . . unsettling . . . in Sam's anger. His muscles clenched, quivering slightly, as though his entire body was a spring about to unleash.

"I've done everything you've asked of me, Captain," Sam said. "But even you can't ask me to trust a damn Songshaper."

"But we have to—"

Sam slammed a fist on the bench.

Without thinking, Susannah threw up a hand to defend herself. She knew that Sam would never hurt her if he was in his right mind. But the lamps were swinging overhead, and a thousand cogs and wheels on the ship were spinning with sorcery. In this wild wash of melody, Sam's mind would be anything but right . . .

"Sam," she said. "Sam, it's me."

Silence.

And then, one muscle at a time, his entire body seemed to collapse in on itself. He sat back down and slumped against the wheel, his breath ragged. Susannah watched, her heart in her throat, as the unnatural fury died in his eyes.

"It's all right, Sam," she whispered. "It's all right."

"No." The word was almost a growl. "No, Captain, it ain't."

Susannah reached slowly into her pocket. She retrieved a tiny lantern, stained with the familiar orange hue of Dot's magic, and held it up cautiously for him to take. "Do you want . . . ?"

He nodded.

Susannah pressed her fingers to the glass bauble, flaring its sorcery into life. It was one of Dot's special lanterns, enchanted with a calming melody, and hopefully its tune would help. Sam took it from her with shaking fingers and clutched it like a lifeline, his breath still ragged.

"I'm sorry," he said, sounding broken. "Damn it all, I'm sorry."

"It's not your fault," Susannah said. "It's *their* fault. They're the ones who did this to you. And in just a few weeks, we can finally make them pay."

"By working with one of them?" Sam shook his head. "No. There's gotta be another way. We'll wait another year, if we've got to. We'll find some kid who's good at music, and *we'll* train him up. Not a kid who's already got Music in his veins."

Silence.

"Dot's a Songshaper," Susannah said quietly.

"That's different. She got rejected by the rest of 'em. Makes her an outsider, like us. And besides, she never—"

"Has Chester ever hurt you?" Susannah said.

Sam hesitated. "No."

"Was he trained at the Conservatorium?"

"No."

"So he's not really one of them, is he? He's probably just some street kid, trained by another bunch of criminals."

Sam stared down at the bauble in his hand. His breaths were slower now, lulled by the throb of the lantern's melody. "He says he ain't been trained at all."

Susannah shook her head. "That's impossible. How else could he connect to the Song?"

"Maybe he's just a natural."

"It doesn't work like that!"

"Well, I'm not the expert, am I? Go talk to Dot about it."

Susannah frowned. As far as she knew, it took years of training to conjure Music—let alone to touch the Song itself. It wasn't enough to be a talented musician. You had to learn the sorcery, to weave your own tune upon the magical rhythm that underscored the world . . .

"I don't believe it."

Sam shrugged. "Guess he's lying, then."

A hill loomed in the darkness ahead. Sam pocketed the lantern and wrenched a nearby lever. The echoship shuddered up the slope. Darkness streamed across the window as rain swirled past in a blur of unnatural droplets.

"How much does he know?" Susannah said.

"Never even heard of the Hush."

"Plenty of low-grade Songshapers haven't heard of the—"

"No idea how to wake up a doped pegasus, either. Not until I told him. And he would've been killed by an Echo if I hadn't told him the tune-reversal trick."

Susannah considered this. "He could just be acting," she said. "Playing the fool. Trying to hide his true talents until he's sussed us out better."

"If he is, he's a damn good actor," Sam said darkly. "Better than Travis, even. He's impulsive, Captain, and he's damn immature. He put his pride above his life in that saloon. And he shouted out the recital in the Hush, too—brought a whole pack of Echoes down on us. I sure ain't ready to trust him."

Outside, the darkness swirled.

"Do you trust me?" Susannah said.

Sam wrenched his head up, visibly pained. "Come off it, Captain. You know I do."

"Then I'll make you a deal," Susannah said. "For now, we'll assume Chester can't be trusted. We won't tell him about the plan, or our real goal." She paused. "But let me bring him on the Linus job. We'll see if he's reliable and if he's good enough to work with. If he proves himself, we tell him the truth about the Conservatorium."

"And if he fails?"

"If he fails," Susannah said, "I'll let you deal with him."

Sam stared at her for a long moment. Then he gave a slow, deliberate nod. "All right, Captain," he said. "You got yourself a deal."

The world beyond the window was black. Susannah had a sudden urge to reach out and grab it—the mist, the rain, the darkness—and shake it all in frustration. She was so close to achieving justice. To pulling off the greatest job in the Nightfall Gang's history. To spitting in the face of the Conservatorium leaders, to making a real difference and showing the world that tyrants could be beaten.

But to do that, she had to be able to trust this new boy. To understand him. To use him. And she couldn't do that yet. She still wasn't sure if he had his own agenda.

For now, she just had to watch. To wait. To pay very close attention to the mystery that was Chester Hays.

CHAPTER SIXTEEN

ONCE CHESTER'S WOUND WAS PATCHED UP, DOT VOLUNTEERED TO give him a guided tour of the *Cavatina*. She smiled and pointed excitedly at everything, steering his gaze toward particularly interesting parts of the echoship.

Unfortunately, Dot's idea of "interesting" didn't entirely mesh with Chester's.

"Oh, I've always loved that sorcery lamp! Look at the shine on the globe—it took me three hours to blow the glass that neatly. Oh wow, do you see that doorknob? Lovely, isn't it? Best parts of the ship, if you ask me: the doorknobs and latches. Sometimes you get these awful swinging handles that are such a pain to open when you've got your hands full of clothes or teacups or something, but this one's very practical, you see . . ."

At first Chester wondered if Dot was being sarcastic, but she was so cheerful and seemed so genuinely enthralled by lamps and doorknobs that Chester eventually gave in and went with the flow.

"So," he said, trying to sound casual, "how'd you end up joining the gang?"

Dot froze.

It was only a moment—a quick break in her step—before she regained her stride. She replastered her usual cheery expression across her face and shrugged. "I got kicked out of my old life, so I found myself a new one."

"Yeah," Chester said, "but most people go to the city or something to start a new life. They don't join a gang of thieves."

"Susannah recruited me," Dot said. "We knew each other when we were little, you see. My family used to spend our summers in Delos, where Susannah grew up. We used to sneak away and play on the docks together. So when Susannah told me what she'd been through and how she wanted to—"

"What she'd been through?"

Dot hesitated, realizing she'd said too much. "Hey, look over there! I really like the floorboards in this corridor. Mostly we've got carpet, but it's fun to scoot along these boards in your socks when no one's looking . . . Oh, and this is your cabin!" She threw open a door at the end of the corridor. "Smallest one we've got, I'm afraid, but we've already all snagged the better ones."

Chester's eyes widened, his questioning interrupted by a sudden glimpse of comfort. The cabin was long and narrow, like the bar in a good-sized saloon. The wallpaper was a rich crimson patterned with tiny black dots, and the ceiling was painted a dusky cream. A weak blue sorcery lamp hung from its center, casting dim light across the room. Finally, the bed looked plush and comfortable, with a heavy blue blanket atop a squishy mattress. All in all, it was better than many places he'd slept of late.

"I always liked these old lamps," Dot said, staring up at the weak globe. "But this is one of the last ones left; I've been replacing them all over the ship."

"It's not very bright," Chester said.

"True," Dot said. "But it reminds me of the moon. We don't get a moon here in the Hush. When I first joined the gang, I used to lie in my room with a sorcery lamp and pretend I was looking at the night sky."

Chester stared at her. "Um . . ."

The lamp didn't look much like a moon to him. Just a faded old lantern, stuttering out its last few flickers of light. But Dot looked so wistful as she stared at it, her eyes as wide as globes themselves, that Chester thought it best not to argue. Then a thought struck him. "Hang on—*you've* been replacing sorcery lamps? You know how to make them?"

"Oh yes," Dot said. "They're one of the first things you learn in training."

"You're a real Songshaper!"

Dot looked at him. "Yes, of course. Didn't you know?"

Chester shook his head. "But if you're a Songshaper, what the hell does your gang need me for? You're much more advanced than me if you made all the lamps on this ship . . ."

"Oh, lamps are easy," Dot said. "I can teach you, if you'd like."

"But if the gang's already got a—"

"We need an *unlicensed* Songshaper. Someone who can audition without being recognized."

"You'd be recognized?"

Dot let out a bitter laugh. It was odd, coming from a girl who usually sounded so cheerful. "Oh yes. My name is on their records; I could never audition again. I'm sure they'd all remember me."

There was a pause. Then the full meaning of her words hit him and Chester almost choked. "Again? You mean—you studied at the Conservatorium?"

Dot turned away, refocusing her gaze on the moon globe. "Yes. I studied at the Conservatorium."

"What was it like?" Chester said. "I always wanted to study there but my father couldn't afford it. Did you learn to play new types of music? Did they teach you real Music right away, or just normal playing? Was the sorcery hard to learn, or—"

"I don't want to talk about it. They . . ." Dot sucked in a quiet little breath, and her voice rose an octave. "They didn't treat me too well, toward the end."

There was a long pause.

"But hang on—if you studied at the Conservatorium, shouldn't you still be there?" Chester frowned. "Seven years of training. You're too young to have graduated . . ."

And with a cold start, he realized the truth. *I got kicked out of my old life . . .*

Dot had been expelled from the Conservatorium.

No wonder they needed him to audition. Dot could never go back there—not with her name on the records, and her face in the teachers' memories. What on earth had she done? It must have been bad . . .

"If I asked what you were expelled for," he said, "could you tell me?"

Dot's gaze lingered on the globe. "I could."

Silence.

"So . . . ?" Chester said.

"I *could*," Dot said. "Not *would*. There's a difference."

She gave him a quiet look, with something hard in her eyes. Chester squirmed a little, suddenly uncomfortable. He had a strange feeling that Dot was trying to read him in the same way that he had been trying to read Sam earlier, to test something about him and his attitudes that he could barely interpret himself. He straightened his spine and tried to look a little more trustworthy.

"What I *would* tell you," Dot said quietly, "is that it was a moonless night, and I was young and stupid, and I was betrayed. I got caught. I got expelled." She took a sharp breath. "And I learned to put my trust in things like moons and doorknobs, and not in people."

She turned to leave.

"Wait!"

Dot turned back, raising an eyebrow. "Yes?"

"I . . ." Chester hesitated. "I'm sorry. I shouldn't have asked. It's none of my business."

Dot stared at him for a long moment. Then she nodded. "You're allowed to be curious, Chester Hays. I'm curious about things, too. That's why I study. That's why I develop theories."

"Do you have a theory about me?"

"All of us have theories about you," Dot said. "Sam doesn't trust you. Susannah thinks you'll be a handy little stooge in this job." A flicker of her smile returned. "Travis thinks you have appalling taste in shirts."

"And what about you?"

"I think," Dot said, "that I can't judge what a thief will be like until I've seen him on a job. I like evidence, you see. Data, statistics, observable results. And as luck would have it, we're due for a job in Linus. Should be a simple little burglary—nothing too dangerous."

Dot turned away, tossing the last few words over her shoulder. "And a good trial run for our newest recruit."

∗

That night, Chester sat alone in his cabin. He knew the others were in the kitchen, chattering about the Linus job and preparing dinner. But a quiet nausea churned his stomach.

The recital.

In the real world, it was likely approaching sundown. During the day, in the rush of action and exploration, Chester had almost forgotten about his withdrawal symptoms. But now his body cried out for relief. He doubled over, clutching his stomach. The jabs inside were hot and hard. It was like a knife being turned around through the slit of his belly button, carving a circle of pain. He half-expected to see blood when he pulled away his fingers, but there was nothing. Just the pain and the silence.

Chester curled his knees up to his chest so that he lay in the fetal position. There was a faint sound of music in his head now, a forgotten tune. A drumbeat and a set of fingers on banjo strings, a sting with every twang. *Pluck, pluck, pluck* . . . The tune flicked pain into his belly and music into his skull.

There was a knock at his door.

"Yes?" he managed.

The door swung open and a head of bright red curls slipped inside. *Susannah.* Chester stared up at her, blinking at the influx of color in his cabin. He hadn't expected the captain herself. He'd thought maybe Dot or Sam or Travis . . .

"Are you all right?" Susannah said.

Another wave of pain hit and Chester curled up tighter. His pain vied with embarrassment, as he suddenly realized he was curled up like a baby in front of the captain. He tried to straighten his limbs but they refused to extend. It was like trying to bend a rifle with his fingers.

Susannah didn't look scornful, though. She dropped onto the bed beside him and placed a hand on his forehead. "No fever," she said, after a moment. "That's good."

"Recital," Chester managed.

"I know," Susannah said. "You should've seen me when I went through withdrawal. Cried for five hours straight." She bent down to look at him, her eyes intense. "You'll get through this. It only lasts a few hours, as long as you don't fall into a fever. If you can beat it tonight it should be over for good."

"I heard of an old woman . . ." Chester faltered, curling beneath the weight of his pain, which pulsed through his body

152

in waves. "I heard of a woman who suffered for days. Lost her mind . . ."

Susannah shook her head. "Just stories to keep you compliant. As long as your temperature stays stable it's just a few hours of pain. We've all been through it."

"Why?" Chester whispered, his voice hoarse. "Why can't we keep doing the recital? Why bother with this . . ."

"This pain?" Susannah looked down at her fingers, steepled in her lap. "Because the Songshapers teach us the recital is necessary. They teach us it's what keeps us alive, what keeps us healthy. They tell us we'll go insane without it." She looked up, expression set. "And they're lying."

"So?"

"So they're lying for a reason." She shook her head again. "I don't know what the recital is for—to control people, to track people, or to keep us compliant. I know it hurts like hell to withdraw. But I also know life goes on afterward. Everyone on this ship has withdrawn from the recital, just in case. And if you want to be a part of this gang—if you want our help finding your father—you've got to pull yourself through this."

Chester fought back another ripple of nausea. "Why . . . why are you here, Captain?"

"Here in the gang? Or here in this room?"

Chester nodded. He didn't care which question she answered, he just needed the distraction of talking. Of listening. Of filling his head with something that wasn't agony.

"I'm here in this room," Susannah said slowly, "because you're in my gang now. This pain is because of my orders. I wouldn't be much of a captain if I didn't try to help you through it."

As she spoke, the pain hit again. Chester let out a strained breath. He wanted to say *It hurts*, or *Make it stop*, but he couldn't afford to look even weaker in front of the captain. He could see that as a

Songshaper he was valuable to them, but their information was just as valuable—if not more—to him. If they decided he was too weak for the job, he might never learn the secret of the vanishings . . .

"I know," Susannah said. "I know it hurts."

Chester cracked a weak smile. "You a mind reader, Captain?"

"Just someone who's been there." Her teeth were very white, Chester noticed. A gleam of white beneath a sea of red.

"Are you okay?" he said. "After the bullet, I mean? You're . . . healing?"

Susannah nodded. "It's amazing what Travis can do."

"Travis knows medicine," Chester said, "and he's good at acting. Dot knows Music and mechanics. Sam's big and tough, and he seems to be the best at flying the—"

His sentence broke midway as he was hit by a clench of agony in his chest. Chester curled into himself, scrunched his eyes shut and breathed through the pain. *Convince the world you're strong . . .*

As the pain faded, he forced his eyes open and continued through gritted teeth. "Sam's the best at flying the echoship. And you're the leader."

Susannah nodded. "And I do the climbing and burgling of places."

"What about me?" Chester said. "Where do I fit in?"

"You're our Songshaper."

"But Dot—"

"Dot's on the Conservatorium records, so she can't do the job. Not this time." Susannah waved a hand, as though casting around for a change of subject. "Anyway, you're a natural. You connected to the Song without any training. That's not normal, Chester. That's . . . valuable." She gave him a careful look, assessing his reaction—as though still not entirely sure whether she believed him. "If you can already hear the Song, I'm sure you can learn to play a bit of Music for us."

"I've been trained in music," Chester said. "Sort of."

"There's a difference between music and *Music*." She put a clear emphasis on the second version of the word.

"Apart from the capital letter, you mean?"

Susannah smiled and Chester's stomach twitched. "Yes. Apart from that. Anyone can be trained to play a tune on an instrument, but not to create their own sorcery." She gave him a curious look. "Who taught you to play fiddle, anyway? Don't take this the wrong way, but you don't look much like a rich man's heir."

"I worked in an instrument shop," Chester said.

"Ah. That would explain it."

Chester let a gasp of pain escape his teeth as another wave of misery shuddered down his spine and into his belly. He curled, then uncurled, like an indecisive wisp of smoke, before he straightened his legs with a grunt.

"I can leave you if you want."

"No, don't. Please. I . . . the distraction helps."

"All right." Susannah placed a hand on his head to check his temperature again then gave a relieved nod. "No sign of fever."

Chester twitched again in pain. He realized he'd bitten his tongue in a thrash of agony and blood welled against his teeth with a new-found sting.

"Tell me about this instrument shop," Susannah said.

Chester swallowed hard. "Just a little shop in Thrace. Ashworth's Emporium, it's called. There aren't many customers, except for the regulars who know the owner . . ."

"The owner?"

"Mr. Ashworth."

Chester had struggled for months not to think about life in Thrace. Part of him was terrified that if he let himself think about it he might just run back and slip into his old life, abandoning his father, leaving him to suffer whatever fate the vanishing had dealt him . . .

Now, though, Chester let himself remember. It was better than the pain of withdrawal. He remembered the crooked little alleyway, the weight of shadow and the stink of old garbage. The wooden sign swinging, welcoming him inside. ASHWORTH'S EMPORIUM. And inside, the light of sorcery lamps, the warmth of the fireplace, and the crackle of flame. The scent of wood and polish, rows of bows and instruments: fiddles, banjos, clarinets . . .

And Goldenleaf.

Goldenleaf was the first instrument he had carved on his own. Chester had stayed awake by lamplight, carving gentle curves into the fiddle and breathing in the sweet scent of mahogany. He remembered stretching the strings into place and coaxing the virgin notes from the instrument . . .

It was more than just a fiddle. It was *his* fiddle.

Of course, Chester could never afford to buy it. Mr. Ashworth had painted gold leaf into swirls on its neck—ostentatious and flashy, but there was no point arguing. Once the old man set his mind to something, he wouldn't budge.

"A fiddle worthy of a lord," Mr. Ashworth had said.

So Chester had watched in silence as the price tag was added—more than a year of his wages—and it was placed in the window display. It was probably still there, with dust on its golden twists and its strings. Chester yearned to place his fingers on the bow and charm a run of fleeting notes to counteract his pain . . .

"What are you thinking?" Susannah said.

Chester blinked and the image shattered. He looked up at her, eyes slightly hazy with pain, and he forced his aching shoulders into a shrug.

"Nothing," he said. "Just remembering Mr. Ashworth, that's all."

"Was he a nice man?"

Chester hesitated. "He paid me well."

156

But that wasn't all of it. Chester had always felt that there was more to Mr. Ashworth. Right now, he didn't have the strength to explain the way that Mr. Ashworth had made him feel sometimes. The way the man's eyes had watched him when he thought Chester wasn't looking. The way Mr. Ashworth had vanished into his back room sometimes and made strange garbled calls on his communication globe. The way the man had spoken so softly, and moved like a coyote on the prowl . . .

Another wave of pain washed over him, but this time, even in the heat of the agony, Chester realized that the pain wasn't as bad as it had been. Was he past the worst of it? Heat rippled through his body and his skin burned. But he could now straighten his limbs and he could breathe more easily. *In, out. In, out.* His breaths came soft and shallow, washing cool relief through his throbbing lungs.

"Getting better?" Susannah asked. "Or worse?"

"Better, I think."

As time wore on, the pain faded. It came in fits and spurts, less frequent and less overwhelming. It came in quiet tugs and squirms of nausea until, finally, it was gone.

Susannah took his temperature again. Chester felt the warmth of her fingertips against his forehead and experienced an irrational stab of shame at the sweat on his skin. He knew she could feel it and he knew she was fighting the urge to wipe her fingers on the bedsheets when she pulled away.

But when her fingers left his skin, despite his embarrassment, part of him wished she would put them back again. Just for a moment.

"You'll be fine," she said. "No fever. You just need a good night's sleep."

"Will it still hurt tomorrow?"

She shook her head. "You got off lightly, all things considered. I've seen much worse withdrawal cases than this." She smiled at

157

him. "Tomorrow, you'll be good as new. And even better—you'll be free."

"Free?"

"Free of the lies. Free of the Songshapers' influence. Free to do whatever the hell you want with your sunsets instead of bowing down and humming a tune for the sake of someone else's stories."

Chester nodded. He was suddenly exhausted, as though all the strength had been drained from his body. The pillow felt soft as a sonata beneath his cheek. He yearned to slip into sleep and to let the coolness of dreaming wash the aches from his body.

"Get some sleep," Susannah said, as she turned to leave the cabin. "Tomorrow, we're going to hit Linus."

Chester stiffened. Of all the things he'd expected her to say, of all the ways she could have changed the topic . . . "Isn't that a little soon?"

Susannah shrugged. "Should be mostly healed by then, as long as we keep using Travis's injections. Besides, there are things we need there. Linus is a town of sugar barons. There are wealthy families with lots of paperwork. Important documents, important jewels."

"And?"

"And we," Susannah said with a smile, "are important burglars."

CHAPTER SEVENTEEN

THE HUSH WAS SILENT.

Outside the *Cavatina*, all was black. The ship had settled on the outskirts of Linus, behind the local Songshaper's mansion. Not as good as a railway line, but the air nearby was tainted with just enough Music to restart the engine for a quick getaway.

"Everyone all right?" Susannah said.

The others nodded. The Hush-rain fell in swirls around them, disintegrating into speckles of unnatural cold. Susannah could just make out a wooden fence topped with a trail of barbed wire, leading into the dark. The earth sloped downward, descending into the town.

"If a Songshaper lives here . . . what if he comes into the Hush?" Chester said. "Won't he see the *Cavatina*? I mean, I think I'd notice if an enormous ship turned up in my yard . . ."

Susannah shook her head. "Most small-town Songshapers are only small fry. They're not senior enough to know about the Hush. Or even if he knows about it, he'll be too scared to set foot inside."

"Only high-grade Songshapers know about the Hush?"

"That's right."

"Why?"

"Because it's a secret," Dot piped up. "And in Weser City, secrets are a currency. They're not the sort of thing you give away lightly."

"Are we here to rob this Songshaper, then?" Chester said.

"No." Susannah glanced up at the mansion then turned her gaze toward the town. "I've got a different target in mind."

At her gesture, the gang members knelt. Susannah placed a hand on Dot's shoulder and together, with a mixture of whistles and hums, they performed a reversal of the Sundown Recital.

As they burst into the real world, Susannah let out a sigh of relief. She hated the Hush. She knew it was necessary, of course: traveling in the Hush was the only reason they'd survived so long. But Susannah was a child of the seaside, of ships and waves, of sunlight and open sky. The darkness made her stomach crawl and the fear of Echoes was constant. They couldn't touch her or Sam, but Dot and Travis were all too vulnerable.

And Chester, she reminded herself. *You've got another gang member to care for now.*

Here in the real world, the sky was a bright peacock blue. Susannah breathed in the fresh air, threw out her arms, and bathed in the luxury of a natural breeze. The air was sweet, with the faintest tang of sugarcane.

She could see the fence more clearly now, marking the back of the Songshaper's property. The sloping earth melted into a dusty road, leading them down into the main street of the town. Really, Linus was more of a city than a town. Restaurants, hotels, gambling halls . . . This was a city of sugar barons, and they had cash to splash around.

Wealthy locals rode in ornate carriages adorned with colored plumes and pulled by pegasi. It was a criminal waste of enchanted creatures, of course, but the sugar barons used them as a show of wealth. *Look at me,* they silently proclaimed. *I can afford to buy the most expensive beasts—and use them for menial labor.* Susannah was disgusted by how the barons had grown so wealthy from the work of their laborers. The whiplashed folk who tended their fields and mucked out their stables. Those who worked without sleep during harvest time and ensured the landowners' fields produced a bounty of corn and sugarcane.

She turned to the others. Travis wore his fanciest frock coat, while Sam and Chester were dressed in dusty shirts and trousers. Dot looked quite content in a starched white bonnet with a long dark skirt and blouse. Susannah had been forced to don a heavy calico skirt of her own, complete with flannel drawers and awkward petticoats. A girl in trousers would likely cause a scandal in polite society. On the bright side, if anyone bothered her, she could use her parasol to whack them over the head.

"Now listen up," she said. "Travis, you're a wheat baron's son from Thrace, keen to invest in sugar. Chester's your errand boy, Sam's your bodyguard, and Dot and I are your maids. Got it?"

They all nodded. Chester looked a little nervous but there was no helping that. Susannah had always believed that courage wasn't a lack of fear, it was how you responded when fear took hold. They'd all been nervous before their first job. All things considered, he was coping quite well.

Almost subconsciously, she found herself watching him. He wasn't feeble. Months on the road had left him fit and lean, with tan skin beneath a rumple of dark hair. He moved with a sturdy sort of grace, his muscles tight, his face determined despite the nerves.

But he was also reckless and a little impulsive. The fact that he was here at all was testament to that. The boy had played a difficult song in front of a roomful of witnesses when he could barely control his own powers. He had placed his life in a stranger's hands, and he barely had a grip on his Musical abilities.

Maybe he wasn't ready for this job.

But Sam met her eyes and Susannah nodded. She had made a deal and there was no backing out of it.

Travis took the lead, with a bold swagger in his step. He raised his nose and placed his hands on his hips as he strutted down the street. He looked for all the world like the arrogant young heir he was meant to be, sniffing out the town's potential for investment.

"Come on," Susannah muttered to the others. "Keep your heads down and don't talk too loudly. They keep their servants tightly reined in around here."

That, of course, was an understatement.

The sugar barons were descended from Weser nobility. Their grandparents had forcibly seized a large swath of eastern Meloral during the failed Oscine Uprising, sixty years ago. The locals had no land left of their own, and no choice but to work the fields for their wealthy overlords. And so they toiled on, painting the landscape with sweetness.

Here, servants walked in garb of soil and linsey cloth. Hair clung in sweaty bunches around their necks and their faces were as red as tomatoes. They bowed in respect, almost spilling baskets of bread, as another carriage rolled past. The pegasi snorted and huffed, their nostrils foaming a little from the stress and the heat.

Someone needs to hose those horses down, she thought. Were the sugar barons so rich that they could afford to run their pegasi ragged and simply replace them if they keeled over?

Susannah kept her head low, traipsing the street in quiet thought. The sunlight, which had seemed so comforting at first, was beginning to sting the back of her neck. She pulled up her collar and let down her hair, allowing a red cascade to spill across her shoulders. The air felt stifling—she could feel sweat pooling in the crooks of her elbows—and the last thing she needed was a sunburn.

162

"By the Song, it's hot," Travis whispered. "I'd hoped to visit that talented tailor I was telling you about, but I wouldn't dare set foot in his establishment when I'm so covered in sweat."

"How tragic," Susannah whispered back.

"Oh it is, Captain," Travis said. "I've heard the Linus sugar barons have some rather pretty daughters, but I'm afraid even *my* charms might not work in my current state." He peered down at himself. "I do hope you've chosen a hotel with decent bathing facilities."

Apart from house servants, there were few poor folk in the city streets right now. They would all be out working the sugarcane fields: hacking at crops with a scythe or hauling heavy baskets. Susannah couldn't imagine their exhaustion. In this weather, it was bad enough just walking down the street. With her long dark skirt and its layers of petticoats, she felt as though she was dragging around a saucepan to slowly boil her own legs.

"So what's the plan?" Chester said.

Susannah pointed past a row of parked carriages. "Our hotel's down there. We'll talk inside."

As they approached the center of town she sensed a stiffening in Sam's movements. There was too much Music in the air, she realized. The carriage lanterns, the kitchen stoves, and even the water pumps . . .

"Are you all right?" she said quietly.

Sam grunted, his expression strained. His fists were clenched together now, tight as boulders.

Susannah reached into her skirt pocket, where she had stowed one of Dot's precious calming lamps. She handed it wordlessly to Sam. He looked away as he seized it, either too furious or too ashamed to meet her gaze.

The hotel's facade was tall and creamy, carved from chunks of polished sandstone. Columns supported the first-floor balcony and windows glinted in the afternoon sun. A pair of finely dressed gentlemen strode out the front door, noses high as they approached their carriage. The entire building reeked of money.

"There?" Chester said. "We're going to stay *there*? But how can we afford—?"

"It's an investment," Susannah said. "I chose it for its location, not its price."

The woman at reception looked more bored than alert. Travis flicked his wrists and sneered at her, playing the role of the snobby heir to a tee.

"You're taking your servants up to the room, sir?" the woman said. "Normally, our guests prefer to—"

"Good grief, woman, of course I'm taking them," Travis said. "I am accustomed to a certain level of service and I can hardly entrust my well-being to a mob of rural ruffians employed by a mere *hotel*."

Five minutes later, they stepped into a fancy room on the hotel's top floor. A four-poster stood as the crowning glory, with fluttering silk curtains of pale gold, and a chandelier hung from the ceiling, tinkling with crystal. When they activated its melody, every fragment of glass shone like a sorcery lamp.

"Wow," Chester said, wide-eyed. "This is amazing."

Susannah glanced at him. It was easy to become blasé about these sorts of things: expensive rooms, ornate hotels. She spent so much time in these places nowadays—either as a guest or a burglar—that she barely noticed the puffery. But the awe on Chester's face made her pause for a moment.

"Yes," she said. "I suppose it is."

Travis pushed past with an eager expression and gave a sigh of contentment when he spotted the adjoining bathroom. "Ahhh," he said. "Civilization."

Susannah stole a surreptitious look at Sam, whose face was torn between elation and fury. Too many melodies, too many emotions. He clutched Dot's calming globe like a drowning man who had been thrown a rope.

Without a word she extinguished the chandelier. Sam seemed to be in control of himself—for now, at least—but it was cruel to make him suffer for the sake of a few fancy crystals. As the lights flickered out, Sam's stiff limbs began to unclench.

Susannah released a slow breath. "Right," she said. "Our target is the house across the street—the home of Charles Yant, a wealthy sugar baron. He's a nasty piece of work: keeps his servants locked in barns overnight so they don't run off and hitch a train to a new town."

"He can't do that!" Dot said. "That's like slavery. That's illegal!"

Susannah sighed. "This isn't Weser City, Dot. There's no real police force. There's just the sheriff and his cronies, same in every town. And whatever the sheriff says is law, that's what the law is."

"But—"

"You've seen worse in other towns, Dot. Remember that family in Oranmor?"

"Yes, but—"

Susannah raised her hand, calling for silence. "Look, you'll have to take my word on this one. This whole town is run by the sugar barons. They provide the money and they own the land. The sheriff isn't about to upset them. And a high-up baron like Yant, who brings in thousands in taxes?" She shook her head. "Well, throw in a couple of bribes here and there and I bet the sheriff would let him get away with murder."

They all stared at her. Sam's expression was dark; Travis's lip curled back, as though he was appalled; and Dot's eyes were as round as buttons. To her surprise, Chester was the only one who didn't look shocked. He sat there, staring down into his hands.

"Chester?" she said. "You with me?"

He looked up, startled. "Yes, Captain. Sorry. I was just . . ."

"Just what?"

"Just . . . I saw a lot of stuff like that, when I was a kid," he said. "Back in Thrace. It was a wheat-belt town, and the people who owned all the land used to . . ."

He trailed off again. Susannah nodded, not needing him to finish the sentence. She could guess.

"Right," she said. "My point's that Yant is not a nice man. But that's not the only reason we're going to rob him. He's got something we need."

Travis stirred, looking a little more interested. "A collection of silver cufflinks, perhaps?" he asked hopefully. "Or a genuine silk undershirt—I've always wanted one of those . . ."

"He's got a huge family," Susannah said. "He has seven siblings, five children of his own, and dozens of nieces and nephews scattered all over the region."

"You want to steal a nephew?"

Susannah rolled her eyes. "No, don't be stupid. I want to steal some paperwork. Birth certificates, farming licenses, wax seals, writing paper . . ."

"You want to build me a fake identity, don't you?" Chester said. "When I audition, I'll be pretending to be part of the Yant family."

Susannah nodded. "You'll need a new name, a wealthy background, a family line . . . You can't waltz in without credentials; the Songshapers'll be too suspicious."

Chester hesitated for a moment, then returned her nod. Susannah found herself watching his face. The boy wore a strong resolve in his dark eyes, despite the evident nerves in his expression.

She forced herself to look away. "We're going in at midnight, when Yant should be asleep. You've got that folding ladder you were working on, Dot?"

Dot patted her coat pocket.

"Good. This is a simple sneak 'n' grab job, nothing fancy. Sam, I want you in the Hush with an echoboat, in case we need a quick getaway. Dot, you're in charge of the ladder from this end. Travis, you're on guard duty." She tossed him a communication globe. "If you see anything, or hear anything, I want to be alerted. Got it?"

Travis tilted his head. "It's hardly a scintillating role, is it? Guard duty . . . It sounds awfully like grunt work. You know, Captain, I hardly think the best use of my talents is to—"

"What else are you going to do?" Susannah said. "Let's face it: you're not exactly a hardened criminal."

"Of course I am," Travis said. "Why, I got up to all sorts of criminal mischief back at medical school. On one memorable occasion, I even spiked my professor's cologne with aniseed." He leaned forward with a conspiratorial whisper. "The man smelled like a licorice cake for weeks!"

"I see," Susannah said. "And what did he do to deserve such a terrible fate?"

"He confiscated my plum cravat." Travis looked indignant, as though this was a terrible injustice. "I had to wear a green one instead, and it clashed terribly with my waistcoat."

Susannah stared at him.

"So you see, Captain," Travis said, "it was a clear case of criminality being used in the pursuit of justice. Rather like our goal tonight, don't you think?"

"Our goal tonight," Susannah said, "is for us to all get home safely. This isn't a night for grandstanding. It's for working together and doing what the job requires. Got a problem with that?"

"Ah," Travis said. "Well, when you put it like that . . ."

"Good," Susannah said. "Chester, got your flute?"

167

"Yes, Captain."

"You're coming with me. I want a Songshaper, and Dot will be busy with the ladder."

Chester's mouth fell open. "But Captain, I don't know if I can—"

"You'll do fine," Susannah said. "You fought off that Echo, didn't you?"

"But that was . . ."

Susannah gave him her sternest look. "Is there a problem?"

"Well, I don't think . . ." Chester must have read something in Susannah's expression because the end of his objection died on his lips. "No, Captain."

"Good."

Susannah peered out between the curtains. Afternoon sun painted the street with light, throwing sharp shadows on to the opposite building. She gazed at the balcony. The windows. The elaborate stone carvings underneath the sill. This would be a simple job. Easy to sneak in, easy to sneak out. All under the cover of darkness, without the complication of an inside man.

She glanced back at Chester with a twinge of regret for her harsh tone. Of course he would be nervous. Agitated. After all, this was his first real thieving job.

"You all right?" she said.

He gave her a weak smile. "Yeah. Thanks, Captain."

Susannah nodded, turning back to the window. With a twist in her belly, she remembered her deal with Sam. She tried to convince herself that her concern was merely practical; after all, the auditions were fast approaching. She needed a Songshaper for her plan to work. If Chester proved himself tonight, she could fully initiate him into the gang.

But if he failed . . .

＊

At sunset, Chester sat in the hotel bathroom. He needed some space from the others. He felt no real agony tonight, just the final cold, dull remnants of the withdrawal ache. As Susannah had predicted, he had survived the worst of the torment already. In another day or so, he should be able to pass his sunsets with barely a shiver.

Assuming he didn't die tonight.

Chester's stomach was tight—not with pain, but with nerves. To distract himself, he examined the gang's burglary trunk, full of knickknacks for various jobs. His fingers brushed the globe of a sorcery lamp and its melody flared on his skin, warm and thick as molasses. There were tiny glass devices, ropes and grappling hooks, a communicator globe, and a box of costume items including a sturdy silver necklace, a carriage-driver's license, and even a false moustache.

A trunk of lies, he thought. *A trunk of secrets.*

Tonight, he would be risking his freedom for the Nightfall Gang. He might even be risking his life. And yet, despite everything, Chester still didn't know for sure if they could help him find his father. It was time for some answers.

With the lantern in hand, Chester ventured back into the main hotel room. Sam had gone for a walk to clear his head, while Susannah was out casing Yant's security, leaving the others to keep watch until nightfall. Dot sat by the window, dunking toast into a cup of tea, while Travis trimmed his fingernails. He held them up to the light, frowned a little, then angled the blade to adjust the curve of his thumbnail.

Chester took a deep breath. He forced himself to remember that although he needed them for their information, they needed him, too—they needed a Songshaper for the job at the

Conservatorium. They owed him information. *Convince the world you're strong . . .*

"I want the truth," he said.

They turned to look at him. Travis leaned back in his chair and raised an eyebrow. "And I want a mansion with a fleet of forty pegasi and a tailor on call," he said. "Tragically, we don't all receive what we want, do we?"

"I have a theory," Dot said, "that—"

"We don't care about your theories, Dorothy." Travis waved a careless hand. "Honestly, the way you blather on, you'd think I'd joined a public speaking academy instead of a gang of thieves."

Dot stared into her teacup, a quiet little smile on her face. "I have a theory," she said again, "that people make demands when they're too afraid to ask favors."

"What do you mean?" Chester said, slightly deflated.

"Well," Dot said, "you could have asked nicely for information about Songshaping and I could have taught you something useful for tonight. Instead, you barge in here and make demands."

Chester forced himself to shake his head. "I don't want information about Songshaping, I want information about the vanishings."

"Well, if you want the latter," Dot said, "you'll have to learn the former first and use it to help our gang. Didn't the captain tell you? Nothing comes for free, Chester. Not even when you demand it."

Chester ran a hand through his hair. He yearned to make an ultimatum: *tell me the truth or I'm leaving.* He could picture it now: his clenched fists, his raised voice, his righteous indignation. But it would be an empty bluff and they both knew it. If he left, he might never find out the truth.

Chester sighed. He threw himself into the chair beside Dot's and placed her sorcery lamp on the table. "Teach me, then. About the Songshaping and stuff, to help your gang. If I'm going to help with this burglary tonight, I need to know what I'm doing."

Silence.

Travis sliced another little curve off his thumbnail then held his hand to the light. Dot gazed down into her cup of tea.

Request, Chester thought, *not demand*.

He drew a steady breath. "Dot, I'm sorry. Will you please teach me about Songshaping?"

She looked up at him. Her eyes were brown, unlike the pale blue shine of Sam's or Susannah's. She looked very young, all of a sudden. Too young for the measured words that had escaped her lips.

"Touch that sorcery lamp," she said, nodding to the one Chester had placed on the table.

Chester hesitated. Was this a trick? He touched the lamp. The warm glass tickled his fingertips and the now-familiar hum of Dot's illumination tune began to trickle through his veins.

"Feel it?" Dot said.

Chester nodded.

"Know how to do it yourself?"

He shook his head. "I've never been trained. I know no one here believes me but it's true."

Dot stared at him for a long moment. Her lips curved into a frown and she tilted her head slightly to the side, almost like a bird would. "What's your instrument?"

"I play fiddle," Chester said. "But it got taken when I was arrested in Hamelin. I've only got this."

He pulled the miniature flute from his pocket. It felt cold against his fingertips. Chester knew he could play it—when he'd worked in the shop, he'd practiced every instrument he could get his hands on—but it wasn't the same as his fiddle. His fiddle was warm wood and familiar strings. It was the purr of a cat and the comfort of hot soup. It was home.

"You don't like the flute?" Dot said.

"It's just not the same."

Dot nodded, looking thoughtful. "I'm not surprised. Every Songshaper has an instrument that comes most naturally to them. Mine is the piano."

"But I've only seen you use a piano accordion."

"Well, yes." Dot smiled. "The problem with pianos, you see, is that they're not very portable."

"Oh, right." Chester felt a little foolish. "That makes sense."

"Anyway," Dot said, with a wave of her toast, "it doesn't matter which instrument you play. Not really. It's easier on your natural instrument, of course, but you can still play Music on another."

"And how do you do that?" Chester sat up a little straighter. "I mean, what's the difference between playing normal music, and Music with a capital 'M'?"

Dot nodded at the sorcery lamp. "You tell me."

Chester paused. "I don't know what I'm doing. Sometimes I'm playing a really tricky song, something that makes me tune out the rest of the world, and get lost in the melody . . ." He trailed off. "And then I hear it."

"Hear what?"

"The Song. It's like another melody, underneath everything. It runs through the air, the ground, the stones, the trees. Even people, and furniture, and buildings." Chester took a slow breath. "It's like . . . like the blood under a person's skin. You can't see it until you've pierced the surface, but it's always there, pumping away, keeping your body alive."

Dot gave him a cautious look. "You need to be careful, Chester. Playing your own Music doesn't mean hijacking the Song. Only the highest-level Songshapers are allowed to—"

"I know," Chester said quickly. "That's not what I meant. I just . . ."

Chester trailed off, suddenly nervous. If the gang realized how often he'd connected to the Song—or that his connections were growing more frequent—they might decide it was too risky to include him in their plans.

He ran a hand through his hair. "It's just . . . Well, I think that's the difference between music and *Music*, isn't it? When you play music, you hear the tune. But when you play *Music*, you *feel* the tune."

Dot's expression relaxed.

"What?" Chester said.

"It seems to me, Chester Hays, that you're a lot more ready than you think you are." She surveyed the window with a slow smile. "And tonight, you'll have your chance to prove it."

CHAPTER EIGHTEEN

THE NIGHT WAS HOT.

A constant buzz rose from the hotel's taproom below. Noise and music, the clatter of dishes and voices. For a brief moment, Chester wished he was down there, playing his fiddle for coins. Had it only been days since the Barrel o' Gold?

His shirt stuck to his back, as heavy as a wool blanket. He didn't bother with a coat—all he needed was the flute. He thrust it into his pocket and tried not to let the nerves show on his face.

"Ready?" Susannah said.

Chester glanced at her. She stood at the window dressed in simple brown trousers, her red hair framed like a fire against the glass. It was dark outside—a truly dark night, with the barest sliver of moon—and she was a riot of color against the black windowpane.

He nodded. "I'm ready."

"Good."

Dot stared out the window, a distant smile on her lips. "I used to like moonless nights," she said. "Good for stories. Good for secrets. Good for sneaking."

"All right," Susannah said. "Put out the ladder, Dot."

Dot kept her gaze pressed close to the glass, piercing their own reflections to stare out into the night. Down in the taproom, the musicians finished their number and there was a roar of shouts and applause.

"Sometimes I think there must be Echoes out there," Dot said distantly. She ran a finger through the air, brushing at some unseen strand of shadow. "Or the ghosts of Echoes. Like mirror images of the Echoes in the Hush, wandering like streaks of light and shadow through the world . . ."

"And sometimes," Susannah said, a little impatient, "I think you should hurry up and put the damn ladder out."

Dot's ladder was made of wood, but not a wood Chester was familiar with. It shimmered at his touch and from it he caught snatches of broken Music—tiny songs, or the faintest whisper of melody. But when his fingers lingered too long, the songs fell silent.

"It'll only work for me," Dot said, as she hooked one end of the ladder to their windowsill. "I enchanted it especially. Wouldn't want another Songshaper to get his hands on it and steal my thunder for my invention."

"Have you patented it?" Travis said, interested. "There's a great deal of money in such things, if you invent something that people will pay to replicate."

Dot waved a hand. "No point now, is there? It was going to be my research project at the Conservatorium until . . ." She trailed off. "Anyway, I can't patent it now. It would mean admitting I've done sorcery without a license."

She began to unfold the ladder, clicking out its extending pieces one by one. "I was inspired by my accordion, you see," she said. "It folds up small but extends into a longer strip."

Susannah pushed the window open. Chester blinked as their reflection vanished, replaced by the black street outside. Hot wind ruffled in through the window, blustering dust and shadow into his face. If he squinted, he could make out the shape of Charles Yant's house, looming on the opposite side of the street.

"Can you see the balcony?" Dot whispered.

"Don't ask me," Travis said, gesturing up at his spectacles. "I can hardly see a page in front of my eyes."

Chester shook his head. "No, I . . . Wait, yes! There it is."

"Can you point?"

Chester squinted, focused as hard as he could, and pointed through the dark.

"Don't move," Dot whispered. "I'm going to put out the ladder."

She retrieved her piano accordion from the bed and hoisted it up into playing position. She opened it with a wheeze of sound and Chester winced. The accordion wasn't exactly a quiet instrument—it was lucky that the taproom downstairs was in such a raucous state or they'd risk alerting half the street.

Dot coaxed the bellows into a dance between her hands. It resembled a lung, inflating and deflating with life and air, and as the instrument breathed, her fingers played. One note, then the next. The melody slipped and lingered, pulling on chords with a wheeze and then exploding out into a tinkle of fast-paced notes.

And as the Music played, the ladder rose.

It moved like a snake. It slithered up from its half-unfolded position and unfurled out the window, as though some invisible breeze was carrying it forward even though the air was heavy, hot, and lank. The ladder folded outward, piece by piece, and the Music flowed, until there was finally the clink of wood on metal.

Dot played a sudden run of tightening notes. She pushed the bellows inward, compressing and locking the Music around a single final chord, and Chester thought he could almost taste the moment when the ladder locked into place.

Dot released her breath. The room fell silent.

Their ladder stretched across the street, from their own window to Yant's upper balcony.

"I'll keep an eye on it," Dot said. "I don't know how long the Music will hold it—I'll probably have to replay the melody every few minutes."

Susannah nodded. "You keep an eye on the ladder and Travis can keep watch for dangers."

Chester knew what was coming. He straightened his back and tried to look confident, just as the captain's gaze swept around to focus on him.

"Ready?" she said.

Chester's heart throbbed. He stared out the window at the darkness. The ladder. The balcony across the street.

"Yeah," he said. "I am."

"Good," Susannah said. "Then let's go."

She jumped onto the windowsill, quick and nimble as a cat. Susannah's hair danced in a mass of curls, swaying with the movement of her body. Then she was gone, scurrying along the ladder into the dark.

Chester stared after her for a moment, then he gave himself a mental slap. This was a time to focus on the job, not . . . other things.

He hauled himself onto the windowsill. He was confident on his feet, of course—you had to be, if you wanted to sneak aboard cargo trains. But this was different. Jumping onto a train as it slowed . . . well, that was all about panic. It was sheer momentum and adrenaline as you leaped up and prayed like hell and grabbed the door handles in the certain knowledge that letting go meant death.

But here? Now? This was a different sort of courage. There was no urgency. No rush of a freight train and no roar of its Music or its engine. No blast of steam to scare him into action. There was just the silence of the night, and the weight of baking air. The ladder stretched out before him, a gently swaying bridge across the darkness.

If he fell, his death would not be pretty.

"You know," Dot said, after a pause, "sometimes I like pretending the whole world is a song and we're all just notes inked onto the staff." She smiled at him. "Nothing real to hurt you, you see? Just lyrics in a lullaby."

Chester flushed. "I'm not scared, Dot."

"Never said you were."

Chester paused, then bent his knees and reached out to grab a ladder rung. His upper body stretched out into the night, fingers wrapping around the farthest rung he could reach. With a sharp breath, he trusted his weight to the ladder.

He was suddenly aware, again, of the noise in the taproom below. If a drunken patron stumbled outside and looked up . . . *No.* He didn't need something else to worry about. That was beyond his control. All he could do was concentrate on crawling and try not to slip.

The climb was slow. He crawled along the ladder, limb by limb, and fought to ignore how it swayed and tilted when his body weight shifted. Sometimes the ladder rolled to one side and he was left hanging sideways, his heartbeat pattering, his fingers slick with sweat. Then—Dot must have played her Music again—it swung back into a flattish bridge and Chester forced himself to move before his courage deserted him.

Susannah had already finished her crossing. She stood on Yant's balcony, peering back at him along the ladder.

"Hurry," she mouthed.

Chester let out a quick breath, suddenly embarrassed. This was ridiculous. If he could hop into a moving cargo train, he could surely negotiate a stationary ladder between two buildings.

He took the rest of the ladder at a faster crawl, a shuffle of lunges, like the unfolding scrunch of a caterpillar. At the balcony rail, he crossed the bars with all the casual ease he could muster.

He forced a grin and thrust his hands behind his back, trying to hide the tremble in his fingers.

"Well," he said. "That was fun."

Susannah returned his smile but pressed a finger to her lips. "Only talk if it's important, all right?"

"Yes, Captain."

Susannah turned her attention to the balcony door behind them. It was locked, of course. A heavy padlock dangled from the shutters. Susannah fished a metal pin from her pocket and jiggled it cautiously inside the lock. It took a minute or so of fiddling, but finally Chester heard a click.

Susannah removed the pin and yanked the padlock open. They crept inside, as slow and quiet as spiders. Chester glanced around the room, alert for any signs of human life, but the room was empty. He let out a slow breath.

Before the balcony door closed, Chester stole one last glance back out into the night. He saw their hotel room across the street, dimly lit by sorcery lamps. Dot's and Travis's faces were silhouetted at the window. Then the door shut and they were gone.

Susannah pulled a pair of tiny globes from her pocket and passed one to Chester. It was barely the size of a marble.

"Hideaway lamp," Susannah whispered.

She buried her globe in her palm and hummed a quiet run of notes. A tiny beam of light shot from the lamp, which was so small that she could hide the shine by adjusting her fingers. She opened two fingers to make a crack that allowed a single ray to light the path ahead.

Chester closed his palm around his own hideaway lamp and tried to feel the Music inside the glass. He sensed it almost immediately: a quiet run of notes, identical to the newer lamps aboard the *Cavatina*.

"Dot made these?"

Susannah nodded.

Chester raised the tiny lamp to his lips and hummed the notes as quietly as possible. A faint sheen spilled from the glass. He could feel the Music now, that familiar hum of a sorcery globe trickling like liquid through his fingers.

They stood in a sitting room. A glass chandelier hung from the ceiling and velvet chairs were scattered around the room. Decorative rugs cascaded over furniture and a crystal chessboard perched on a marble table. The pieces glinted in the shadows. *Crystal.* Just one of those chess pieces was worth more than he'd earn in a year of playing his fiddle in saloons.

Chester jerked his head in the direction of the chessboard. "Can we . . . ?"

Susannah shook her head. "Might be a honeypot."

"A honeypot?"

"Sometimes people leave valuables in the open, rigged with Musical alarm systems," Susannah said. "Perfect way to catch a lazy thief. Stick your hand in the honeypot and you risk getting stung."

They crossed the room on tiptoe. The hideaway lamp felt warm in Chester's palm as he let a tiny crack of light escape between his fingers. Unfortunately, the lamp soon proved something of a distraction. As Dot's melody tinkled into his palm, the Music spilled a constant flutter into his flesh. It was enough to make him wish for a pair of gloves.

He stole a look at Susannah but she didn't seem bothered by the Music's touch. Perhaps she was very good at tuning out distractions—or perhaps she just couldn't sense it. The touch came naturally to Chester, like his accidental forays into the Song when he played complicated music. It felt simple. Natural. Just like breathing.

They tiptoed along a winding corridor and down a flight of stairs. Whenever the Music grew too intense, Chester switched his lamp from hand to hand. Each time, it took a good minute for the tune to build up into a crescendo again.

Susannah walked in utter silence and with utter confidence. Actually, Chester decided, she didn't walk. She prowled. She seemed to know instinctively where to step and how to navigate the floorboards without making a creak. She was light on her feet, but determined. A master burglar.

Chester, on the other hand, felt rather flustered. He remembered the time he'd crept downstairs the night before Harvest Parade, to sneak a peek at the present his father had scrimped all year to buy. His stomach had curled the entire trip, both with the fear of discovery and the knowledge he was doing something wrong. Every step was tortured.

Now, those feelings were magnified a thousandfold. If Chester was caught tonight, he wouldn't just face a scolding from his father. He would likely die.

But still, there was something else . . .

Another feeling. Another emotion. It squirmed below the surface, dipping and diving with every nervous step. What was it? Chester felt tight with frustration, unable to place a label on the twisting in his gut.

Then he realized what it was. Excitement. It was the thrill of being naughty, of taking risks. It was a stupid thing to feel, and probably suicidal. But even so, he couldn't quite fight down that giddy little rush that came from breaking the rules. *One step, two steps, three steps* . . . Each step was another risk, another transgression.

They turned another corner and Chester froze.

A guard stood at the end of the corridor.

CHAPTER NINETEEN

SUSANNAH REACTED FAST. SHE GRABBED CHESTER'S SLEEVE AND yanked him back around the corner. They flattened themselves against the wall, keeping their breaths low and quiet. Chester's limbs felt so tightly coiled that he feared his body might explode. He tightened his fingers around the hideaway lamp, blocking even the smallest rays of light from escaping.

Silence.

"Didn't see us," Chester mouthed.

Susannah nodded, ghostly in the shadows. She bent in close and whispered in his ear. "We'll have to pass him in the Hush."

Her breath tingled warm on Chester's neck. It took him a second to refocus. "Okay."

They dropped to the floor, seeking something solid to hold onto. In unison, they hummed the backward Sundown Recital, as quietly as possible, so that each reversed run of notes was barely a breath in the still of the corridor.

Chester felt a tingle as the final note brushed his lips. The air rippled around him and he lurched. It felt as though an invisible hand had yanked him off kilter, leaving him to teeter on his knees and splayed palms.

Darkness filled the corridor. It wasn't the usual dark of a building at night. It was a stronger shadow, a deeper black. It

182

exploded into the air like ink spilling from a broken bottle. It tasted bitter, casting an unnatural tang of cold onto his tongue.

And to Chester's surprise, it swirled with rain. He had never entered the Hush inside a building before—for some reason, he'd half-expected the Hush-rain to stay outside, like in the *Cavatina*. But unlike the echoship, this corridor had not been designed to withstand conditions in the Hush. Here, the unnatural rain slithered and smacked and sizzled at odd angles, striking sideways, dancing through the air. And as always, it left him dry.

Susannah opened her palm, allowing the full light of her hideaway lamp to bloom. It glinted off raindrops and the corridor's ornaments; it glimmered off golden picture frames and lit their path around the corner.

And this time, when they turned the corner, there was no guard in sight.

"Why didn't we do this whole job in the Hush?" Chester said, as they moved down the corridor. "If none of the guards know about the Hush, wouldn't it be safer to—"

"Too dangerous."

"Worse than getting caught by guards?"

"Yes," Susannah said emphatically. "Echoes are worse than guards."

"But we just spent days in the Hush and I only saw Echoes once in all that time. They can't be *that* common . . ."

"We were out in the countryside," Susannah said. "Out where we were traveling, there wasn't much human influence in the real world—not much sorcery around to leak through. But it's different in towns and cities. The Hush is more dangerous here."

"Why?"

"Too much Music in the air," Susannah said. "It leaks through and poisons the Hush. We know there's at least one trained Songshaper in this town, and there's sorcery all over the place. In the lamps, the water pumps, the kitchen stoves . . ."

"That means more Echoes in the Hush?"

She nodded. "And worse things, too."

"Worse than Echoes?"

Susannah hesitated. "The Hush is a dumping ground, so it gets tainted by things that are dumped here. When you get too much magical disturbance in an area, the Hush can get . . . tricky. Twisted."

"What do you mean?"

"I mean it's not just Echoes you have to look out for," Susannah said. "It's where you put your feet. Whether the floor is solid or made of shifting sands. Whether the air is toxic gas, or whether—"

Chester froze. He stared down at the floor, searching for signs of trickery in the wood. Nothing. Just empty black and the swirl of mist and rain.

"Don't panic," Susannah said. "I've been keeping my eye out and this corridor looks okay. But I know what to look for. I know the signs. Don't ever go into the Hush on your own. Not in the country and *definitely* not in town. And if you try it in Weser City . . ."

Chester felt a little queasy at the thought. "Got it."

"Right," Susannah said, as they rounded another corner. "Let's get back to reality."

They dropped to their knees. A few hummed notes later and the Hush melted away. Rain vanished, blackness receded. They knelt upon an ordinary floor, in an ordinary corridor.

The Hush was gone.

Chester let out a slow breath. He pressed his fingers against the solid floorboards.

Susannah leaned in close. "Better keep moving."

They covered three more corridors and a flight of stairs. No sign of another guard. Perhaps Yant saw no need to post guards here, deep in the inner sanctum of his mansion. After all, there was no way for a thief to sneak past the earlier guard, not without knowledge of the Hush, at least.

The corridors were dark now, and more sparsely decorated. Chester held a fist before him, letting the barest crack of light shine between two fingers. This part of the house seemed more for function than show. No more paintings on the walls. No more decorative carpets on the floor. Just silence and darkness and the nervous huff of his own breath.

They reached a heavy wooden door, carved with dozens of floral patterns. It held a series of interlocking deadbolts, with twisting iron bars that melted down into an ornamental treble clef above the door handle.

Susannah shook her head. "What a show-off."

"What?"

"It's a Musical lock. They're rare and expensive, so Yant gets the end shaped into musical notation to show his friends that he can afford such a luxury." She shook her head. "Completely defeats the point, mind you, since it tells us what we're dealing with."

"You can pick the lock, then?"

"No. But you can."

Chester stared at her, confused. Then he realized what she meant. If it was a Musical lock, it must require . . . "Music?"

Susannah nodded. "Sam said you fought off an Echo, didn't you? By reversing its tune?"

"Yeah."

"Well, this is similar. That's what Dot says, anyway—you can usually undo Music by playing it backwards."

Chester drew out the silver flute. It felt cold and hard in his fingers, so unlike the familiar warm wood of his fiddle bow. "People will hear me."

"So play quietly."

It's not that simple, Chester wanted to say. He wasn't very familiar with the flute. It took enough concentration to hit the notes right and prevent them from squeaking, let alone to adjust the volume as he played . . .

But Susannah looked at him with expectant eyes, and the sight of her face in the shadows was doing funny things to his stomach. She raised a hand to scrape red curls behind her ear and Chester's insides did a tiny flip.

He blinked and tried to clear his mind. This wasn't the time for sorting out his feelings. He had more important things to worry about. He remembered what Dot had said about making demands, but he forced her words to the back of his mind. He had to be confident. He had to be strong.

Or at the very least, to put on a show of it.

"If I do this," he whispered, "I'll be taking a big risk."

"So?"

"So I want something in return."

Susannah's lips curled into a frown. "I treat all my gang members equally."

"I just want information," Chester said quickly, before she could get the wrong idea. "I want to know about the vanishings and what might have happened to my father."

Susannah hesitated. "Chester, I . . ."

"My father is the only reason I'm playing along with this gang," Chester said. "And if I don't start getting answers soon, I don't see any point in sticking around."

It wasn't entirely true, of course. After endless weeks of wandering the wilderness and hopping trains with lies on his lips and secrets in his belly, it was a massive relief to have a feeling of home. To feel as though he belonged. And despite himself, he was starting to enjoy the gang's company.

But even so, his father came first.

"All right," Susannah said. "When this job is over—if all goes well—I'll tell you what I know about the vanishings."

"Everything?"

"Everything I know."

Chester eyed her suspiciously. "Aren't you worried I'll run off before the Conservatorium job?"

"You won't. Not once you've heard what I've got to say."

Chester stared at her, hungry for more information. But he could still feel the flute, cold in his hands, and the lock hung, dark and twisted, in front of his eyes. This wasn't the time for an interrogation.

He pressed a finger to the lock and strained to hear the tune within the metal.

Nothing.

Chester frowned. Was he too distracted to focus? He touched the lock again. No. Still nothing. The only Music he could sense came from the hideaway lamp, still clutched with the flute in his opposite palm.

He opened his eyes to stare at Susannah, who looked a little perplexed by his hesitation. "What's wrong?"

"I can't feel any Music in this lock. Normally when I touch enchanted things, I can feel the tune run up my fingers . . ."

Susannah swore under her breath. "We should've brought Dot along. I'm not a Songshaper—I don't know how to deal with this sort of thing."

"Hang on," Chester said, "I'll try again."

He pressed his fingers back to the lock. It felt dead against his skin, a curve of empty metal. No thrum of sorcery, no hint of a melody. And still his lamp played on, a tickle of notes into his opposite palm . . .

"This metal isn't enchanted," Chester said, opening his eyes. "There's nothing there."

"Try again," Susannah said.

"There's no point! If I can't feel the Music, I don't know what notes to play in reverse . . ." Chester paused. He could still feel the thrum of the hideaway lamp, like an itch on his palm. "Hang on. Hold this for me, will you?"

He passed the lamp to Susannah, who quickly closed her fist to stifle the flash of light. Chester took a second to refocus, shoving aside any lingering remnants of the lamp's melody. He needed to be fresh. Clean. No interference from another source of Music. He took a deep breath and sent a silent prayer to the Song. He pressed his hand to the lock.

And this time, he felt it.

Chester almost let out a whoop of triumph; instead, he settled for a wild grin at Susannah. Music spun inside the metal—a quiet tune, tight and spiraling, darkly closing in on itself with a C diminished chord. It sounded like locks. Like closed doors. Like stifling fear and a choking of the throat . . .

Chester rolled up one sleeve then raised the flute to his lips. He knelt on the floor beside the lock, so that his exposed elbow could press against the metal while his hands played. And with a quiet breath, he reversed the tune.

It was hard to keep his Music quiet. He allowed only the slightest breaths, more like whispers than proper notes. A few were slightly off-key, distorted by the quaver in his breathing. But he slowly settled into the tune and ran it backward, again, again, again. Notes flowed like a rearranged song: somehow broken, yet somehow whole. It was odd to play them against the tune of the lock; the whole affair sounded painfully disjointed, until—

There it was. The Song.

Dee duh. Dee . . .

"No!" Chester hissed, and his exclamation turned the note on his flute into a squawk. He stifled it quickly, conscious of Susannah's worried glare, and took a moment to steady himself.

He couldn't afford to connect to the Song. If anyone in Linus had radar equipment, or if any Songshapers were in nearby towns hunting for him . . .

"Is everything all right?" Susannah said.

"Oh, yeah," Chester lied quickly. "Fine. I'm just figuring out the tune in my head, that's all."

Deep down, he knew he should tell her the truth. If he couldn't control his connection to the Song, he would put the entire gang in danger. But he couldn't let Susannah think that he was weak. This job was now his chance to find the answers, to save his father. He had to impress the captain, no matter what.

Chester pressed a finger to the lock once more. Its tune was quiet and stifling, tightening in upon itself like a noose. He returned his fingers to the flute, took a shaky breath, and attempted once more to reverse the tune. The music spiraled backward, coiling and weaving, a run of notes that tinkled back around to brush itself with melody . . .

And then it happened.

Click.

It was a moment just like when he'd fought the Echo, back in Sam's echoboat. A moment when the bars met in rhythm and in harmony and the tunes somehow clicked together. Like one mirror staring back into another, their reflections slotted into place.

A chill rippled up Chester's elbow, rising from where his skin pressed the lock. The air throbbed around him. The lock groaned. There was a clanking sound behind the door and the mechanical scrape of metal on metal. Bolts creaked back as the treble-clef door handle turned.

The door swung open.

The room inside had no floor. At least, so Chester thought when he first glimpsed it. It was a room of chestnut walls with a crimson ceiling, as rich and dark as chocolate. But no floor.

Then he realized: the floor was made of glass. It was utterly clear, without a single crack or chip in the facade. He wouldn't have spotted it at all, if not for the glint of Susannah's lamp on the glass. Chester doubted it would take a human's weight.

In the center, a marble column rose from the room below. It was topped with a pedestal, flat and white—large enough for six people to stand on. Atop the pedestal sat a massive wooden chest.

"Damn," Susannah muttered. "I should have known he'd have a shattervault . . ."

"A what?"

She gestured at the floor of glass. "It's called a shattervault. You can't reach the chest without breaking the glass and falling down into . . ." She hesitated. "Into whatever nasty trap he's laid underneath."

Chester swallowed. What lay below the shining floor? There was no way to see from this angle. Perhaps metal spikes, or a chamber of sorcery gases, or just a long dark fall onto stone . . .

"This must have cost a fortune," he whispered.

"All the Linus sugar barons have got fortunes," Susannah said. "And Yant's the richest of the lot." She took a cautious step forward, to the edge of the solid floor.

Chester fought an urge to grab her arm and haul her back to safety. "Don't step on the glass!"

"I wasn't planning to. I was trying to figure out the trick."

"Trick?"

Susannah nodded. "There's got to be a secret way to reach the platform, so Yant himself can access it. If we can figure out how he does it . . ."

"Maybe he flies across on a pegasus," Chester said, only half-joking.

Susannah shook her head, looking distracted. "Have you ever seen their wings up close? They're two yards long each, at least. No room to fly around in here."

"Well," Chester said, "maybe he climbs along the ceiling and drops down onto the platform."

They both peered upward. It was a plain wooden ceiling without the slightest sign of a handhold. There weren't even brackets in place for sorcery lamps. It was bare.

"Yant's pretty old," Susannah said, "and he's getting fat nowadays, from what I've heard. I doubt he's doing spider walks across the ceiling every time he wants to open his vault."

They both stared into the room. The glass floor winked at them and Chester fought down a surge of frustration. Had they come this far—and risked this much—only to be thwarted by a sparkly floor? This job was his ticket to information about his father, and he'd be damned if he gave up on account of Yant's flooring materials.

"Does Yant know anything about Songshaping?" he said. "Maybe you have to cross the room in the Hush."

Susannah glanced at him. "I don't think so. Our background research said he inherited his sugar fields from his father, and he grew up here in Linus—except for a few years he spent in Weser City as a young man, to visit his uncle . . ."

There was a pause.

"Weser City?" Chester said. "The Conservatorium's in Weser City . . ."

"He wasn't there for seven years, though," Susannah said. "Not long enough to graduate from the Conservatorium. Anyway, we keep a list of licensed Songshapers and his name wasn't on it—I check that sort of thing before we start a job . . ."

"So he's not a Songshaper," Chester said. "Maybe it's his uncle who's a Songshaper; maybe his uncle set up this vault for him."

"Maybe," Susannah said. "But I don't want to go into the Hush in this room. There's too much Music around here—in the door locks, for a start, and I bet there are other sorcery traps around, too."

"But can you think of a way Yant could use the Hush as his trick to cross the glass floor?"

Susannah hesitated. "I suppose it would be possible . . ."

"Yeah?"

"Well, you can build things in the Hush that don't exist in the real world. Things like echoships, for instance."

Chester sucked down a deep breath. "You think whoever designed this vault could have built a solid floor in the Hush?"

"Maybe," Susannah said. "Or a ladder, or handholds on the ceiling, or a bridge across to the platform. Something that doesn't exist in the real world."

"Good way to keep out thieves," Chester said, nodding. "If hardly anyone knows the Hush exists—"

"—and if most of those people are listed in the license registery—" Susannah added.

"—then your chances of being robbed have gone down to a tiny, tiny pool of potential suspects. Right?"

There was a pause.

"Then it's Yant's bad luck," Susannah said slowly, "that two of those potential suspects are standing at the edge of his vault. You know, I almost feel sorry for the man."

"Almost?" Chester said.

"Not enough to quit this job." She smiled at him, eyes alive with nervous energy. "Ready to pull off your first burglary?"

Chester pressed his hands to the floor. "Ready when you are, Captain."

CHAPTER TWENTY

As THE LAST NOTE ROLLED OFF HER LIPS, SUSANNAH PLUNGED INTO the Hush. Darkness swelled around her, cool and thick and bitter on her skin.

She blinked. Fog and rain slipped like lids across her pupils. The room looked sinister now, in the depth of the shadows. Raindrops swirled and danced through the air, teasing this way and that, as darkness danced a silent quadrille across the floor.

The floor.

The floor was still made of glass, glinting and deadly. Chester's guess had been wrong, then. There was no solid pathway built in the Hush.

"Up there," Chester whispered.

Susannah followed his gaze. It took a moment to make out the shape through the darkness. It was a basket seat, dangling from ropes and pulleys. Above it, a row of metal tracks ran like teeth along the roof, ready to winch the basket across to the platform.

Susannah let out a low whistle. "Whatever Yant's hiding in that chest," she said, "he's going to some serious lengths to keep it safe. It's either very valuable, or very secret."

"All the better for us, right?"

She glanced at him, a little surprised. Chester grinned at her, his teeth shining white beneath his mop of black hair, and

Susannah felt a strange little surge of pride. Here he was, on his first ever job and already talking like a member of the gang. If the boy was afraid, he wasn't showing it. In fact, he was the one coming up with good ideas. He was thinking on his feet, even in the heart of the wasp's nest.

Susannah returned his smile. "Right. All the better for us."

She took a few steps toward the edge of the opaque floor then reached for the seat, swinging it down toward them, letting its ropes extend as a pulley clanked overhead.

"Not enough room for both of us," she said. "I'll go first and send it back for you."

Chester nodded. "Be careful. If you fall onto the glass . . ."

Susannah felt a little clench in her gut. He sounded genuinely worried about her. She gave him a reassuring smile. "Don't worry. I'm our resident cat burglar, remember? If there's one thing I'm good at, it's keeping my balance."

She leaped up into the basket seat. It swung wildly at the jolt of her weight, but Susannah grabbed the ropes to steady herself.

A long rope dangled in front of her with a metal contraption on its end. Susannah studied it for a moment. It was a handle to wind the rope, like the handle on a fishing line. She had seen plenty of fishing lines in her youth spent by the sea, so it wasn't hard to figure out how to work the contraption. She wriggled a little to make herself comfortable, then cranked the handle. The rope slipped around the winding device, the cogs creaked, and her basket jolted forward.

It wasn't a smooth ride. Her basket jerked and bucked like a drunken horse as her legs swung high above the glass. She stole a fleeting look behind her, just in time to see Chester vanish into the black.

She was alone.

All around her was the Hush, cold and black and swirling. It felt a little as though the world had vanished and there was nothing but this basket and its creaking attempt at flight . . .

Then she saw the platform. It appeared at the edges of her vision, a pillar of white marble erupting out of the darkness. Susannah gave the handle a final crank and tipped herself out of the basket onto the platform.

She knew she should probably stay as quiet as possible but couldn't help her call. "Chester? You all right?"

"Yeah." His voice was distorted in the Hush—almost as though it was dripping or dissolving, like a half-melted candle.

Susannah held the basket for a moment before she realized the problem. "I don't know how to send the basket back. Wait there and I'll come back once I'm finished with the chest."

"All right."

Susannah suppressed a shiver at the melt of his voice. Then she told herself off for being silly. She spent half her life in the Hush nowadays, didn't she? *Nothing to be scared of,* she told herself. But that was different. In the confines of the *Cavatina*, she could almost pretend she was in the real world. There was light, and she felt protected, and the rural Hush was mostly empty.

But here, in the middle of Linus . . . Well, it was different. Here, the Hush was potent. It could twist a voice, a breath, a soul. It could—

Stop it, Susannah told herself. *Focus on the job.*

She released the basket. It hung limply in the shadows. Susannah crossed to the middle of the platform where the massive wooden chest sat on its pedestal.

It wasn't locked.

She frowned, staring at it. Why would Yant go to all this expense—the Musically locked door, the vault, the glass floor, the basket seat that only existed in the Hush—and leave his chest unlocked at the end of it?

Maybe he didn't expect anyone to get this far. Maybe he considered the room to be amply guarded, since so few would know how to reach this platform, and those who did wouldn't take the risk. *Arrogance.* It was the flaw that had delivered countless treasures into Susannah's hands. Why should Yant be any different?

Still, something didn't feel right.

Susannah placed her hands on the chest. The wood felt normal and natural. A little cold, perhaps, but that was just the chill of the Hush. She hesitated for a moment, then shoved open the lid. It swung up in silence, like an opening jaw, and Susannah blinked at the darkness within.

It took a long moment for her eyes to focus. She pulled out a fistful of papers. The deeds to Yant's farmland. Some stock certificates. The deeds to a mansion in Weser. None of it was useful so she placed each paper back into the chest as she dismissed it.

Once she'd moved through the business papers, she began to find more personal files. A birth certificate. A marriage license. A family tree . . .

"Got you," she whispered.

Susannah slipped the pages into her pocket. With all the other forms and papers in the pile, it would be a long time before Yant noticed they were missing. All they had to do now was escape in silence, and the man might take years to realize he had been burgled . . .

Then her eyes fell on a beautifully decorated wooden box. It was carved from dark mahogany, with an imprint of the family crest on its top. It sat beneath the pile of papers, right at the heart of the chest.

Susannah frowned, running her fingers across its bumpy surface. What was inside? It must be valuable, to be kept in a vault like this one. She knew she should leave it—after all, the identity papers were her goal tonight. But a peek couldn't hurt, could it? What if it contained the rarest of jewels? Gold? Diamonds? They could feed an entire town of beggars with such a prize. Her fingers lingered on the wooden carving . . .

She opened the box.

She had time to glimpse its contents—empty—before the music started. Deep inside the box, something mechanical plucked a quiet little tune . . .

The Sundown Recital.

It was playing the Sundown Recital in the Hush.

Susannah's skin turned cold. She shut the music box and shoved it back into place before slamming the entire chest shut with a bang. But she could still hear the music, tiny and tinkling, from deep inside the chest.

"No," she whispered. "No, no, no . . ."

She had been wrong. There had been a lock of sorts on the chest after all. Except it wasn't a lock in the traditional sense. It was a booby trap. A honeypot. And like a greedy child, she had fallen for its lure.

"Captain!"

She whipped her head around, startled by Chester's mangled shout. All she saw was blackness: the roil and ripple of the Hush. All she felt was the unnatural rain, dry as whispers on her skin.

Chester shouted again, terror and the Hush distorting his voice into a strangled choke. "Echoes!" he cried. "Captain, they're coming out of the walls!"

Susannah's throat tightened. This vault was not an echoship. It wasn't built with protective layers of Music, designed to shield against the rain or the monsters of the Hush. In only moments, the Echoes would be upon them.

"Get out of the Hush!" she shouted back. "Chester, get out of the Hush!"

No response. Susannah didn't know if he had heard her. The sound in here was already distorted, and with Echoes floating around . . . Well, her voice may well have simply dissolved into the slosh of magic.

Susannah lunged for the basket. She had to get back to Chester. The Echoes couldn't touch her—not since that terrible night at the Conservatorium—but she knew that they could kill Chester.

She reached for the basket—but at that moment, it jerked away. Susannah swore, almost toppling off the platform onto the glass. She threw out her arms to steady herself and staggered backward onto solid floor. The basket continued to move away, winching itself back across the ceiling in a jerky mechanical dance.

So this was the rest of the trap. The final snare. To catch a would-be thief on the platform, while the Echoes crowded in around her. To leave her no choice but to plunge through the glass floor . . .

No. Susannah couldn't stay here. If she didn't get to Chester fast she would be too late. He couldn't fight a dozen Echoes alone—not when every creature had its own unique melody to counter. Chester only had one set of lungs and one flute. He could fight one Echo, perhaps, but the others would destroy him while he played.

The thought of the Echoes reaching Chester, crowding over his body, touching him . . . it made her knees feel weak. And to her shock, she realized it wasn't just the fear of losing a pawn, of losing her deal with Sam, or losing a piece in her plan.

It was the fear of losing Chester.

She stumbled backward, giving herself space for a running start. Then she dashed to the edge of the platform and jumped, straight upward, like a cat launching itself from its haunches. She swiped up with a desperate hand to where she hoped the basket would be. Instead, one of her hands seized a greasy cog with coils of rope and chain around its belly. Desperately, she held on.

Below her stretched the glass floor, as mysterious as ever. It shone, painted almost silver by her bubble of Hush-light. Susannah gritted her teeth and swiped out with her other hand, grabbing a line of the pulley that ran farther along the ceiling. Then she swung again and again. Her feet dangled wildly above the glass floor and her hands felt as raw as a sunburn on the slippery grease of metal cogs.

She was halfway across when she saw the first Echo. It faded into her circle of vision, pale and ethereal, a ghost in the dark of the Hush. It glided toward her. She knew that its melody—the tune that powered its supernatural existence—would be piping forth, but Susannah could not hear it.

She swung again and the creature reached her, cold and slithering, a snake of silent gas. It slid through her like water through cloth. There was a freezing sensation as it melted through her flesh—a terrible sense of frost, of death, of *violation*—and Susannah almost lost her grip on the pulleys and ropes. But she clenched her eyes shut and dangled, determined to endure its touch.

"You can't hurt me," she whispered. "You can't hurt me."

The words gave her strength. They were a distraction. They let her know she was alive. She clung to her words, and she clung to the machinery, and the moments passed like slow-moving molasses . . .

And finally, defeated, the creature drifted away.

Susannah didn't give herself a chance to feel relief. She took another wild swing then another. She had to keep moving, to relieve the throb of her fingers and to return to solid ground. One of her hands slipped and she caught a fistful of sharp metal. The pain was hot and the blood made her fingers more slippery. Susannah cursed, dangling from the other hand for a moment as she paused to wipe the blood across her shirt.

Ahead of her—at the very edge of her vision—something melted from darkness into her circle of light. Susannah took another swing, jolting her bubble of Hush-light forward. She grunted, hands slick with blood, and felt her stomach drop as the scene came into view.

Chester stood in the doorway, feet on solid ground.

And before him floated the nebulous shapes of three Echoes.

Three. Susannah was hit by a stab of panic. No one could fight three Echoes at once. They would be upon him in a moment. They would lunge forward and kill him with a touch, melting his flesh with their Musical toxins . . .

But they weren't moving. They floated as though hypnotized—they weren't dissolving, but they weren't at their full strength, either. Chester's flute was at his lips, piping out a melody, and his elbow was smacking out another rhythm on the doorframe. At the same time, his feet stomped and kicked a raucous beat on the floor.

Startled, Susannah realized what he was doing. To destroy an Echo, Chester would have to play its tune backward on his flute. But he had only one flute, and no other way to make Music. So he had gone one level less deep; a level more basic. Instead of playing Music back at them, he was playing the rhythm—the beat and the bars behind their tunes. His elbow thumped out a three-beat loop, while his feet stamped down the beat for a fast little ditty . . .

And before him, the Echoes remained frozen. They seemed confused, as though they'd never confronted such a thing before. The rhythm wasn't their melody, so it couldn't destroy them, but it was just enough to paralyze them . . .

"Chester!" Susannah cried. "Get out of the Hush!"

He looked up at her, eyes wild with terror. But when he met her gaze, his expression shifted into something like relief. Susannah froze, struck by an unsettling thought. Was this why he had remained in the Hush—to wait and ensure that she was safe? No, surely he wouldn't . . .

She realized with a lurch that Chester's arm was bleeding: the thumping of his elbow was too much for the recently healed wound. But understanding flashed in his eyes and he gave her a nod. He dropped to his knees and hummed the tune.

And he was gone.

Susannah dangled from the pulley system, high above the glass floor. Her hands slipped and slid, raw with blood and pain. The Echoes were turning on her: the only human left in the room. But she couldn't leave yet. This ceiling contraption only existed in the Hush—if she slipped back into the real world now, she would be left clutching thin air . . .

She sucked down a breath and swung forward. The creatures converged, encircling her with translucent limbs. They began to pass through her, frozen splinters in her flesh, her veins, her eye sockets. She felt sick. Her hands shook and slipped. As the Echoes slid through her, her world turned to cold nausea and her fingers skittered until—in a disorientated panic—she was half-convinced that she was already falling . . .

"No!" she choked.

She was almost there. Another swing, and another, and . . .

Susannah reached the basket seat, which had swung back to its original position at the edge of the glass floor. She clambered into it and sat for a moment, sucking down desperate breaths. Then she hurled herself forward onto the opaque flooring. Crouching there, hugging her knees, the notes fell like sweat from her lips and the world around her crunched. Darkness faded, the rain fell away, the Echoes vanished, the basket melted . . . all replaced by empty air. And there was Chester, offering a hand to help her to her feet.

Susannah ignored the hand. She forced herself to stand, wincing in pain as she kept her bloody palms away from the floor. They couldn't afford to leave any traces. Their entire plan depended on Yant taking a long time to figure out that he'd been burgled.

"Think we set off any alarms?" Chester said. "To alert Yant, I mean—not just to call the Echoes."

Susannah shook her head. "Automatic communicators can't work between the real world and the Hush." She tried to steady her breath. "How did you hold off those Echoes by yourself? Didn't the beats all run together and get messed up in your head?"

Chester shrugged. "I don't know. Music just . . . works for me. If I hear it, I can play it. It doesn't get messed up in my head." He looked at his feet. "It would be like messing up the faces of my friends."

Susannah stared at him. "You're a very interesting person, Chester Hays."

There was a long pause. Chester seemed unsure how to respond to that, so Susannah decided it was time to take charge again. She'd messed up tonight and she needed to remind the boy why she was captain of this gang.

The boy? a small voice inside her said. *You're barely a year older than him, if that.*

She gave him her best commanding look. "Come on," she said. "Let's get out of here."

Quietly, they locked the door behind them. As they crept back down the corridor, Susannah kept her eyes on Chester. He moved with a strange sort of grace—quick and nimble, like an arrow in the dark. He might not be good at climbing, but the boy could sure as hell move his feet on solid ground. His eyes glinted in the light of her hideaway lamp and he flashed her a smile.

Susannah's belly gave an odd little twinge. She found her gaze drawn inexorably toward Chester, even when she told herself to pay attention to the corridor. He was bright, she knew. He was talented. And again, there was something about the way he moved . . . She could tell he would be perfect for the Conservatorium job.

Suddenly, Susannah wished she had been wrong. She wished that Chester had failed this job, that he was a hopeless thief and too inept for the role she had planned for him in the upcoming heist.

Because Chester's role was the key to her plan.

And if all went to plan, he would die to complete it.

CHAPTER TWENTY-ONE

AN HOUR LATER, CHESTER LAY ON HIS BED IN THE *CAVATINA*. HE could feel the gentle hum of the machinery, down in the engine room below.

His body still buzzed with adrenaline. With the thrill of sneaking back through the mansion, of clambering along the Musical ladder, of collecting Dot and Travis, of fleeing into the night and into the Hush, where Sam waited with their echo-boat . . .

In the last few months, Chester had committed his share of reckless deeds. He had left his home, he had begged on the streets and once, when a guard had caught him riding trains without a ticket, he had even been beaten and dumped on the roadside. He'd chased a trail of rumors from Jubaldon to Leucosia, played "The Nightfall Duet" in the middle of a packed saloon, and landed himself in a prison cell in Hamelin.

But sneaking into a Musically protected vault owned by a wealthy sugar baron? Well, hopping trains and playing his fiddle seemed banal by comparison.

And he had almost ruined everything. If he had fallen for the Song's lure tonight, he'd have blasted a signal to the radar of every Songshaper in the region. He could have gotten the entire gang killed. If he couldn't even pick a lock without connecting to the Song, how the hell was he supposed to audition for the Conservatorium without doing it?

He had hinted it to Dot earlier in the night, but even she had no idea just how shaky his grip on his powers truly was. His connections to the Song were growing more frequent. Two months ago, it had taken the most complicated musical piece to engage the Song—but now, even a simple lock-picking tune could coax him into blasphemy.

Chester couldn't tell the gang the extent of the risk. They had promised him information in exchange for his Songshaping. What if they decided he was more trouble than he was worth? Then he would never find out about the vanishings.

✳

Chester stepped into the kitchen.

It was dim and cozy, lit by a single dangling lamp and warmed by the scent of oatmeal. Dot sat at the table, her hands wrapped around a bowl, her expression downcast. She poked the lamp and sent it swinging, so that light danced across the tabletop.

Dot glanced up as Chester entered the room. "Can't sleep?"

He shook his head.

She pointed to the stovetop, where steam rose in tendrils from a copper saucepan. "More oats in there, if you want a snack."

Chester slid into the seat beside her. "Thanks," he said. "Not really hungry, though."

Dot gave a slow nod. She didn't look surprised. "I have a theory," she said, "that when we forget our hunger for food, it means we're busy hungering for something else."

She reached up to touch the lantern, halting its swing.

"It's the Music," Chester said. "I can't control it. Tonight, I got so distracted by the tune of that damn hideaway lamp . . ."

Dot tilted her head. "You can't tune it out?"

He wanted to tell her the real problem—that he couldn't stop himself connecting to the Song. But his insides tightened and he knew his trust didn't yet stretch that far.

"Not really." It wasn't a lie; he was just omitting part of the truth.

"Why didn't you say something earlier?" Dot said.

Chester shook his head. "I don't know. I . . . I guess I didn't want to seem weak. When I was a kid, this man told me . . ." He shook his head. "Doesn't matter. Forget I said anything."

For a long moment, Dot stared at him. Then she pushed her bowl of oatmeal away, slid back her chair and stood. "Come on."

"What?"

"Come on." She looked amused by his hesitancy. "I want to show you something."

She led him to a narrow cabin on the highest level of the *Cavatina*. It was a comfortable nook with a velvet couch and a smattering of little glass stars across the ceiling. They glinted when Dot lit the sorcery lamps, reflecting orange light across their points.

The room's most striking feature, however, was the piano. It took up half the floor space and arched with a sleek grand blackness that seemed quite determined to out-glint the stars. Whoever owned this instrument clearly loved it. They cared for it deeply, polished it daily, dusted the pure white shine of its keys. Chester felt a sudden yearning for his fiddle. The yearning was so sharp that his fingers ached. The pang wasn't just regret for a lost object. It was more like mourning for a lost friend.

Dot slid onto the piano stool and patted the space beside her.

Chester sat. The cushion was thin and threadbare, worn down by countless uses. Even so, he couldn't help noticing the fine lace skirting around its edges and the gold embroidered patterns across the seat. The piano and stool combination must have cost a fortune.

"Where's it from?" he said, a little awed. "Did you steal it?"

Dot looked down at her fingers, resting on the keys. "Someone gave it to me. Someone I . . . cared for. Very deeply. When I passed my first exam at the Conservatorium, she bought it to congratulate me."

Chester opened his mouth to respond then spotted Dot's expression. He closed his mouth again.

"Have you played the piano before?" Dot said.

"Not as well as the fiddle, but I used to work in an instrument shop so I learned to bang out a tune on most things."

"Good. That will make it easier to listen."

Dot's fingers were strong and confident on the keys, like the legs of a spider roaming across its web. Notes bounced softly around the room before she launched into a familiar tune. Chester picked it out immediately, before her fingers had completed the second bar. "The Nightfall Duet."

As Dot played, a strange tingle ran through the air. Chester glanced around, startled. It was as though an invisible person had run her fingers across his skin. He shivered a little then returned his gaze to the keys, just in time to see the first wisps of smoke.

"Hey!" he said. "What . . . ?"

Dot smiled at him.

The smoke curled up from her fingertips, tinged with the faint aroma of honey. It spiraled up into vertical whirlpools, slow and silent, then faded like breath into the air.

"You know the duet, don't you?" Dot said. "Sam said you played it in Hamelin."

Chester nodded.

"I want you to play it now with me," she said. "And I want you to listen for the Song."

"What?" Chester said, startled. "But they'll find us! If our Musical signatures aren't registered, they'll . . ."

"No," Dot said gently, "they won't. Their radars are in the real world. They can't pick up what we're doing in the Hush."

"But why . . . ?"

"You're having trouble with focus," Dot said. "That's why Songshapers study the Song. They don't disrupt its tune, but they use it as inspiration when they paint their own melodies into the air—it's a source of strength and focus. I think it could really help you, Chester. And this is the safest place to try."

Chester wanted to argue. He wanted to tell her the truth—that the Song wasn't an inspiration to him or a source of focus for his own Music. It was a deadly intruder and he couldn't keep it out of his head.

But Dot was waiting for him, a quiet expectation in her gaze as her fingers brushed a verse across the keys. Chester drew the flute from his pocket and placed the cold metal against his lips. He waited until Dot reached the end of the verse then launched into the chorus with her. Music flowed from the flute, high and haunting. Dot provided the chords while Chester played in the melody—usually performed by a vocalist—on the flute. He closed his eyes and let the Music fill his ears, his throat, his lungs. There was nothing but the Music and the stillness of the air . . .

And then he heard it. The other rhythm. The other melody. It lurked beneath their own duet—a constant thrumming, a constant tune. It slithered through the stool beneath his body, through the floor beneath his feet. It trickled like molasses and it sloshed like whiskey. It was hot and cold and silent and loud, all at once, and Chester felt as though every cell in his body might explode with the sound.

No, not the sound. The Song.

Chester hesitated.

"Go on," Dot said. "Don't be afraid of it, Chester. It's a part of you. It's a part of all of us."

And so, his fingers stiff, Chester raised the flute back to his lips. Note by note, they eased back into the duet. Their melody floated upward, swirling around them, brushing their skin. And note by note, the second rhythm returned. The beat of the Song. After the initial rush, it felt slightly distorted in the Hush, or oddly distant—like a cry echoing across a deep crevasse. It wasn't the clear, compelling peal he had touched in the real world. But still, Chester could sense it. The heartbeat of the world . . .

"Can you hear it?" Dot said. Her own voice sounded distorted, now. Almost like a whisper. A memory of a voice, or a cry from far away. "Don't touch it, Chester. Don't interfere. Just listen."

Chester didn't respond. He was afraid to lower the flute, afraid that he might break the tune, even for a moment, and the Song would be lost to him forever. It felt so perfect on his lips. So light on his fingertips. So sweet in the air, and so—

"Light up the stars," Dot said.

Chester almost dropped the tune to say *What?* but he caught himself. He played the next note instead, and opened his eyes to meet Dot's gaze with confusion.

"The stars on the ceiling." She nodded up toward the smattering of tiny glass shapes. "I made them from leftover glass from sorcery lamps, but they're not enchanted yet. I want you to play a song of light. Of shining. And direct it into those stars."

Chester let his gaze roam upward, toward the stars. They still glinted in the light of the sorcery lamps, but they themselves were empty of light. Just translucent glass. He felt a faint jolt in the tune as Dot fell silent, her fingers falling away from the piano keys. It was just his flute now, and just his choice. He could play whatever he wished . . .

The choice came to him at once. A memory flashed into his mind and for a moment he was young again, a child in a cradle, with his father singing softly.

Into the night, child,
Into the sleep;
Where the stars fly free
And your soul flies deep . . .

It was a lullaby from his hometown, Thrace. Chester hadn't heard it for years, but his fingers settled into that familiar starting note. He blew it like an owl's hoot, before a whole bar of notes tumbled out into the smoke. He could still feel the Song in his veins, and the Music on his fingers. He focused on the stars and let his vision blur until all he saw was the glint of glass.

Then he slowed. The Song felt quiet at the moment: a deep, rolling beat. Chester shifted his own Music down to fall into the same rhythm, until the two melodies were kissing in his ears. They rolled around each other, clutched at each other's notes and pulled each other's tunes into a spin of quiet embraces. A moment of touch. A moment of connection.

The stars, Chester thought, staring up at the glass. *Where the stars fly free . . .*

And then he saw it. A faint gold cord, threaded from light. It rose slowly from the end of his flute and, like a snake charmer coaxing a snake up from its basket, he made the gold sway toward the ceiling. It was hard to focus on it: the light resisted Chester's eyes as though he was observing it with the wrong sense, so he closed his eyes and opened his ears and let the Music flow up in a ribbon of sound.

Dot gasped. "Look!"

Chester opened his eyes again and blinked. He dropped his flute. The Music stopped. He felt his connection to the Song snap and the world was silent again. He felt naked, as though something had been stripped from the surface of his skin.

But above his head, the stars were shining.

"You did it," Dot said, sounding stunned. "On your first try, you . . ." She turned on him, suddenly looking furious. "You've been lying to us! You've been trained already!"

Chester shook his head, mouth dry. He stared up at the stars. They glimmered with a pale gold light, like the splinters of a broken galaxy. Then he stood, stretched on his tiptoes, and reached up to touch one. Music rippled back down through his fingertips into his body, and he felt his own lullaby being played back to him. *Into the night, child, Into the sleep* . . .

Chester sat heavily on the stool. "I swear, I didn't know this would happen."

He forced his gaze down to meet Dot's accusing eyes. There was a long moment of silence.

Dot dropped her fingers back onto the piano keys. She didn't play, however. She simply rested her fingers, as though contact with the ivory was enough to calm her.

"It took weeks of classes at the Conservatorium for me to learn that," she said, sounding awed. "Even the best students in my class couldn't do it on their first try. Nobody can."

Her tone told him that she believed him.

"Are those stars all sorcery lamps now?" Chester said.

Dot shook her head. "The Music should fade in a couple of minutes. It's much harder to make permanent sorcery objects than to enchant something temporarily."

They both stared back up at the stars.

Chester blinked again, still slightly startled at the thought that *his* music had breathed the light into those stars. No, not his music. His Music. His sorcery.

"You started playing Music without permission, didn't you?" he said. "That's why they kicked you out?"

"No, Chester," Dot said quietly. "They kicked me out because of what I am. Who I am. Because of the person I loved."

Chester blinked. "Huh?"

Dot leaned back farther, holding the piano rim with her fingers. "Her name was Penelope. Penny, I called her. We used to sneak up onto the Conservatorium roof, at night," she whispered. "We used to watch the stars together."

Chester didn't know what to say. He settled for silence and kept his own eyes fixed firmly on the ceiling.

"She gave me this piano," Dot said. "It was her parents who found out. Who had me expelled. They said we were blasphemers. Sinful. Unnatural. That it was against the Song itself for us to love each other."

Chester wet his lips. His heart was hammering. This was why Dot had been expelled?

"But it wasn't against the Song," Dot whispered. "We loved the Song. We used to play Music together, up on the roof, under the stars."

There was a pause.

"She wanted to come with me," Dot said. "To leave her parents, leave the city. But I made her stay. It was her dream, you see. She'd worked all her life to get into the Conservatorium. I couldn't let her throw it all away."

Another pause.

"I'm sorry," Chester said.

Dot glanced at him. Her eyes shone a little, but Chester couldn't tell if it was from moisture or the light of the sorcery stars. She blinked, shook her head, and looked down at her fingers. "It was a long time ago," she said. "Over a year."

"But it still hurts?"

"Every day."

There was a long silence. They both looked down at the keys. Then, slowly, Dot's fingers pressed down. A note rang out. For

212

the first time, Chester noticed a tiny curl of faint brownish ink on each hand: a treble clef, but painted backward, as though the symbol had been reflected in a mirror.

"What are those?" he said. "Those . . . tattoos?"

Dot glanced down and her expression went dark. "They give you these when you're expelled from the Conservatorium," she said. "They stop me from crossing Musical thresholds. I suppose they don't want failed students to sneak back in and sabotage other people's work."

"What? But you—"

"Oh, I can still play Music," she said. "I can still create my own sorcery—even the Shapers can't stop me doing that. I can make trinkets and play my tunes into lamps and ladders and engines. But I can't cross a Musical barrier—not without someone else to pull me through. You've seen—I can't even move in and out of the Hush without help." She looked down. "The captain has to help me."

Chester stared at the tattoos, horrified. Crossing into the Hush was so simple that even Travis could do it, and he hadn't a musical bone in his body. It was just like switching on a lamp, or using a sorcery map: the Music was already active, so all you needed to do was to hum the right notes. The idea that Dot couldn't manage it, with all her wit and her flair for Songshaping . . .

He remembered their arrival in Linus. Just before they had burst into the real world, Susannah had placed a hand on Dot's shoulder. At the time, Chester had thought they had just been steadying each other—but now he realized the truth. Without that hand, that connection to Susannah, Dot would have been left in the Hush, trapped and alone.

"Can't you get rid of them?" he said, gesturing at the tattoos.

"Of course." Dot gave an unexpected smile. "That's easy. If I chop off my hands, I'll be cured. But I won't be able to play piano anymore, so it'll be a pretty useless cure, won't it?"

She ran her fingers along the keys in a ripple, coaxing a wild roar of notes from the ivory. Then she looked up at the artificial stars, an unreadable distance in her eyes.

"Chester," she said, "strength isn't just about putting on a show. It's not about tugging on the strings, manipulating your audience." She lifted her fingers from the keys. "And it's not about lying to your friends."

"I know," he said.

"No," Dot said gently. "I don't think you do. But you will." She smiled at him, a quiet understanding in her eyes. "Sometimes," she added, "I think true strength is admitting when you're vulnerable."

CHAPTER TWENTY-TWO

JUST AS THERE WAS NO SUNDOWN, THERE WAS NO DAWN IN THE HUSH. When morning arrived, only the chime of Chester's alarm clock split the shadows. He rolled out of his bed, pulled on his clothes, and shuffled into the kitchen.

He poured himself a coffee from the pot on the stove then slipped into a spare seat at the table. Dot, Sam, and Susannah already sat there, sipping coffee with bleary-eyed faces. Dot had cooked up a mess of beans with fried potatoes, but no one seemed particularly hungry. Five minutes later Travis arrived, his hair and clothing impeccably styled as always.

"Look at you all," he said, with a touch of disdain in his voice. "Honestly, you'd think you'd just walked off a battlefield."

"Don't mind him," Dot said, as Travis helped himself to the coffee pot. "He's sulking because we had to leave Linus before he visited his favorite tailor."

"I'm not sulking," Travis said, "I'm indulging in a fit of righteous indignation. Do you have any idea what a rare opportunity—"

"All right," Susannah said. "Enough."

The others fell silent. Chester closed his fingers tightly around his coffee cup.

Susannah stood and tugged the cloth covering the blackboard. Her wounded hands were already scabbing over, thanks to a series of Musical injections when they had returned to the *Cavatina* the night before.

A list adorned the blackboard's surface: *money, enchanted charges, identity documents, escape route . . .*

"Right," she said. "This is our checklist for the Conservatorium job. But before we get to that, we need to debrief from last night."

For the sake of Dot, Sam, and Travis, she briefly outlined what had occurred inside the mansion. "We should've investigated Yant's time in Weser better," she finished. "That was my fault. I assumed that because he hadn't attended the Conservatorium himself, he would have no knowledge of the Hush."

"You think it was his uncle, Captain?" Sam said. "Who set up the shattervault and the basket seat?"

Susannah nodded. "If only I'd dug a little deeper . . ."

"Don't blame yourself, Captain," Dot said. "None of the rest of us thought twice about it, either."

"What'd you end up stealing?" Sam said.

Susannah dropped a pile of papers onto the table. "Identity papers," she said. "Birth certificate, a family tree . . . Travis, think you can craft a false identity for Chester out of this stuff?"

Travis picked up the papers and flicked through them slowly. His lips curled slowly upward. "Oh yes," he said. "That won't be a problem." He pointed at the family tree then glanced up at Chester. "I can make you a son of Yant's cousin, here—he seems to have an overlarge brood as it is."

"How long will it take you to forge the papers?"

Travis waved a hand casually. "Oh, a couple of days. I'll need to work out a background story and train the boy in that, which might take a little longer." He gave Chester a frank look. "How good is your memory?"

"Good enough," Chester said. "And I'm not a boy. No more than you are, anyway."

"Oh, don't be such a dullard," Travis said. "You should be celebrating your youth, not denying it. In a few years' time, or so I've been assured, we'll all wake up with enough wrinkles to—"

"That's enough," Susannah interrupted. "So we've got Chester's identity under control." She picked up a piece of chalk and ticked off *identity documents* on the blackboard. "But we need to work on our escape plan. It's one thing to get into the Conservatorium, but getting out won't be easy."

"I still favor the bait-and-switch," Travis said. "Wait until we're ready to escape, then alert the Songshapers to the presence of intruders. That should make them activate their alarms and deactivate the inner shield long enough for us to sneak through." He rubbed his hands together. "And it has a certain flair to it, doesn't it? It's delicious, the irony of their own security system—"

"Yes, but we can't just *tell* them we're intruding," Susannah said. "They'll realize they're being played."

"Anonymous note?" Dot suggested.

Susannah shook her head. "They're not stupid. We need the information to come from a legitimate source, so they think someone's helping them by alerting them to the break-in."

"How about a servant?" Sam said.

"No," Susannah said. "It's an issue of timing. We need someone with enough authority to go straight to the top. A servant would waste time reporting to someone more senior, who could then pass on the report to the bosses . . ."

"So we need a real Songshaper on our side," Travis said. "Someone with a proper license from the Conservatorium— someone who can make an urgent report without raising his colleagues' suspicions."

Sam snorted. "What kind of Songshaper's gonna help us break into his own damn Conservatorium?"

"Well," Susannah said, "how about one with a grudge against his bosses?" She paused. "Dot, can you think of anyone at the Conservatorium who might help us? Someone with a full license, preferably."

Dot shook her head. "I mostly hung out with other students; I never knew the teachers well. And my old friends wouldn't trust me, anyway. Not since I got expelled."

Susannah nodded. "Well, it's another thing to think about, anyway. We've still got time to iron out the details." She added *Recruit licensed Songshaper* to the blackboard. "Now I was thinking—"

Chester gave a little cough.

Susannah paused mid-sentence, and looked at him. "Are you interrupting me?"

"Yes, Captain."

The others sucked in a trio of breaths. Chester felt a little of his bravado dissipate, but he forced himself to go on. "We made a deal, Captain. You promised me information if I picked that lock for you."

Susannah stared at him. "We're in the middle of a meeting. It can wait until later."

Chester shook his head. "Last night made me realize how dangerous this job will be. If a rural sugar baron's vault was *that* well protected, how do I know what I'll be up against in the Conservatorium, itself?"

Susannah didn't speak.

"If I do this job," Chester said, "I'll be taking a hell of a risk. I need to know what's in it for me." He tightened his grip on his coffee cup. "I'm not going to pretend that I'm some tough guy giving you a grand ultimatum. I'm not going to stomp my feet and pretend I'm a brawler like Sam, or a leader like you." He offered Dot a wry little smile. "I already tried that routine and I got put back in my place quick enough."

218

He paused. "But I'm going to be honest with you, Captain. I can't do this anymore. Not without the truth. Not without knowing for sure that you know something about the vanishings."

The silence stretched. It felt almost heavy, now, as though a fistful of awkwardness had pummeled the space between them.

It was Sam who finally spoke. "Tell him, Captain. He deserves to know."

Chester turned to him, taken aback.

Sam gave him a level look from under the rim of his cowboy hat. His blue eyes glinted, pale and eerie. Just like Susannah. What were the odds that two members of the gang would share such an unusual feature?

"Last night, you proved yourself," Sam said. "You won your place at this table."

A strange look passed between Sam and Susannah. There was a long moment of silence, as tense as a fiddle string, and Chester had the distinct impression that he'd just missed something important.

Finally, Susannah dropped into her chair. "I did promise, didn't I?"

Chester nodded.

"All right, Chester," she said. "I keep my promises."

Chester hesitated. He felt as though he should thank her, but really, she did owe him this information. He didn't want to imply that she was doing him a favor or that he was putting himself in her debt. So he closed his mouth, took a sip of half-cooled coffee, and forced himself to wait out the silence.

"The vanishings started two years ago."

Susannah's voice was shaky, with a little too much staccato in the syllables. Chester frowned. She spoke as though this was personal to her, as if it was more than just a rumor she'd heard. Had she lost someone, too?

"The process starts with a virus," she said. "It's a sickness that comes from Music. They can play it into your skull or your food or even your clothing. The tune rubs off into your skin, so soft that you don't even notice it."

"It works on your mind. It makes you weak. It makes you compliant. Then they come to you at night, through the Hush."

Chester felt his heartbeat racing. "Who?"

"The recruiters. The first thing you see is a shadow in the darkness and a hand to muffle your screams. They pull you in and out of the Hush, to test how well you endure it. If you try to struggle, they just tell you to hush."

She gave a bitter laugh. "They inject you with more Music until you stop fighting. Until you stop caring. After a few nights, the whole world is a blur of shadow and fear and pain and you can't even tell what's real anymore. And then . . ." Susannah looked down at the table. "And then they take you." There was a long pause. Susannah glanced up at Sam, as though seeking his opinion on whether to continue. They stared at each other for five long seconds before Sam gave an almost imperceptible nod.

"They drag you into the Hush with them, when you're in the depths of your fever. They take you back to their headquarters, and they turn you into . . ."

She swallowed. "They turn you into a Silencer."

"What's a Silencer?"

"Someone the Echoes can't hurt," Sam cut in, his tone abrupt. "The Echoes can't even touch them, see, 'cause a Silencer's own damn body's like a ripple of Music reflecting back at them."

Chester froze. A memory came back to him. He thought of his first night in the Hush, in the echoboat with Sam. The Echoes had passed right through Sam without harming him . . .

"Like you," he said, mouth dry. Then he turned to Susannah. Susannah, who had those same pale blue eerie eyes. Eyes that were almost like mirrors . . .

"Yes," Susannah said quietly. "Like us." She took a deep breath. "Sam was one of the first to vanish. An early test subject."

"They used me for experimenting," Sam said. "But it didn't go quite right."

"What do you mean?"

Sam just looked down at the table.

"They made a mistake in their Musical dosages," Dot said, "so Sam's transformation didn't work properly. Most Silencers lose their ability to connect with Music. Even if they're trained Songshapers, they can't sense the tune in a lamp or make a sorcery map anymore. But with Sam, they made him emotionally sensitive to Music. When he goes near Musical objects, they yank his emotions around like crazy."

There was a long pause.

Chester breathed out slowly and turned to Dot. "That's why you wrote your own melodies to replace all the lamps . . ."

Dot nodded. "I would've used the normal tunes for sorcery lamps if I could, but those tunes turned Sam into a stomping ball of fury whenever he heard them. Not that it's your fault, Sam," she added, glancing at him. "But I used calming tunes instead, so they help to keep him more peaceful."

"Creating a Silencer is painful," Susannah said. "Long and painful. And tricky. They tie you down for weeks, keep you wrapped in your fever, and pump your body with Music. They paint a melody into your flesh, your skin, your bones, your muscles."

Chester stared at her, horrified. "But why? What do they want you for?"

Susannah shook her head. "Once they've turned you, they lock you in a prison in the Hush. They've been recruiting for two

221

years now, perfecting their techniques. They've got hundreds of Silencers locked away, ready to deploy."

"But you don't know what for?"

"No idea. Must be something to do with the Hush, though. Why else would they need an army of people resistant to Echoes?"

"They've got my little sister," Travis said unexpectedly. He was looking down at the table, his expression grim. "Penelope. She was a student at the Conservatorium, and she used to invent things. Beautiful things. Sorcery decorations and Musical light beams and doors that played melodies when you walked into a room . . ." He shook his head. "She vanished from her bed one night, just like all the others. They must have seen her potential and they snatched her away."

Penelope. The name was vaguely familiar; it stirred something in Chester's memory. He turned to Dot. "Hang on—wasn't Penelope the name of your girlfriend? Is it the same person?"

Dot nodded, looking bleak. "That's how I met Travis in the first place—through Penny." She paused. "I'm the one who made her stay at the Conservatorium. I'm the one who left her there, alone. And now they've got her."

It hit Chester so suddenly that his gut seemed to snap with the impact. "And they've got my dad. They've got my dad, and they're going to turn him into one of those Silencers."

No one denied it. No one offered false reassurances. His father had been snatched into the Hush. He had been taken to these recruiters' headquarters and tortured. He was probably a blue-eyed Silencer by now.

"But you got away." Chester wrenched his gaze up to Sam and Susannah. "You escaped, didn't you?"

Sam shook his head. "They dumped me. I was too damaged and no good to 'em. They figured my mind was gone, so it was easiest to chuck me in with a bunch of regular prisoners for

Execution Day. But normal prisons ain't built to hold Silencers, so I snuck out through the Hush."

"But how did you know how to do it?"

"Heard 'em hum the recital backwards when they dragged me in and out of the Hush in the first place." Sam shrugged. "Even with your brains all jumbled, it's the sort of thing that sticks in your head once you get your bearings back."

Chester swallowed back a queasy twist of disappointment. Sam's case looked unique. His father wouldn't be able to escape that way.

He turned to Susannah. "And you?"

She hesitated. "Well, they kept us in a cage. I've always been flexible. And I'm good at climbing."

Chester tried to picture it: a cage in the Hush, brimming with hundreds of prisoners. He pictured Susannah clambering up to the roof, searching for a way out, for a gap between the bars, a patch of metal malleable enough to twist aside . . .

"A few people escaped with me," Susannah said, "but not many. Most were too broken—in their bodies and their minds. Only the fittest and the strongest made it. Even then, I spent days alone in the Hush before I figured out how to break back into the real world. I lost track of the others in the dark . . . I'm guessing most of them died of dehydration before they learned the trick."

Chester nodded. His coffee was cold now, but he clutched the cup more tightly than ever. He imagined his father, climbing out into the blackness and wandering, alone and dying, in the unnatural mists and rain of the Hush . . .

No. That couldn't have happened to his father. His father was too old and his arthritis too painful. He would still be in the cage, withering in agony as the days stretched on.

He felt like vomiting.

"I can't do this Conservatorium job," he said, finally. "I can't waste time stealing jewels. I have to find my father."

Silence. He could sense Susannah looking at him but he didn't want to raise his eyes. He didn't want to see her disappointment or hear the accusations of broken promises.

"I know," she said quietly. "And that's why you're going to help us on this job."

"What do you mean?"

"There's one last thing we haven't told you. The recruiters are the highest ranks of Songshapers. Their headquarters are in Weser City. And their prison in the Hush? It's right in the middle of the Conservatorium."

"You mean . . . ?"

Susannah nodded. "This job was never about the money, Chester. We don't want to rob the Conservatorium of its jewels or its gold. We want to rob it of its Silencers. Of Penelope. Of your father."

She took a deep breath. "Chester, this isn't a jewelry heist. It's a prison break."

CHAPTER TWENTY-THREE

FOR DAYS, THEY CHURNED THROUGH THE DARKNESS.

The *Cavatina* wound slowly westward, keeping close to the railroad line as it rambled along in the direction of Weser City. A mile became a hundred miles; a hundred became a thousand. The world was black. The Hush was silent.

Chester roamed the ship alone, his mind wrapped up in visions of a metal cage with screaming bodies trapped inside, weakened, weary, half-starved. He imagined his father as just a body, slumped on the ground, his face pale with exhaustion as he wrapped his knuckles around the bars and screamed and screamed until he fell into a final twitching collapse and—

No, Chester told himself. *I'm going to save him.*

Sometimes he helped Susannah with her captain's duties in her office. She showed him her logbook of income and expenditure. Chester tried to keep his voice steady and casual but their proximity in the tiny office made his stomach flip. Susannah's hair fell in messy ringlets across the desk and she smelled faintly of cinnamon, which was her favorite topping for her morning oatmeal.

Chester forced himself to concentrate on the logbook, clenching his fists under the desk. He noticed a series of strange notes in the expenditure column, marked by an asterisk instead of a word like *food* or *medicine*.

"Donations," Susannah said. "To the poor."

Chester stared at the column for a moment and felt his eyes widen. So much money. The gang had given away *so much* money. How many lives had they saved with their donations?

For a moment, Chester wondered if they were doing the right thing. If they risked breaking into the Conservatorium, the Nightfall Gang might be killed or captured. They might never pull off another job and never donate more money to the poor of Linus or Bremen. People might starve who otherwise might have been fed. In the long run, more lives might be saved if they gave up on this suicidal mission at the Conservatorium.

But when Chester imagined his father screaming in that cage, his stomach knotted with new resolve. Perhaps it was selfish, but he had to save his father, no matter the cost.

Sometimes Chester sat with Travis at the kitchen table as he drilled Chester on the life experiences of Frederick Yant, the invented persona he was to take on. Travis forged identity documents by examining the papers from Charles Yant's vault, testing six different inks until he found a color that matched, then adorning a blank sheet of paper with perfect calligraphy.

As he worked, Travis boasted of his various romantic conquests. Barmaids, young ladies of Weser, and farmers' daughters from a dozen minor towns. He spoke in a loud whisper, as though these stories were naughty secrets that shouldn't be divulged. Chester tried to mimic Travis's conspiratorial tone, and deliberately turned the conversation back to Travis whenever it veered uncomfortably close to Chester's own lack of romantic experience.

Eventually, though, Travis brought up the subject that Chester had been hoping to avoid.

"I see the way you look at her," Travis said slyly, as he pulled a dripping stamp from his fresh wax seal on a document.

"Her?"

"The captain, of course. It's painfully obvious."

Chester's face burned. He stammered for a moment then looked back down at the table. After a few awkward seconds, he steered the conversation back to Travis's pursuit of a buxom barmaid in Delos. The moment seemed forgotten but from then on, Chester felt a little awkward in Travis's presence, as though the older boy was secretly laughing at his every word.

Of all his new jobs, Chester's favorite was helping Dot in the engine room. In the steam and smoke and screaming metal, he felt almost invisible. It was hot and exhausting and his body ached by the end of every session. He loved it. The confines of the *Cavatina* were beginning to feel like a prison and it was sheer relief to wear his body into exhaustion. It helped him feel alive; it reminded him that this whole trip wasn't just a hazy dream.

But even with all these jobs—and the endless other chores that filled his hours, from cleaning the bathroom to scrubbing the dishes—Chester felt somewhat useless on the *Cavatina*. He didn't have a single job that was solely his own.

You're not useless, he told himself. *Your role just hasn't started yet.*

His role, of course, was the audition. Now that his goal to find his father had aligned with the gang's own scheme, Chester was beginning to realize what he'd signed up for. It was beginning to feel real, and he couldn't believe that the audition was under a fortnight away.

Everything rode on his ability to impress the Songshapers, to win a place at the Conservatorium. It was the most prestigious institution in Meloral, with an entrance process so difficult that children who'd grown up with expensive lessons and professional tutors wept in failure. Chester thought he could beat them? It was ridiculous. He pictured himself on the audition stage, the flute against his lips, an off-key note squeaking into the silence.

Despite Dot's lesson, he still couldn't control his connection to the Song. If anything, it was growing more compulsive. For hours each night, Chester practiced with the flute to ensure there would be no off-key squeaks. But every time he played well on the instrument, that *dee duh, dee duh, dee duh* of rhythmic breaths slurped down into his throat and he felt the tingle of the Song in his veins. In the Hush, its tune was often distorted, as though he was trapped at the bottom of a black lake, hearing the howl of the wind above the surface.

But every day the wind grew stronger.

If Chester stood on that audition stage and connected to the Song, he would put the entire gang in jeopardy. And still, he couldn't bring himself to tell them the truth. If they rejected him, he would be back at the beginning, with no way to find his father.

*

At dinner one night, Chester took a nervous slurp of stew and put down his spoon. "I'm going to need a fiddle."

The others looked at him.

"What?"

"A fiddle. I can't pass this audition on the flute—I'm not good enough. I don't even know if I can do it on a fiddle, but it's the best chance I've got."

"You should have mentioned it earlier," Susannah said. "We could have picked one up in Linus."

"We'll need to stop in Thrace anyway," Travis said. "I should post these application documents as soon as possible, to ensure they reach the Conservatorium before you arrive."

Chester's throat tightened. *Thrace?* "That's my hometown," he said, trying to keep his voice even. "I mean, that's where I grew up."

"It's also the largest town between here and Weser," Travis said.

Chester nodded. He tried not to look too affected by the news, but it was hard to maintain a casual expression. He took another gulp of stew to keep his mouth busy, and sloshed the warm mush between his teeth.

Thrace. He was going back to Thrace.

He hadn't been home in months, not since his father had disappeared. Chester had sworn that he would never return until he'd rescued his father, but surely this wasn't breaking his vow—he had to visit for the sake of the rescue.

Another thought hit him.

In Thrace, he would find Goldenleaf.

"All right," he said. "If you give me some money, I know where to buy a fiddle."

Susannah gave him a shrewd look. "The shop where you used to work?"

Chester nodded. "There's a fiddle there I carved . . ."

He trailed off. How could he explain how he felt about Goldenleaf? It wasn't just wood and string: to him, it was so much more.

"You sure that's a good idea?" Susannah said. "If the sheriff in Hamelin put out a name and description for you, word might've reached Thrace by now. Locals could be on the lookout, if the reward's big enough."

Chester's stomach twisted. The idea that his old neighbors might sell him out for a sack of gold was nauseating. He thought of the old lady at the bakery, the men who sold meat in the market square. He thought of Mr. Ashworth, with his thin white eyebrows and drooping skin. He pictured them at the sheriff's office, eyes gleaming and fingers grasping at the gold as they reported seeing Chester on the street . . .

They wouldn't, would they? They would know they were selling him to the executioner's block . . .

But they also had children, parents, friends. Folks with empty bellies and hunger in their eyes. If it meant selling out an old acquaintance for the sake of filling those bellies—well, not everyone would have the guts to refuse. Especially if they'd heard what Chester had done. If they knew he was a blasphemer who'd connected to the Song, they might decide he'd earned his execution.

"I'll be careful, Captain," he said. "I can disguise myself, or—"

"No," Susannah said. "Pick another shop, Chester. Somewhere the staff don't know you."

"But my fiddle—"

"Watch it, Hays," Sam cut in. "You don't get to argue with the captain."

Chester flushed. He nodded, muttered an apology, and looked back down at the table. It was sometimes hard to remember that Susannah was in charge of things. She seemed so friendly and open to discussion that he had let himself get a little carried away. But Sam was right. There was a line between discussion and disobedience, and he had almost crossed it.

He couldn't mention the real reason that he wanted Goldenleaf so badly. If he had his favorite fiddle—with its reassuring weight, how it felt against the crook of his neck, the way it rested on his shoulder—he wouldn't have to focus on getting to know the instrument like he had to with the flute, or with any other fiddle. With the reassuring weight of Goldenleaf in his hands, he could focus on finally controlling his Music and resisting the lure of the Song . . .

Chester bit his lip. He knew that he should tell them. He should admit the truth, admit to Susannah that he was randomly connecting to the Song whenever he tried to play. But he couldn't do it. If Chester hoped to save his father, he had to keep his role in the gang. And if he hoped to keep his role in the gang, he couldn't let them know he was a liability.

"Right," Susannah said. "When we get to Thrace, we'll go in and out fast. Sam, Travis, and I will head for the post office to post the identity documents and to do a money drop in the beggar districts. Dot, you're a musician—you can help Chester pick a new fiddle."

Dot nodded, a distant look in her eyes. "I have a theory that instruments have souls, you know," she said. "And different keys bring out different emotions in those souls. When my piano plays C minor, she feels lovesick. When she plays D major, she feels triumphant."

"What's your point?"

"Well," Dot said slowly, "if an instrument has a soul, perhaps it has a soulmate. I know I can never play another piano with as much feeling as my own. If Chester feels a bond with this particular fiddle, perhaps—"

"No," Susannah said. "If the shop owner recognizes Chester, he could shoot him dead for the reward money as soon as you step inside."

"But I could buy it for him, Captain," Dot said. "If Chester points it out to me, I could—"

Susannah shook her head. "Too suspicious. If it's been sitting there for months with no interest from other customers . . ." She turned to Chester. "We can't risk drawing attention to anything related to you. I want you to choose a shop with *no* links to your old life. Understood?"

"Yes, Captain," he said.

Chester caught Dot's eye and gave her a tiny nod, trying to indicate his thanks. Dot understood. She knew what it was like to rest her fingers on a set of keys and to *know*—not from logic, but from something deeper—that this was the instrument for her.

"All right," Susannah said, after several moments. "If no one else has any objections, we should get some rest."

They rose to gather bowls and cutlery. Chester volunteered to wash the dishes, lingering in the kitchen when the others had left. He wasn't ready for bed. He ran the water—heated by the Music of the engine—over his fingers, and let its warmth trickle across his skin.

He imagined himself walking through Thrace. The sights, the smells, the faces. He imagined Goldenleaf waiting for him, his fingers on the strings and the music flowing fast and warm as water. A new mastery over his music, and the confidence to finally keep the Song at bay . . .

And Chester knew, in that moment, that he was going to disobey.

CHAPTER TWENTY-FOUR

THREE DAYS LATER, THEY ARRIVED IN THRACE.

It was a growing city: the most densely populated area outside Weser. Its streets were hot and narrow, like strands of heated wire. They swerved and bent, this way and that: alleyways, courtyards, rooftop paths, all brimming with sweaty bodies and brickwork that hoarded the heat.

Chester moved quickly, light on his feet as he retraced old haunts. He wore a loose flannel shirt and Sam's cowboy hat sat low on his head, cloaking his face in the shadow of its rim. If he bent his head low, no one would recognize the scrawny boy who'd run away so many months ago.

"Is it always this cramped?" Dot whispered.

Chester nodded, darting to the side as a trio of burly men shoved past them. "You get used to it."

"I don't think I want to get used to it," Dot said, wrinkling her nose at the men's body odor. "I feel like an ant scurrying around in an anthill . . ."

Chester smiled. "At least we get some air."

That was debatable. There was indeed a chink of sky overhead, startling blue in the mid-morning sun. But sheets of laundry hung between the buildings above their heads, muffling the breeze and intensifying the stale weight of alleyway air.

As they passed a row of garbage bins, even Chester had to hold his breath. The air didn't just smell bad, he could *taste* the stink on his tongue. Rotting eggs, old cabbage, maggoty meat . . .

Had Thrace always been like this? It must have been. So many months away had spoiled him.

"Okay," Dot said, when they burst into a market square. "Where are we going?"

Chester hesitated. The market was a bustle of activity, obscuring his view of the nearby streets. Farmers sold tomatoes and corn from their stalls, children squealed and darted around, and butchers shouted prices for their freshest cuts. A wrinkled busker played "The Captain's Cat" and coins clinked into a hat by her feet.

One man was trying to sell a shabby old griffin, which slumped in a metal cage on the back of his cart. The beast looked thin and mangy; its beak was cracked, its feathers were dull, and its fur was gray with age.

"Caught this one wild, up in the mountains!" he informed a potential customer. "He's a real bargain, and strong as a—"

"I could buy three pegasus foals for that price!"

"True, true," said the salesman, raising a finger, "but they're gettin' common as muck nowadays, ain't they? It's still a damn rare chance to get your hands on a griffin. If you're after a real impressive beast to pull your carriage, can't go past—"

"That old thing?" The customer sniffed. "It couldn't pull a wheelbarrow. You'd have more luck selling it to the slaughterhouse."

As they passed, Dot offered Chester a sly grin. "What do you think the captain would say if we brought back a griffin instead of a fiddle?"

"She'd probably try to make me play it," Chester said. "Just to make a point." He looked around, trying to remember the details of the city. "There's a pawn shop on that street down there. They might have an old fiddle, I suppose . . ."

Dot shook her head. "You're one of Yant's spoiled nephews, remember? It has to be a shiny new instrument."

"Well, there's a piano shop in the eastern district," Chester said, "and a woodwind shop near Rattenfanger Bridge. But they're not going to have many fiddles to choose from."

Dot raised a suspicious eyebrow. "Are you looking for an excuse to go to your old workplace?"

Chester felt himself flush a little but he stammered a denial. "No, really—there aren't many other instrument shops here."

"In a city this size?"

"I'm just telling you what I know. I figured we'd go to a pawn shop, to be honest, but if that's out . . ."

Chester held his breath. He knew Dot was considering it, that she was weighing up the risks of disobedience. She knew what it was like to fall for an instrument. It was exactly one week until Chester's audition, and he would never perform as well on another fiddle as he would on Goldenleaf.

Dot stared at a sausage stall for a long moment, her eyes fixed on the smoke that painted patterns on the air. The town smelled cleaner here: there was a whiff of sizzling corn and fresh bread, and dry wind rustled through the market like a sheet.

"All right," she said. "But you'll have to wait outside—and don't you dare tell the captain about this. We'll say you bought the fiddle from that place near Rattenfanger Bridge."

Chester stared at her. "Thank you."

She gave him a hard look. "Don't thank me, Chester. I'm only doing this because we need your audition to go well next week." She glanced back at the filthy alleyway and wrinkled her nose. "And because I don't plan to spend a minute longer in this city than we have to."

"I know," Chester said. "I just . . ."

He shook his head, unable to quite believe this was happening. After all those hours dusting the fiddle, polishing it, tuning its strings and buffing the gold leaf as it sat on display in the window . . .

A nasty thought hit him. What if it had been sold? He'd been away for months, after all—perhaps a wealthy traveler had passed through Ashworth's Emporium and plucked Goldenleaf from its nest.

There was only one way to find out.

"Let's go," he said.

*

The Emporium was nestled in the corner of a side street, in a fog of flatulent air. Garbage bins lined the alley outside, and a fading wooden sign swung forlornly in the shadows.

"This is it?" Dot said, clearly unimpressed. "You've got your heart set on a fiddle from *this* place?"

Chester shrugged. "I know it doesn't look like much, but Mr. Ashworth makes quality instruments. Besides, *I* made this fiddle."

Dot didn't look convinced but she nodded. Chester moved toward the door but stopped when Dot suddenly grabbed his forearm. "What?"

"I told you: you're staying out here."

"But you'll need me to point out which fiddle—"

Chester stopped. He had caught a glint of gold in the shop window, behind a layer of dust. He stepped forward and laid his fingers against the glass.

There it was.

It sat in the same position as always: high upon a pedestal, sur-rounded by velvet cushions. The gold decorations looked garish, but the wood underneath shone dark mahogany. Goldenleaf. Chester stared at the strings, picturing his fingers upon them.

He imagined plucking out a note, a scale, a melody. All that lay between him and this fiddle was glass and dust.

Mr. Ashworth needs to hire a new assistant, he thought, remembering all the hours he'd spent scrubbing those windows.

"Is that it?" Dot said.

Chester nodded.

"Wait here, then." She strode across to the door and gave it a push, but it refused to open. Dot frowned then jangled the doorknob. Nothing. "It's locked!"

"Hang on," Chester said. He turned to the alleyway wall and retrieved the spare key from behind a loose brick. "Here you go."

"I can't just break in," Dot said. "If your boss catches me, he'll think I'm a thief." She paused then amended this: "He'll realize I'm a thief."

"So I'll come in with you," Chester said.

Dot gave him a hard look. "Do you trust this man with your life?"

In all honesty, Chester wasn't sure. Mr. Ashworth had always sent a shiver up his spine. He had always asked about Chester and his father in the tone of a taxidermist inquiring about a burrow of rabbits in the area. But the old man had never hurt Chester. He was just a little odd, that was all. Having a strange personality didn't make you a murderer . . .

Even as he ran along with these thoughts, Chester knew he was lying to himself. He was making up excuses to walk into that shop. Now he was here with Goldenleaf in his sights, he couldn't bear the thought of walking away.

"Yeah," he said. "I trust him."

And before Dot could protest, Chester unlocked the door and led the way into the shop.

"Mr. Ashworth's probably having lunch in the back," he said. "He locks up when he doesn't want customers."

A bell jingled overhead as they entered. Chester inhaled the scent of the shop: wood and polish, as familiar as the salty cheese sandwiches his father would pack for his workday lunches. But there was an added touch of dust now, and a mustiness in the air.

"Mr. Ashworth?"

No response. Chester frowned, then turned to Dot. To his surprise, she had picked up a nearby clarinet and was holding it to her lips. Her eyes were narrowed and she looked on edge. If they came under attack, did Dot really think she could get out a defensive tune in time? A bullet would always move faster than a melody.

"Mr. Ashworth?"

Something crunched beneath Chester's feet. He looked down to see the broken shards of a sorcery lamp. The shards were covered in dust, as though they'd lain untouched for weeks or even months.

A cold prickle brushed his neck. This wasn't right.

Chester reached up to the ceiling, where another sorcery lamp hung. He brushed it with his fingers in a clockwise swirl, coaxing up the Music that would bathe the room in light. As it began to glow crimson, shadows ran the color of blood.

"I don't think anyone's been here in a while," Dot said.

Chester took another step forward, wincing at the crack beneath his feet, passing a rack of piano-tuning keys to reach the back room. He pushed the door open, fingers strung with tension, and slipped inside.

The room was destroyed. The tapestry hung in tatters from its railing, desk drawers were upside down on the floor, their contents discarded in an avalanche of papers and stationery. Chester waded forward through the wreckage, heart sinking as he realized the extent of the destruction.

Half-finished instruments lay smashed in their stands. The air stank of mildew, and more broken glass crunched beneath his feet. Following his nose, he discovered the source of the stink: an upturned cup of milk, its contents long since soaked into the rug beneath the desk.

"Mr. Ashworth always drank hot milk," he said, a little stunned. "He always . . ."

"Chester," Dot said, grabbing his arm. "I think we should leave."

"What? Why?"

Dot pointed. Chester looked up from the mess of the mildewed rug to see a dark spatter on the wall. Almost like . . .

"Blood," he whispered.

"How come no one's been here to clean up?" Dot ran a finger across the desk and held it up to examine the grime. A thin layer of dust blanketed the disorder, much like the dust on the shop's front window. "Someone must have noticed that the shop's been closed for weeks . . ."

Chester shook his head. "Mr. Ashworth was a strange man. Sometimes he'd go away for months without telling anyone—he'd head off to study new Musical developments in Weser City, or he'd go foraging northward for new types of wood to make his instruments."

"So even if the shop was locked up for months—"

"—the neighbors might not see anything odd about it," Chester said. "We might be the first people to set foot in the shop since . . ." He wet his lips, stunned by the horror of the scene. "Since whoever did this to Mr. Ashworth."

"We'd better get out of here," Dot said. "In case they come back."

"But if this happened weeks ago . . ."

"They might have set security spells."

Chester tensed. Dot was right. When they'd unlocked the door, or when he'd been foolish enough to light the sorcery lamp . . .

any of those actions might have triggered a remote alarm globe. Mr. Ashworth's attacker might already know they were here.

They hurried back into the main shopfront. Fighting the urge to run, Chester thought about the risks they'd already taken to be here. He couldn't leave with nothing! He unlocked the front window display, fingers trembling a little, and grabbed Goldenleaf from its perch. He had only a moment to relish the feel of the fiddle against his skin—that familiar old friend, with the waiting hum of its strings—before Dot slammed an empty fiddle case onto the countertop.

"Hurry," she said, voice low.

Chester snatched a packet of spare strings from a display rack. He pocketed the strings, placed the fiddle and bow into the case, then closed the lid and buckled it up. Just as he was clicking the final buckle into place, the front door flew open.

A figure stood silhouetted in the gloom of the alleyway. The figure took a slow step forward—and suddenly Chester's mind was back in Hamelin as he and Sam had fled through the corn-fields. As a Songshaper had pointed a gun at his head. The same Songshaper who stood before him now.

It was Nathaniel Glaucon.

CHAPTER TWENTY-FIVE

SUSANNAH LEFT THE POST OFFICE WITH A LIGHTNESS IN HER STEP, with Sam and Travis trailing behind her. The city of Thrace stank as badly as usual—rotting garbage, overflowing drains, a sweaty morass of human bodies—but in an odd way, it reminded her of home. As a fishing port, Delos was home to its fair share of unpleasant smells.

Chester had grown up here. It was a strange thought. She imagined him as a child, laughing and playing in these tangled streets. He might have run errands in the market, or scampered through the nearby alleyways . . .

As she thought of Chester, the lightness in her faded. She could picture him here, his dark eyes marked by an innocence so different from the cynicism in Travis or the hardness in Sam . . . Or the ruthlessness she tasted in herself.

For Chester, a song was more than just music. More than melody or rhythm, sound or beat or the silence in between. It was air. It was food and water, life itself. He inhaled each note as though it might fill his belly, soak through his skin and paint his bones with starlight.

In a way, Susannah envied him. She had never been a musical girl. Growing up poor on the docks, she'd never had the chance. Her father was a sailor and Susannah's first love was the sea. As a child, she had clambered high up the masts of ships in harbor. She had learned to scamper up ratlines and swing from the yards, just as Chester had learned to coax a tune from fiddle strings.

Now, they both found themselves turning those talents to thieving. They had seized the skills they learned and loved as children and turned them into tools as practical as knives or lamps or lock-picks. There was something cold in that, perhaps. Something hollow.

She remembered Chester at dinner, playing with his stew bowl. He had such long fingers: the fingers of a violinist, fingers that could coax music from a bow, or a song from silence. It was that music that made him useful to the gang. It made him valuable.

It made him vulnerable.

With that thought, Susannah's breath turned cold. Ever since Chester had arrived, she had tried to avoid thinking about his role in the plan. It was a role she'd set out so long ago, so coldly, so utterly without compassion or emotion. The role was to be filled by a Songshaper who was to be a pawn, to be sacrificed in her final game with the Conservatorium.

But now . . .

Well, now that Songshaper was Chester and she didn't know what to do. She couldn't go through with her original plan, she knew that now. For over a week she had been in denial, refusing to consider the flaw at the heart of her scheme. To ask Chester to throw his life away . . . the thought made her chest seize up in a terrible tightness, like the howl of a badly tuned banjo. She *knew* Chester. She knew him as a person, as a friend. Perhaps, even, as more . . .

But they were running out of time, and she was out of ideas. She couldn't think of any other way to achieve her goal in the Conservatorium. How else was she supposed to finish the plan? Only a week left until the auditions . . . If she postponed the heist, they wouldn't have another chance for an entire year. She had to find a way to—

"All right, Captain?" Sam said.

Susannah blinked, startled. She realized she must have been staring into space, and gave him an apologetic look. "Just tired, I think."

Sam frowned a little, as though trying to assess the creases in her eyes. "You just looked a little . . . upset."

"I'm fine." She hated the snap in her own voice but shook her head sharply to reinforce the tone. She didn't want to talk about this. She couldn't afford to talk about it. She would think of something. Another option. Another plan.

There was still time.

"Where to next, Captain?" Travis said.

Susannah turned to Travis, grateful for the change in topic. "We could kill some time in the market before we meet with the others."

Travis brightened. "I once met a lovely girl at a market stall— Annie, her name was. Gorgeous blonde hair, all tumbling over her shoulders while she sold hot sausages to the riffraff . . ." He sighed. "Shame her voice was as shrill as an off-key viola."

"No one's good enough for you, are they?"

"Oh, it's not like that," Travis said. "I can't expect every girl to meet my own standard of perfection." He gestured down at his own impeccable outfit and winked at her. "I mean, can you imagine the girl who could live up to this?"

The market square was hot and dusty but thankfully smelled of fruit and sausages rather than trash. They bought a loaf of bread, so fresh that steam rose from its insides when they cracked it open. It was sweet—laced with sugar and currants—and the taste made Susannah's tongue tingle with pleasure.

After a moment, she realized that Sam wasn't eating. He was surveying the crowd with narrowed eyes, his limbs as tense as trip-wires.

"Sam?" she said. "What's wrong?"

He didn't answer. For a moment she feared it was the music of the nearby busker, manipulating Sam's emotions. But she was sure it was only music, not Music with a capital "M." And besides, the tune was upbeat and cheerful—if Sam's behavior was down to melodic interference, shouldn't he be smiling and bouncing around in response?

No, it wasn't the music. Something else was wrong.

She touched his arm lightly, trying not to startle him. "Sam? What do you see?"

Sam's eyes were fixed on a figure in the crowd. Susannah followed his gaze, frowning, and settled on a man in an olive-green coat. A neatly trimmed goatee curled below his lip, and he wore a silver pendant in the shape of a nautilus shell. *Songshaper*.

"Nathaniel Glaucon," Sam hissed.

"Who?"

"The Shaper that chased us out of Hamelin," Sam said. "Damn near put a bullet in Chester's head."

Susannah stiffened. Her body was tense and alert, now—ready to charge, or pounce, or flee. Survival instinct flooded her veins, screaming at her to run for it . . .

But she couldn't run. Two members of her gang were still here, somewhere in the sprawling mass of the city. She was their captain and she was their friend. She wouldn't leave them. And until she knew the Songshaper's purpose here, she wouldn't let this danger out of her sight.

The marketplace bustled around her, a sea of shouts and clanks and the sizzle of roasting corncobs. Susannah followed Nathaniel, who wove through the crowd like an expert, dodging and weaving through groups of passing shoppers. He moved ever closer to the edge of the square, shifting in the direction of a particular side street . . .

"He's not here to go shopping," Susannah said, pausing a moment for the others to catch up. "He's looking for something."

Or someone, her mind added.

Susannah stamped down on that thought and countered her panic with another dash forward. For a moment she lost sight of him as he slipped into the crowd, just another shadow in a tangled knot of limbs. "Where . . . ?"

"That way," Travis pointed. He was taller than her by at least a foot and he peered over the heads of the bustling shoppers. "Down that street to the right."

They hurried after the Songshaper, ducking and weaving through the crowd. People swore as Susannah shoved past, but she waved them off with a muffled apology. After almost a minute of elbows, protests and assorted curses, she was funneled by the crowd into the side street.

"Down there, Captain!" Travis called, somewhere in the crowd behind her. "To your left, just near—"

His voice was drowned out in the rush. Susannah cursed under her breath. They were too close to the market and it was nearing noon, the busiest time of the day, when local workers swarmed to purchase lunch from the stalls.

She pushed into the side street, where the crowds mercifully thinned. This street was narrow but mostly deserted. The main source of life was a row of garbage bins, buzzing with the wing-beats of tiny black insects.

"I assume this isn't a popular shopping area," Travis said in distaste, holding his nose as they passed a doorway.

They reached the end of the street and peered around the corner. Susannah spotted the Songshaper immediately: a lone silhouette against the bricks of the next alleyway.

"Come on," she whispered. "This way."

She peeked into passing windows, studying the types of shops in the area. Taxidermist, embroiderer, glass blower . . . These weren't popular mainstream shops, like bakeries or tailors. They were curiosities, mostly, selling odds and ends and offering peculiar services. Such shopkeepers couldn't afford the rent in more popular areas.

Susannah couldn't imagine an instrument shop in this part of the city. Were they barking up the wrong tree? Perhaps it was just a coincidence that Nathaniel Glaucon was in Thrace; perhaps he wasn't looking for Chester after all . . .

Up ahead, Nathaniel vanished through a doorway.

Susannah turned to the others, the question on her lips.

"Don't reckon there'd be an instrument shop down there, Captain," Sam said, frowning. "In all them shadows. How's it supposed to get any customers?"

"Perhaps it isn't an instrument shop," Travis said. "It could be a secret meeting place for Songshapers or something. Perhaps he's sending a message to his superiors in Weser."

The others gave him incredulous looks.

"What?" Travis said. "It could be."

Susannah shook her head. "Well, only one way to find out."

A minute later she stood in front of the shop. Dust clung like skin to the window, but she could still make out the shapes inside. A clarinet, a banjo, a gleaming silver triangle. Above the door, a faded old sign read Ashworth's Emporium.

"I'm going to kill them," she muttered. "Both of them."

"Is this where Chester used to work?" Travis said.

She nodded.

"Well, I can hardly imagine it had many customers, down here in—"

He was cut off by a shout inside the building. They froze. Susannah looked through the window and saw two figures: Dot and Chester, posed defensively behind the counter . . .

Nathaniel Glaucon stepped into her line of sight.

"Well, boy," he said. "Long time no see."

Susannah held her breath and listened. The shop door was partially ajar, allowing the indoor conversation to trickle out onto the street. Sam moved toward the door but Susannah held up a hand to halt him. If they simply barged inside, Nathaniel might shoot someone in the chaos. They needed time to think, to assess their options . . .

Chester clutched a fiddle case to his chest defensively, like a father protecting his baby. "What the hell are you doing here?"

"Looking for you, boy." Nathaniel stepped forward. Glass crunched beneath his boots. "Did you really think you'd get away so easily?"

"What have you done to Mr. Ashworth?"

"Who?"

"Mr. Ashworth! The man who owned this shop, you—"

Nathaniel Glaucon glanced around the shop, as though noticing his surroundings for the first time. "This? You think I had anything to do with this?" He shook his head. "Oh no, boy. I have no interest in this shop. This is the first time in my life I've set foot in the place."

"Then how did you know I'd be here?"

"Because it's my duty, boy." Nathaniel pulled a sphere from his cloak. "I'm here to bring a fugitive to justice."

His fingers stroked the glass surface, coaxing out a quiet gold shine. A faint trickle of light concentrated in its center. A swirl of golden smoke rose from the globe, fizzling and hissing, as its tendrils melted into the shape of a familiar face.

Susannah stared at it, horrified. This globe wasn't just a radar designed to pick up illegal connections to the Song. This device was personalized. It was programmed to locate a specific person.

Chester.

"Do you like it?" Nathaniel said. "An impressive little device, is it not? And right now it is screaming through my fingertips that my target is right here in this room . . ."

"That's a locator globe!" Dot's voice was high, but she sounded more excited than afraid. "They're not supposed to exist! It's impossible to lock a tracking device onto a single soul's melody—there's too much interference from the Song!"

"Oh, it's possible." Nathaniel took another step forward. Even through the dusty window, Susannah could make out his smirk. "Quite a recent invention, but certainly possible."

He drew a pistol from his belt and aimed it straight at Chester's head.

"And do you know what else is possible?" He flicked off the safety catch. "Ensuring that justice is served."

Susannah jerked to action. "Go, go, go!"

There was a terrible bang as the pistol fired, so sharp and shocking that Susannah's head jolted backward as the sound slapped her ears.

Sam was on Nathaniel in an instant, knocking him to the floor, his beefy hands wrapping around the Songshaper's throat. Dot was shouting, stumbling aside with a cry of outrage. But in that moment, Susannah was barely aware of them. She staggered forward, her entire body so tense that she felt ready to shatter. In the aftermath of that gunshot blast, all that mattered was Chester. *Where is he? Where is he?*

He couldn't be . . .

Then she saw him. He stood behind the wrestling figures, his arms still tight around the fiddle case. He was pale with shock, but still standing. Still alive. Susannah let out a breath—more of a cry, really—when she spotted the bullet hole in the wall.

It had been close. Too close.

"Captain!" Dot said. "How'd you find us?"

Nathaniel Glaucon gave a furious screech, thrashing wildly as Sam threw his own weight upon Nathaniel's heaving chest. The pistol skittered across the floor; Travis scooped it up with a cry of triumph. Nathaniel kicked and writhed, snarling like a feral dog, but it was no use. He was trapped. He pursed his lips to hum a melody but Sam slapped a hand across his mouth.

"Don't even think about it," Sam growled.

Nathaniel's eyes widened in recognition. "You!" he managed, muffled by Sam's coarse fingers.

"Yeah," Sam said. "Me. And I thought we'd made clear last time that I don't like you shooting holes in my friends?"

From the corner of her eye, Susannah saw the flicker of surprise in Chester's face. She was a little startled herself by the venom in Sam's voice—and, more strikingly, to hear him refer to Chester as a "friend."

Sam pressed harder on the Songshaper's mouth then nodded at Susannah. "All yours, Captain."

"Thank you, Sam." She took a deep breath, trying to steady herself. "You did well."

Susannah stepped forward to survey their captive, who still clutched at the locator globe in his hand. It took every ounce of self-control she possessed not to kick him.

"So," she said. "Let's say you're telling the truth and that globe really can pinpoint Chester's location. You've been hunting him ever since he escaped in Hamelin. But that was over two weeks ago. Why's it taken you so long to find him?"

Nathaniel spat out something angry, but the sound was muffled by the flesh of Sam's palm. Sam loosened his grip a little, allowing the Songshaper's words to leak between his fingers.

"What was that?" Susannah said.

"I said the globe can't just locate anyone on a whim! You need a sample of their Musical residue."

"Musical residue?"

Nathaniel just glared at her.

"Dot, do you know what he's talking about?"

"People leave Musical traces, Captain," Dot said. "If you play music somewhere regularly, and you've got a gift for Songshaping, you can leave a trace of your own natural melody behind." She waved a hand, struggling to explain. "It's like when you live in a house for years and you leave your own touches in the design, in the paintwork, in the furniture . . ."

Susannah nodded, turning back to Nathaniel Glaucon. "That's why you're here, isn't it? When Chester was arrested in Hamelin, he gave you his full name. You looked into the official birth records, and found out that he grew up in Thrace."

The Songshaper didn't speak.

"So you came here," Susannah said, "and you figured you'd find some of this . . . residue . . . in his old hometown, perhaps? His old workplace?" She glanced around the shop. "You found traces of his music here, to make the locator globe work. And then, of course, the damn thing told you that Chester was heading toward Thrace anyway. You could just sit here until he strolled right into your clutches."

Nathaniel let out a low chuckle. The sound was somewhere between glee and fury, distorted by the curl of Sam's fingers. "I knew he'd come back here. That's what criminals do, my dear. They run back to their little nests, their old hidey-holes. Like a rat's nest in a gutter."

Susannah fought back the disgust that was welling in her throat. She knew the man was trying to provoke her but she couldn't stop her mind from ticking over with a cavalcade of memories. She thought of Chester, trying so hard to help out on the *Cavatina*. She thought of their shared meals, of their work together on the logbook. She thought of the way he'd held his nerves together on his first burglary job.

She thought of the way he smiled at her.

And all that time, this worm of a man had been holed up in a Thrace hotel. He'd been watching the locator globe . . . watching Chester travel closer and closer to Thrace . . . waiting to put a bullet in his head.

Susannah drew a deep breath. *Calm down*, she told herself. *Take it slow.*

"All right," she said. "You're working alone?"

There was a long pause.

"No," Nathaniel said. "I'm working with the Conservatorium. I'm an undercover agent in the Hamelin region. I've got a backup team nearby, and they'll be on the way if they don't hear from me in—"

"You're lying."

"I'm not lying! You've got about thirty seconds before they burst through the door, and then—"

"I know you're lying," Susannah said, "because if that were the truth, you would have just thrown away your only advantage. And you don't strike me as the sort who would throw away advantages lightly, Mr. Glaucon."

She bent a little closer, studying his face. His pendant glinted in the light. "I don't think you're working for the Conservatorium. I think you're doing this job on your own."

Nathaniel's expression briefly shifted but he quickly schooled it back into fury. "You'll be sorry," he spat. "When they burst through that door with pistols firing, you'll—"

"There won't be any pistols," Susannah said, hoping like hell that she was right. "Because you don't have a backup team. You're not working on orders from the Conservatorium. I think you're just a little no-name rural Songshaper who couldn't make it in the big city. You were good enough to graduate but not good enough to make a name for yourself. A small fish in a big pond. So you moved out to Hamelin—a tiny little town, where you could be the biggest fish around."

She leaned in closer. She was right in front of his face now. "Somewhere you'd be the only Songshaper around for miles. Somewhere you could feel special."

Nathaniel's face curled. He tried to spit at her but the effect was ruined somewhat by the intervention of Sam's fingers. Sam let out a curse as the spittle sprayed across his skin, but didn't remove his hand.

"And then you had a lucky break," Susannah said, moving a bit farther away. "An unlicensed Songshaper waltzed right into your town and got himself arrested, and you were the only person for hundreds of miles who could use Music to help retrieve him.

"This was your moment to shine, wasn't it? Killing Chester . . . this was your chance to win some respect from the bigwigs at the Conservatorium. Maybe they'd even bring you back to Weser City, give you a position. A medal. A reward for your bravery."

Nathaniel began to writhe again, the hatred evident in his eyes. "Someone else will kill him!" He spat the words between Sam's fingers. "You can't hide him from the Conservatorium forever; as soon as he touches the Song again, they'll sense the boy on their radars and send someone to get him. You can do what you like to me, but you've already lost, you stupid little—"

"I know the Conservatorium can send someone," Susannah said. "They've already done it. We met a Songshaper in Bremen who was using a radar to track Chester down. But she didn't know Chester's name—just that someone was connecting to the Song without a license. It was safe for us to let her go."

She paused. "But you, Nathaniel? You're different. You know Chester's name. You've got his Musical residue. You know how to track him down." Susannah drew back up to her full height, looming directly above his head. "It's not safe to let you go."

The Songshaper's eyes widened. He began to squirm again, apparently convinced that she was about to stomp a heavy leather boot on his face. But in truth, she had no idea what to do with him. Here he was, entirely at her mercy, but she wasn't a murderer. No matter what he'd tried to do, she couldn't imagine killing this man in cold blood.

But she couldn't let him leave, either. His silver pendant seemed to wink at her: a nautilus shell, the symbol of the Songshapers and a mocking reminder of where his allegiance lay. He would hunt them down and they wouldn't be able to complete their job at the Conservatorium . . .

The job!

Her mind flashed back to the kitchen of the echoship. To their careful plan, and the blackboard full of notes for the job. To the words that read *Recruit licensed Songshaper* . . .

Susannah glanced at the others, who were all watching her in silence. They didn't see it. They didn't yet realize what an opportunity they had just stumbled into.

"Mr. Glaucon," she said quietly, "I want to offer you a deal."

The others gasped but Susannah raised a hand to silence them. Nathaniel looked up at her, his eyes flickering with fear and fury.

Susannah drew a deep breath. "We have a very important job next week, but there's one big hole in our plan. A hole that needs to be filled by someone who's graduated from the Conservatorium." She paused. "A hole you're going to fill for us."

Nathaniel glared. "And what do I get out of it?"

"Your life, for a start," Susannah said. "And if you play along nicely, you might even get a reward from the Conservatorium bosses. If we plan this right, we all get what we want." She gave him a falsely sweet little smile. "Now wouldn't that be nice?"

"I don't work with—"

Susannah bent low, so that her face was barely inches from his. "Listen up, Mr. Glaucon. You tried to kill my friend. Any other gang leader would have you strung up from the nearest lamppost. But I'm not a murderer, and I don't plan to start being one right now. All I want is your help on one little job. What I'm offering you is a chance to live—and to improve your blasted life while you're at it," she added.

There was a pause, as thick and textured as the dusty air. Nathaniel swallowed loudly, twitching a little under Sam's weight.

Finally, he closed his eyes. He rested his head back against the floor, as though he hated himself for the words that were about to leave his lips.

"What kind of job?"

PART THREE
THE SECRET

CHAPTER TWENTY-SIX

WESER WAS A HARBOR CITY, SQUATTING IN A SOUTHWESTERN CROOK
of the coastline, over a thousand miles from Thrace.

For six long days, the *Cavatina* rolled through the Hush. It was
a lonely beacon in a sea of black, traversing an endless parade of
cold and damp, of shadows and silence. Occasionally, the proximity bells would chime to warn of another vessel, but in the swirling
darkness, the ships never came close enough to spot them.

On the third night, they left the Hush to set up camp beneath
the stars. After days of inhaling the Musically twisted darkness,
Chester felt a strange prickle in his veins, as though every instinct
in his body yearned for purer air. Sam settled the *Cavatina* near
the railway line, which pointed like a gleaming finger toward
Weser City. The gang dined on hard cheese, pickled eggs, and ash
cakes. They slept by the crackle of a campfire, wrapped up tight in
blankets, dirt, and bracken.

When morning came, they plunged back into the dark.

As they sailed from open fields into the southern prairies, navigating the Hush became more dangerous. The gang lost a full day
of travel when Sam insisted that they detour around the Sawgrass
Marshes, a vast terrain of swampy fens down in the lowlands of
the prairie.

"Honestly, Sam, it hasn't rained in weeks," Travis said. "The prairie should be drier than a—"

"I ain't taking risks with this ship." Sam wrenched the wheel aside. "Or do you *want* to get swallowed by an overgrown puddle?"

Travis frowned. "But—"

"I grew up 'round here," Sam said. "My pa's ranch was just north of here, up in cattle country. You saying you know these prairies better than me?"

"I suppose not."

"Good," Sam said. "Then go play with your mirror and let me do my job."

Chester spent countless hours in the driver's cabin, gazing out through the windows. As they drew closer to Weser City, he began to spot occasional signs of life in the darkness. A glimmer on the edge of a hill. A flash of unnatural movement in a gully. A flicker of silent lightning in the distant sky.

"Getting close to the city," Sam said. "The Hush's even worse 'round here."

On the sixth day, Chester began to spot signs of other echoships. These weren't just dings on a proximity bell; they were huge and glinting. Every few hours, a ship would loom out of the darkness—a streak of light, the flutter of sails, the groan of old wood in the breeze—and then vanish again into the black.

Finally, it was time.

Chester sat alone in his cabin, legs curled beneath him. Weser City. They were finally here, floating through the fields on the outskirts of the city itself. His audition was tomorrow night and though his fingers should have felt light, they felt like lead on the strings. He wasn't ready. He was going to fail, or make a terrible mistake, and the entire plan would fall to pieces . . .

His fingers rested on the neck of his fiddle, where the gold leaf bumped like goose flesh at his touch. Chester longed to rip away the decoration and return the instrument to its original form but Susannah had forbidden it.

"You're playing the role of a spoiled little brat," she reminded him. "A bit of gold on your fiddle will help convince them you're Yant's nephew."

Chester hadn't argued. He didn't want to push his luck, especially after his mistake in Thrace. It had been his choice to disobey his captain and stray into Ashworth's Emporium. His greed had put the entire plan in jeopardy. He hadn't just risked his own life, but also Dot's—and the lives of all the vanished prisoners the gang hoped to rescue.

Chester pressed his bow to the fiddle. He didn't want to dwell on Susannah's fury. On the way her spine now stiffened when he entered the room, or how she avoided his eyes, and gave him orders in short, snappy tones.

He had made a mistake. He knew it now. He had disobeyed an order from his captain, and betrayed the trust of a friend. Any fragile web of unity between them had been shattered when he had stepped into Ashworth's Emporium.

Afterward, he had insisted on taking the blame. He had told Susannah that he had tricked Dot into visiting the Emporium— not that she had been his co-conspirator. After all that Dot had risked for him, it seemed the least he could do.

But his choice had come with a price. When Susannah looked at him now, she didn't see a friend or an ally. She only saw the fool who almost ruined their entire plan. Before, Chester hadn't been able to bring himself to tell Susannah about his connections to the Song. He certainly couldn't now.

And it had all been for nothing.

During their week of travel, Chester had practiced playing fiddle. Each time, his veins still thrummed with the rhythm of the Song. He felt it call to him, luring him through the deep, reeling

259

his emotions out until his entire body tingled. Deep down, he had always known he was fooling himself. Goldenleaf was no better than the flute. He still felt the Song behind every note and, if anything, it was getting worse. Its notes were fast and frantic, like the final gasps of a dying man.

At least one good thing had come of his mistake. Nathaniel Glaucon.

Chester didn't trust the Songshaper for a moment: if Nathaniel thought it was in his best interests to betray them, he would do it. But Susannah had convinced the man it was in his best interests to help the gang, and he had agreed to meet them in Weser City. Chester had even sweetened the deal by telling him he'd return the stolen flute if he played his part right.

"All you have to do is raise the alarm at the right time," Susannah had told him. "When we give the signal, just tell your bosses in the Conservatorium that someone's broken into their inner sanctum. We get the alarms tripped, you get to be a hero. Win-win."

"What makes you think I won't sell you out beforehand?" Nathaniel said. "Tell them that you *want* to trip the alarms and I'm part of your plan?"

"Because if you do it our way, the other Songshapers are going to be responsible for a serious failure. Those are the Songshapers who ostracized you, Mr. Glaucon. The ones who made you feel like you were never good enough. The ones who made you run off to Hamelin, just so you could stop feeling like a failure."

There was a pause. Something hungry seemed to stir in Nathaniel's eyes.

"And you'll humiliate them?" he said.

Susannah nodded. "We'll waltz out of there with some very valuable loot, and it will be their own security system that lets us get away. And when the bosses are looking for heads to roll the next day . . ." She paused. "Well, they'll need to promote *someone* to replace those failures. Who better to lead than the hero of the hour?"

"Me?" Nathaniel said.

"Yes, Mr. Glaucon." Susannah gave him a satisfied smile. "You."

Chester remembered the look on Nathaniel's face. The dawning realization. The knowledge that if this plan worked, helping the gang would solve all his problems.

And Susannah standing over him, tall and triumphant, red hair flowing over her shoulders . . .

There was a knock at the door.

Chester dropped his bow and the memory shattered. He blinked a couple of times then jolted his mind back into the present. "Come in."

It was Dot. She looked very small in the shine of the sorcery lamp, almost elfin, with her sharp nose and dark eyes. She had slicked back her hair into a blonde smear, keeping it away from her eyes, and she wore a wool peacoat over her blouse.

"Time to go," she said. "We can't risk sailing any closer to the city."

Chester nodded. He laid Goldenleaf carefully in its case, the bow alongside it. Then he pulled on his own coat, gathered the fiddle case under one arm and reached for his suitcase. He took a deep breath.

And he followed her up to the deck.

✶

Chester slipped down a rope ladder, his boots thudding in the dirt. The *Cavatina*—which Sam had settled by a sloping hill—loomed above him: a spectral bulk of wood and sails.

"How far to the city center?" Chester said.

"Five miles," Susannah said. Her tone was as cold as the air.

Chester nodded, although his insides had shriveled at her words. The world swirled, raw and bitter. Just five miles away, the Conservatorium brimmed with students and Songshapers. They might be jostling for dinner, or finishing up their lessons for the day. A riot of chatter, of music, of crowds and corridors.

Tomorrow, if all went to plan, he would be joining them there.

"I still say we should have sailed closer," Travis said. He was dressed even more impeccably than usual, in a silk waistcoat with a silver pocket watch pinned to the front, his black hair slicked with oil and a polish to his spectacles. "I hardly think it fitting to waste our strength trekking into the city, especially when the job is—"

"Too risky," Susannah said. "There are other ships around here. And there are too many Songshapers. And . . ." She trailed off, then gestured at the blackness beyond their bubble of light. "And I don't trust the Hush around here."

Dot nodded. "Too much sorcery in the air."

Chester peered out into the darkness. The rain was almost gelatinous. It fell in cold sheets, a quagmire of blackish custard. In the distance, something glimmered. It was just the briefest flash—a curl of flame, like the flicker of an old-fashioned candle. Chester watched the darkness where it had vanished, waiting. And there it was again, so sharp but so soft. His skin began to prickle . . .

Without thinking, he stepped forward.

"No!"

Someone grabbed his arm, their fingers tight and violent. Chester whipped his head around to see Susannah, her face so pale in the Hush-light that she looked almost sickly.

"Don't move," she hissed.

Chester blinked down at the dirt around his boots. Now that he focused, he noticed that the dusty earth was curling and swaying up into unnatural tendrils around his ankles, like a pit of swaying vipers carved from sand . . .

"How . . ." Chester swallowed, his throat dry. "How much Music is leaking through here, exactly?"

Susannah released her grip on his arm. "A hell of a lot more than I'd like."

As one, they bent to their knees. Chester tucked his suitcase and fiddle case up under his armpits, ensuring they would be carried into the real world alongside him. He had to force himself to touch the dirt. It felt strange as it rippled, softly swelling beneath his palms. He fought down a shudder. In his peripheral vision, he saw Susannah place a hand on Dot's shoulder.

"Three," Susannah said, "two, one . . ."

In reverse, they hummed the notes of the Sundown Recital.

The world shrank. Chester's skin sucked down on his flesh, his veins, his bones. His body ached as the wind whipped past, as the air itself sucked and gushed and roared. The darkness here seemed determined to fight him, and he clutched the earth with every last bit of strength in his fingertips. He couldn't breathe. He couldn't think. All he could do was hold on tight and clench his eyes shut until—

It was over.

Chester opened his eyes. He knelt in the dirt by the railway line, the sun beating hot on the back of his neck. He clambered unsteadily to his feet, blinking at the sudden influx of daylight. The air was dry; it smelled faintly of dust and sand, with an after-taste of burned grass.

The *Cavatina* had vanished. In its place, there was nothing but the sloping hill he had seen in the Hush. The hill was no longer black; it was thick with pale brown grass, with wild wheat and tangled dandelions. Above it, the sky was blue. When a breeze brushed the hilltop, it carried with it a salty whiff of the sea.

Chester swallowed. Beyond that hill, he knew, the world would melt from wheatfields into streets, from streets into mansions, all the way to the harbor.

Weser City. He was really here.

And tomorrow night, he would either have his father by his side . . . or silence for a heartbeat.

CHAPTER TWENTY-SEVEN

WESER CITY WAS THICK WITH HUMID AIR.

Its roads and bridges caressed the sea, like a fiddler's fingers on his strings. On the eastern side of the bay, shanties and hovels ran down almost to the waterline. Children ran through the streets, shrieks filled the air, and the world flapped with gulls' wings and the stink of rotting seaweed.

On the western side of the bay, the streets brimmed with mansions. They rose from the earth like crags on a cliff: tall, white, ornate. Lavish pillars propped up their balconies, and on each rooftop rose marble statues: dragons and pegasi, griffins and dancing ladies. Fountains danced with bubbling water in the squares. People rode in carriages along the streets, faces clean and clothing cut from the finest lace and leather.

The real showpiece was the Grand Square, rimmed by palatial buildings and expensive restaurants. Many patrons dined outside, where dozens of circular tables were adorned with cloths of silk and lace.

The Conservatorium loomed at the back of the square, vast, tall, and breathtaking. Marble pillars curled with carvings of musical notes, and the balcony railings shone white with sorcery lamps.

The Conservatorium. After years of impossible daydreams, this was it.

When evening fell, Dot asked for a few hours to scope out their target. She and Chester sequestered themselves in a fancy restaurant, just across the street from the Conservatorium. Dot took notes on a scrap of paper, which she surreptitiously slid beneath her napkin whenever a waiter appeared to refill their water glasses.

Chester swirled a spoon slowly in his bowl. He wasn't hungry. He had only come to escape the chill of Susannah's stares—and to sneak a better look at the Conservatorium. He'd had a vague idea that it might calm his nerves, somehow, to get a good look at the place before tomorrow night.

So far, it wasn't helping.

"Need any help?" he asked Dot, searching for a distraction.

Dot shook her head. She was jotting numbers onto her notepad, performing some kind of mathematical calculation. Chester knew it had something to do with her sorcery for tomorrow night, but the numbers were beyond him.

Just sitting in the restaurant, Chester felt distinctly out of place. He had grown up on simple foods, such as stew and cornbread, eggs and beans. The closest he'd come to a restaurant was a saloon, where the patrons slouched in grimy shirts and shouted for whiskey.

Here, however, the diners wore cravats and fancy hats, and the waiters served pale sherry and champagne. The menu proclaimed such oddities as lamb tenderloin, baked trout with anchovy sauce and something called "purée of grouse." When Chester had received his menu, he had stared at it, utterly dumbfounded, until he finally ordered the mushroom soup. At least he had a vague idea of how to eat it.

Now, he swirled the spoon in a slow rotation through his soup and glanced back up through the window. He no longer felt much like eating.

At its peak, the Conservatorium rounded upward to a huge central dome, which curved like half a melon beneath the moon. A rooftop stable encircled the dome, providing a home for the city's finest pegasi. Chester could imagine the beasts up there, pawing their hooves as the stars streaked overhead and the rooftop breeze played a rhythm on the dome.

"Beautiful, isn't it?" Dot said.

Chester realized that she had stopped writing and had shifted her attention to him.

"Well, you know . . . it's the Conservatorium." He took a sip of water. "Never thought I'd get the chance to see it."

Dot didn't respond.

"Is it hard for you?" Chester said, feeling a little awkward. "Being back here, I mean?"

"Well, you know how it is," Dot said. "It's always the worst parts you remember most." She rolled the pencil between her fingers. "I have a theory, you see, that our memories are songs. It's the big dramatic chorus that gets stuck in your head, isn't it? Not the quiet rhythm beneath it all."

There was a long pause.

Dot looked back down at her notebook. "On the bright side," she added, "at least one good thing came of me being expelled."

"What?"

"Well, it was a huge scandal. And Susannah and Sam were here in Weser, recruiting members for their gang." She looked up at him with a smile. "They couldn't help but hear about it."

"That's how you got recruited?"

"Susannah said we were going to help people. We were going to change things." Dot leaned forward, as though she was about to divulge a secret. "At first, I thought she'd gone crazy. I told her that a flock of moths had flown in her ear and fluttered her brain into lunacy."

"Until . . . ?"

"Until two weeks later, when we sailed from Weser in an echoship we'd stolen from the Songshapers' fleet. My first trip on the *Cavatina*. That's when I knew we were onto something special."

"Well, yeah," Chester said. "When you've stolen a ship worth a thousand times the average annual salary, you know you're onto a good thing."

"It's not about the money, Chester." Dot set her pencil down on the table. "Being part of the Nightfall Gang . . . I'm part of something bigger. Something more important."

"I know, but—"

"We've been to Bremen, to Oranmor, to Leucosia. We've been to the deserts and we've been to the sea. In winter, we went to the northern mountains, where it's cold enough to snow. Can you even imagine it? Real snow, just fluttering down from the sky. I never thought I'd see such a thing." Dot shook her head in wonder. "And everywhere we've gone, we've tried to help people."

There was a long pause.

"The job tomorrow . . . it's everything we've worked for," she said. "It's what we've been practicing for. What we've trained for." Dot looked down at her tattooed hands. When she looked back up at him, her voice was a little shaky. "Tell me, Chester. Tell me honestly. Can you do it?"

Chester hesitated. He pictured himself inside the Conservatorium, his fingers sliding over the strings of the fiddle. He pictured the Songshapers, sharp with judgment, just waiting for him to slip up. He pictured himself floating into the melody, drifting note to note like a ship at sea, until the Song called him and he sank like a wreck into its embrace . . .

"Yeah," he said. "I can do it."

Dot stared at him for a long moment. "You don't have to lie, you know."

"What?"

"You're not the only performer in this gang," Dot said. "Travis does the same thing, in a way. The winks, the vanity, the smarmy comments about his appearance . . ." She looked down at her plate. "It's all just an act, you know."

"So why don't you lecture him about it, then?"

"Because it makes him happy," Dot said simply. "To Travis, it's just a game. It gives rhythm to his life and gives him something to focus on. He wears his bravado like a carnival mask."

"And me?"

"You wear it like a pair of handcuffs."

Chester looked down at his soup. He wanted to change the topic, to steer their chat away from these uncomfortable waters, but he had no idea what to say. Part of him wanted to argue, to deny it, but the polite atmosphere of the restaurant crawled like fingers down his neck and he felt so hopelessly out of his depth . . .

"The audition," Dot said. "Can you do it?"

Convince the world you're strong, he thought for the hundredth time, *and you're halfway to being there.* But he was tired of lying and tired of performing. Dot was right. At this point, a lie would put them all at risk.

Chester released a faltering breath.

"I don't know," he said. "I just . . . I don't know."

And he pictured the fury of the Songshapers, as they raised their guns and pulled the trigger to destroy a blasphemer.

✳

The following day, Chester woke to a churn of nausea.

The gang had booked a suite of rooms in a nearby hotel. He sat by a window and clung to his fiddle case, struck by a vague idea that he should be practicing. Right now, however, he felt more able to produce a pile of vomit than a melody.

The city was hot but his nerves were hotter. By nine o'clock, the air in their hotel room was thick enough to slice and butter. By noon, his breath felt like a fistful of stuffy blankets in his throat.

"You look nervous," Susannah said.

Chester shrugged.

"You should go for a walk," she said. "Get some fresh air. Here," she added, tossing him a pouch of coins. "Go and buy yourself lunch."

Chester wondered if she simply wanted to be rid of him. Even now, a week after the debacle in Thrace, she seemed as stiff as a bow in his presence. But still, he laid Goldenleaf on the table and nodded. "Thanks."

She didn't respond.

As Chester left the suite, he passed Nathaniel Glaucon. The man had fulfilled his end of their deal, meeting them in the hotel lobby. When he had arrived, Chester had fulfilled his promise and returned the flute, which Nathaniel had seized with greedy fingers, as if the weedy little instrument was made of gold. Now Nathaniel sat stiffly in a corner of the living area, fiddling with his flute, a scowl on his lips.

The street outside was hot and dusty. The only relief was the scent of the sea, a salty tang that Chester sucked into his lungs. It seemed to help a little with his nausea.

Chester paced the streets in silence, trying to distract himself with the sights and sounds of the city. A sweet scent wafted from around the corner, where a street vendor sold stewed fruits, spice cakes, plum pudding, and fruit pies. Chester bought an apple from the man, although he still didn't feel like eating.

Step by step, Chester followed the curve of the bay. As he moved from the wealthy west into the poorer eastern district, he began to feel a little more at home. The city here was a network of streets and alleys, which looked as if they had grown organically from the earth itself. It was the sort of place that sprang up strand by strand, like the tangled knots of tumbleweed. Wagons and hay carts rumbled down the widest streets, with a clatter of wheels and the faintest whisper of a melody.

A sweaty cowboy rode past, one hand on the saddle, as he shouted prices for the cattle in his master's herd. "Over in the east market, folks! I got fifty head for a damn good price, rode 'em all the way from Molpeton . . ."

The locals in this part of town weren't aristocrats. They were sailors and carpenters, fishermen and dockworkers. A pair of barmaids strutted out of a saloon, long skirts swishing on the cobbles. A horde of washerwomen bustled down the street, enormous baskets in their arms, while a blacksmith grunted over the bellows in his workshop.

Back home in Thrace, only the affluent districts could afford sorcery. But in Weser, it seemed that even the poorest of folk could fill their lives with Music. Chester heard it in the rattle of the wagons. He tasted it on the breeze, as he stepped between a pair of jangling wind chimes. He touched a glinting street sign and a series of banjo chords twanged into his ears, tingling through his veins.

Even so, these were the cheapest of Musical objects, held together by a lick and a promise—the leftover dregs from the students' training, perhaps, or trash that was tossed into the alleyways behind the Conservatorium. Some of their melodies were slightly off-beat, or badly tuned—and the effects of the Musical objects were therefore not always predictable.

One misshapen sorcery lamp hung above a doorframe, its globe looking more like a puddle than a sphere. When Chester's curiosity drew him close enough to touch it, it blasted out a screech of wild notes and a rush of pain shot through his fingertips.

"Hey, you!" A man threw open the door from inside, a shotgun ready in his grip. His breath stank of corn liquor. "Get the hell off my stoop! You want your damn hand blown off?"

Too late, Chester realized that the man was using the broken lamp to warn him of trespassers on his property. Chester gave an apologetic shrug and stumbled back into the crowd. Although the pain in his fingers ebbed, the encounter left him shaken. He couldn't risk an injury—not today, of all days.

And so, as nervous as ever, Chester slunk back to the gang's suite in the hotel. He didn't speak as he sidled inside, but simply returned to his chair by the window. Nathaniel Glaucon was still in the corner, his expression surly. The rest of the gang was munching bread and cheese, taking turns to recite the plan—apart from a few choice details that weren't suitable for Nathaniel's ears.

After a while, Chester retreated to his room: if he had to hear the rundown one more time, he feared his nerves might physically shatter.

An hour after sundown, he changed into his audition outfit. Travis helped him fold his cuffs, stiffen his collar, and slick back his hair. The suit was uncomfortable and itchy on his limbs. Chester tried to force a confident swagger—as though he were a rich man's heir—but he mostly felt like a child in his father's clothes.

"Hmm." Travis examined his handiwork with a critical frown. "Well, you're hardly the prince of style, but I suppose it'll do. After all, Frederick Yant is supposed to be from Linus. The rigors of fashion in rural towns are less demanding than those in the city."

Chester picked up his suitcase, fingers shaking, and hefted his fiddle case under his arm. Susannah was staring out the window, her spine straight, her back to him. He was vaguely aware of Dot wishing him luck, but her words washed past like the refrain of a forgotten song. His skin felt clammy, although he wasn't sure how much of that was fear and how much was simply the cling of the humid night.

He had left the suite and descended to the hotel lobby when he heard a cry. A whirl of figures passed by, a clatter and chatter of footsteps and voices, porters and guests, clicking boots and clacking tongues. But one voice rose above the crowd and it roped him with all the force of a lasso around his midriff. "Chester, wait!"

It was Susannah.

She stood with one hand upraised, her bloom of red curls and pale eyes stark against the cold black marble of the lobby. They met in the center of the floor, halting abruptly when a yard of marble tiles remained between them.

"Chester," she said, so quietly that he almost lost her words in the noise of the crowd. "I just . . ."

There was a long pause. Chester searched for animosity in her eyes, for a hint of the chill that had defined their relationship since Thrace. But Susannah's mood had shifted, as though the dangers of tonight had somehow shattered the wall between them.

Susannah shook her head. "No matter what happens tonight, I want you to know that . . . that I'm glad we found you. That I'm glad you're on our team."

He stared at her. "Me, too."

Susannah wet her lips, hesitant. "Are . . . are you feeling all right?"

Automatically, Chester opened his mouth to say *yes, of course*. But then he thought of his lies to Susannah in Thrace, his deception. Of how close his dishonesty had brought them to ruin not just in Thrace, but even back in Linus when he had almost connected to the Song during the burglary. He thought of Dot's words as her fingers roamed those piano keys. *I think true strength is admitting when you're vulnerable.*

273

And so, with a deep breath, Chester told her the truth. "No," he said. "I'm not."

"Your music?" she said.

He nodded and lowered his voice even further. "I don't know if I can control it. I kidded myself into thinking Goldenleaf would help, but it hasn't—there's a chance I might connect to the Song."

"Goldenleaf?"

Chester realized he'd never even spoken the name to the gang. Had he been that reverent toward the fiddle? Put that much hope in one instrument?

He gestured to the case under his arm. "My fiddle."

Susannah's face was unreadable.

"I should have told you sooner," Chester said. "I'm sorry."

Susannah gave an odd little twitch. She clasped her hands together before her, knuckles tight, and looked down at the floor. She seemed to be debating with herself, as though there was something else she wanted to say. Finally, she raised her eyes to meet his.

"You know," she said, "I don't know much about music. I don't know anything about flutes or fiddles. My father was a sailor, and he told me that a ship is only as good as its captain. Even when the whole sea's a storm and the waves are high enough to sink you." She paused. "I don't think it's about your instrument, Chester. I think it's about you."

"You're saying I should act more confident?" Chester said. "That I should have more faith in my skills, or something?"

Another pause.

"No, Chester," Susannah said quietly. "I'm saying you should have more faith in *you*."

Chester watched her leave, a lump in his throat. It wasn't until she had disappeared up into a stairwell that he found the strength to turn away.

CHAPTER TWENTY-EIGHT

OUTSIDE, THE CITY WAS DARK.

A massive fountain sat out in front of the Conservatorium. From its base, water spewed from the mouths of a dozen marble fish and pegasi. Above this, the next layer of the fountain rose: arches in the shape of musical symbols—treble clefs, minims, quavers. And above it all there stood a beautiful lady, carved from stone to represent the Song. She held a viola and played light and water high into the air above the square.

Chester stopped for a moment, staring up at the fountain. He could feel the cool of water spray across his skin. He knew it was silly, of course, but the touch was somehow reassuring. As though the Song itself was reaching out and playing a tune to soothe his fears . . .

Don't be stupid, he told himself. *It's just a statue.*

A pair of guards stood at the front of the Conservatorium, resplendent in crimson uniforms. Beside them stood a man in a clerk's uniform, with a finely starched collar and a pencil in his fingers. He was a portly fellow, in his mid- to late thirties, with a scraggly blond beard.

Chester took a deep breath. "My name is Frederick Yant," he said. "I'm here for my audition."

The clerk raised an eyebrow. "You're registered?"

"Yes."

"You've paid the fee?"

"Yes." Chester's throat was dry. "I sent my papers ahead last week."

The clerk pulled a gilded scroll from his pocket then ran down the list of names. He frowned, then nodded as his finger hit Chester's false name. "Proof of identity?"

Chester took a deep breath and handed over his forged birth certificate. The clerk seized it, turning it over in his fingers as though he half-expected a forgery. He held it up to the light, frowned, and nodded.

"All right. Better head in, then." He crossed Chester's name off the list and offered him a tiny silver token. "You'll need this to audition. Don't lose it, or you'll have to reapply next year."

Chester nodded and took the token. It was surprisingly light: a fragile slip of silver paper. He put it in his pocket.

"Thank you," he said. "I'm honored to be here."

And with that, he walked into the Conservatorium.

∗

Susannah stood by the hotel window.

Chester looked so small from here, just a boy clutching his suitcase, lit up by the fountain display. When he moved into the shadows of the Conservatorium, Susannah lost sight of him for a moment. Her fingernails cut into her palms and she felt her body stiffen until he reappeared in the light of the doorway conversing with a group of uniformed figures.

Her insides were tight. She hated how Chester seemed able to twist her emotions, how he could undermine the plans that she had made so carefully, for so many months. Ever since Thrace, he had stirred in her such a violent tumult of feelings that she had barely been able to look at him, let alone hold a private conversation.

There was fury at his foolishness, at nearly getting himself killed and putting her gang in danger. There was horror at the memory of that gunshot and the terrible moment when she thought it had found its mark. Yet above all, there was a quiet pride in how he had claimed the guilt for his mistake. His clear remorse—and his loyalty to Dot—had diluted any final pangs of anger.

Besides, Susannah knew how it felt to yearn for something so desperately that it seemed worth any price.

"How's it going?" Dot said, appearing by her shoulder. "Is he in?"

"Still talking."

There was no hope of making out the words, not from this far away and with the roar of the fountain and the outdoor music and the chattering of diners. But they could see the exchange take place.

Susannah watched as a man examined Chester's papers, then handed him something. "What's . . . ?"

"Audition token." Dot sounded a little tense, as though this scene was bringing back unwelcome memories. "You give it to the judges to show your application was approved."

Susannah felt her fingers unclench a little. "So we're in?"

"Looks like it."

Below, Chester stepped through the doors and into the Conservatorium. Susannah ran a nervous hand through her hair then forced herself to turn away. There was work to be done.

"Right," she said. "Everyone ready?"

The others nodded. Susannah flicked her gaze between them, one by one, to check their preparations. Travis wore a servant's outfit, stolen from the laundry where Conservatorium uniforms were sent for cleaning. He had resisted the urge to spruce it up—apart from the little glass baubles that he had substituted for the buttons on its sleeves. The globe on his left wrist was a hideaway lamp. The one on his right was a signaling globe. Susannah pulled the matching globe from her own pocket and pressed a finger to the glass. There was a flash of warmth on her skin, and Travis gave a little jerk as the glass button heated against his wrist. Unlike a proper communication globe, they could use it for signaling only.

"It's working, Captain," he said, a little irritated. "No need to test it again."

"Don't you trust my inventions, Captain?" Dot said.

"Of course I do," Susannah said. "But I'm not taking any risks, Dot. If anything goes wrong tonight, people could die." She gave Travis one last glance up and down. "Ready?"

He nodded.

"Remember, don't cross the threshold until Chester comes to fetch you," Susannah said. "The security spells will detect you unless an authorized person brings you over the boundary."

Travis nodded. He looked as though he was barely restraining an eye roll, and Susannah bit back her next barrage of warnings. They had gone over the plan a dozen times and her gang members knew what they were doing. If she badgered them over every little detail, they might suspect how terrified she really felt. She had to be strong for them. Fearless. A job like this needed confidence. If the gang let doubt destroy their nerve, they might as well shoot themselves before they began.

"All right," she said. "I'll give you the signal."

Travis nodded. He bade a quick farewell to Dot and Sam before slipping out of the hotel suite and out of sight. Susannah listened to his footsteps on the stairs for a moment, then turned back to the others.

"Dot?" she said. "Are the charges ready?"

"Ready to be laid, Captain."

"Good. Sam, how are you holding up?"

Sam gave a short nod. He held one of Dot's calming lamps, his grip so tight that the glass was on the verge of cracking. Even so, its tune would be a mere whisper in the storm of Sam's mind. The hotel was bright with sorcery lamps, all of which would be blasting emotions into his head. More untamed Music floated up from the square as outdoor lights and the Music of the fountain piped melodies into the night.

By now, Sam would be a riot of conflicting emotions. Susannah's own skull ached at the thought of it. She could only hope that he held it together until this was over. She needed Sam on this job. She needed his strength and she needed his courage.

Nathaniel Glaucon slouched in the corner, chin resting unhappily in his palms. His nautilus pendant hung limply at his throat. Susannah knew he felt just as conflicted as Sam right now—but instead of blaming the effects of Music, the Songshaper could only blame his own choices. He was about to betray the people who had trained him. From his perspective, he would be about to betray the Song itself. It took a serious ego to risk a charge of blasphemy all for the sake of a promotion. But still, the man had made no moves to betray them.

Susannah held up another of Dot's signaling globes. "You remember how this works?"

Nathaniel looked up at her, his expression stained with distaste. "Yes."

"When we signal you, you make your report. Not a minute earlier. Understood?"

He hesitated. "I . . ."

"If you screw up our plan," Susannah said sharply, "the Conservatorium Songshapers will get to be the heroes. They'll be the ones who stop us, the ones who defeat the Nightfall Gang. You'll just be the oaf who tattled on us. And when we're captured and being interrogated, we'll be sure to tell them that you were in on it.

"But if you work with us tonight, you get to be the hero. And the arrogant fools who left you feeling like a failure your whole life? They're the ones who'll get blamed for our break-in." She let a new intensity enter her voice. "Don't you forget it, Mr. Glaucon. Don't forget why you're here."

There was a long silence. Nathaniel rolled the little glass ball in his palm, his expression stony. Then, with a slow nod, he slipped it into his pocket.

Susannah took a final glance around the room. Somewhere in the depths of that building—just across the square from here—lay a cage in the Hush full of screaming prisoners. A cage she had once been thrust into. A cage she had never wanted to see again.

She remembered the cold, the fear, the pain, and the burning in her eyes as they buckled her down to that laboratory table and *changed* her . . .

This was it. There was no turning back. Susannah had devoted almost a year to planning this heist, to gathering her gang and putting all the pieces into place. To saving the prisoners from their cage. To fulfilling her dream of justice.

And tonight, she would achieve it.

"All right," she said. "Let's go."

CHAPTER TWENTY-NINE

The entrance hall was white.

White stone, white marble. White walls and ceiling, with a grand staircase winding up at the back of the hall. A massive chandelier made of platinum metal, with sorcery lamps on each limb, hung from the ceiling. Their light shone a spectral blue.

Chester's footsteps slapped echoes on the floor, sounding out of place and clumsy in this world of shining silence. He tried to step more regally—the way Travis moved, like an aristocrat—but he knew he wasn't cut out for it. With every step, he winced at the clunk.

At the top of the staircase, he ventured down a corridor. Its walls were a glorious emerald green, lit by lamps of gold. When Chester breathed, he tasted honey-smoke on the air. Faint music called him toward the ornately carved door at its end.

This was it. He had to stride in proudly, to look the part of a wealthy young gentleman. He placed a nervous hand on the door. The wooden carvings were sleek, a cold touch of reality beneath his fingertips. There was no point wishing or regretting. Chester had to face the situation he was in and fight to make the best of it.

Frederick Yant, he told himself. *You're Frederick Yant and you belong here.* He stepped inside.

The audition hall was not what he had expected. The circular room had the same aroma of honey-smoke, only more intense. He had entered at the ground level. Looking up he could see seats looped on a high platform, surrounding a shallow pit of gleaming wood. If he squinted, Chester could make out silhouetted figures through the smoke. His stomach knotted. *Songshapers.* They must be the Conservatorium's teachers, here to judge the auditions.

A round stage coiled in the center of the pit. A young woman, perhaps four years older than Chester, stood on the stage. Her hair fell in silver-blonde ringlets, as pale as winter sky, and she held a flute to her lips. The tune that escaped was light and carefree, like a breath of wind among the fields.

Then suddenly, it changed. It was not the wind but a storm, a torrent of rain, a cry of crumpled roofs and screaming children. Chester heard the story in the music. The terror. The crack of lightning. The whip and the whistle of rain. The music grew louder, louder, whipping up into a frenzy of notes and fear and panic.

Chester's breath caught in his throat and he clutched his fiddle case to his chest. The woman was good. Too good. If this was the standard expected of those here to audition . . .

The smoke changed. Its scent of honey faded and a stink of coal and fumes and charcoal blasted into Chester's mouth. The room turned dark and his skin felt as though a thousand tiny sparks were crawling across its surface. Was she even *allowed* to play Music like this? No one had tried to stop her; perhaps she came from a family of Songshapers. So long as she didn't touch the Song itself . . .

In the air above the stage, a bolt of lightning flashed. Chester jerked back. The room was bathed in sudden light and just for a moment, he saw the faces of the Songshapers sitting high up in the stands. Dark eyes and cold mouths, twisted into unreadable lines. Then the flash faded, and they were gone.

The young woman lowered her flute. The Music stopped. There was a long silence, and the smoke began to clear.

Chester exhaled. As the smoke faded, the rest of the room grew clearer and shapes materialized out of the gray. He wasn't the only spectator watching from ground level; a dozen or so other teenagers stood on the far side of the pit. Clutching their music books and instruments, they looked as pale and startled as Chester felt. These had to be his fellow applicants. One or two began to clap but shut up hastily when there was no sign that the Songshapers overhead would join their applause.

"Thank you, Bethany," said a voice from overhead. "You may leave."

The young woman gave a neat little curtsy before turning away. On her way out, she passed Chester and raised one perfectly plucked eyebrow at the sight of him. Chester felt his face burn but he didn't look away. He waited until Bethany had passed into the corridor before he scurried forward to join the other applicants.

"Well," said the voice overhead. His voice was neat and crisp, every syllable like a bite of dry cracker. "I hope you all understand why we must be so selective. The power of a Songshaper can't be entrusted to just anybody."

Chester sensed a few muscles clenching in the bodies around him. He felt his own throat go even drier and he licked his lips to moisten them.

"Bethany is a third-year student of Music," said the voice. "She is an example of what you might achieve here, should you have the talent and perseverance to succeed in your studies."

A third-year student. The panic in Chester's stomach lessened a little. So it had been a demonstration, not an audition.

He squinted up at the balcony to see where the voice came from. The smoke of Bethany's Music had mostly cleared now and he could make out the faces of the Songshapers once more. The speaker was a middle-aged man with a beard the color of straw. Dark-rimmed spectacles graced the arch of his nose and he peered down at the applicants through tinted lenses.

"Someone start, then," he said.

A few people shifted their weight. There were a couple of nervous coughs and whispers. No one stepped onto the stage.

"Go on," said the man. "Hurry up. Anybody."

Chester glanced at the others. He had expected a schedule, a list of names, and auditions in order. But instead, there was silence in a sea of anxious breaths that sloshed around him, hot and nervous.

A boy stepped forward.

"Token?"

Trembling a little, the boy held up his silver ticket. Up high on the balcony, a female Songshaper gave a melodic little whistle. The token quivered in the boy's hand. He gasped and released the paper as it twisted from his fingers and floated up and out of his grasp.

Above, the woman's whistle twisted into a quiet tune. A scale of notes danced upward, coaxing the paper toward her. Craning his neck, Chester saw it float up like dust through the air, a twist of flittering silver, until it landed in her outstretched hand.

He realized he was holding his breath and released it. The Songshapers passed the ticket around among themselves, taking note of the boy's name and family. Finally, they nodded and gestured for him to begin.

And so began the auditions. One by one, Chester's companions stepped onto the stage. Some played violin or flute or harpsichord. One boy sang a perfect scale and Chester could see clearly that he'd had operatic training.

The Songshapers made requests occasionally: "Play a chromatic scale," or "Transpose that into F." Some students played perfectly; others blew off notes, or squeaked out a horrific mistake in their timing. Whenever this happened, Chester saw the attitudes change in the Songshapers above. Their mouths tightened. Their eyes hardened.

The minutes wore on. The group dwindled. When each audition drew to a close, Chester dug his fingernails into his palms. Finally, he knew he couldn't put it off any longer. This audition was only the start of tonight's plan and he couldn't waste hours on the sidelines. He dropped his suitcase to the floor and stepped forward, fingers wrapped around his fiddle case.

"Token?" The woman sounded almost bored now, as though the night had dragged on long enough already.

Chester fished the silver scrap from his pocket and offered it up, trying to hide the tremble in his fingers. The Songshaper whistled her summoning melody and the token floated up into her outstretched palm.

"Very well, Mr. Yant," she said, a moment later. "Play me a run of major scales."

Chester took a shaky breath. He tucked his fiddle beneath his chin, raised his bow and began to play. The first note was hesitant, but as soon as it rang out—alive with music, rich with the sound of the instrument he'd helped carve—he felt his fear leave him. *Just another performance.*

He ran his bow along the strings and carved out the scales. C, then G, then D, rising higher and higher as his breath grew tighter in his throat and suddenly there was nothing but the sound and his fingers and the dust-streaked yearning of the air, and—

"Enough," said the woman.

Chester fell silent, halfway through his F scale. He glanced up at her, uncertain. Had he made a mistake?

"Play me something . . . difficult," she said.

Chester blinked. *Difficult?* He cleared his throat. "Do you mean a song, ma'am?"

There was no response from up high, just the arch of staring faces, stern and silent. Their eyes bore down like weights and Chester fought the urge to crumple under their pressure. He cast his mind around—*something difficult, something difficult* . . .

There was only one thing to do.

Chester pressed his bow to the strings. He couldn't afford to lose himself in the music, or fall into the trap that had ensnared him last time. He couldn't afford to show them the truth: that he could already connect to the Song. Because if they found out what he could do—without any legal training—he'd be lucky to live until the end of the chorus.

He cleared his throat again. "'The Nightfall Duet.'"

And he began. The notes fell away, rolling from his strings into the air. He moved his bow like an extension of his fingers—long and lithe, with all the subtle flexibility of human flesh. One note, then the next. With every note, Chester forced his eyes to stay open. He forced reality to stick in his head.

He found himself speeding up, racing ahead from the opening to the verse, from the verse to the chorus . . . Then he heard the Song. It was halfway into the chorus when it happened: the faintest wisp of another tune. Something more, something deeper, awoke in his mind by the frenzy of his own music. He felt it in his fiddle first, then in his fingers, his breath, his limbs. In the curve of the floor and the dust of the air . . .

No!

He forced the sound away and refocused on the music in his fingers. He couldn't let it happen again. He knew the lure of the Song, but as he played, Susannah's final whisper echoed in the back of his mind.

You should have more faith in you.

This wasn't a moment to bluff. It wasn't a moment for false confidence, for lies and bluster, for the clickety-clack of bravado on his tongue. He knew he was nervous. He knew he was afraid. His stomach felt ready to revolt, with the thundering cavalcade of notes and nerves all writhing deep within his belly.

But this tune was part of him. It was *his* tune. His music. His fingers on the bow.

He ignored the lure of the Song and tightened his focus, pulling in his mind to lasso the music in his fingertips. It felt surreal, as though he was half-awake, half-dreaming. The audition room seemed to vanish around him, as dark as the Hush. All he knew was the fiddle, and the bow, and the melody. The Song was a trespasser. It was the tune of the external world and Chester didn't have to heed its call.

The final verse rang true and he pulled his bow from the strings. The last note lingered, long and mellow. Chester realized suddenly that he'd closed his eyes without even meaning to. He blinked, startled at how deeply he had lost himself. But there was no taste of honey on the air and no one was shouting for a pistol, so—

"Thank you," said a man, in the darkness above his head. "That will be all."

Chester took a long, deep breath. He bent to open his fiddle case and laid Goldenleaf down in the velvet folds. He did it gently, as if he was laying a child down to sleep.

Somehow, he had done it. He had kept the Song at bay. He had kept himself alive, and kept the plan in action.

CHAPTER THIRTY

A RED-BEARDED SERVANT WAITED OUTSIDE THE AUDITION ROOM. "This way, sir."

"When do I find out?" Chester said, slightly perturbed at being addressed as "sir." "If I got in, I mean?"

"In a moment, sir," the servant said. "I'm here to lead you to the results room. If you'll step this way . . ."

Chester followed the man down the corridor. Shadows moved in the lamplight around him, tinged by the cold surrealism that had settled on Chester when he had played the duet. He felt as though part of him was still tainted by his near connection to the Song, as though the very air was thrumming at his touch, waiting for him to reach out and seize it. To listen for it and hear its melody.

He shook his head, struggling to clear it.

The results room was small and plush. Leather sofas curved into its corners and a gold-framed painting of an orchestra covered an entire wall. A man sat behind a marble bench, fingers resting on the edges of an enormous wooden tray.

The tray was compartmentalized into two dozen open segments, each containing a small glass bauble. Most of the baubles glowed red while about a third of them glowed green. Chester noticed with a lurch that the last few baubles remained unlit, cold and lifeless in their little nests of wood.

The man glanced up at Chester then picked the first unlit bauble from its tray. "This one is you," he said. "The result hasn't come through yet. They're taking a while to deliberate."

Chester felt his throat tighten. "How will I know if—"

As he spoke, there was a flash of light from the bauble. In the man's fingers, it shone with a strange little spark of gold. Then it faded into a quiet green, the color of leaves in the cornfields.

The man nodded, and slipped the ball back into its compartment. "Congratulations."

"I got in?"

"Yes, lad. You got in."

Chester stared at him. The relief hit him with an almost physical blow. He hadn't failed. He hadn't let the gang down. He hadn't let Susannah down.

He hadn't let his father down.

But the relief was flirting with terror now, and Chester half-suspected terror was leading the dance. Passing his audition was only the first part of tonight's plan. The only thing that counted as a triumph was to survive the night and to flee this city with his father by his side.

"Well?" the man said. "Are you going to take it?"

Chester blinked. He realized that the man was offering him a silver ring. He took it with a nod of thanks, expecting to feel just the lifeless cold of metal.

To his surprise, the metal wasn't cold. As soon as he touched it, Chester felt the Music run up through his veins. It wasn't just the lullaby of a sorcery lamp. It was fast and charged and aching, like a torturous song that would make you dance until your feet bled and your breath faltered. It shivered into his flesh, through the skin of his palm, and Chester fought a sudden urge to hurl it back onto the desk.

"Put it on, lad," said the man.

Chester realized, too late, that the man was watching him closely. He took a quiet breath and forced a smile, trying to hide his reaction. He wasn't supposed to be trained in Songshaping yet, and he wasn't supposed to sense the Music in sorcery objects. If the man knew what a rush he'd felt from touching the ring . . .

He slipped the ring onto his finger. Its Music pulsed around him, brushing against the fingers on either side to send a trio of shivers through his body. Chester gritted his teeth and forced his smile to widen. "What an honor, sir."

The man nodded, relaxing a little. "That's your official student ring, lad. Don't lose it—or sell it—or you'll find yourself out on the streets. We don't give them out lightly."

"Does it have any powers, sir?" Chester said, trying to sound innocent.

The man shook his head. "It's just ornamental. A symbol of what you've achieved—of earning your place in the Conservatorium."

Liar, Chester thought. He felt the Music pulsing up through his skin, his veins. This ring was the entire reason he'd needed to audition for the Conservatorium. It was his ticket to bypass the intruder alarms, his route past the security spells, and his pass into the inner rooms.

It was his ticket to his father.

"Any formal activities tonight, sir?" he said.

The man shook his head. "You're welcome to take refreshments in the hall if you fancy it but most new folks just head up to bed. You've earned a good rest, I'd say."

Chester gave a silent snort. Rest? The only way tonight was likely to prove restful was if a Songshaper blew his head off and his resting was of the eternal variety.

"So it's okay to just go up to bed?" he said.

The man nodded. "Fourth floor for new recruits. Davidson here will point you toward your room." He gestured toward the servant, who gave a neat little bow and beckoned for Chester to follow.

"Thank you, sir."

The man waved a dismissive hand. "Oh, don't thank me, lad. You earned your place here." He gave a tight little smile. "Welcome to the Conservatorium."

*

Susannah dangled from a balcony. Her fingers streamed with cold, her hands burned raw from the weight of her body, and the shadows sloshed a sea of eerie rain.

The balcony protruded from the side of the Conservatorium, stained black by the darkness of the Hush. Echoes congealed in the air around her, swarming in packs around Weser City. Their translucent bodies ebbed and flowed, a pack of ghostly monsters.

"Damn this city," she whispered.

There was too much sorcery in the air. Too much Music, too much magic. Too much runoff and residue, leaking through into the Hush and staining the shadows with sorcery. Ten minutes earlier, she had almost slipped when a solid handhold had dissolved into a gritty, shining powder. Moments after that, a spectral creature had swooped at her face, a vicious rake of claws and molten bronze.

But Susannah had no choice. If she was going to lay these charges, she had to do it in the Hush. She couldn't climb up the Conservatorium walls in the real world: even at night, there were shoppers, diners and shift workers who might spot her silhouette.

She took a deep breath, pulled another charge from her pocket, and pressed it into a crack in the mortar.

"Is that right?" she said, bending her mouth down toward her shoulder.

Two glass communication globes adorned her collar, one transmitting her voice to Dot. She could just glimpse Dot's face from the corner of her eye: a shine of distorted blonde in the glass.

"Move it a brick left," Dot said. "The charges have to be spaced as evenly as possible around the building. If my calculations are right, you're about a foot off target."

"Got it."

Susannah shifted her weight onto her right arm, ignoring the strain in skin and muscles. She sucked back the pain and dug her left fingers into the gap in the mortar, fishing around in the crack until she located the little metal strip and yanked it out. It almost slipped from her grasp, but she swiped with a desperate grab and snatched it between two fingers.

She swore aloud. That was one good thing about working in the Hush. You could make as much noise as you liked, and mostly it was only the Echoes that could hear you.

"Left, you said?"

"Yeah," Dot said. "About the same height, if you can."

Susannah gritted her teeth and edged along the balcony railing, ignoring the burn in her fingertips. She prodded around until she found a slightly crumbling section of mortar around the requisite brick, then shoved the metal charge into the gap. "Better?"

There was a pause, and Susannah guessed that Dot was comparing her blueprint against her sorcery map of Susannah's location.

"Yeah," she said eventually. "That'll have to do, I think. Okay, now the next one goes twenty bricks to your right . . ."

As Susannah clambered along the wall, she fought back a surge of envy for Dot: sequestered in the hotel room, warm and safe with her maps and cocoa. Better than throbbing fingers, dark, and rain.

But if she was honest with herself, Susannah's main discomfort wasn't the climbing. Despite the pain and the fear and the darkness, it made her feel useful. It made her feel alive. No, it wasn't the climb that worried her. It was her own brain, and the countless disasters it was dreaming up. It was the fact that a gaping hole remained at the heart of her plan . . .

Chester.

Her brain seized upon the distraction. Would he have completed his audition yet? Or was he playing right now, pressing his bow to the strings in front of the judges? Was he hitting an off note and receiving his rejection?

Something buzzed against her shoulder. It took her a moment to register that it wasn't Dot's communication globe. It was Chester's.

Susannah stopped swinging and her fingers jolted painfully at this jerk against momentum. She reached up for the next balcony and clambered onto it, releasing her fingers with a litany of hissed curses. This release from her bodyweight made the sting even worse, erasing the numbness to leave only pain.

"Chester?" She unbuttoned the globe from her shoulder and cradled it in her palm, allowing herself a proper view of its contents. "Chester, are you all right?"

It took a few seconds for the image to form. There was a swell of light and a jerk of heat against her palm . . . and there he was. Tanned face, dark hair. Dark eyes staring up at her from the depths of the glass. For a moment, all she could do was stare at him.

"Captain?" he said. "I got in."

Susannah leaned her head back against the wall. Hush-rain fell around her, swirling and cold, its touch as insubstantial as a breath. She clutched the globe tighter and leaned forward again, showing Chester her smile of relief. "Where are you now?"

"I'm in my room," Chester said. "I think I can sneak off without anyone noticing. I told them I was going to make it an early night."

Susannah nodded. "You remember where to let Travis inside?"

"Yeah. I remember."

"He's there now," Susannah said. "You'd better hurry—I don't want him lingering too long around the entrance. People might get suspicious."

"On my way, Captain." Chester hesitated. "Are you all right?"

Susannah couldn't hold back her smile. Her fingers burned, her muscles ached, and Echoes swirled through the night like storm clouds. But their plan was on track, and they were all still alive.

"Yeah," she said. "I'll see you soon. Be careful."

"You, too, Captain."

And then he was gone and Susannah was left with an empty glass bauble in her fingers. She stared at the globe and her mind floated back to what her thoughts had been before the interruption—to the gaping hole in the center of her plan, one that all her tossing and turning and nightmares had proven unable to fill. It was a gap that had originally been filled with Chester's sacrifice, but that option was no longer on the table. She could barely even *think* of it—the cold, calculated horror of her original plan—without a bitter sting of self-loathing.

Yet even with the plan incomplete, they had no choice but to proceed. If they had missed tonight's auditions, they'd have been forced to wait an entire year for the next admission period. It was too late to back out now, too late to delay. The prisoners in the cage wouldn't last another year.

She would think of something. She still had time. When she was down there, in the dark of the Hush, faced with the cage itself . . . *then* she would find the answer. She would spot a loophole, or find another angle, another way to break the Music.

She still had time.

Susannah pinned the globe back to her shoulder, giving it a rough little jerk to ensure it was safely secured. Then she rubbed her hands together, winced at the pain, and launched herself back over the balcony. There was no time to soothe her aches.

She had a pocketful of charges to lay.

CHAPTER THIRTY-ONE

THE CONSERVATORIUM BRIMMED WITH MUSIC.

The red-bearded servant left Chester at the top of the staircase. "Just along this corridor, sir, and take a turn right," he said. "Your room should be the seventh door down. Will you require assistance in—"

"No, thanks," Chester said. "I'll be fine."

The servant nodded, gave a little bow, and finally scuttled off to deal with the other auditionees.

Now that Chester was alone, he allowed himself to revel in the building's flush of Music. When he brushed a hand across the wallpaper, a whisper of warmth buzzed into his skin. When he stepped through an ornate crimson doorframe, he was hit by a scent of smoke, burned butter, and honey. A drumbeat tingled at the back of his skull.

This was where the Songshapers trained. Where they practiced, where they studied, and where—hour after hour, year after year—they carved their craft from their fingertips. After centuries, their Music had left a mark on this building and on every object inside it.

Around the corner, a dozen sorcery lamps dangled along a chain from one end of the corridor to the other. Each was a different color: emerald green, bloody crimson, sea sapphire. As Chester stepped into the glow of each colored shine, a new lick of sorcery played itself into his veins. When he accidentally brushed a lamp of green, he heard a distant gust of wind in the trees and the scent of prairie grass. When he prodded the red, a shock of heat rushed through his limbs. When he touched a lamp of shining blue, his entire body flushed with a chill of water, as though he had plunged into the sea.

And when he retreated, his clothes were as dry as a bone.

Chester's bedroom was small but luxurious. A crimson tapestry covered the wall, depicting the Song: a beautiful lady, woven of pure gold thread. She stood atop a mountain, her arms spread wide, as musical symbols tumbled down from her fingers and glinted with all the shine of sorcery.

After Chester gave his report to Susannah, he opened his suitcase on the bed. Inside lay an assortment of expensive clothes and reams of sheet music: perfectly innocent luggage for a new student to carry. But he brushed all that aside, tossing waistcoats and sonatas onto the bed until the bottom of the case was exposed. Chester ran his fingers along its edges, pressed a little dimpled button in the leather and whistled a quiet run of notes.

The hidden compartment clicked open.

He retrieved the folded servant uniform and began to change as quickly as he could from waistcoat to crimson vest, from silk shirt to cotton. Chester transferred the contents of his pockets to the new outfit, but the only external sign he kept of his status as a student was the ring on his finger.

Servants wore rings, too, though they gave more limited access. Unfortunately, however, servants' rings were bronze, not silver. Hopefully no one would look too closely.

Chester relocked the hidden compartment, bundled his belongings back into the suitcase, and checked himself in the mirror. His dark hair was still slicked down with the oil that Travis had applied to make him look like a cultured aristocrat. Chester ruffled his fingers through his hair, breaking up the clumps and coaxing his hair back into its normal disarray. He was a servant now, not a nobleman. He shouldn't be able to afford such luxuries as hair oil.

When his hair was back to its usual dark rumple, Chester nodded to himself. He was ready. No more putting it off. Travis was waiting for him and for every second he wasted, his friend's risk of exposure increased.

Chester glanced one last time around the room and gave it a silent farewell. His experience of life as a student of the Conservatorium had been very brief.

He swept his fiddle case into his arms, took a deep breath, and slipped back out into the corridor.

*

He found Travis by the building's back door, down in the dark of an alleyway. It took ten minutes of skulking and sneaking to find the place—ducking down corridors, creeping down stairs, and avoiding eye contact with passing servants.

At one point, he had grabbed a doorknob to pass between hallways and it flared beneath his skin with a whisper of forgotten Music. Chester felt a vivid flash of thousands of other hands, over hundreds of years, who had touched this lump of metal. He yanked his hand away, startled.

A couple of servants tried to talk to him but Chester waved them off with an explanation that he was taking his master's violin down to an expert in the city for polishing.

"You working for a new student?" a maid said. "Been sent from home to look after him, eh?"

Chester nodded, trying to look casual. "My master wants to make a good first impression tomorrow, so . . ." He waved the fiddle case in the air to finish his sentence.

"Oh," she said. "Well, it's nice to see some new faces around here."

She gave him a little wink and a giggle then slipped away down the corridor. Chester blinked, stared after her for a moment, then continued on his way, telling himself firmly that the brief flurry of his heart was just the twinge of nerves.

"What took you so long?" Travis said, when Chester reached the doorway. "Honestly, I've been standing here for half an hour; I have to keep ducking behind those piles of trash when I see someone coming. And let me assure you, that trash isn't likely to win the Weser perfumery's Scent of the Year award anytime soon."

"Sorry," Chester said. "I had to wait to get my result . . ."

Travis waved a hand. "Just let me inside, would you? Do you have any idea how hard it's been, watching through the windows as all those pretty maids flounce around—and here I am, dressed perfectly to woo them—while I'm stuck out here in the cold? Pure tragedy, I tell you."

"I'm sure," Chester said.

"Honestly," Travis went on, "the captain should offer me extra compensation for pain and suffering. I was almost at the point of sneaking in myself, security spells be damned."

Chester tucked his fiddle case securely under one arm. With the other, he grabbed Travis's wrist, pressing his flesh against the older boy's own. "Ready?"

"Yes, yes, of course I'm ready. Haven't we already established—"

Chester closed his eyes and focused on the silver ring on his finger. Dot had explained how this ring worked. He knew about the security spells, about the invisible locks on the Conservatorium thresholds.

He just had to figure out the key.

Chester blocked out the night, the chill of the doorway, the smell of garbage. He blocked out the distant clangs and clamors

299

from the kitchen, and the gleam of lamplight on the cobblestones. He tuned out Travis's babbling and let the Music of the metal trickle up his finger. It ran across his skin, into his veins, through the pores and creases of his flesh. He could hear it like a drumbeat, or like the amplification of his own pulse.

Dum, de dum de de, dum, de dum de de . . .

And for a moment—for the briefest of moments—he caught it. It was like trying to catch a butterfly with your fingers: too hesitant and it would flitter away, but too rough and it would be crushed in your palm. He felt his mind wrap around the tune and he let it run through his mind.

He had it.

Chester opened his eyes. "Now!"

They crossed the threshold. As Travis passed from outside into the corridor, there was a faint little twang in the air, like the feeling of reins being pulled too tightly, yanking a horse into a backward jerk.

Chester knew the security spells were registering them, sensing his ring. He ran the tune through his mind, hummed it under his breath, and kept his hand gripped tightly on Travis's skin. He could feel the Music in the ring, and he coaxed it up his arm, and used the tune to push it out through his skin into Travis's . . .

No alarm bells rang. No traps fell from the ceiling, and no guards came running. They were through.

Chester let out a deep sigh, relief as sharp as the night air.

"Thank the Song for that," Travis said, as Chester let go of his wrist. "To be perfectly honest, I was worried there for a moment. Glad to see that our investment in you wasn't entirely a waste."

"Not entirely?"

"Well, your taste in shirts still leaves rather a lot to be desired—but I suppose we can work on that when this job is over."

"More important things to worry about tonight?"

300

"Or rather, more *pressing* things," Travis said, looking smug. "Aha! Do you get it? 'Pressing'—like you press a shirt?"

Chester rolled his eyes but couldn't hold back a smile. "Come on. We have to lay the inner charges."

Chester tried to shake the feeling that they were walking into a trap. He found it hard to concentrate with nothing to distract him from the Music of his ring. He wished he could yank it off—just slip it into his pocket, and make the melody stop churning. But the ring helped him sense when security thresholds were approaching—the rhythm of its Music increased in pace, and its metal burned hot against his skin—so he didn't dare remove it. He gritted his teeth, blinked his eyes, and tried to refocus on the world beyond its tune.

They hurried back along the corridors, mentally following the maps that Dot had drawn for them. Chester yanked Travis back a few times when he sensed a security threshold, and repeated his performance with the ring and its melody. These were terrifying moments: one little slip in the Music and they would be done for. But Chester kept his mind clear and his focus clean, and the melody flittered from his lips like the beating wings of a sparrow. Quiet, rhythmic, natural. His lips tingled at the tune.

The corridors resembled a maze, layering inward in a spiral. They constantly turned left, moving closer to the center of the Conservatorium until plushness of the corridors faded: the deeper into the building they ventured, the sparser the decor grew. No more carpets or tapestries. No scent of perfume on the air or sound of clanging in the kitchen. Just shadow and stone, cold and dark.

And finally, they found what they were looking for.

Travis spotted it first. He grabbed Chester's sleeve and Chester froze, struck by a sudden fear that they were under attack. But the other boy pointed, his eyes narrowed through his spectacles. "Look."

Chester looked. It took him a moment to realize what Travis was pointing at, because the thrum of the ring's melody was so strong in his head. He wrenched it off and pocketed it, breaking its contact with his skin. Then he stood, dizzy for a second, trying to readjust his senses to a silent world.

A shimmer. It was a shimmer on the air, like the heat waves that rose from a hot road in summer.

"The flame wall," Chester whispered.

Dot had warned them about the wall: a barrier of invisible flame, woven from magic. There was a rumor bandied about among students—those with family high in the Songshapers' ranks—that the wall was the ultimate protection, a shield of Music to keep the innermost core of the Conservatorium safe. There were whispers of strange experiments, of ancient secrets, of conspiracies and secret organizations beyond the flames . . .

But Chester didn't need to rely on rumors. Sam and Susannah *knew* what went on beyond the wall. It shielded the cylindrical core of the building, a vast chamber that reached up to the domed roof of the Conservatorium. Chester had no idea what it held in the real world, but he knew what it held in the Hush: a great cage of screaming souls, hundreds of prisoners weeping into metal bars and shadow . . .

Chester put down his fiddle, fished into his pocket and pulled out a dozen tiny metal strips. Dot had designed them herself. She called them "extinguishers," but really they were Musical interference devices. When activated in a loop, they would break the chain of Musical heat that formed the flame wall. It would only last for a moment—just as long as the extinguishers were active—but in that moment they should be able to break through.

At least, that was the theory.

"Dorothy had better be right about this," Travis muttered, as they laid their metal strips in a line along the floor.

302

Chester felt the buzz of Music as he handled each extinguisher, and he marveled for a moment at Dot's abilities. "They should work," he said, sounding more confident than he felt. "I can feel the Music in them. They should counteract the flames—like when you're fighting an Echo, and you play back their song in reverse, or—"

"I know how it's supposed to work," Travis said. "I'm just hoping it actually works like that, instead of turning us all into tomato pudding or something."

"Tomato pudding?"

"You should see what Dorothy dreams up when she's not in the mood for kitchen duty."

They stepped back to inspect the line of extinguishers. Two bodies were needed to jump-start the mechanism, which was why Chester had been forced to sneak Travis inside with him for this part of the plan. He lined up his hands to measure, stepping sideways to check that the metal strips were properly aligned.

"Remember what to hum?" Chester whispered.

"Contrary to popular belief, I'm not a complete idiot," Travis said. "Just because I'm not a musician doesn't mean I can't remember a simple tune."

"Sorry. Just making sure." Chester retrieved his fiddle and stood toward the leftmost end of their line. Travis stepped in the opposite direction, standing at the rightmost edge. They stared at each other, spaced barely two yards apart. The silence stretched.

"Three," Chester said, "two, one."

They hummed. It was a four-note bar, hummed only once: a simple quartet of tones. But Dot had enchanted the extinguishers well, and it was enough. There was a faint buzz in the air, a sudden snap of cold, and for a moment the shimmer in the air before them vanished . . .

Chester and Travis didn't hesitate. They threw themselves over the line of extinguishers, through the blank space of air where the shimmer had been. A moment later the cold was gone and the air was moving again, the extinguishers' energy spent.

They were through.

CHAPTER THIRTY-TWO

CHESTER STARED BACK AT THE FLAME WALL. IT LOOKED THE SAME from this side: a haze of heat in the air, nothing deadly, nothing special. But now, for perhaps the first time in history, an unauthorized intruder stood on its inner side.

Chester felt a slow grin cross his lips. They had done it. He glanced up and down the flame wall, catching its glint in the corners of his eyes. It was all just Music, really, when it came down to it.

He let out a slow breath. "I guess any tune can be tinkered with, if you know what you're doing."

"Remind me to shake Dorothy's hand when we see her," Travis said.

Chester turned to assess what lay before them: the shape of a vast doorway, hewn from a curving wall of stone. They were truly approaching the inner sanctum now.

Chester placed a hand on the stone door. It was cool beneath his fingertips, but there was no sign of a lock. "How do we . . . ?"

Travis shook his head. "Don't look at me. I thought you were the one who was good at Musical lock-picking."

"But I need an actual lock to pick. I can't hear anything . . ."

Chester ran his fingers across the stone again, to be sure. Nothing. There was no sign of Music. No sign of sorcery. Just blank stone. His skin began to tingle.

"No doorknob," he whispered. "No handle. No lock."

They both stared at the door. This wasn't good. They had devoted their planning to crossing the flame wall; it hadn't occurred to them that there might be something as mundane as a door in their way. If they couldn't break through quickly, their timing to meet the others would be thrown out of kilter . . .

"Hurry," Travis whispered, as though sensing his thoughts. "The longer we make the others wait, the more likely they are to be spotted . . ."

"I know."

Chester pressed a palm against the door. He sucked against the back of his teeth, throwing every inch of concentration into the touch of the doorway. Nothing. Just cold stone.

"There has to be a way," he said. "I mean, it's obviously a doorway. But if there's no physical lock, and there's no Musical lock . . ." They stared at each other. "We have to go in through the Hush, don't we?"

Travis gave a slow nod. "I don't see what other answer there could be. If the door doesn't work in the real world, then—"

"—it's designed to work only in the Hush," Chester finished.

He didn't need to speak his fears aloud; he saw the same anxiety written on Travis's face. Susannah had made it clear they were not to enter the Hush until the very last moment. There was too much Music in the Conservatorium. Too much sorcery, leaking through to poison the Hush. There could be Echoes, or sinking floors, or hidden drops into darkness . . .

They dropped to the floor. Chester heard a sharpness in Travis's breath, betraying his tension.

"Three," he whispered, "two, one."

They hummed. The world melted into black.

Chester wrenched his head up, alert for signs of danger. He half-expected to see a hundred Echoes encircling them like a pack of translucent wolves, but he saw nothing but the dark swirl of Hush-rain, as dry as falling leaves.

He glanced up at the door and his body stiffened. The door was gone, replaced by an arch of empty air.

They crossed the threshold into a vast, black room. The inside was mostly invisible, tainted by the mist and rain. Chester strained his eyes through the little bubble of light that surrounded him, but, again, all he could make out was shadow.

He moved forward but as soon as he was inside the room, there was a yank behind his belly button. Chester let out a cry and the room spun violently before color and life flooded back into the world. He blinked and almost slipped backward, slightly stunned by the sudden light.

The real world. They had been yanked out of the Hush, back into the stark white shine of reality. "What . . . ?"

"This room," Travis said, glancing around. "It must be the final protection, to stop people from finding the prisoners. You must not be able to access the Hush in this room unless the security system's shut down."

The room was a vast cylinder that reached all the way up to the top of the building. The space was massive. In Chester's estimate, an entire saloon could fit comfortably inside. It stretched up for four or five stories and was capped by an enormous copper dome. Chester remembered seeing the dome atop the Conservatorium when he'd stood outside; it was odd to think that he was *here*, now, in the belly of the building, staring up at its underside.

There was no sign of life in the room, just vast white walls and a floor of polished marble. On the far side of the room, a round basin was carved into the floor: an artificial pond full of rippling water.

A row of trundle beds arced around the curve of the walls. The bedside tables were littered with strange implements: metal vices, strange knives and contraptions, silver needles, and bags of dripping fluid. And above each bed, a brass pipe protruded from the wall, feeding down into a pair of mechanical earpieces that lay upon the empty pillows.

"So this is where they do it," Chester whispered. "Where they turn people into Silencers."

He thought of Susannah, strapped to one of these beds, screaming as they forced the Music into her ears and the toxins into her veins. He thought of Sam, writhing as the sorcery went wrong and tainted his mind . . .

And he thought of his father.

His father had been here, buckled to one of those beds. Chester tried to imagine how it would feel to be abducted from his home, deep in fever, and dragged through the Hush to this place. To this bed. To this torture.

His stomach churned. He doubled over, fighting the sudden urge to retch.

"Are you all right?" Travis said, alarmed.

Chester clutched his fiddle case tightly, taking a deep breath. He forced himself back up. "Yeah. Sorry. It's just so . . ."

"Awful? Bleak? Depressing?"

"Yeah. That."

"Come on." Travis sounded shaken. "The others are counting on us."

Chester nodded, but it took all his effort to pull his gaze away. He glanced up at the ceiling once more, at the copper dome, so deceptively calm in its metallic gleam. There wasn't time to reflect on the horrors of this chamber. Susannah, Dot, and Sam were waiting to break through, but he and Travis still hadn't laid their charges underneath.

He wrenched his gaze down to the floor, where a ring of rough stone tiles hugged the wall. The rest of the floor was smooth marble. Did he dare step out onto the marble? It looked solid, unlike the glass in Yant's shattervault . . . But surely the Conservatorium would be better protected than a sugar baron's house . . .

"There must be a trap," he said. "It's too easy."

They both stared at the empty floor.

"Maybe there's a pattern in the marble tiles," Chester added. "You know: you can only step on certain ones, or . . ."

Travis shook his head. "I doubt it. If Songshapers are bustling around doing experiments on the prisoners in those beds, wouldn't they want to know that they can trust their own feet?"

"Well," Chester said, "maybe you need special boots. Or a ring with higher level permission spells built in."

He glanced down at the student ring on his finger, shining silver. Had the judges at his audition worn silver rings, too, or had theirs been made of a different metal? Gold, perhaps? He couldn't remember.

"I hope not," Travis said, "or we'll be stuck here for a very long time."

Chester realized that he was right. Retreat was no longer an option. The only way to pass back through the stone door was in the Hush—and the security systems prevented them from entering the Hush inside this room. They were trapped. Either they completed the gang's plan, or they waited here for capture.

"There's got to be something we're missing," Chester said. "Something to keep out intruders who don't know the secret."

He scanned the blank walls, the white tiles. His eyes roamed up to the copper domed ceiling then down to the glint of metal instruments beside the beds.

And then he noticed the mirrors. Circular sheets of glass and metal barely a foot in diameter adorned the walls above each bed. "What are those for?"

Travis shook his head. "No idea, I'm afraid. I wish Dot was here—she'd spot a mechanical trap in a jiffy."

Chester risked a hesitant step to the side, a little closer to the nearest bed. He studied the mirror with suspicious eyes. There was nothing outwardly dangerous about it. It was a circle of glass, no more deadly than a painting or tapestry. But every mirror pointed to the center of the room, as though their reflections might meet at some invisible point.

Chester laid Goldenleaf at his feet and wriggled out of his vest.

"What are you doing?" Travis said.

"Testing something."

Chester pulled off a boot and draped the vest over its end, allowing him to hold out the vest without touching it. Cautiously, he edged a little closer to the bed—and extended the dangling vest in front of the mirror.

It happened so fast that Chester almost dropped the boot. With a screech of sound and scorching heat, beams of light shot from every mirror in the room, blasting into the center where they met in a blazing point.

Chester gaped at the boot in his hand. A trail of smoking fabric hung from it, half-disintegrated by the force and heat of the blast.

"Well," he said weakly, "good thing we checked before we stepped onto the marble."

Travis stared at the smoking vest. "Good thing I didn't lend you one of my quality waistcoats."

Chester shook the charred remains of the vest onto the floor. He waited a moment for his boot to cool then shoved his foot back into its folds. The leather was warm against his toes, but it didn't seem to be at risk of catching fire.

"Look!" Travis said.

Chester looked up and his stomach sank. The light beams that crossed the room had not faded or retracted into the mirrors.

They had begun to move.

The beams roamed up and down, moving and crossing one another at odd angles. Each beam shone out from its mirror in a straight line, but each line moved its destination point from up to down and side to side in a slow-spinning dance of danger. The lines of light swerved and crisscrossed, like ever-changing partners in a silent ballroom.

Beautiful and deadly.

Chester stared. They seemed to be safe on the ring of stone tiles, but they couldn't cross the room. There was no way to predict the path the light beams would take; there was no way to dodge or weave. Beneath the heat of the dancing beams, they would be fried to cinders.

"There has to be a way to turn them off!"

Travis didn't respond. Chester waited a moment, still staring at the lights. "Travis?"

Still nothing.

Chester turned to look at the older boy, confused by his silence. Travis had backed up against the wall, his eyes as wide and white as the marble flooring. His hands were pressed against the wall and he didn't seem to be breathing.

"Travis?" Chester placed a hesitant hand on his shoulder. "Are you all right?"

The older boy nodded but his gaze did not leave the light beams. Inch by inch, his back slid down the wall until he was almost crouching. He watched the beams like a mouse watching a cat, as though he didn't know whether to freeze or run.

"Penelope," he whispered.

Chester stared at him, confused. "What . . . ?"

Travis wet his lips. "My sister, Penelope. The one who vanished—the one they took. I told you she was an inventor."

Chester nodded. "Just like Dot. That's part of the reason they fell in love, wasn't it?"

"Penelope was an artist," Travis whispered. "She didn't invent practical things, like Dot. She invented beautiful things. Musical wallpaper and light displays and enchanted dinnerware for the most fashionable Weser parties . . ."

"What's that got to do with—"

Travis raised a shaky finger, pointing at the beams of light. "She invented those lights. You see the way they move? The way they dance? That was Penelope's last invention—the last thing she showed to me before she vanished. She was so proud; her dancing lights were going to revolutionize ballrooms, she said . . ."

Chester stared out at the light beams. His stomach twisted as he realized what Travis was telling him. "You mean, they stole her invention? Twisted it into some kind of killing machine?"

"My sister's lights were beautiful," Travis said. "They were designed to feel like cobwebs when they touched you; soft and fragile and shining."

His eyes hardened behind his spectacles, melting slowly from shock to fury. "But these *people* . . . It wasn't enough for them just to take Penelope. They had to take her greatest triumph and poison it and turn her lights into weapons that burn people's flesh."

There was a long silence.

Travis slid back up the wall, jerking up onto his feet. "Well," he said. "They didn't predict one thing."

"What?"

"My sister showed me how to work the light beams." Travis clenched his fists. "And I know how to shut them down."

CHAPTER THIRTY-THREE

THE SKIN OF THE DOME WAS COLD AND GRITTY. SUSANNAH RAN HER fingers across its shell, searching for a seam in the copper sheeting. She didn't dare risk a sorcery lamp up here on the roof—not when pegasus riders soared high above, riding their mounts through city skies. All she had to work with was moonlight.

The dome wasn't the Conservatorium's only rooftop feature. Pegasus stables looped around her in a circle. The scent of dung mixed with quiet nickering to paint the air with a decidedly equine flavor. Here they were, atop the Conservatorium itself, in Meloral's largest city—yet all Susannah could hear and smell was *horse*. She might as well be back in a country town.

Dot and Sam waited beside her, looking out of place on the rooftop. Dot wrapped her arms around her torso, looking almost defensive, while Sam stood as still as a mountain. Neither had enjoyed the climb up the fire escape; their talents lay in areas other than cat burglary. But Susannah needed them for this job and this was the only route inside.

Her fingers played across the copper and she strained her eyes to pierce the dark. She had expected the dome to feel smooth and cool, an arch of perfect metal. But it felt almost powdery beneath her fingers—a tactile echo of the greenish tinge it took during the daytime, stained by time.

"The others are late," Dot whispered. "They should have contacted us by now."

Susannah nodded but didn't break her concentration. Her fingertips roamed to the right, searching, searching . . .

There! The seam was subtle: a textured line, trailing down the side of the dome. It was a sign of where two sheets of copper had been Musically melded together. A sign of weakness.

"Got the charge?"

Dot nodded, her face barely visible in the dark. She pulled out a ball of something that looked like wire. It was long and thin but glinted in the moonlight. "I made this one longer," she said. "To reach all the way along the joint."

"Good thinking."

Susannah took one end of the wire and unspooled it. She tied it to a bolt at the bottom of the dome's joint then trailed it upward, clambering onto the dome itself—wincing at the quiet little clangs of copper beneath her weight—until the wire ran all the way to the apex.

"Sam," she said, struggling to keep her grip on the powdery metal slope, "can you run it down the other side?"

Sam hurried around to the other side of the dome. He reached up and, stretching his oversized limbs, grabbed the strand of wire she dangled down toward him. He trailed it down the copper slope, right along the opposite seam of the one Susannah had started with, before he knotted its end to another bolt at the base of the dome.

Susannah slipped back down to roof level and dusted off her hands. "Okay," she said. "We're all set, then?"

Dot nodded. "As long as I've calculated the angles right . . ."

"Good," Susannah said. "Well then, I guess we've got to wait for the signal."

As she spoke, a throbbing heat sparked in the communication globe on her shoulder. She yanked it down and clutched it in

314

her palm, swallowing in relief as the light and fog eddied into an image of Chester's face.

"Chester! What's going on down there?"

He gave her an apologetic look. "We've hit a bit of a setback, Captain, but we're working on it. Can you give us a few minutes?"

Susannah glanced around the rooftop. The pegasi were getting nervous, now, confused by the presence of strangers near their stables. They nickered and pawed at the hay. The noise could bring someone out to investigate—and, of course, there was always the risk of an overhead rider glancing down at the roof . . .

"What's the setback?" she said.

"They've built a trap out of light beams—they fry anything that passes in front of them. But Travis says he knows how to switch it off; he's using some of the medical tools to adjust the angles of the mirrors . . ."

"Travis?" Susannah said, startled. "But he doesn't know the first thing about—"

She cut herself off when she caught sight of Dot's face. The blonde girl was pale as the moon, her eyes wide and her lips slightly open. "Dot, what's wrong?"

"Penny," Dot whispered. "She invented a show with beams of light. That's how Travis knows how to deal with it."

Susannah let out a low breath. "All right. Just tell him to hurry up, will you?"

"Will do," Chester said. "Look, Captain, I should be helping him—I'll signal when we've got our charge in place."

Susannah nodded. "Go on, then. Just . . . be careful. Don't get fried."

"Wasn't planning to," Chester said, "but we'll keep it in mind."

He threw her a nervous little grin before the light of the communication globe faded to nothing. Susannah kept her fingers wrapped around the glass for a few seconds, clinging to the remnants of its warmth. Then she pinned it back to her shoulder and forced her face into a neutral expression.

"We might be stuck up here for a little while," she said.

The minutes dragged. The gang melted back into the shadows of the rooftop stables, trying to keep out of sight of any pegasus riders overhead—but their proximity to the stalls sent the horses into a tizzy. The closest beast, a gleaming black stallion, pawed nervously at the door of his stall.

"He can tell we're stressing, I bet," Sam said. "Horses always figure out when something fishy's going on—it's instinct."

"Shhh," Dot whispered, reaching through the wooden bars to stroke the stallion's quivering side. "It's all right, baby. Aren't you beautiful? Don't be scared of us. Shhh . . ."

"Stop hissing at him," Sam said. "He'll think you're a damn snake."

"I wasn't hissing! I was hushing him, like a baby. Isn't that how you calm babies down?"

Sam snorted. "Do I look like a nanny to you?"

"Shut up, both of you," Susannah whispered. "Forget the horse and keep your eyes on the sky. We'll have to do this quickly, as soon as—"

The globe on her shoulder shuddered. She saw the others jump, too, and knew that Chester had sent the signal to all three of them.

The others looked grim now; all hints of silly argument had fled from their eyes. They stared at each other for a long moment and Susannah had a sudden thought that this could be the last time she saw them alive. If anything went wrong with the charges . . .

"You're sure about your math, Dot?"

Dot nodded. "I'm sure, Captain. It should all be lined up properly—as long as Chester and Travis put their charge right underneath the middle of the dome."

"All right then," Susannah said. "Let's go."

They crept out from under the stables' eaves into the central round of the Conservatorium roof. The dome loomed before them, shadowed in the night. Their line of wire glinted along its seams, just waiting for the Music to begin . . .

"Wish we all could've snuck in with Travis," Dot said. "I could've pretended to be a servant, too."

"Too suspicious," Susannah said. "Two servants skulking around together is one thing, but five of us?"

Dot nodded. "I know. And I guess Chester couldn't have pulled us all through the security spells at once with just one ring. Even if he took us one by one, it'd take forever—and just one little slip-up would trigger the alarm . . ." She sighed. "Still, it would've been nice to keep our feet on the ground."

"This job was never going to be *nice*," Susannah said.

She positioned herself at one end of the wire while Sam hurried around to the opposite side. His face was strained, tense with the churn of nearby Music. Dot stood back a little, her arms outstretched, and she closed her eyes to concentrate. Her face strained, as though she was fighting to hear a distant sound, something on the very edges of her hearing that was delicate enough to be washed away by the slightest breeze.

Susannah knew what she was straining for. The Music of the charges. If they wanted enough power to snap the copper's joining magic, they needed a serious tune of interference. Dot was listening for the Musical pattern, to ensure they activated the charges at the strongest point in the melody.

Dot's expression changed and Susannah knew she had found it. She had heard the call of her own Music in the darkness and her mind had latched onto the rhythm of the tune.

"Five," Dot whispered, "four, three, two, one."

Susannah hummed. She had no idea what she was doing, or how the enchantment worked. All she knew was that Dot had taught her what to hum and she was damn well going to hum it. She heard the same notes resonate from Sam's lips on the far side of the dome, and from Dot's as she mentally activated the charges . . .

There was a groan in the metal. Light sizzled along the wire, like captured lightning, white and hot and thin as a fingertip. The copper groaned.

The seam snapped.

It was more dramatic than Susannah had expected. The entire line of metal gave way, splitting one half of the dome from the other. It was like cracking an egg—a vicious smack of sound in her ears—and she winced: what if someone had heard?

But there were no shouts of alarm and no cries from the sky. The city was home to too much general racket: restaurant music, carriages on cobblestones, laughing diners and splashing fountains. In all that whirl and bluster of noise, the crack of the dome would sound like a hiccup in a storm.

Susannah reached out to touch the dome. "You're a genius, Dot."

Dot smiled. "I know that, Captain. Isn't that why you hired me?"

The dome still sat in the same position, but for the enormous crack that had opened along its seam. There wasn't enough room to slip through on the lower parts of the slope—the crack was barely as wide as Susannah's hand. But up on the peak of the dome, where the crack was at its widest, a human body could *just* squeeze through. Even Sam, if he held his breath.

"I'll go first," Susannah whispered, "and set up the pulley system for the rest of you."

The others nodded.

Susannah clambered up the side of the dome, slipping and sliding a little on the copper. She kept as quiet as she could, but still winced at the occasional clank of metal as her boot nails hit the sides.

She reached the top and saw the massive hole open beneath her. Down in the room below, she saw sorcery lamps shining in the dark and—if she squinted hard enough—the shapes of two figures, waiting in the center of a white marbled floor.

Susannah unfastened the rope from where it was tied to her belt and strapped a harness around her torso. She dropped one end of the rope through the hole and received a flash of light from a hideaway lamp to signal that Chester and Travis had hold of the end. She waited a few moments, knowing they were securing the rope to their own belts to counteract her weight.

She bent down, thrusting her upper body through the crack while her knees remained securely gripped to the outside of the dome. She retrieved a pulley ring from her pocket and pressed it against the inside lip of the dome, where an iron frame ran in lines beneath the copper. Her magnet gripped the iron like a kiss. It was strong enough to hold the pulley in place but she wouldn't yet trust it with her body weight.

Susannah wriggled back out into the open air and nodded at Dot. The blonde girl raised her hands and whistled a quiet little run of notes. The melody was tight and fast; it reminded Susannah of a hammer thwacking in an obstinate nail. Three, four, five bars of melody and Dot's whistle faded away.

"Done," she said. "It should hold for a good hour, at least."

Susannah reached back down under the dome and gave the pulley a tug. It held fast to the sturdy iron frame, secured by the power of Dot's melody.

Time to go.

She fed her end of the rope through the pulley, before securing it to the harness system around her torso. Then, with a deep breath, she slipped the rest of her body through the gap.

There was an almighty jolt. For a moment, Susannah was falling, plunging down toward the marble below. There was nothing but empty air and the terrible upward kick in her stomach . . .

The rope caught.

And then she was swinging, hanging from the rope as it fed through the pulley above her head. She let out a deep breath and tugged on the rope. Then she waved down at Travis and Chester, who were digging in their heels against the marble below.

"Go." Her voice echoed through the empty chamber. "Let me down."

They winched her down slowly, her body dropping a foot or so at a time, jolting down through the airspace of the chamber. Susannah threw out her arms and tightened her core muscles, trying to balance her body and minimize the swinging.

Finally, she reached the bottom. Her boots landed on solid marble and Chester grabbed her arm to steady her. "You all right?"

"Yeah," Susannah said. "I'm fine."

But she wasn't fine. Now that she stood on solid ground, she could see the room around her much more clearly. White floors, pale walls, empty beds. Glinting silver tools and tilted mirrors. She had been here before.

"Captain?" Chester said.

Susannah barely heard him. The air was sharp and hollow in her chest. She was younger. She was screaming, she was writhing and fighting, she was cursing as they buckled her down into that bed and forced those needles under her skin . . .

Chester tightened his grip on her arm. "Susannah?"

The sound of her name jolted her out of it. She was disoriented, her eyes fixed on the bed and the buckles. She took a deep, shuddering breath, and nodded. "Sorry. I'm all right."

She didn't look at him. She didn't look at either of them. She didn't want to see the judgment in their faces—or worse, the pity.

She was supposed to be their captain. She was supposed to be strong.

With another breath, Susannah bent down to fiddle with the harness buckles, pulling the contraption free from her torso. As they hoisted it back up toward the ceiling, ready to lower the others down, she stared up at the sliver of night sky visible through the dome crack.

I survived, she reminded herself. *They didn't beat me.*

They had tortured her, changed her, twisted the natural Music of her body. They had turned her into a Silencer, and they had locked her into a cage. But they hadn't beaten her.

This time, she was here on her own terms.

This time, *she* would beat *them*.

CHAPTER THIRTY-FOUR

FIVE FIGURES STOOD IN THE CENTER OF THE WHITE-FLOORED ROOM. Chester clutched his fiddle case and watched as the others caught their breath. Sam and Dot, fresh from their swing down the rope. Susannah, a mask of careful blankness as she surveyed the room. Travis, his eyes still hard behind his glasses.

Chester had been impressed with Travis's handling of the mirrors. The older boy had used medical tools and trembling fingers to readjust the reflections, manipulating their angles into a careful pattern. Finally, the light beams had vanished and the room had been left in a smoldering haze.

Travis had been forced to use his fingers at one point, twisting a mirror into the exact angle that would interrupt its Musical flow. The edge of the mirror had been sharp and his fingers had bled from the contact, trailing blood across the white of his shirt cuffs. He hadn't seemed to care. In fact, he had wiped his fingers on his vest and forced a smile. "Lucky I had to wear this hideous servants' outfit, eh?"

Dot produced a coil of bandage from her pocket, snipped off a couple of feet, and bound his bleeding hand. As she worked, she glanced up into Travis's eyes. "Was it really Penny's design? The light beams, I mean?"

Travis nodded.

"Well, doesn't that mean she's alive? If they're forcing her to work for them, then—"

322

"Not necessarily . . ." Travis said. "She had plans in her bedroom—blueprints, material lists, patent diagrams . . . I'd say they just stole the plans when they took her."

Dot's face fell. "Oh."

"But that doesn't mean she's dead," Susannah added quickly. "She's probably in the cage, still. And that's why we're here, remember? To break everyone out of the cage?"

Dot looked unusually serious now, with a wistful distance in her eyes. She cast her gaze across the room—at the beds, the equipment, the mirrors—and her expression hardened. "Yeah, you're right. We're going to get them out."

There was a pause.

"So where's the cage?" Chester said.

"Here," Susannah said. "Right here, but in the Hush."

Chester stared at her. "But we can't get into the Hush from this room! It's blocked off—the security spells . . ."

Susannah gave him a grim smile and pulled a signaling globe from her pocket. She pinched it carefully between two fingers. "Ready?"

It took a moment for Chester to realize what she meant. Only one person could be holding the matched pair of that globe.

Nathaniel Glaucon.

Susannah closed her fist around the globe. There was a flash of light between her fingers. Chester stared at her hand, stomach churning. Somewhere in this building, Nathaniel's matching globe would be flashing. He would run to the Head Songshaper's chambers, report an emergency, and . . .

"The Conservatorium's got an emergency shutdown system," Susannah said. "It locks the building externally, so that no one can get in or out. But it also shuts down the internal Musical boundaries so Songshapers can reach the scene of the crime more quickly." Her smile tightened. "And it will shut down the Hush blocker in this room."

Chester gaped at her. He had known that Nathaniel would be reporting them at some stage . . . But *this*? Setting off the alarm *before* they'd rescued the prisoners? Their chances had been slim before, but were definitely worse now. How were they supposed to make it out of here alive, with countless prisoners to care for and dozens of Songshapers on their trail?

Susannah caught his look. "It's the only way, Chester. We've been planning this for months—there's no other way to shut down the blocking spell."

Chester glanced at the others. None of them looked surprised.

"You all knew?" he said, his voice a little hoarse. "No one thought it'd be a good idea to warn me?"

Dot gave him an apologetic look. "Well, we didn't know you at first and we didn't want you chickening out on us."

Chester felt sick. "I thought I could trust you."

Dot looked taken aback. "Of course you can trust us! It was just a little . . ."

"You're the one who told me to be honest!"

"I told you not to lie to *yourself*," Dot said. "To be honest with *yourself*—to stop pretending to be someone you're not. And until we knew you were reliable, we couldn't risk . . ." She trailed off. "Chester, we told you the truth about everything else. I swear it."

Chester wanted to believe her. Her eyes were honest and she looked genuinely shocked at the idea that he might consider this a serious breach of trust. Had she just made an honest mistake of judgment? Or was she still lying?

"I swear," Dot said again, her voice quiet. "I swear you know everything I do."

And despite himself, Chester believed her.

He looked at the others. Travis was still tidying up the bandage that Dot had wrapped around his hand and didn't seem to be listening. But when he looked at Susannah, she was gazing down at her feet. Only Sam met his eyes. Shadowed and stone-faced under his cowboy hat, the older boy looked as weathered as the dome above.

"Chester," he said slowly, "there's something else we gotta tell—"

A high-pitched wail cut him off, slicing the air like Penelope's light beams had. But the wail wasn't made of light; it was a wave of rippling sound, harsh and discordant, and Chester dropped to his knees with his hands over his ears. He caught a glimpse of the others doing likewise before he scrunched his eyes shut. His very pupils seemed to burn with the sting of the sound.

He doubled over, face pressed down onto his thighs, and curled his body as small as it could go. Some animal instinct screamed that he must shrink himself, he must hide, he must shield his face and hands and chest from the agony . . .

And then it was gone.

There was a long moment of silence. Chester heard nothing but the haggard rasp of his own breath and the gasps of those around him. He forced his eyes open and slowly uncurled his limbs. "What . . . ?"

Susannah glanced around the room. "It must've been the alarm. They're activating the security shutdown—come on!"

They all pressed their palms to the floor. Susannah placed one hand on the floor and the other on Dot's shoulder. Chester closed his eyes and clenched his fiddle under his arm, struggling to subdue the crash of emotions in his chest. The Songshapers were coming. The others had lied to him. And Sam still had one more secret . . .

"Three," Susannah said, "two, one!"

They hummed the notes. The air lashed out and Chester's breath turned cold.

And when he opened his eyes again, he stared into a swirl of darkness.

CHAPTER THIRTY-FIVE

THE HUSH STRETCHED OUT BEFORE HIM, BLACK AND COLD. THE LASH of dry rain, the whirl of mist and shadow. Chester breathed in its chill and let the bitter taste slip back across his tongue and teeth.

"Watch your step," Susannah said. "This is the most Musical building in the country. I bet the Hush'll be twisted here in all sorts of deadly ways."

"Starlight and shadows." Dot sounded distant, almost dream-like. She raised a hand and brushed it through the air, a peculiar look in her eyes. "I had a theory, once, that the Hush was more than leakage. That it was a layer, a trick, a dream . . ."

Her voice trailed off and her hand brushed silent air.

"A nightmare, more like it," Susannah said. "Now come on—I'm sorry, Dot, but we haven't got time for theories. Follow me."

She strode forward, a hideaway lamp shining in the palm of her hand. Chester followed. His insides were still churning from shock at discovering their plan, but he forced his emotions to the back of his throat. All he could think about now was survival.

"You've been here before, Captain," he said. "Don't you know what traps we'll run into?"

Susannah shook her head, looking grim. "These aren't permanent traps set by the Songshapers. They're just surges of

Music—side effects of the magical leakage. It all depends on what Music's leaked through recently. There's no way to predict it."

Chester nodded. He drew his own hideaway lamp from his pocket and the others echoed his movement. Soon they all clutched sparks of light: five tiny fireflies, flickering in a swarm as their fingers shifted. It made little difference to the dark of the Hush: even with the globe in his hand, Chester could barely see two yards through the black. But it was better than nothing and it helped him feel a little safer.

At least, until he heard the scream.

He whirled around, his ears registering the voice in a panic. Dot. It was Dot. Her arms and legs were splayed backward, pinned out against the limbs of a shadowed tree.

Chester reeled. *A tree?* There were no trees in the Conservatorium . . .

But it wasn't solid. The tree didn't loom with the heavy weight of bark and wood and ringed years inside a groaning trunk. It flickered. It shifted. It was made of shadow, darker even than the air around them, and its branches moved like water through the air. Leaves and twigs reached around Dot's limbs and she screamed again as the darkness stretched her.

"In the name of the Song . . ." Travis whispered.

A moment later they were on her. Sam and Susannah grabbed at Dot's arms, struggling to pull her free, but she only screamed more and sobbed as the magic pulled at her, stretched her, abused her body like it was a piece of taffy. Travis hacked at the tree with his signaling globe—forgetting that it was fragile glass—but it floated through the trunk as though it was made of smoke.

Chester tried to help, thrusting his hands into the shadow, but he quickly yanked them back. His flesh felt as though it was boiling in a surge of heat and light and agony. But in that brief instant, that second of contact between his hand and the tree, he heard it. He heard the Music of the tree, distorted and twisted like a jolting nursery rhyme being played by a broken-down music box.

The others were still screaming, fighting, pulling. Dot's head lolled forward as she sobbed and Chester realized for the first time that she was trying to hum a tune through her pain. She was fighting to save herself. Her sobs and cries came in a strange rhythm, which she fought to work in opposition to the quaver of the tree's melody—but her voice was too shattered, and her notes too shaky.

Chester dropped to his knees and wrenched open his fiddle case. Goldenleaf came up into his arms and he rested it beneath his chin and pressed his bow to the strings, so quick and desperate that he didn't even think to tune it. If one of the strings was out of tune, he would have to work around it. He had no choice.

With a quavering breath of his own, Chester began to play. He started on the last bar of the tree's four-bar melody and ran it backward, trickling back into the third bar, the second, the first. He could barely hear his music over the screams, the whipping, the thrashing and cursing, but he pressed on, the world a whirl of rain and pain and darkness.

His melody leaped up from the strings, almost alive, and he felt a hum of heat through his fingers as it melted from music to Music. It filtered through the air until it hit the shadowed trunk of the tree. The Music lodged there, curling around the trunk like a woodchopper's blade. Chester stared through the blackness, eyes straining as he opened them wide, trying to let his pupils drink in any smidgen of light they could scavenge.

And in that grayish light, he saw the tree fall.

It seemed to happen in slow motion. The trunk leaned a little to one side, creaking under the weight of his Music. Then it began to unravel. It groaned and it bent farther sideways, its limbs unknotting from around Dot like a ball of twine. Its shadows twisted from tree limbs into ribbons then collapsed to the ground like a nest of writhing snakes . . .

Dot fell to the ground with a cry. The others rushed to surround her, pulled her up into their arms and urged her to breathe. But Chester kept his focus on his fiddle and the Music. He played on and on, coaxing another four bars from his strings, until those slithering snakes had faded completely into the black of the Hush.

Then, and only then, did he fall silent.

Dot groaned in Susannah's arms; she was frail and shaking and looked as small as a child. But her fingers moved and her eyes were alive, and she staggered back onto her feet.

" 'M all right," she murmured, her voice almost swallowed by the Hush-rain. " 'M all right."

Chester took one of her arms and Susannah took the other. Together they supported Dot, helping her limp forward into the dark. Every step drew from her a sharp little intake of breath, as though her muscles burned with every stretch and retraction. But she gritted her teeth and staggered onward, and Chester felt a surge of admiration for her. Dot might *look* like a little blonde pixie, but by the Song, she was tough.

"Look," Travis whispered. "Up ahead."

Chester looked. The edge of their light bubble was brushing something different now, and it solidified as he took another step forward. His throat tightened.

Bars. Tall metal bars, stretching like corn stalks into the dark. And around the bars, fingers. White fingers. Brown fingers. Fingers in the tattered remains of gloves. Fingers with wedding rings, and fingers covered in scars. All desperate, all grasping. A snippet of the souls trapped beyond, as they clawed at the bars on the outside of their cage.

As the gang ventured closer to the cage, their circles of light lurched to encompass more of the bodies within it. They weren't just hands now. They were arms, torsos, shoulders. Faces. Starved and weathered, lined with wrinkles and cries and screams that refused to sound from their muted throats. Some had scratched at their eyes and others had torn chunks from their hair. Scars on their scalps and blood on their cheeks and—

"It's so quiet," Chester whispered.

Somehow that was the most disturbing thing of all. Here they were, barely a yard from the cage—one more step and he would be able to touch the prisoners' grasping hands—and yet there was no sound. No cries, no moans, no screams for help.

Just . . . hush.

"Their voices are gone," Susannah said. Her own voice was hoarse, almost stunned. "I forgot. I forgot what they do to you . . ."

"But you've got a voice!" Chester said, desperate. Was his father in there, trapped in that writhing mess of hands and bodies? Was his father doomed to be mute forever?

"They've been in the Hush for too long," Susannah said. "Weeks, for most of them, or months. Maybe even longer." She took a shuddering breath. "That's why we never stay in the Hush for more than a few days at a time. There's too much Musical pollution. The air is twisted, tainted. It does things to you . . . to your body. To your soul."

"But they'll get better, right? Once they've had some time back in the real world?"

"I think so." She paused. "I mean . . . Yes. Of course they will."

Chester stared into the morass of hands and bars and his stomach twisted. He wished Susannah's voice had sounded as certain as the words she produced with it.

Then he noticed something odd. The prison bars were spaced at least a foot apart—it was plenty of space for a body to squeeze through. "Why don't they leave? Why don't they slip through the bars?"

"The real trap isn't the bars." Susannah sounded strange now, her voice wound tight with some unknown fear. "It's the Music. It runs between the bars and it holds back anyone who can't hear it. You have to touch it, connect with its rhythm, to pass between the bars—that's how the Songshapers get in and out. But these people . . ." She waved at the writhing mass of hands and faces. ". . . they're Silencers now, like me and Sam. Even if they'd all been trained as Songshapers, they still wouldn't hear the melody."

"So how do we break them out? Chester said. "There isn't time to drag them through the Music one by one . . ."

Susannah hesitated. She exchanged a glance with Sam then looked down at her feet. It wasn't just her voice strung into a tight sort of coil, now: there was an odd tenseness to her body language, too. It looked and sounded as though she were about to face a moment she'd been dreading. Chester thought suddenly of Sam's words before they'd stepped into the Hush: *Chester, there's something else we gotta tell* . . .

Sam hadn't been able to finish the sentence, but Chester could guess what word had been coming: *you.* They were keeping something else from him. Another risk. Another secret.

"Chester." Susannah's voice was so quiet that he had to strain to hear it. "We had another plan, to start with. When we were looking for an unlicensed Songshaper, we wanted you for something else, more than just the audition. But . . ."

She took a rickety breath. "But I don't want to do it that way anymore. We're *not* going to do it that way anymore. Not now . . . now that I know you. Now that *we* know you. It means we've got to find another way, without you going into the cage, but I haven't quite come up with another plan—"

Travis grabbed her shoulder. "What do you mean? You never said anything about this—I thought we'd just pick the lock!"

331

"Pick the lock?" Susannah gasped out a raspy laugh, although it was stained more with hysteria than amusement. "Pick the lock? You really thought it'd be that easy?"

There was a muffled shout from the darkness behind them. Chester winced and sensed the indrawn breaths around him as the others did the same. The Songshapers were coming. They were running out of time. He swallowed the roar of wild emotion that was churning in his throat.

"My father's in there! Tell me what to do, and I'll do it!"

Susannah clenched her fists, closed her eyes, and took a deep breath. When she opened her eyes again, they glistened with moisture in the light of her hideaway lamp. She ran a hand through her curls then shook her head. "I saved some of the charges; I thought we could try blasting open the cage—"

"It won't work, Captain," Dot said. "The charges only work on physical targets, like the dome. You can't blow up a melody."

"But your extinguishers worked on the flame wall . . ."

Dot shook her head. "They can quash external manifestations of Music, things like flames or heat. But this is a wall of pure melody, conjured by the best Songshapers in the country. Nothing I've built could erase it."

"All right," Susannah said, sounding desperate. "All right, so we'll just have to trick the Songshapers into unlocking the cage. Quick, hide! I'm going to grab their attention and . . . and . . ."

She faltered, one hand half-raised, as though the darkness itself might drop a solution into her palm.

Chester stared at her for a long moment. Then it hit him. What had she said? *We've got to find another way, without you going into the cage.* Did that mean the cage could be opened from the inside? So there was something in there that could break the Music, something in there that could set the prisoners free . . .

And he alone could reach the key.

Chester knew how to connect to a piece of Music. He could cross the threshold between the bars and enter the cage. Only he could do it. Not Travis, who didn't have a musical bone in his body. Not Susannah or Sam, who were impaired by their status as Silencers—and who had never been Songshapers anyway. Not Dot, whose tattooed hands prevented her from crossing Musical thresholds.

It had to be him.

And if Susannah's plan required someone to go into the cage, he'd damn well do it. He hadn't come this far and survived this much to walk away and leave his father in a world of silent screams.

Behind him, he heard a charge of footsteps as the Songshapers drew near. He heard the shouts, the bangs, the wild firing of pistols.

Before the others could stop him, Chester lunged to touch the cage. The air gave a violent surge, clearly designed to repel him, but he could feel its melody now; it surged through his veins like water and he breathed it in, every muscle shifting in time with its tune.

He could taste it. And he could defy it. There was a single, deliberate flaw in the rhythm—a choke between Musical bars when the melody faltered and a person connected to its tune could force their body through . . .

With a breath like fire, Chester plunged between the bars.

CHAPTER THIRTY-SIX

SHE WAS A MOMENT TOO LATE.

The noise had distracted her—the bangs, the shouts from the dark, the snarls of Songshapers as they hunted their prey. Susannah had whipped her head around to seek out their hunters, but in that moment, she felt the brush of fabric against her arm. She felt the rush of breeze as Chester's body shifted—as it moved from inhabiting the space beside her own, to vanishing. When she whirled back—grasping around her, desperate to pull him back— he was already gone.

Susannah screamed.

She threw herself against the bars and tried to smash her own body through the gap, but it was like trying to float through a solid wall. The space between the bars thrust her backward like an almighty slap and she fell to the ground. Staggering to her feet, she tried again, but again the cage repelled her.

"Come back! Chester, come back! We'll find another way!"

She beat her fists against the bars, again and again, but the Music shoved her violently backward. With every useless punch she swore a litany of curses against her own mistake. Why had she told him? Why had she let the original plan slip from her lips? She had promised herself that they would find another way. They could break down the bars with one of Dot's inventions, perhaps.

Or they could trick the Songshapers into opening the bars for them. Something. *Anything* . . .

Anything but this.

Because Susannah knew what it took to escape from the cage. It wasn't just a matter of climbing up the bars and out of the top—that had been a lie, a desperate lie. It had taken a death for her to break free. And once Chester realized what needed to be done . . .

She glanced from Travis to Dot and for a single moment she hated them. She hated them both for their innocence, for their ignorance. All along, she had fed them a sanitized version of the plan. She hadn't told them the true reason she wanted an unlicensed Songshaper on the team. She hadn't told them that Chester's original role was to sacrifice himself. They had waltzed through the preparation for this job with clean hands and they would walk away with clean consciences.

Not her, though. She and Sam had planned it all.

Inside the cage, the Silencers writhed. They clawed at each other, fighting to reach the bars, their futile hope of escape. Did they guess that a real chance of freedom was coming?

"Chester, come back! Ches—"

Someone thrust her aside. Her head crashed against the floor and the world swam. There was blackness, and shouting, and the sting of shame and horror and—

Susannah took a shuddering breath and raised herself onto her elbows. She blinked, struggling to get a grip on her vision. The world slowly drifted back into focus, looking like a broken shadow-puppet show. Her eyes fixed on her companions. Travis. Dot.

Sam. Where was Sam? She spun around, the movement sending a new surge of dizziness through her veins. She saw him. He gave her one last look. One last glint of pale blue. And then he was gone, following Chester into the maelstrom of bodies behind the bars.

"Sam! Sam, come back!"

But her voice was choked now, strained with disbelief. He was a Silencer, like her. He shouldn't be able to slip between the bars. He shouldn't be able to . . .

"He can hear the Music," whispered Dot. Her face was paler than ever and her eyes were red with shocked tears. "I can't believe I didn't see it before. They messed up his transformation—that's why he's so affected by Music, why it changes his emotions." She stared into the dark of the cage. "He's not a proper Silencer. He's . . . something else."

And suddenly, Susannah thought of Sam's words in the driver's cabin. The memory jolted back, so sharp that it hurt. Sam's fingers on the wheel as he plunged the *Cavatina* into the dark. The pain in his eyes. The resolution in his voice.

It's getting worse . . . Every day it hurts a bit more . . . I can still feel it in my head. All the time. Just the Music, running over and over and over . . . I'm gonna be the one who takes 'em down . . . Whatever it takes.

"Something else?" Susannah knew she sounded hysterical but she couldn't hold back the surge of words. They clattered against the back of her teeth, fighting for release like the souls in the cage. "I don't care what he is—we've got to get him back! We've got to get both of them back!"

Travis grabbed her arm. "Captain!"

She didn't want to see what he was looking at. Didn't want to know. All she could think was that Sam was going to die. He was going to throw his life away, to quash the living hell of Music playing in his brain . . .

But the rest of her gang needed her, and she was still their captain. She wouldn't let them down. So she turned her gaze away from the cage—hating herself with every jolting breath—until her eyes fixed on the darkness ahead. On the Songshapers—and their pistols—at the edge of their circle of light.

"Well, well, well," said their leader. "What a fine place to meet old friends."

It was Nathaniel Glaucon.

*

Chester staggered into the dark. The space between the bars had seemed tight at the time, a cold scrape of metal along his back and his chest. But now, compared to the crush of the crowd, it seemed like nothing. Here, he could barely breathe.

There were bodies everywhere. They pressed around him, hot and heaving and bloody. They scratched at one another, crazed in their desperation to escape the cage. Once they saw him they pushed harder, shoving, shouting silent whispers into one another's ears.

Could they hear one another? Could they hear their comrades' silent screams? All Chester heard was the weight of the silence and the rush of his own panicked breath as he pushed into the fray.

Shoulders battered him; elbows knocked him down. Chester almost fell to his knees but he forced himself—with every inch of strength in his limbs—to stay upright. To fall down here would be to never rise again. He would be trampled, a fallen calf in a buffalo stampede, and he would be a bloodied mess before he died.

He pushed on.

Every step was torture. A hand swiped dangerously close to his eyes. A woman gouged a bloody gash into his side and he swore at her, shoving her aside—but there were too many bodies to push her more than a few inches away. For a second he thought she was going to lash out again, to retaliate with another swipe of her gore-flecked fingernails, but then the crowd washed to one side and she was carried away in a tide of flesh.

Was his father here? Was Penelope here? Chester felt a burn of terror in his chest, worse than anything he'd felt since the night of his father's vanishing. He hadn't known it would be like this. He'd thought the cage would be filled with weary prisoners: broken bodies, souls in need of rescuing. Not this. Not this writhing, desperate, animal mass of bodies.

And somewhere in the mass, his father. Would he be cowering on the floor, trampled and broken by the viciousness of his peers? Or would he be one of those clawing and fighting and shouting silent screams?

Chester didn't know. He didn't *want* to know. He just wanted a clear space, a space to breathe, to open up his arms, to feel as though every inch of world wasn't pressing in to smother him.

But Susannah had planned for him to enter this cage. Which meant that here, somewhere, was his key to setting the prisoners free. As Chester staggered forward, his bubble of Hush-light traveled with him. He had lost his hideaway lamp in the crowd—trampled and shattered underfoot, no doubt—and so his only light was the natural sphere of vision that always traveled with him in the Hush. All that he held was his fiddle case, which he clutched desperately against his chest.

Chester pushed onward and something new crept into sight. Something that wasn't floor, that wasn't marble in the real world. Something that rippled. *Water*. A pool of water, black as coal in the darkness.

As he approached, the crowd thinned until Chester staggered out into a haze of empty shadow. He drew a shaky breath, startled by this sudden rush of personal space. Even the Silencers, in their state of writhing desperation, were sane enough to avoid the water.

Chester stopped. He didn't dare allow his own reflection to fall upon its surface. He remembered the night that Sam had taken him to join the others on the *Cavatina*. The way the water's reflection had caught the ship in its grip and how it had tried to drag the vessel down into its mirrored depths . . .

Sam's words came back to him.

Can't trust water in the Hush . . . The ripples, the gurgles, the way it sloshes on the shore—all of that's making a tune . . . It grabs you . . . It drags you down . . .

Chester looked up from the water, his gaze rising to the space above it. High above, at the very edge of his vision, he saw the roof of the cage. Glinting dark silver bars crossing the blackness. Right in the center, above the pool of water, the bars met in an arch of joining lines.

Why was the pond here? And why wasn't it pulling down the bars?

In an instant, Chester knew.

They were counterweights. Opposites. Opposing forces, pushing against one to keep the other in check. It was an ingenious design. The pond and the cage worked like magnets, north poles turned toward each other, strengthening each other with their mutual repulsion. It was how the cage's Music kept running, day after day, month after month, year after year. It pushed against the pond and the pond pushed back, and that clashing energy traveled in an invisible wall between the bars to keep the prisoners in place . . .

But if the water was disturbed . . .

Chester knew what he had to do. He had to touch the water. He had to hear its melody, feel it, sense the ripple of its song and the rhythm of its tune. He had to touch it so that he could reverse it.

But, if he touched it, it would consume him.

Chester tightened his grip around his fiddle case. It was hard and sleek and dug into the flesh above his ribs. Goldenleaf lay tucked inside, waiting to be summoned. Once he touched the pond and sensed its tune, he could play it backward. Unravel the power of its Music, like unraveling an Echo. He could break its connection to the cage's walls and the prisoners could claw their way between the bars . . .

He inched forward. How long would he have, once he touched the water? Would it suck him down right away or would he have time to belt out a few repetitions of its melody as he sank? Once Chester—thrashing and gasping—stopped playing, the water would return to its earlier state of calm and the cage's Musical shield would be reinstated, trapping any remaining prisoners inside its shell.

How long could he give them? How long would it take him to drown? Would playing underwater work? *Could* he still keep playing underwater, while the last breaths in his lungs eddied out into black and bubbles . . . ?

Chester felt sick. He shut down the train of thought and forced himself to take several long, slow breaths. He couldn't do this. He wasn't brave enough. The thought of slowly drowning in that pool, unable to fight the pull of water as it sucked him down into the dark . . .

He wanted to run. He wanted to run and run and never look back.

But there were hundreds of souls in this cage. His father. Penelope. They were here somewhere, caught in a silent scream and a tangle of desperate limbs. They were scratching and clawing— and Chester was the only one who could save them. He imagined Dot ladling soup between Penelope's lips. He imagined Susannah helping to care for his father, nursing him back to health . . .

Susannah. The thought hit him hard, like a kick to the gut. She had planned this all along. She had recruited him, then she had tested him. She had known all along that his role would be to die.

Chester felt almost numb, now, as if a heavy wool blanket had been wrapped around his heart and squeezed. It felt hot and itchy and tight and sore. Susannah had planned for him to die, and she was right. There was no one else who could take his place, no one else who could make it through the bars of the cage, no one else who could reach this pond.

There was no time for goodbyes. No time for emotion. The alarm had been triggered and the Songshapers would surely be closing in on them by now.

Chester crept forward. His limbs were trembling. He pulled Goldenleaf from its case, and pressed the chinrest into his shoulder. He raised his bow. He took a deep breath.

And he lifted his foot, ready to touch the water.

CHAPTER THIRTY-SEVEN

NATHANIEL GLAUCON SMILED. IT WASN'T A COLD SMILE OR A VICIOUS smile. In a way, that made it more chilling. It was benign. So quiet. So . . . pleased.

"What are you doing here?" Susannah's tongue felt like dust. "You were supposed to report us to the Head Songshaper—"

"Oh, I did." Nathaniel took a step forward. The other Songshapers stood behind him, all with dark-cloaked smirks. "I did. And he set off the alarm, like you wanted."

His eyes were bright now, alight with a joke he was going to reveal. "And then he sent for the head of the Hush Initiative. He sent for the man who really plans this nation's future. The man behind the curtain. The man who pulls the puppet strings."

Silence.

"Me."

Susannah stared at him. She watched the word roll off his tongue, but it didn't make sense. Nathaniel Glaucon, head of the Hush Initiative?

"It can't be you!" she said. "I mean, you don't even live in Weser City! You live in Hamelin, of all places!"

Nathaniel cut her off. "I chose to live in Hamelin. I happen to like it there. It was my hometown, once. A long time ago."

There was a pause.

"You see, my dear, you made a terrible mistake. You assumed that a Songshaper living in a tiny town must be a failure. Someone too humdrum to make it in the big city. Someone with no accomplishments, no career, no prospects.

"But you forgot the other reason that a Songshaper might live in a tiny town: because he's a success. He's someone with enough clout and power to live wherever he likes. He's someone with the wealth to buy long-distance communication globes and enough pegasi to travel to and from Weser whenever he pleases. He's someone who hires underlings to do his dirty work. He's someone with a great career and limitless prospects."

He tightened his smile. "He's someone like me."

"You're lying!" Susannah said. "If you're such a high-up Songshaper, why the hell would you let us break into the Conservatorium?"

Nathaniel shrugged. "I was curious. I wanted to see what your plan entailed and what flaws you'd discovered in the Conservatorium's defenses. Nice job on the dome descent, by the way. I shall have to remedy that one. And I'm impressed that you dismantled my light-beam trap. I must admit, I wasn't expecting—"

"You stole it!" Travis shoved himself forward, anger on his face. "You stole that trap from my sister, just like you stole her—"

Nathaniel raised his pistol and Travis froze.

"Ah, ah, ah." Nathaniel wagged the finger on his other hand. "One more step, my boy, and I'll be forced to use this. And that would be such a pity, wouldn't it? I have so many questions to ask you all. So many things to learn."

"You stole my sister!" Travis snapped, breathing heavily. "You stole her away in the middle of the night, and you stole her ideas and turned them into weapons."

"We steal many things," Nathaniel said calmly, "and many people. You can't expect me to remember the identity of every soul we gather up for our mission."

343

"What mission?"

"Why, our mission to keep the Hush populated, of course. Our mission to replenish the supply of Echoes."

Susannah stared at him. "What are you talking—"

And then it hit her. She twisted back around to face the cage. *The cage.* The cage full of writhing bodies, of grasping hands, of silenced throats. The cage full of Silencers, twisted into something less than human, pumped with warped Music and imprisoned for months in the Hush . . .

And she understood. She understood it all.

"The Silencers," she whispered to herself, her throat barely managing to form the syllables. "We're not finished transformations . . . We're just . . . just . . . unfinished Echoes."

Susannah stared at the cage bars. At the grasping hands. *Unfinished Echoes.* The Songshapers were building an army of Echoes. They were stealing people from their beds, sparking the transformation with drugs and melodies, and then somehow letting the Musical toxins of the Hush do the rest.

"That's why we're immune to Echoes," she whispered. "We're half-baked Echoes ourselves."

It all made sense. The truth throbbed; a pulse of terrible realization in her brain. Echoes were people. They were all just people who'd been taken and twisted and driven insane by the Songshapers' schemes.

She looked up at Nathaniel. "But how . . . ?"

"Oh, the process is simple," Nathaniel said quietly. "We take a man and we impregnate him with a melody. A melody of control. The tune is only a seed, at first; it hasn't yet germinated. At this stage, he is what we call a Silencer. He still retains his mind, his memories, his free will."

"Then we lock him down here in the Hush. The tune inside him will slowly germinate, nurtured by the twisted Musical pollution of the air. As long as he never leaves the Hush, the melody inside will awaken. Little by little, day by day. The melody prevents him from connecting to other Music—even if he has studied Songshaping—so he cannot escape the cage."

Susannah could not breathe.

"Eventually," Nathaniel said, "the man will lose himself. His natural qualities will remain intact—strength, courage, resilience—but he will use them on our behalf, not his own. He will forget his past, his future. He will forget everything but the tune in his veins. The Music inside him will grow and strengthen, gradually hijacking his mind and body, until nothing is left but a hazy ghost of humanity.

"Finally, when his mind is gone, he will regain the power to detect other melodies. He will not only detect them, but he will crave them, just as a starving man craves nourishment. He will drift out between the bars of the cage, hungry for a new source of Musical energy. He is now an Echo. He is a slave, ready to roam the Hush on our behalf."

"But why?" Susannah's voice was hoarse. "Why would you—"

Nathaniel took a step toward her. He didn't lower his gun. "Ah, now—that's the question you should have been asking all along, isn't it? Not so clever as you think you are. Not so clever by half."

Susannah could sense Dot and Travis on either side of her. The entire world seemed to take a giant breath, teetering on a precipice, as she waited for more horror to unfold.

Part of her wanted to leap forward, to throw herself onto Nathaniel and tackle him now, to shut him up, to stop him from revealing whatever terrible gloat was about to drop from his lips. Because she could tell from the twist in his smile that it wasn't good. Part of her didn't want to know.

But the rest of her—the part of her that had propelled her on this mission to form the Nightfall Gang, to fight back against the cruelty of the Songshapers, to release the Silencers—that part of her burned for the truth. It hungered for knowledge, for answers. For the reason this had been done to her.

So she took a deep breath and forced her feet to stay steady. "Why do you care about making Echoes?" she said. "The Songshapers are more powerful than the government! You've already got power in the real world—you don't need the Hush to—"

"The real world?" Nathaniel's lip curled up higher, revealing his teeth. "Ah. That's an interesting label, isn't it? The thing about reality, my dear, is that it's all so relative."

"What do you—"

Nathaniel's teeth were white as lightning. "What if I told you that the *real* world is the Hush?"

✳

A hand grabbed him.

Chester's body was jolted, caught by this tug against momentum as he leaned toward the pond. He jerked backward, startled by the strength in the arm that held his shoulder. Then a thought hit him and he almost couldn't turn around. He was certain that it was him. *His father.* It had to be. His father had found him and saved him and how was Chester supposed to sacrifice himself when his father was standing right—

But when Chester turned, it wasn't his father.

It was Sam.

Chester choked. The pale blue eyes of a Silencer, eerie and shining in the dark. Sam held him so tightly that his fingertips stung against the bone of Chester's shoulder, but the older boy showed no signs of letting go.

"Don't," Sam said.

It was such a simple word. *Don't.* One little syllable. How could one little syllable hold so much meaning?

Chester shook his head. "It's part of the plan . . ."

"No, it ain't. She's back there screaming for you, Chester. She wants you to come back until we figure out something else."

Chester stared at him. "She?"

"The captain."

They met each other's eyes for a moment and Chester had no idea what to say. Susannah had planned this. It was the only way. How could she want to back out now, when they were so close to victory?

"This is her chance for justice," Chester whispered. "This is what she wants."

Sam shook his head slowly. There was a strange expression on his face, a slow kind of weariness that Chester had sometimes glimpsed in his eyes, when the older boy thought no one was watching.

"It's the only way to save my father," Chester said. "And Penelope. And all these other people, too."

"Ain't the only way." Sam's voice sounded gruff now, choked with something left unsaid.

"I've got to disrupt the melody," Chester said. "It's what's holding the cage's Music together. If I can touch the tune, then I can reverse it . . ."

"Don't need a fiddle, then," Sam said. "You're just planning to break the water's tune, ain't you?"

"I guess so," Chester said, "but—"

"Remember when we crashed into that river? Dot said maybe we could just throw in an Echo. A creature with Music inside it." Sam gazed down at the water. "She figured it might be enough— the mixture of its Music and its dying life-force, or something like that."

Chester shrugged, helpless. "Yeah, but we haven't got an Echo to throw in there! There's just me and you."

"I'm a Silencer," Sam said. There was a haunted look in his eyes. "Know what Silencers are? Know what we're really made for?"

Chester felt his heartbeat stammering. He could tell that there was something very wrong in Sam's voice. Another secret? Another revelation?

"No," he whispered. "I don't know."

"Silencers ain't the final product," Sam said. "We're just a step along the way. A half-baked recipe. A work in progress."

A glimmer of understanding brushed the edges of Chester's mind. "No," he whispered. "It can't be . . ."

"A Silencer," Sam said, "is an unfinished Echo."

The glimmer became a shine, then a fire. Chester's brain lit up with too many understandings to bear. It all made sense, a horrible, calculated kind of sense. Silencers were immune to Echoes' touches; in fact, the creatures floated right through them. Silencers were kept in this cage for months and months, in the twisted air of the Hush, as if they were seeds being kept in a greenhouse to develop . . .

"No," he said. "It can't be."

But it was. He knew it now, as sure as he knew his own breathing. Susannah was halfway to being an Echo. His *father* was halfway to being an Echo. Penelope was halfway to being an Echo, alongside all the other half-mad souls that clawed their way through the thick of the cage. Their voices were gone, their minds were being twisted, their memories were slowly fading . . .

All the Echoes he'd encountered on his journey through Meloral—the one he'd killed on his first night in Sam's echoboat, the ones he'd fought in Yant's vault—they had been *people*, once. Vanished people, turned into monsters by the Songshapers . . .

"Why? What do they make them for?"

Sam shook his head. "Don't know." He was staring at the pond now, at its quiet ripples, at its sheen. His fingers flexed on Chester's shoulder and a new twinge of pain ran up Chester's collarbone.

"I only know 'cause I heard 'em talking when they chucked me onto death row," Sam said. "After they stuffed me up with their experiments, they figured I'd never end up a proper Echo so they might as well be rid of me. And since they were getting rid of me, they didn't figure I'd live to spill their secrets. I did live—but I never told a soul. Not even Susannah. Figured she'd be happier not knowing what she really was."

"But you're not a full Echo," Chester said, breathless. "It's just the start of the process—you're still human, mostly . . ."

"Maybe," Sam said. "Maybe not. Either way, they put a melody in me. It ain't properly developed, yet, but it's there. It whips me 'round like a damn lasso. It fills up my head with . . . with fear, or hate, or happiness, or fury—all just from hearing a bit of Music . . ."

Sam sucked down a breath. "I ain't even sure what I am anymore. I feel like . . . like a bull at a rodeo, all roped down and trembling in the dust. Nothing left but the whip." His voice cracked. "But I know one thing for sure. I'm gonna make the bastards pay for what they done to me."

Chester stared into Sam's pale eyes. For the first time, he saw not just anger but pain. Anguish. Chester and Travis weren't the only members of the Nightfall Gang to have put on a false show of strength.

And with a terrible rush he realized what Sam was about to do. "No! No, Sam you can't—"

Sam shoved him backward, so violently that Chester crashed against the floor. He struggled back up and launched forward to try to snatch a fistful of Sam's shirt. But Sam's headstart had been too much, and Chester's fingers were still inches from—

Sam hit the water.

The splash was a roar. The moment seemed to freeze in front of Chester: the strangled cry, the wild determination in Sam's eyes. Chester had one last glimpse of Sam's face, those ghostly blue eyes, the scars, the stubble, and a final cry from his mouth as the black smoke rose around him, engorged him . . .

The air gave an almighty yank and hurled Chester backward again. He heard the clatter of bodies as hundreds of prisoners staggered sideways, tossed violently in the cage. He knew they would be shouting, screaming, but their silent lips held back the sound.

The cage that held them flashed a hot, violent white. Its bars lit up like a broken sorcery lamp and for a moment Chester saw everything. Then the scene unfolded in staccato jerks as bodies poured between the bars, shoving out into the darkness beyond the cage . . .

"Sam!"

Chester forced himself onto his knees, reaching forward. If he could just grab the boy's disappearing hand, if he could drag him back out onto the Hush-blackened floor . . .

Flickering light shot down from the top of the cage. It sizzled like lightning, a tongue in the air, and hit the pond with a crash louder than a gunshot. The pond exploded with sorcery and Chester was slammed backward a third time. He rolled to the side, gasping and cursing and forced himself back up onto shaking knees. He caught a final glimpse of Sam's hand—charred, broken, and unmistakably dead—before it vanished beneath the sheen of the water.

Chester stared at the pond. It was still sloshing, still electrified. He knew it was too late to rescue his friend. Even if he threw himself in after Sam—even if he fought the Music and managed to drag him out—the boy was already dead.

Chester felt a cry rise in his chest and he fought it down. He clenched his fists so hard that his fingernails left bloody marks in his palms.

Later, he told himself. Later, he could fall to pieces. Later, he could deal with the horrors of the cage, with Sam's sacrifice, with the fact that Susannah had betrayed him. For now, he had to hold himself together and do what he could for the rest of his gang.

CHAPTER THIRTY-EIGHT

Susannah was still struggling to process what Nathaniel had just told her. The *Hush* was the real world? But that meant Meloral was . . .

"It's a grand piece of Music," Nathaniel said. "The greatest symphony ever performed. Isn't that what music is, after all? Conjuring emotion out of sound. Conjuring stories from the air. Well, why not increase the scale? Why not conjure a whole world out of the air?"

Susannah stared at him. She opened her mouth to argue, to deny it. But her mouth was so dry that it felt like paper, and her lips stuck together in a prickly suction seal. She licked her lips and tried again, but still the words would not come.

"This place," Nathaniel said, gesturing at the Hush, "was our real world, once. It is so rich in magic, you know. So rich in power, so rich in fuel to increase the strength of our Music. Down in the depths of the earth, there are rich deposits of liquid sorcery just waiting to be harvested.

"The earliest Musicians learned to exploit those resources," Nathaniel said. "They were seen as herocs, as innovators. They learned to mine for liquid sorcery, to carry it with them, to enhance their own abilities beyond their natural limits."

Nathaniel's spare hand roamed up toward his throat. His fingers settled on his nautilus shell pendant, which curved upward like a silver vial. Susannah stared at it, her pulse pounding violently as realization hit. The pendants weren't just symbols of the Songshapers, they were vials of liquid sorcery, worn around their necks to enhance their powers.

Nathaniel smiled. "Unfortunately, as the liquid evaporates with use, we needed more of it. The process of extraction is . . . difficult. We dug through shafts of toxic sorcery, through rock and shale and veins of Music. We released gases and twisted melodies into the air. The process stained the air dark with fumes and pulled unnatural rain from the skies.

"My people were no longer seen as heroes. We were villains. We were called polluters and we were shunned. We had power in Music, but no power in society. And we wanted both, my dear. We wanted it all."

Nathaniel's eyes were alight now, bright with mania. He tightened his grip on the pistol with one hand, while the other clenched greedily at his pendant.

"We needed people to forget," he whispered. "To live in ignorance."

"The real world isn't real?" Susannah whispered.

"Oh, it's real enough," Nathaniel said. "It exists. It's a physical place. But we created it. We *all* created it. You created it, my dear: you and every other soul in Meloral."

"The Sundown Recital," Dot whispered. It was the first time she'd spoken since Nathaniel had revealed himself. "That's what it's for, isn't it? Thousands of souls, humming that tune every night in unison."

"Oh yes," Nathaniel said. "Five hundred years ago, the world's Musicians created the largest Musical enchantment in history. They didn't just build a sorcery lamp, or a shield, or an echoship.

They built an entire world. They gave themselves a new name: *Songshapers*. They built the largest Musical enchantment in history and most of the musicians don't even know they're part of it.

"Just think of it, Dorothy. You're a clever girl. You'll see the genius in it. Thousands of souls to replenish this world, feeding back into the enchantment, renewing the sorcery for us. Thousands of souls rebuilding their own prison for us, night after night."

Susannah felt sick. No wonder withdrawal caused such agony. They weren't just quitting a nightly habit. They were quitting the song that had defined their entire existence.

"It's the Song," Dot said, looking stunned. "That's what holds the fake world together, isn't it? It's just another piece of Music—like the Music of a sorcery lamp but on an enormous scale. *The heartbeat of the world . . .*"

"Of course it is," Nathaniel said. "Why do you think we treat unlicensed Songshapers so harshly? We can't afford to have amateurs interfering with our masterpiece. They could blunder in and play an off-key note into the sorcery. They could cause ripples in our melody, or even expose the truth . . ."

"But why not just *tell* everyone the truth?" Susannah said.

"The Hush is still ripe with resources, my dear," Nathaniel said. "We can't afford for anyone to interfere with its extraction."

"The Echoes!" Dot breathed. "They're made to protect the secret, to kill any trespassers they find in the Hush. They go into the most dangerous places, the places twisted and ruined by your pollution—"

"—and tell us where to dig." Nathaniel was smiling again now, a tight, thin smile that looked more suited to a predator than to someone showing pleasure. "Oh yes, very good. They're naturally attracted to Musical energy, you see—not only to the leakage that accumulates near cities, but to the natural Music of the earth itself. When they find a deposit of liquid sorcery, we set off in our echoships to harvest the loot."

Nathaniel paused. "Unfortunately, over the centuries, the number of Echoes has slowly dwindled. Natural attrition, you see."

"That's why you've started vanishing people." Susannah's voice was hoarse. "To replenish your supply."

Nathaniel nodded. "By the time I took over the Hush Initiative, almost half our Echoes had dissolved into the dark. It's been a hell of a job replacing them. Unfortunately, the methods our ancestors used to create Echoes have been lost over time. A few . . . experiments . . . were required to refine the process."

Susannah's stomach knotted. *Sam.*

"Eventually we got it right," Nathaniel said. "We selected people carefully to become our new Echoes. People with resilience, with drive, with courage. People strong enough to endure the transformation and to survive for longer in the Hush. We relied on informants in the towns and cities—people who could identify likely candidates, who could tell us who to vanish next.

"In fact, that was where you found me, wasn't it? In the shop of one of my ex-informants. Mr. Ashworth. A loathsome little man, but he had his uses. In fact, he led us to your friend Chester's father.

"Of course, once Mr. Ashworth's usefulness ended, he had to be disposed of. I couldn't leave loose threads, you see. I couldn't leave clues behind. I've always prided myself on being neat and tidy in my work."

Nathaniel adjusted his grip on the gun. "But Chester's father . . . Ah, I have high hopes for that man. A great asset, he'll be. The man has a real knack for survival. Just like his son. But he's not as dangerous to us. Not *too* talented, you see. Not enough to pose a threat. Not like Chester."

Susannah started. "Chester?"

355

"Oh yes," Nathaniel said. "A very rare boy, that one. It took me a while to realize it, but he was never trained, was he? Just connected to the Song on his own, as though his subconscious latched onto the strongest piece of Music it could sense. A Natural, the historians call them. Hasn't been a Natural born in hundreds of years. No wonder he turned up on my agent's radar."

He nodded toward the group of Songshapers behind him and one of them stepped forward. It was a woman in her late thirties who wore her dark hair tied into an intricate knot. With a lurch, Susannah recognized the Songshaper from Bremen, the one who had chased the *Cavatina* through the darkness of the Hush . . .

"She was working for you?"

Nathaniel gave a cold smile. "You don't understand yet, my dear? I run the Hush Initiative. *Everyone* is working for me."

"Not us," Susannah said, throat tight. "We don't do the recital. We don't work for you."

"Oh, but of course you do." Nathaniel's voice was patronizing, as if he was a master speaking to a foolish pet. "You're the ones who tested the security for me. You're the ones who helpfully discovered the flaw in my defenses. And you're the ones who brought Chester Hays into my grasp."

"You—"

Nathaniel's smile broadened. His teeth gleamed, spectral in the Hush-light. "I'm afraid that I can't let a boy like that keep breathing. He's a threat to the Song and to the order we've worked so hard to create."

Susannah was enraged. It was all tied together: the lies and the poverty those lies had created. "You mean the system where only rich people can become Songshapers?" Susannah snapped. "The system where *you* control who gets power, and you run roughshod over anyone who's not lucky enough to be born with filthy rich parents?"

"Why, yes," Nathaniel said. "That system exactly. The Hush Initiative is not cheap to run, my dear. We need students who can contribute to our cause—not the sort of riffraff who would dare audition with empty pockets." His eyes narrowed. "But now I come to think of it, where *is* our dear little prodigy? I have a score or two to settle with the boy."

Susannah stared at him. Didn't he know? Her heart hammered a little faster and she tried to hide the twist of hope that threatened to show on her face. If he didn't know that Chester was here, that he was already inside the cage . . .

"I said, where is he?" Nathaniel repeated, and there was a new edge to his voice now. "I want him to be part of this little conversation."

"I . . ." Susannah hesitated. "I don't know."

"Liar." Nathaniel stepped toward her and raised his gun. It pointed directly at Susannah's face now and she swallowed down a throat full of bile. She stared right down the barrel into that shadowed tube of silver metal and all she could imagine was the roar of a bullet to her face . . .

"I don't know! He didn't come to the Conservatorium with us!"

"You're lying," Nathaniel said. "I know he auditioned. I know your plan. I was part of it, remember?"

His finger hovered over the trigger. Susannah flinched, thinking for a moment that he was about to fire, but she kept her lips sealed. Her heartbeat felt as fast as a rush of fingers on piano keys. There was still hope that Sam might find Chester somehow, might bring him out of this alive . . .

"I don't know where he is!" she said, stronger this time.

"You're lying." Nathaniel ran his tongue across his teeth. "Interesting. You know that I could shoot you dead, but still you're lying. You obviously care for the boy."

357

He considered her for a long moment. "But how much do you care for him? More than you care for your friends?"

He swung the pistol sideways so that it pointed straight between Dot's eyes.

"Five seconds," Nathaniel said. "Five seconds to tell me where the boy is, or I'll blow dear Dorothy's brains all over the marble."

No one spoke.

"Five. Four."

Susannah tensed. She prepared to leap sideways, to shove Dot aside at the moment of firing . . .

"Three."

Susannah tightened her muscles. She felt as though the world was running in slow motion, and at any minute—

"Two."

There was an almighty crash. Lightning smashed across the bars of the cage and Susannah heard screaming. The next thing she knew, the world was a blur of bodies and clawing fingers.

*

The crowd surged around Chester, wild and frothing in the thrill of the lightning. He was knocked aside as a huge man barrelled past, then someone kicked him. The world spun around him like the curve of a fiddle.

A fiddle! Where was Goldenleaf?

He found the fiddle lying near the edge of the pond, mercifully untouched by the rush of bodies. Even in their half-crazed state, the Silencers knew to avoid the water; they poured around it like living molasses, a parted sea of frantic limbs. Chester clutched Goldenleaf to his chest and let the crowd carry him, stumbling and gasping as the silent bodies surged toward the bars.

At the edge of the cage, he was slammed against the bars. He let out a cry of pain as the metal bruised his ribs but, raising the fiddle above his head, he twisted aside and squeezed through a gap in the bars. They were still lit by sorcery, painting brightness into the Hush, and Chester strained his eyes for a sign of his friends.

The crowd had spat him out on the wrong side of the cage. He whirled around and looked to both sides but there was no sign of the others. He tried to shove Goldenleaf back into its case, but the bodies surged again and his fingers lost the case and bow in the turmoil. He heard an awful crack and splintering as the case vanished beneath stampeding feet, and he was left clutching a naked violin in the lightning's glow.

He heard a scream in the distance, from the other side of the cage. Chester pressed his fiddle against his body and shielded it with his arms, then charged into the melee. Desperate and confused, he burst around the curve of the cage and through the crowd until finally, he saw them.

Susannah stood in the rain, her face half-lit by the glare of the cage bars. She was grappling with someone in the darkness: a fully grown man, with the glint of a pistol in his upraised hand . . .

Nathaniel Glaucon.

Chester charged. The pistol shrieked, blasting a bullet up into the air. Nathaniel swore and fumbled, struggling to aim at Susannah's face, but Chester rode the crowd like a wave and in a second had hurled himself onto the man's back and yanked back his arm, jerking the pistol skyward once more. His fiddle slipped from his arms.

Chester forgot the crowds, the dark, the rain. His whole world was just this moment, this clutching of limbs, this fighting for control of the gun. All he knew was that he had to grab that gleam of silver, to point it away from his friends, to—

All of a sudden, Nathaniel stopped fighting. He stood motionless and stared out at the Hush around them, as though he could barely grasp what he was seeing. Chester, still clutching at Nathaniel's back, turned his blinking eyes outward to survey the scene.

Hundreds of bodies stood around them. Hundreds of Silencers, freed from their cage, loomed in the flickering light of the cage bars. They stood still. They stood silent.

And their eyes were turned on the Songshapers.

Chester slipped down from Nathaniel's back. The Songshaper seemed hardly to notice. His expression was numb with panic, as if he was barely able to comprehend the hundreds of haunted faces surrounding him.

Unable to think straight, Chester picked up Goldenleaf. The fiddle was damaged—its scroll was shattered, one of the tuning pegs was gone, and broken strings spiked outward in a tangle—but his shock was too raw for any new emotions to register. He staggered back to his friends and felt the painful squeeze of Susannah's hand on his shoulder. Her breathing was sharp and heavy as though she didn't know whether to sob or shout. Chester felt the same terror building inside himself: a terrible mixture of fear and hope and something else. Something like the first bar of a folk song, just waiting for the melody to kick in . . .

The nearest Silencer opened her mouth. She was as tall as Travis and she shared his high cheekbones and thick black hair. She stood in front of Nathaniel looking thin and ragged, but still she was beautiful. Her eyes glinted with the pale blue gleam of a Silencer.

Penelope.

"You stole us," she said, and the words were not silent. The sound left her lips, hoarse and tight. "You did this to us."

Her accusation hung on the air.

And as one, the Silencers charged.

CHAPTER THIRTY-NINE

THE SONGSHAPERS DIED QUICKLY.

For a moment, Susannah thought they might all go down screaming—not just Nathaniel and his comrades, but her own friends as well. But they were buffeted backward, carried on the sea of frantic bodies.

She didn't see Nathaniel die. She heard his screams, then there was a moment of quiet broken by the howls of the Silencers as they charged into the darkness, voices returning, alive, free, and unconstrained.

Susannah stumbled sideways but caught herself and grabbed Chester's arm before he could be swallowed by the crowd. Before Susannah knew what was happening, she had wrapped her arms around him and she was breathing into his neck, his shoulder. There was nothing but the scent of him, his warmth against her, the knowledge that he was here, he was alive, he was *Chester*.

"I'm sorry," she whispered. "I'm so, so sorry. I never meant to go through with it, Chester. I thought we'd find another way . . ."

And then he was returning her embrace and his face was warm and damp against her cheek. "It's okay. I know why you . . . it was the only way. But Sam . . ."

She didn't need him to finish the sentence. If Sam wasn't here—if the cage was broken and Chester was alive and Sam was

361

missing . . . well, there was only one answer. Shock and sorrow welled in her like liquid fire and she pressed her face closer and breathed the scent of Chester's living body. He was alive but Sam was dead. Sam. He had been like her brother.

She looked up and saw hundreds of Silencers. They needed her. They needed someone to lead them out into the light, into the real world—or the false world, or whatever you wanted to call it. To lead them back into Meloral. Their world might have been carved from a melody, but it was still real, in a way, wasn't it? It was still a version of reality. And it was a hell of a lot better than this one.

She would finish the plan. She would get these prisoners out of here and give them a chance to take back the lives that had been stolen from them.

With a startled cry, Chester broke free of her embrace. Susannah's heart stuttered. Had the full weight of her betrayal hit him? Did he want nothing more to do with her? But then she saw him slipping through the crowd, his hands outstretched as he lunged toward an older man with dark hair and gleaming eyes . . .

His father.

The man was limping and staggering about with a haggard look of sickness in his face. How long had he been down here? Months, from what Chester had told her. She helped Chester support the man and they hauled him up between their shoulders.

"Captain!" Travis shouted.

They met in a patch of open floor on a newly vacated stretch of marble, as the Silencers swarmed outward in their desperation to escape. Dot and Penelope were in each other's arms, lips locked in the tightest of reunions, filled with so much longing that they looked ready to dissolve from the sheer intensity. Dot was crying, tears streaming down her face.

Susannah was overwhelmed. They had done it. They had released the Silencers, they had Chester's father, they had Penelope, and they had finally achieved justice.

But Sam . . .

She drew in a breath. "Start the melody!"

Travis placed one hand on Dot's shoulder and the other on Penelope's. Together, they began to hum. A run of quiet notes, bursting from pursed lips. Chester joined them and suddenly the music was spreading, ebbing outward, floating like a wave through the crowd. One man would stop in his panic and pick it up, then another. Each person passed it to his neighbor like a secret on the tongue. Sweet and succulent, it rippled outward, their twist on the Sundown Recital, the tune that would pull them back out of the Hush . . .

One by one, the people disappeared. Susannah watched them vanish, winking out of the Hush to return to their real world. As others saw what was happening—as they realized that the melody was their escape route—they took up the tune like a man in the desert grasps for water. The notes rolled outward and bodies vanished into the haze of shadow as the cage behind them shone.

Susannah waited until they were all gone, every body, every soul. Just darkness hugged her. She let the Hush-rain play upon her skin.

She stared down at the Songshapers' bodies. Broken. Crushed. For a second she could see their features, then the light from the cage behind her flickered out.

She had seen this cage once before. The last time, she had escaped when a fellow prisoner had tripped into the pool, when he'd let the water snare a taste of his ankle. He had crawled out again, dying slowly from the shock of the magic, but the water's Music had broken for a moment—and in that moment, Susannah had slipped between the bars.

This time, Sam had bought the prisoners more time. He had thrown his whole body into the water, had let his Music churn and writhe in violent death throes through the dark, so that the spell would stay disrupted until the last of his body burned away.

Sam.

Susannah let the melody slip softly from her lips. He was gone. She would never see him again.

✳

For Chester, the next few minutes were a blur. The marble floor was white again, and the beds and medical equipment punctuated the curving walls.

People were screaming, kicking over the beds, smashing canisters and trays and needles and tearing buckles free from the walls. Mirrors splintered and bodies shoved and all Chester could think was that it was so *bright* in here, after the black of the Hush. His eyes burned and he wondered how the Silencers would cope after months of darkness . . .

The Silencers.

His father.

Chester still had Goldenleaf pinned under one arm. With the other shoulder he supported his father. He looked like a broken man, hunched over, his breath ragged against Chester's neck.

"You found me," his father whispered. "Chester . . ."

"Shhh," Chester said, and hoisted him a little higher. His legs felt like they were about to buckle under the strain but this was his father, dammit. Chester wasn't about to let him fall, not even if his legs shattered and his arms turned to sawdust. No matter what, Chester would not let him fall.

When Susannah appeared he let out a little choke of relief. She was pale and dishevelled, her red hair a mess of tangles more than curls. When his gaze fell upon her, Chester was struck by how wild she was. Wild and beautiful. She looked back at him and there was a desperation in her gaze that made his insides flip. And he knew—in a tangle of hurt and hope and fatigue—that Susannah had told the truth when she apologized. She didn't mean to go through with the plan tonight.

She didn't mean to betray him.

People were pouring out of the chamber now, pushing and shoving through the door into the corridors beyond. The shield systems were still shut down, deactivated by the emergency alarm that had allowed Nathaniel to find them so quickly. Bodies pushed out into the corridors, spilling like sand through the neck of an hourglass.

"I believe," Travis said, "that this is the part where we flee the city."

Chester nodded. Every Songshaper in Weser would soon be dashing from their beds to investigate the chaos. It was too risky to leave with the crowd; the gang looked too clean and healthy to fit in with the escaping prisoners, and half the gang lacked the pale blue eyes of the Silencers. Besides, it would take too long to navigate the corridors, let alone to escape onto the streets of Weser. If anyone identified them as suspects . . .

Susannah produced a final charge from her pocket. It looped into a perfect silver ring. "Ready?"

They nodded.

Susannah laid the charge on the floor, right beneath the center of the dome. It would connect to the charges she'd lain on the outside of the building: they were double-use charges, ready for one last bang.

They cried out the notes together—the notes that Dot had taught them, which were programmed into her final system of charges—and the metal twist came alive with light. It spun and sputtered, shooting sparks into the air, and there was a sudden tremendous bang.

Above them, the dome exploded into tiny fragments.

The residue fell softly, like a sandcastle dissolving in the wind. It poured down around them, soft and harmless, and Chester felt for a moment that he was back in the Hush and the air was made of dry rain. Overhead, all that remained of the dome was its iron frame, a skeleton in the sky. Their pulley ropes—deliberately attached to the frame rather than the dome itself—still dangled down to greet them.

The room was almost empty now, and Chester found himself staring at his friends in the sudden quiet. The absence of Sam made his throat clench. But there was Susannah. Dot. Travis. There was Penelope, and there was his father.

"Come on," Chester said. "There'll be more Songshapers here in a minute—when they hear all the—"

"I think they'll be busy for a while." Travis stared at the disappearing remains of the crowd. "They've got a few unexpected visitors."

They all stared at each other for a moment and—against all odds—Chester found himself laughing. It was an exhausted, wild laughter that bubbled up from his stomach to his chest, and tumbled from his lips. They were almost free. The Conservatorium was in chaos, the prisoners were escaping, and they were almost out of here.

Almost.

They used the pulley to winch themselves up, two at a time. Dot and Penelope went first, then Chester and his father. Chester left his fiddle for Susannah to carry, since she had no injured Silencer to occupy her hands. Chester supported his father's drooping body, barely aware of the ache in his limbs and simply relishing the warmth of his father beside him. They were a family again, father and son caring for each other, struggling to survive in the chill of the world.

They clambered out onto the rooftop, where the pegasi were screaming panicked neighs, whinnies, and shrieks into the night. The explosion of the dome had been too much for the beasts and they kicked wildly in their stalls. Chester left his father leaning on the side of a chimney stack and ran along the stable front with fumbling fingers, unlocking the stalls one by one. The horses charged out into their new-found freedom and took to the skies, flapping wildly, another contribution to the chaos in the city.

Down below, he heard screams and shouts as Silencers poured out onto the streets, disrupting late-night diners and overturning tables as they rushed into the freedom of Weser City's streets and alleyways.

"Their minds will be returning, slowly," Dot said. Her eyes were bright and more vivid than he'd ever seen them, and she clutched Penelope's hand as if it was a lifeline in a storm. "They'll remember themselves and they'll go back to their families."

"How long will it take them to recover?" Chester said, glancing back at his father. "If they've been trapped in the Hush for weeks . . . some for months . . ."

"It will take time," Dot said. "But not forever."

Beside her, Penelope gave a weary smile. She looked a little distant, a little lost, but her eyes were shining like her girlfriend's, and she leaned her head on Dot's shoulder as if it were a pillow.

"Home," she whispered.

"Yes," Dot said. "A new home. A home where they can't find us."

When Travis and Susannah had clambered up onto the roof, they seized the last of the pegasi—three shining beasts that Chester had left in their stalls—and took to the sky in pairs. Susannah rode with Travis, Dot rode with Penelope, and Chester rode with his father.

And as the wing-beats threw a breeze across their faces, they flew toward the stars.

EPILOGUE

One Week Later

CHESTER SAT IN HIS HOTEL ROOM, STARING THROUGH THE WINDOW.
A quiet town rolled out before him, gleaming in the early morning light. Behind him, his father snored quietly on the bed, a curling frame of messy hair and wrinkled eyes. There was gray in his hair now, which hadn't been there before. Chester sometimes caught himself staring at the man in disquiet. He had aged so much in just a few months. Suffered so much.

"It's just stress," Travis had assured him, checking vital signs and blood pressure. "Once he's recovered, he'll start looking better again."

But there were some things that time couldn't fix. Time couldn't erase the wrinkles, or the gray, or the trauma. Chester's father had aged before his time, and the knowledge made Chester sick to his stomach.

There was a knock at the door.

"Come in."

It was Travis. He carried a medical kit under his arm and gave Chester a reassuring nod as he entered.

"How are the others?"

"Better," Travis said. "Penelope is healing much faster than your father, although I imagine her youth has something to do with that."

Chester turned back to the window. He could hear Travis behind him, rummaging around for needles and equipment as he performed his daily tests on Chester's father's body. The man had slept almost constantly since their escape from Weser City.

Occasionally his father woke for a few minutes at a time. Chester snatched at those minutes like the berries atop dessert: little bursts of sweetness before the heaviness set back in. Chester tried to talk, to ask questions, to reassure, but his father would slip back into his dreams and Chester would slip back into loneliness.

He didn't blame the others for not keeping him company. They were busy with their own problems. Dot barely left Penny's side, and Travis stayed with them. Penelope was his sister, after all—what else did Chester expect?

Chester fixed his eyes on the sun-streaked sky. It was early morning and out in the town, people were beginning to awaken. They dribbled onto the streets, yawning and calling to one another, bustling out to buy their morning bread and paper.

As for Susannah . . .

Inside this hotel, in another room, Susannah kept silent.

Chester had tried to visit her, once. But when he knocked on her door, she hadn't answered and he'd slunk back to his own room, back to staring through the same damned window. Back to watching the same damned streets. Because Susannah didn't want him here. She wanted Sam. And deep down, Chester knew she would trade his life for Sam's in a heartbeat if it would bring the older boy back.

He traced a finger across the window, blotting out his view of people on the street. One by one they vanished, then reappeared as his finger moved on. That was how it felt, sometimes. Like some huge invisible finger was moving through the heavens, stealing random people from the world before their time. Stealing Sam, and leaving Chester.

Why? Why had the older boy done it? Chester knew they'd grown to understand each other a little more as time wore on, but this? To throw away his life for Chester's sake?

It didn't make sense. It didn't—

"He's fine," Travis said, interrupting this train of thought. "Blood pressure's about what I expected, and I've given him another set of injections. Just a matter of waiting for him to wake up properly, I'm afraid."

Chester yanked his gaze away from the window and turned back to Travis and his father. The latter lay quietly on the bed, so still that he looked more dead than sleeping. His breaths were deep, though; his chest moved up and down with the quiet rhythm of his lungs.

"Thanks," Chester said.

"Don't mention it. If you need anything else, let me know, all right?"

"All right."

The bed creaked, the door swung. Chester was alone again.

He crossed to the foot of the bed and slid onto the blanket by his father's feet. He pulled Goldenleaf from its perch on a nearby chair and began to tune the strings. Chester had carved a new tuning peg from a lump of firewood, mended a crack in the pegbox, and replaced the broken strings. He had even ventured out to buy a bow from a shabby little instrument shop across the road. The fiddle's scroll was shattered and its gold adornments were gone, but those were only decorative. Goldenleaf was ready to be played.

Yet despite these repairs, Chester hadn't played music for days—for a week, actually, now he came to think of it. Not since the Conservatorium.

All he had done was tune the strings, again and again. Often they weren't out of tune in the first place, but Chester would twiddle the knobs until they sounded like cat screams. Then he would fix them, one by one, coaxing the fiddle back into wholeness of sound once again. He did that now, one string at a time: a plink, a howl, and then a perfect twang.

But no music. No songs. He didn't feel like it. Not when he thought about his father, unconscious on the bed, or Sam, dead in that black pond in the Conservatorium.

Or Susannah, shut away in her room, not wanting to see him.

Chester's fingers grew heavy. He dropped the fiddle back onto the chair. He ran the bow between his palms for a moment, then placed it beside the instrument and returned to the window. The sun was a little higher now, and the streets fuller. He raised his finger and blotted out another random passer-by. Here. Gone. Just like that.

The next knock startled him. Chester frowned at the window, but refused to look back in the direction of the door. He didn't want to get his hopes up. No one had visited him in days, apart from Travis. Who else . . . ?

"Come in," he said.

The door slid open. Even without looking, he knew it was her. It was the way she moved through the air, sleek and stealthy, so light on her feet. He caught a glimpse of red reflected in the window and knew he was right.

Chester turned slowly to look at her. Susannah had changed in the days since he'd seen her. She was thinner, more brittle. Her skin was paler and her eyelids puffy. She had pulled her hair into a bun atop her head and it balanced there like an angry red bauble.

"Chester . . ."

They stared at each other. The sadness hit Chester unexpectedly. He had thought he'd be happy to see her, or shocked, or perhaps just hurt and angry at her for ignoring his knock on her door. But this? Sadness? It wasn't what he'd expected. It was too quiet, too cold. It started in the depths of his gut, rolling up like an incoming tide, slow and subtle, but with a lapping progress that seeped all the way to his scalp.

"Chester," Susannah said again. "I . . ." She trailed off then cast her eyes around the room. "How's your father?"

"Travis says he's better," Chester said. "Looks the same to me. I'm just waiting to see if he wakes up."

"If?"

"Hopefully 'when.' Maybe 'if.'"

She nodded. There was a pause.

"I'm sorry," she said.

Chester didn't answer. Was she talking about his father? Or did she mean she was sorry that he'd survived—that Sam was gone?

"I'm sorry about our original plan." Her voice was barely a whisper now. "It seemed like the only way. But once I got to know you, I knew we had to change it, and I kept trying to think of another solution but it seemed impossible to—"

"Why didn't you tell me?"

"I don't know. I thought you'd run. I thought you'd leave our gang behind and we'd be back where we started, with no way into the Conservatorium."

"I'd spent months on the road looking for my father," Chester said quietly. "Did you think I'd just up and run when your plan might save him?"

Susannah hesitated. "Yes. No. I don't know." She dropped into a nearby chair and looked down at her steepled fingers. "I just . . . maybe it was something else. Maybe I was afraid."

"Afraid of what?"

"That you'd think we were your enemies. That you'd hate me—us, us!" she corrected herself quickly, flushing. "That you'd hate us."

Chester stared at her. She was behaving so oddly, flexing her fingers, staring at her lap, head bowed low to hide the red in her cheeks and the puff in her eyes.

"Captain, I wanted to . . ."

"Susannah," she said wearily. "Just call me Susannah. I'm not your captain anymore."

"What do you mean?"

"The Nightfall Gang's over. We finished what we set out to do. The Conservatorium's in an uproar, the prisoners are free. You've got your father, and Travis and Dot have Penelope. No more gang. No more thieving. No more schemes."

"Susannah," he said, after a moment's hesitation. It felt strange to address her by her name. "I wanted to apologize, too."

"For what?"

"For what happened in the cage." He took a breath. "For Sam."

A breeze played on the windowpane, light and hollow.

"That wasn't your fault."

"I should have stopped him. I should have jumped in quicker, in front of him or something, or gone for it before he even caught up to me, or—"

Susannah stood, the movement jerky. "Don't say that. Don't you ever say that."

Chester blinked.

"There are lots of things I regret about that night," Susannah said. "Things I'd go back and change if I could . . . But not that. Not the fact that you survived." She took a ragged breath. "Do you have any idea how I felt when you ran into that cage?"

He stared at her for a moment then quietly shook his head.

"It felt like my insides were being pulled out." Her voice was hot and serrated, stained with the effort of holding back tears. "I thought I'd killed you, that I'd cared more about justice for the past than for what the future might've been. I thought . . . I thought I'd never see you again."

They stared at each other and Chester realized that his own eyes were damp now. How long had they been like that? He hadn't even noticed the saltiness welling. He raised a sleeve to wipe at his face, too exhausted and sad and drained to even feel embarrassed.

Chester waited for Susannah to break the gaze, to look away. To pull her eyes from the boy who had let her friend die. But she didn't. She stared at him, and he stared back, and the whole room shrank into the line of light and dust and quiet air that stretched between them.

"Sam was always going to die fighting," Susannah whispered. "He threw himself into battles whenever he had a chance. He couldn't bear it anymore—the Music in his head, messing with his emotions. He was always in that cage, in a way. Not a physical cage, but a cage in his mind. In his veins. He knew he'd never leave the Conservatorium alive."

She took a shaky breath. "He wanted to be the one to bring them down, Chester. *Whatever it took*, he told me. And he did it. He got his revenge and he saved a friend. I think he'd be happy, if he knew."

"But I wasn't his friend. He shouldn't have—"

"You were a part of his gang, Chester. It took a while for him to realize that, but then he accepted it. And once you were part of his gang, you weren't just a friend. You were family."

Chester broke the gaze. He couldn't help it. The words were such a jolt that he took a faltering breath, crossed to the window and rested his hands on the sill. He stared out through the glass, his mind awhirl with the weight of her words.

She joined him a moment later. Her fingers rested beside his own. They were long and slender, with nails worn down to stubs. A couple of scars marked the backs of her hands, and they glinted white in the morning sunlight.

"What happens now?" he said.

"What do you mean?"

Chester nodded out the window, to the milling streets of people down below. "We have to let people know the truth. About the Hush, and the recital. About which world is real."

Susannah followed his gaze. "They're both real," she said. "In their own way."

"But this one . . ."

"This one was built by sorcery, yes. But that doesn't mean it's not real. It just means it's newer. And it's where people have made their homes, their lives, their families." She let out a slow breath. "It's real, too, Chester. They both are."

"So what do we do?"

"We get the word out, I suppose. We get the word out and we let people make up their own minds."

"You think people will stay here?"

"Most will, I think. The Hush might have been our world once, but it's been ruined. Not many people would want to live there now. Not now that we've got a better home."

"But we'll give them the choice."

"Yes." Susannah's voice grew tight now, and a twist of hard determination clipped her syllables. "We'll give them the choice, and the Songshapers and their secrets can be damned."

"But won't the Songshapers try again?" Chester said. "Vanishing people, making Echoes . . ."

"When the whole world knows their dirty secret?" Susannah shook her head. "I'd like to see them try."

They stood and stared out through the window, their fingers unmoving on the ledge. Chester glanced down at the street outside, at the people moving from houses to bakeries, to markets and mills. People going about their business. People who had made a home for themselves, in a world they had sung into existence.

"Susannah," he said again.

"Yes?"

"I . . ." Chester was a little startled to realize he'd spoken aloud. His gaze shifted across to Susannah's hand, pale and slender beside his own, and he fought a sudden urge to shift his fingers sideways and touch it. To see if her skin felt as soft as it looked.

And before he could move a muscle, her hand twitched. Chester's hand twitched back and they made the move together, at exactly the same moment: two hands locking together, in a clasp as tight as a treble clef. Her skin was warm and as soft as he'd imagined, and her fingers slotted between his own like a tune into a padlock.

For several long minutes they stood there, gazing into the streets beyond. Chester did not let go. Neither did she.

"Play me a song?" she whispered.

They retreated to the foot of the bed and Chester picked up his fiddle. He reluctantly released her hand, but Susannah just smiled at him and nodded toward Goldenleaf. The fiddle was scruffy—a mismatch of repairs and scratches—but Chester knew it was playable. He pressed the wood beneath his chin and pressed his bow to the strings.

Focus, he told himself, suddenly nervous. It had been over a week since he'd played, and he'd never played a song for Susannah before. Not for personal reasons, at least, beyond the scope of his role in the gang. He hesitated. But his bow brushed the strings and suddenly he knew what to play.

"The Nightfall Duet" soared up from the fiddle, and Susannah's smile curved up a little higher. Not entirely sad, but wistful.

"They changed that song's name, you know," she said. "Just for us. Just for our gang."

"I know."

Chester teased out the first verse. His fingers tensed in preparation for the frenzy of the chorus, but Susannah spoke before his bow could make its slide across the strings.

"We did a lot, didn't we? The Nightfall Gang. We made a name for ourselves. We helped people."

Chester let his bow fall. He thought of the stories of the Nightfall Gang. The money they'd given to the poor. The Songshapers whose plans they'd ruined. The prisoners they'd freed.

"Yeah," he said. "You helped people."

"*We*," she corrected.

Chester gave a quiet smile. "We helped people."

Another breeze brushed the windowpane. Outside, the sun was rising higher into morning blue.

"It seems a waste," Susannah said slowly, "to throw away all that history. All that reputation. When we could still be using it to do some good."

She looked up at him, eyes a little too bright. Chester knew what she was asking and what she was too afraid to say. Sam was gone. He was gone and he was never coming back. Would it be wrong to carry on without him?

"Sam helped you start the gang, didn't he?" Chester said. "I mean, he was one of the original members?"

"Yes."

376

"So he believed in it, then. He wanted it to achieve something."
She nodded.

"Well," Chester said, "I didn't know him as well as you did. And I don't think it's my place to tell you what he would have thought. But . . ."

Susannah looked at him for a moment, then down at Goldenleaf. She gave a slow nod. "He gave everything he had to this gang. It was all he had left in the world."

She kept her eyes low on the fiddle. "He would have wanted us to keep going."

Another pause. Chester glanced at her, then at his father. The older man had shifted in his sleep a little and his mouth was slightly open. He wasn't yet awake but he looked . . . better. More like a man sleeping than a man dead. And Chester knew, with a sudden certainty, that he was going to awaken.

When, he thought. *"When," not "if."*

He looked back at Susannah. Her face was still red and puffy, but there was something new there, too, a glint of the old determination behind her eyes. She nodded at him and gave a pointed look at his bow.

"I asked you for a song, Chester. You haven't finished it yet."

Chester picked up the bow and pressed it against the strings. "From the chorus?"

"No, I want to hear it again. From the top."

He met her eyes and there was a moment of silence. He smiled. She returned it. The sunlight glinted through the window. Chester pressed the bow against the strings and it felt as warm as another hand inside his own.

"Yes, Captain," he said.

And with that, he began to play.

ACKNOWLEDGMENTS

As ALWAYS, THANKS TO MY AGENT RICK RAFTOS FOR FINDING MY manuscript a home.

Without the team at Random House, *The Hush* would still just be a Word document on my computer. I am especially grateful to Zoe Walton, for her passion, guidance and expertise; Pas Lazzaro, for his terrific insight into the manuscript; Bronwyn O'Reilly, for her awesome editing skills; and Sarana Emerton, Dot Tonkin, and Zoe Bechara, who are marketing and publicity ninjas. Thanks also to Julie Burland, Nerrilee Weir, Angela Duke, Rebecca Diep, Jo Penney, Janine Nelson, Jeremy Vine and all the other lovely people at RHA—as well as to Anthony Morais who designed the gorgeous cover. I also owe a massive thanks to Alison Weiss and the talented team at Sky Pony Press, who produced the American edition of this book.

Thanks to my beautiful grandparents for their love and support, and to my parents and sister, who read this book first (and who were exceptionally patient when I needed to babble to someone about plotting issues or fictional geography).

Above all, thanks to my readers. This book could not exist without you.